WAKING

BEAUTY

WAKING
BEAUTY

SARAH E. MORIN

PUBLISHING

Waking Beauty by Sarah E. Morin
Published by Enclave Publishing
5025 N. Central Ave., #635
Phoenix, AZ 85012
www.enclavepublishing.com

ISBN (paper): 978-1-62184-043-5

Published in the United States by Enclave Publishing, an imprint of Third Day
Books, LLC, Phoenix, Arizona.

This is a work of fiction. Names, characters, places, and incidents are products of
the author's imagination or are used fictitiously. Any similarity to actual people,
organizations, and/or events is purely coincidental.

Cover illustration by Kirk DouPonce – DogEar Design

Printed in the United States of America

DEDICATION

To Sherry, who grows roses.

And to the Conner Prairie Youth Spinning Team,
who taught me spinning wheels
are only hazardous to your health
if your name is Sleeping Beauty.

Part One

All that we see or seem
is but a dream within a dream.
Edgar Allan Poe

To explain truth to him who loves it not,
is but to give him the more
plentiful material for misinterpretation.
George MacDonald

1

Arpien

His princess was dusty.

Arpien should have expected that. Anything lying undisturbed for a hundred years would gather dust. He'd crossed the ocean to find the right sword for this venture, but neglected to pack a feather duster.

Great Grandfather Herren had always referred to the enchanted princess's beauty as ethereal. It was, at least, unnatural. Her form outlined under the sheets was slender, the face delicate under the layer of grey. Her skin would be fair and clear, though the only evidence of that was the two streaks under her nostrils, where her breath had blown the dust away.

Arpien hovered over his enchanted princess. He had thought of her as his since childhood. Beautiful, ageless. The air would shimmer with magic as he kissed her soft lips, broke the evil fairy's spell, won a kingdom and her heart.

The anticlimax exhausted him. He was not going to put his mouth on hers until he mopped her off.

Arpien scanned the tower bedroom for a rag. The gauzy tatters of the pink and off-white bed curtains disintegrated at his touch. Oh. They were mostly cobwebs. He wiped the clingy strands on his trunk hose. The fibers twisted together like sticky grey yarn and finally fell to the floor. The age-swollen wooden dresser drawers complained and squeaked when he jimmied them open. Absent mice had long since shredded and remodeled the clothes inside into bedding. Absent, too, were the birds who had left a buildup of dried grass in the narrow openings of the archers' slits. White-purple droppings splattered the tapestries.

Sweaty, his arms scratched up by thorns, Arpien was still the cleanest thing in the room.

Arpien wadded the baggy, torn puff of his dark blue sleeve in his fist and wiped off the princess's mouth. She looked silly with that streak of white across her face, even less like a living human being than before. With clumsy hands he brushed off the rest of her face. Under one hundred years' filth, she was beautiful, he admitted. Even familiar, if beauty so extreme can ever be familiar. It made it easier to lower his lips over hers—

—and sneeze.

"Thorns and thistles!" He sneezed again. This was supposed to be romantic and exciting. Instead it was musty and about as warming as courting a corpse. In Great Grandfather Herren's name, he ought to at least free her from the Curse. Besides, he was a third son. He needed the kingdom. He bent over and planted a quick and decisive kiss on her lips.

Princess Brierly's eyelids flitted open and closed in an erratic rhythm, as though her eyelashes were a butterfly's wings. How long would it take eyes that had been sealed shut for one hundred years to adjust to the light of day? Her lashes stilled and framed two startling pools of blue-green. Her contracted pupils moved up to the headboard, left to the dingy bed curtains, and finally locked on Arpien, where he hovered post-pucker.

He straightened.

The princess's lips moved, but only a rasp came out of her mouth, as though her throat were lined with sackcloth. The line of her slender throat bobbed as she swallowed and tried again. This time she croaked.

It was enchanted princes that turned into frogs, right? Not enchanted princesses.

She must be scared and disoriented. He really ought to say something. "Hello."

Thorns and thistles, this wasn't the speech he rehearsed at all.

"Fair Princess Brierly, my name—" He glanced away and back. "Uh, are you all right?"

Princess Brierly croaked at him again.

Arpien picked up a porcelain pitcher by the washstand. He scowled at the cobwebs and desiccated husks of bugs in its bottom and set it back down. He dug around in his battered doublet and extracted a skin of water. "Here."

Her head strained a few inches forward, just long enough for Arpien to notice the permanent indentation in her pillow. She flopped back down, and at last Arpien understood. Her atrophied muscles were too weak to allow her to sit up.

Curses left their marks.

Arpien eased down beside her. He cupped a tentative hand behind her head. Her hair slipped through his fingers like tangled silk, except for one matted clump. He tilted her head up so she could swallow the water he offered without choking. She grimaced and sputtered as though it were vinegar.

"Sorry." Arpien helped her roll on her side so she could finish coughing. "Are you all right now?"

She shrugged her eyebrows.

He took that as regal permission. He stood and cleared his throat. "Fair Princess Brierly." He whipped off his cap in the *Half Bow of the Potential Wooer Upon First Stage Introductions* and began again. "Fair Princess Brierly, my name is Prince Arpien Teric Elpomp Herren Trouvel of Conquisan."

Her rosebud lips quirked. Ah, his name must impress her. As it should—in Conquisan all young nobles practiced their names until they marched off the tongue with a military rhythm.

He puffed up and went on. "I have traveled many miles, across land and sea, valley and mountain. Many months, nay, years, have I sought this tower to fulfill a vow made long ago. In all my peregrinations, no woman's name but yours has ever rested on my lips. Now I humbly beseech your permission and claim the privilege of saving you."

She coughed, this time on her own dust. "Thanks."

Not the response he'd imagined for twelve years. The awkwardness of the situation drained his vocabulary, and he was left with no other recourse than to stare at her.

"Did you want to save me now or does later fit better into your schedule?" his princess said.

"Uh, now is fine."

He slipped his arm under her upper back and helped her sit up. He enjoyed the feel of her well-formed body in his arms, but his mind was equally occupied with the impolitic mechanics of it. He extracted her feet from under the blankets and planted them on the floor. It didn't even look like a natural sitting position, more like her legs were bent fork prongs.

She sat like that for a minute and narrowed her eyes.

"What are you doing?" he asked.

"Imagining standing."

"Allow me to assist you."

She raised a finger to stall him. A pink circle, the size of a pinhead, scarred its tip. "No. Let me see if I can bend the rules."

She was like a newborn filly, but after several minutes she mastered her shaky limbs. She transferred her grip from the bedpost to his arm. They wobbled across the tower floor like a pair of knock-kneed dancers. The stairs that coiled up the highest tower of Castle Estepel had not seemed so narrow when Arpien climbed them as they did going down now. It didn't help that the points on the princess's shoes stuck out beyond her toes a full five inches. Arpien had never seen poulaines except in old paintings.

By the time they reached the bottom of the tower, Princess Brierly's legs trembled. She sank down on the last step and flashed a tentative look of triumph at him. The tiny smile awakened a new awareness in Arpien. She really was, somewhere under all that flaking cloud of dust, Beautiful. Capital-B Beautiful, in the way only a fairy Gift could make her.

"See? All I have to do is believe hard enough," she said.

"You're very strong, my lady."

"I haven't been this weak in years." She wiped her damp forehead on her sleeve and left a grey spot on the pink silk. She frowned at it.

Arpien knelt down in front of her. "My horse is waiting for us outside the gate. I can carry you there if you like."

"No. I'll conquer this."

Oh, but she really was strong. He smiled at her.

She blinked at him, as though taking him in for the first time. "You're too tall. And your eyes are the wrong color."

She had hero specifications?

"What's wrong with brown?" he said.

"Nothing. You've looked weirder. Remember that time you had antlers? Or the time you had an extra arm? Or my favorite"—her nose twitched—"when you melted into a puddle?"

"Uh—no."

She sighed. "Of course not."

After a few minutes' rest, she rose and they inched toward the stone archway. Thorny vines sealed the entrance.

"No." Arpien dug the fingers of both hands into the cloth of his already bedraggled cap. "No, no, no. I just cut a path through these." He gestured at the blocked entrance. "I thought once the Curse was broken, the thicket was supposed to vanish. How did the briars grow back in less than an hour?"

She shrugged.

"I planned this rescue years in advance. This can't happen."

Princess Brierly cocked her head. "Can't?"

Arpien straightened his spine. He wanted to play the part of the rescuer, not some defrauded little boy. "We'll have to restock our food supplies. Though with what, I don't know."

"I don't need to eat."

"You are most selfless, Princess, but I hope such sacrifice will not be necessary if we ration our supplies. I calculated an hour to cut a path from the front gate to the castle walls. Instead, it took me four days. According to my research, the vademecum sword was supposed to cut through the briars like cobwebs. But chances are it'll take another four days to cut through the briars again. I only brought enough food for three days, not eight. Once we're out of Estepel I can hunt game in the forest. Until then, we have half a loaf of bread."

"Herren, we could see what's in the larder."

"Herren?" The clues started to click together. "You mean my great-grandfather. Thistles, people always said I took after him, but I didn't think—"

Would she mourn Herren? Was it sick to think of his own great-grandfather as a romantic rival?

Arpien cleared his throat, removed his cap, and pressed his palms together in the *Fifth Stance of Bereavement for Distant Relatives and Especially Good Cooks*. "Lady, it is with deepest sorrow that I must relay to you the eternal departure of your betrothed, King Herren Trouvel of Conquisan."

Brierly sighed. "All right. What name do you go by, again?"

"Prince Arpien Teric Elpomp Herren Trouvel of Conquisan." His name lacked the vigor of cadence it had earlier in the day. "Herren was my great-grandfather."

"My condolences."

"It must be a shock to you, that your betrothed is dead, but you've slept one hundred years."

"That explains the neck crick." She pressed her ear to her shoulder. Arpien heard a pop.

"So did you want to check the larder or would you rather try eating the briars?" she asked.

"My lady, didn't you understand? It's been one hundred years. There won't be anything left in the larder."

Her idea defied logic, but that didn't seem to bother her. They found the larder as he'd predicted it—empty except for mouse droppings and some ancient stems of herbs left to hang overhead. A skeleton of a chicken hung on a spit over cold ashes in the hearth, every last bit of flesh picked or rotted away.

Princess Brierly squinted again, this time at the table.

"Now what are you doing?"

"Imagining a feast. Brambleberries and clotted cream and yeast buns with the steam still rising from them. Do you have any requests?"

"Thinking of food makes me hungrier."

"Come, what's your favorite?"

"Goose liver in stewed fruit." It wasn't, but he preferred to think of foods that squelched his appetite.

"If you like." She narrowed her eyes for a full minute, then shrugged. "Sorry, didn't work."

This childlike game of pretend was enchanting. Wasn't it?

They found several bottles of wine, but the only food left in the castle was a crock of pickles. Arpien sniffed them and singed his nose hairs. "Ugh. What is that?"

"Grandmother pickles. A Rosarian delicacy. You're supposed to bury them in the ground on your tenth birthday and when your first grandchild is born, they'll be ready to eat." She nibbled on one. "Still good. Try one."

The mere odor was spicy and pungent enough to make tears run down Arpien's face. "I'll have to be a day or two hungrier before I'm ready for those." But he found a cloth bag for the crock and carried it back to the entrance for her.

Arpien drew his sword from his scabbard and hefted it like an axe against the tough vines of thorns. It took him a couple dozen swings to slice through each one. Brierly leaned against the wall and watched him. He reinvested himself in hearty blows that engaged all his muscles.

"Let me see if I can sharpen that for you," Princess Brierly said.

Arpien frowned but handed her the sword. It looked like a large but commonplace steel sword, nothing of note except a small ruby cut in the shape of a teardrop and inlaid in the blade near the hilt. She pressed the blade between her palms and slid her hands from hilt to tip.

Arpien flung a hand toward her. "Don't cut yourself."

Brierly handed the blade back. "Sorry. Can't help you."

"That was supposed to sharpen the blade?" Arpien said.

"Not today," Brierly said. "So that's a—vademecum—sword?"

"Aye." He started swinging again. "I would have been here months ago but I had to find it first. It was no mean feat. You must seek the sword, and it must seek you, that's how the ballads go."

"Hm."

"They say the Prince of Here and There fashioned it himself, centuries ago when he ruled."

He went on about his sword as he chopped briars. When he paused to look back at her, she was slumping as though she were the one who made a habit of melting into puddles.

"Am I boring you?"

"I'm a little tired."

After a hundred years of sleep, the first thing his princess wanted to do was take a nap? "Is that safe? Falling asleep?"

"I don't think I have a choice."

He relented. "Of course you're exhausted. It will take some time to regain your strength. Sleep in peace, fair princess, knowing I will guard you. Sweet dreams."

She exhaled a half-laugh. "Goodbye."

2

Arpien

This rescue wasn't going as Arpien planned.

Arpien paused to shake out his numb arms and gazed at the napping princess. The worst of the dust had fallen off her. Even smudged here and there, with a bad case of bed head, she was still the most gorgeous creature in the known world. He wished he were worthier of her. He wished his rambling conversation didn't put her to sleep. It never occurred to him that it would be a problem. The legends said only true love could wake her from the Curse. True love was never at a loss for poignant words, was it?

His oldest brother Cryndien always said that perception was everything. Be forceful, be articulate, be proud. How else will people know your worth?

Maybe Princess Brierly wasn't smitten with him because he lacked eloquence. As she snoozed, Arpien practiced several possible speeches in his mind. He had a bad habit of mouthing along as he rehearsed, which made it all the more embarrassing when he noticed Princess Brierly watching him.

"Who are you?" she said.

"Prince Arpien Trouvel of Conquisan." That kiss hadn't been as memorable as he'd anticipated, but how could she forget him completely?

"Just checking."

"Did you sleep well, my lady?" Arpien winced. *In six words, prove to her you are neither sensitive nor eloquent.*

Princess Brierly cocked her head at him like a bird. She gave a tiny, high-pitched "hm" of mild fascination.

He fed her a slice of stale bread and several of the sweet nothings he'd been practicing. She seemed more interested in the bread. While he regrouped his loquaciousness, he told her the rest of his plan. "As soon as we're through the briars, we'll ride for Boxleyn. That's the new capital of Rosaria. We can make it through Sentre Forest in less than a week, but we can take longer if you need. Do you think you can ride?"

"All right."

Lunch was over too quickly, and he picked the sword back up again. "A distant cousin of yours is King of Rosaria now, but once he confirms your identity, he can transfer control of Sentre Forest to us. I was thinking we'd rule out of Castle Estepel, but now that I've seen these briars"—he hacked at a leathery vine—"I'm dubious. This property may not be the most conducive to launching a new kingdom. The budget may be tight our first few years of marriage, until we can manage our exports more effectively, but overall, it might be wiser to build a new place instead of investing in this old one. I imagine you have sentimental attachment to the place, though. What do you think?"

"All right."

"All right we move or all right we stay?"

"Whatever makes you happy."

"I want you to be happy, too, Princess."

"It doesn't matter to me."

That was the way the rest of the day went. He shared with her his long-cherished dreams for their life together, and she shrugged. Maybe she was still tired, but wasn't her complete lack of interest in her own future a little—odd? Was there something wrong with him—or with her? He was relieved when the dimming daylight gave him an excuse to quit chopping and talking. His arms, tongue, and mind ached.

"Time to go to sleep," he said.

"All right." Was that amusement in her voice? Too dark to read her face.

Now that he'd stopped moving, his body cooled enough to feel the chill spring air. "Are you warm enough? I did plan for this, at least." He pulled a wool cloak from his pack. He'd ordered it from Conquisan's finest weavers and toted it around the entire eight months since he'd left home. Even on snowy nights in the mountains, he'd resisted taking it out for warmth. He wanted his first gift to her to be new and unspoiled, the finest Conquisan had to offer.

In this, at least, her reaction was everything he'd anticipated. She drew it around her shoulders and marveled at the colors, the slightly felted texture, the lightweight but warm weave. Blue and green zigzags played tag with each other, and her slender fingers traced the intricate pattern. She thanked him with a pretty curtsey.

The fading sunset cast her face in an attractive glow. Or maybe it was the fact that she was at last showing some animation. It made Arpien want to try that wake-up kiss all over again, and this time do it differently. He steeled himself to play the gentleman. Luckily, he was too tired for fantasies to keep him awake.

He was awakened by a growling beast. He leapt to his feet and drew the vademecum sword. The briars had grown up around them overnight. Whatever was hiding in the thicket—he could feel eyes upon him— would have them at a serious disadvantage.

Princess Brierly sat up and stretched. "What are you doing?"

He motioned for silence. "I heard a bear."

"No bears out here. No animals at all in this thicket."

"Shh."

A low guttural growl came again, close by. Brierly grinned. "It's your stomach."

Arpien lowered the sword. "I thought I saw something move. Probably the vines."

"The vines are dangerous enough in themselves, Arpien." She said this last with a lift of an eyebrow, as though to verify she'd gotten his name right. Was he so forgettable?

He didn't silence the beast in his stomach with breakfast. Only four slices of bread left, and just the smell of the grandmother pickles made his stomach turn.

They didn't talk so much today. Er, he didn't talk so much. He needed to concentrate on hacking a path through the briars while he still had full strength. Finding his way out of the thicket was much harder than finding his way in had been. On the way in, it'd been easy—just head for the spindly sandstone tower rising out of the briars. But the gate in the wall that surrounded the property was only ten feet high and obscured by the briars from here. He could cut his way to the outer wall but miss the gate. Although she was moving more fluidly today, Princess Brierly didn't look quite ready to vault thirty-foot walls yet, so the only way out of Estepel was through the hidden gate. And by every five feet he missed the gate, it would add another hour to their escape.

His sword might be as effective as a wooden spoon against the briars, but it had other uses. He stepped back from the briars, held the blade in front of him, and closed his eyes.

"What are you doing?" Princess Brierly said.

"Finding the gate."

"Your sword is a compass? Handy."

Truth be told, the vademecum sword wasn't a much better compass than it was a hedge-pruner. Sometimes it pointed him where he wanted to go, sometimes it ignored him, and sometimes it sent him in the wrong direction entirely. Today it tugged him forward without any pother. Another three hours of chopping and he could see the end of the briars. Another three hours after that, and the pair broke into a sunlit clearing.

This wasn't the gate. This was a gravesite.

Two gravestones lay at the center of a twenty-foot patch of grass. They were surrounded by a perfect circle of briars, as though an invisible wall held back the thicket. Arpien flung the vademecum sword on the ground and himself beside it. He hadn't run across any graves on the way into Castle Estepel, so this meant they were going the wrong way. If he didn't find the right path immediately, his strength would give out before they reached the gate.

Princess Brierly drifted around the clearing and admired the scenery.

"Well?" Arpien said. "What poor fools will we share our graves with?"

"Read for yourself."

He read the names on the tombstone. "Justin and Golda Steward." Her parents. Thorns and thistles. "I'm sorry. I didn't mean to remind you—though I guess this is new to you, them being dead—"

Bite your boasting tongue, hero.

She turned her head away.

Good job, rescue the princess and bring her to tears.

Arpien didn't like tears. On the few occasions he'd tried to ease a maiden's tears, she inexplicably started producing more. How to fix this? He assumed the *Sixth Stance of Deep Mourning* and flourished the *Bow of Esteemed Members of Foreign Nation-States.* "My condolences on the loss of your—"

"Pickle?" She offered him one from the clay crock.

He aborted the bow and shook his head no.

Brierly plopped down beside a headstone. She bit into the rejected pickle herself, her eyes as dry and unaffected as though she were sitting at a tea table, not on her own parents' graves. The lack of tears disturbed him more than real ones would have.

"I hink you eading us the ong ay." Cucumbery munching obscured her words.

Courtesy was becoming difficult. "Where would you have us go, Your Highness?"

She gestured with the pickle to something behind him. "I wager he knows."

Arpien readied his sword as he whirled and looked into a pair of brown eyes. Living eyes, not the mummified hollows left behind in the dried-apple faces of other would-be rescuers he'd found trapped in the briars.

"What is that?" Arpien asked.

"The Thorn King. One of Voracity's servants."

Arpien had only read about Voracity, the evil fairy who'd laid the Curse on Princess Brierly. Seeing one of Voracity's minions made her seem more real, a threat that snaked from one century into the next.

"He's a king?" he said.

"I just call him that because he can get the thorns to obey him. Watch him."

The creature crept through the thicket. The vines directly in front of him split apart and rejoined as soon as he passed through. His path was diagonal to their position, bringing him neither closer nor further away. As he passed through more sparse parts of the thicket, Arpien discerned more of his form. He had a reddish-brown pelt. At first he appeared to walk on all fours, but observation proved he walked on two feet, his back stooped as though under a heavy load. Not all of him was covered in the brownish pelt. When he passed through patches of sunlight, Arpien caught flashes of skin like his own, only striped in red. The stripes were irregular, uneven, almost smeared.

Not natural stripes. Gouge marks outlined in blood.

Arpien swallowed. "The thorns don't obey him very well. Look how many times he's been cut."

"I think he must be clumsy. Voracity never orders him to attack me. Perhaps he's inept. I've seen him in dreams before, but the only thing he does is spy from a distance."

"Is he human?"

"If he was once, he doesn't look much like it anymore."

Arpien might have described him as a living corpse. No human who had received such wounds would survive. Thorns pierced his flesh so deeply it was hard to tell whether the thorns had fused to his skin or had grown out of it. What Arpien had taken for a pelt was a cloak on his back. It was mottled brown, maroon, and a bruised rose color, as though it had sopped up blood, dried, and sopped up more blood, layer after layer. Even his eyes spoke of pain so deep Arpien was amazed he could stand at all. Had Voracity killed some man and then reanimated him? Did fairies have that power? If he was not dead, he would be soon. His very repulsiveness made Arpien want to stare and avert his glance at the same time.

The Thorn King didn't come any closer to them, but dragged himself in a wide arc around them. At a certain point in the circle, he turned around and began retracing his steps. Was he guarding them? The creature didn't have to attack if he could keep them there long enough for the evil fairy to arrive.

Arpien considered their position. The briars covered the entire lawn from the castle walls to the gate, with the exception of this twenty-foot diameter clearing around the graves. At best, Arpien could chop through enough briars to progress maybe five feet an hour. The Thorn King, even injured as he was, could move that same distance in a matter of seconds. Plus, inside the thicket Arpien wouldn't have enough room to maneuver his sword and body in a fight. The gravesite was the best defensible position. What would be easier—to engage an injured Thorn King and his briars or to wait around for the more powerful adversary?

If the Thorn King controlled the briars, they'd have to go through him to escape. Could they negotiate?

Arpien splayed his feet and lifted his chin in the *Stance of Military Threat Lightly Veiled by Decorum*. "Excuse me." Arpien walked to the edge of the clearing and tried again. "Pardon."

The Thorn King took no notice.

Arpien turned to Princess Brierly. "Does he understand speech?"

"I don't know. I've never wanted to get close enough to talk to him. He's one of hers."

Arpien straightened his shoulders, tried not to feel ridiculous, and addressed the briars at large. "We know who you are and whom you serve. That need not make us enemies, if you do not act against us. Grant us safe passage through the briars."

The Thorn King altered his path to move straight toward him. The vademecum sword buzzed in warning. Arpien tightened his hand on his sword but held his ground.

A gouged hand reached out from the thicket as though asking for payment. Arpien dug in his pouch for one of his last coins.

The Thorn King shook his head. "No," he rasped. "Give me your thorns."

Couldn't he find his own? He lived in a briar patch. Maybe he was inept. Arpien pulled down a vine and hacked at the base of a thorn with the vademecum sword.

"No. Your thorns," the creature said.

"I don't have any thorns."

"Then I can't help you." The Thorn King limped away.

Arpien took a step after him. "Come back!"

There was one path and one path only through the thicket, and it was rapidly closing on the Thorn King's heels. Arpien grabbed Brierly's hand and darted after the Thorn King. All around them the vines stirred in hunger and reached out to taste their flesh.

Short-lived negotiations.

A foot-long thorn bit Arpien's sleeve. Brierly yipped behind him. Had she tripped over those long toes on her shoes? Arpien saw a vine snap around her ankle. He walloped the vine with his sword, severed the empty cloth toes off her pointed poulaines, and yanked her forward. They had to follow the Thorn King closely or they'd be trapped in the briars. Just like all the other princes who'd tried to rescue her and been swallowed by the thicket. He'd always thought those other princes idiots, to blunder into plants and die. Wasn't the power of Voracity's Curse supposed to be broken now that Princess Brierly was awake? Or perhaps it would not be broken until they killed the Thorn King. Her jailor.

The passage narrowed and they fell further behind. They had to turn sideways and sidle through shoulder-first. There was no helping injury now. They'd just have to run and hope the scratches wouldn't dig deep. If she stayed close his body would take the most damage.

"Cover your eyes," Arpien said, "and run."

He shielded his own face with his forearm as they ran. Positioned like that, he couldn't see the Thorn King, only a few feet in front of him where the Thorn King's feet left a vanishing path. Brierly slowed—a hundred years of sleep would leave anyone out of shape—and Arpien dragged her forward. Thorns nipped at his clothes and dragged their pace even more. He heard the ripping of fabric as he broke free of the vines, again and again. Arpien pushed forward with all the strength he had left.

All resistance vanished. They tumbleweeded over each other through long dry grass. He released Brierly's hand for fear he'd crush her. The princess rolled some feet beyond him.

As soon as he could move again, Arpien pushed his nose out of the dirt and looked for Brierly. She'd landed in a much more graceful position than he had. She sat with her legs stretched in front of her and supported her weight on the heels of her palms. She might have been lounging at a picnic. Blue-green eyes studied him, then the scene behind him. She gave another tiny, high-pitched, "Hm."

He flipped over to see what she saw: an open gate of twisting iron rods set in an archway in the sandstone outer wall. It was a good thing he'd lost track of the Thorn King. In fighting to free themselves from the briars, they'd stumbled through the gate. He must have inadvertently used the vademecum sword to find the way out, and this time it decided to cooperate.

Brierly leaned forward. "I broke something." Arpien rushed to her. She dangled a broken piece of crockery between brine-soaked fingers.

"You brought the pickles?" he said.

"I like pickles."

As weak as the one hundred years of sleep had left her, she'd expended the strength to lug a thirty-pound clay crock. And he'd had to drag both her and the crock.

"THOSE PICKLES COULD HAVE COST US OUR LIVES!"

The longer the announcement hung in the air, the stupider it sounded.

A corner of Brierly's mouth twitched. Thistles, he hadn't made her cry, had he? But the woman who shed no tears at her parents' graveside wasn't going to cry over a little royal bellowing. "I've never died by pickle before," she said.

Arpien exhaled. Now that they'd made it out, it was a little humorous to think of death by pickle. "You still haven't."

Brierly peered at him. "You haven't, either."

"Uh—no."

"Hm."

She smelled of spice and vinegar and her ankle bore some scratches from the vine, but otherwise she was unscathed. "I have Fleetsome Feet. It was a christening Gift from a fairy godmother." She wiggled her toes. Arpien could see them through the holes in her poulaines.

Nor were the shoes the final clothing casualty. The beautiful cloak, his first gift to her, bore a twelve-inch rip down one side. Arpien sighed. Third sons, even third sons of kings, didn't have a lot of money, and he'd spent a good deal of his savings on that cloak. It touched him to see how Brierly took it to heart, too. Until he noticed she mourned more for the single rip in her cloak than for the multiple rips in him. This was why you shouldn't wear your best doublet to rescue princesses. Arpien wove a hand in and out of the strips of his sleeves. He could imagine what his older brother would do if he saw him now. Cryndien would thump him on the back, too hard, too jovial. *Well, Fumbleshanks, I guess I did tell you the ladies like a man in a well-cut outfit.*

Arpien had left the bulk of the supplies—utensils, maps, letters of introduction—outside the castle gate. "Fearless!" Arpien whistled. "My horse," he explained to Brierly.

"What does he look like?" Brierly asked, as though he'd lost a ring or a shoe and she could help him search while she lounged on the grass.

"Large, white, very intimidating."

Brierly leaned forward so her weight rested on her fingertips, not her flat palms. "You own a Conquisani Bleacher?"

Arpien nodded. "Since I was thirteen."

"Who would give a boy a Conquisani Bleacher?"

He bristled, although he'd heard the objection since the day he'd gotten Fearless. A cavalry of the renowned Bleachers could shake down a mountain.

"Don't you think I could handle him?" He didn't tell her Fearless turned out to have the temperament of a friendly collie.

"I'm just surprised. That warhorse's bloodlines are probably more noble in the horse world than yours are in the human world, Herren."

"Arpien." He whistled again. He'd trained Fearless better than to mosey off at a little delay in adventuring. The Peerless White Steed was not only a hero's best tool, it was his best accessory. "He was a birthday present from Cryndien, all right?"

"Who?"

"The king. My brother." It seemed odd to have to tell her, but why should she know who Cryndien was?

"You two must be close."

Close? His middle brother Bo had called the gift attempted fratricide.

Fearless didn't come, but Arpien had more urgent problems. He was so hungry he feared that if Fearless did come he'd eat his own horse. He and Brierly shared the remainder of the dry bread. Arpien set out with a crossbow to find small game. "If you need me, whistle three times like a capary bird. It sounds like this—"

Before he could demonstrate, Brierly puckered her lips and let loose a deafening bird call.

"Uh—yes, exactly."

He returned an hour later with a rabbit and a squirrel. The supplies were all there, but now both horse and princess were missing. "Princess Brierly!"

In answer he heard three capary bird calls from within the forest. He dropped the catch and ran after the sound. "Brierly!"

"Why aren't you whistling?" she said.

She lounged on a mossy fallen tree trunk, in a row with a whole flock of birds. Oh, if he had his crossbow now. The birds glared at him as though he'd stumbled into a council meeting to which he was not invited.

"You said to whistle," she said.

"I meant if you were in trouble."

"Oh. I'm not. Are you? I heard you shout."

"No, I just couldn't find you."

She tilted her head at him. "Hm."

The birds flew off as he extended his hand to her. He led her back to their supplies and skinned and cleaned his catch. He asked Brierly to find nearby fuel for a cooking fire. She acquiesced without complaint, but brought back a number of unhelpful items—a piece of eggshell, a hornets' nest, a rock.

After some explanation and effort, they produced a meal of roast meat and wine. Arpien wanted to fall on the food like a beast, but he tried to show some manners to please his lady. He wasn't convinced she appreciated his effort—she licked her dainty fingers and wiped grease down her pink skirts.

When they were full and comatose, Brierly said, "Your horse is over that hill."

Arpien squinted. "You can see him?"

"No. The birds told me."

The birds—?

She arranged her dust-and-grease-streaked skirts in a decorative circle around her knees. "I'd send the birds to bring him, but horses don't take orders well from birds. Insults their dignity. As there's no point in us both taxing ourselves with the climb, I'll just wait here."

She was already settling against the tree, so there was little Arpien could do but do as she suggested. Just as she predicted, as he crossed the crest of the hill, a white horse gamboled up to greet him. Arpien scolded him, and Fearless wagged his long streaming tail back and forth like a sheep dog.

Arpien slapped him on his broad side. "Insult your dignity? You have none, sir."

Reunited horse and master joined Brierly at the fire.

"Hello, Fearless," Brierly said. Fearless lowered his neck and pushed his face in front of Brierly. Brierly patted his neck. "Well, it's fine now, I found him for you."

"Are you talking to me?" Arpien said.

"Fearless says you got lost several days ago. He was worried."

"You can talk to my horse? Just like you can talk to those birds?"

She nodded.

"How?"

"I suppose if you need a reason, it's because of the Gifts the good fairies gave me at my christening—among them the Gifts of Music and Speaking to Animals. I can talk to any animal, but birds best of all."

"So you speak—Wild Boar? Electric Tree Eel?"

"All the usual."

"Then why didn't you ask the animals to help us get out of that briar thicket?"

"There weren't any to ask. Besides the Thorn King, I seem to be the only resident these days."

Up to this point, Arpien had imagined Brierly a lady of few words. Why then did she find plenty to say to his horse? From the opposite side of the fire, Arpien watched Brierly brush Fearless and listened to the sweet low sound of her voice.

"Your horse talks almost as much as you do," Brierly said.

Arpien wanted to ask what his horse was saying. Then again, maybe he didn't. Judging by obscure glances both horse and princess cast at him, they were talking about him. If you could believe that.

Even more unbelievable was the realization that Arpien was jealous of his horse. Didn't he deserve at least a fragment of the attention Brierly lavished on Fearless? He'd heard Rosarians were too backwoodsy to understand proper forms of behavior and rank. While he didn't expect her to fawn over his efforts, he had at least expected warmth, or at a minimum acknowledgement.

Maybe she showed no gratitude because he was Conquisani. He hadn't expected her to hold to the old prejudices. She'd been willing to marry a prince of Conquisan once, why not again? But why would Brierly look on him with favor when so far she had shown more concern for his horse, her cloak, even the accursed pickles?

"You could thank me for rescuing you."

Brierly blinked wide blue-green eyes at him. "Thank you," she said, the way he thanked his old nurse every year for knitting him a new pair of woolen stockings on his birthday.

Exhaustion made him cranky, so he went to sleep before he said something unfortunate.

The next day continued the decline begun the moment they met in the tower. Six days of lopping briars had taken their toll, and Arpien outslept Brierly, who was missing again. His sword didn't seem concerned about her absence, as it didn't point him anywhere. Nor did she answer his whistles. He packed in a whirlwind, and Fearless led him into the woods.

He was stunned that she'd traveled so far. Her body was fast regaining strength. He was even more stunned that she was dancing when he found her. An ensemble of multicolored birds swirled in graceful circles around her and provided the necessary music. To Arpien it sounded like cacophony, but Brierly closed her eyes and whirled to the sound as she might an ensemble of musicians. She looked eerie and enchanted, in that rumpled antique ball gown. Did she imagine a partner as she twirled? Arpien was tempted to cut in, but doubted he'd add much to the visual effect. Brierly danced as though she were the only person in all Sentre Forest—unashamed, solitary, and ingenious in her creativity.

As much as Arpien enjoyed watching her, he doubted she'd appreciate him spying on her private fantasy. He cleared his throat.

Brierly and the birds cocked their heads at him.

"We should be on our way, my lady."

She blinked. "Ah. Boxleyn."

"Yes, to claim our half of the kingdom."

Brierly addressed the birds. "Sorry, I have to be rescued right now. Maybe later."

Fearless was an immense stallion and didn't seem to notice the addition of Brierly's slight body. Certainly Arpien noticed it. Riding with Princess Brierly's arms around his waist was one of the most delectable and uncomfortable experiences of his life to date.

Brierly seemed to agree with the uncomfortable part more than the delectable part, because a few hours later she stole a horse.

It came about like this. Here and there patches of Sentre Forest had been cleared away to create farmland. It was at the edge of one such plot of farmland that the pair stopped for lunch. All during lunch a dark brown horse peered over a fence at them.

"Feed him one of those grandmother pickles and he'll go away," Arpien said.

Brierly crossed her arms over the split rail fence. "He's just seeing what we have to offer him."

Arpien reloaded their supplies, mounted Fearless, and reached a hand down for Brierly. She wasn't where he'd left her. Typical. She was on the other side of the fence on the dark brown horse's back.

"What are you doing?"

"Getting my own horse." In a mighty leap the pair vaulted the fence.

"That's stealing."

"Neef wanted to come with me."

"Neef?"

"That's his name."

"What, you asked him?"

It seemed she had.

Arpien sighed. "What about the farmer?"

"What farmer?"

"The farmer who owns this horse."

"Why does there have to be a farmer?"

Where were her morals? "Fine, you want your own steed, I'll buy it. Wait there."

By the time he negotiated a fair price for the horse and some of the farmwife's bread and boiled eggs, Brierly and Neef had wandered away.

This was getting tiresome.

He didn't need to draw the vademecum sword because his ears guided him to her. A snatch of melody filtered through the trees. He edged Fearless toward it. Now and again he stopped to listen for her voice. Her voice was lovely, if a bit rusty. His muscles tightened even as his chest turned to pudding. He'd been following this song for years, in dreams.

So he followed it a while longer.

3

Brierly

Neef was a social climber and a flirt. The moment Fearless told him Brierly was an enchanted princess on her way to inherit half a kingdom, Neef enumerated with all his equine charm the advantages of a peerless steed like himself. She'd been locked in a tower; he was stuck here on this pathetic farm. Both of them were too handsome for common society. They were destined for each other.

Well, why not?

Neef was so delighted with his new freedom he galloped through the forest. But exertion mussed his mane, Neef said, so he soon settled into a frisky trot. Brierly caught his high spirits and began singing. It was a song she'd made up as a child, all about her beloved Sentre Forest. Over the decades it had evolved into thirteen melodic variations and one hundred twenty-six verses. Today's variation was *con brio*, in A Major. Neef's hooves provided percussion.

She had only made it to verse thirty-seven when Herren—Arpien— caught up with her. "That was—impeccable. Beguiling." He shook his head in self-censure and tried a third time. "Exquisite."

"Thanks."

"You shouldn't wander off on your own, though."

Only one real danger, and Brierly hadn't seen her for years. "I heard you coming."

"What if it were a giant mantiz instead of me?"

"I'd talk to it."

The analytical look was a good one for him: ramrod posture, piercing intelligent eyes, quizzical brow. He would make a fine statue for any palace lawn: Prince Ponders the Situation. Her favorite detail was that his lower jaw didn't quite line up with his upper, as though he were chewing the inside of his cheek as he thought.

The statue broke pose. "How about a cutpurse?"

"I'd tie him up. Join his band. Fly. Turn into a tree. Turn him into a tree. There are so many options."

"Aren't you afraid of anything?"

"Nothing in this place. I started getting to know my future subjects long before my parents made Sentre Forest part of my dowry."

"But are your future subjects equipped to protect you from dragons or electric tree eels?"

"Dragons and electric tree eels would be my future subjects." At least they would have been in a life without fairy Curses. All of Rosaria would be hers someday, her parents once said, but Sentre Forest would be hers on the day she married. It would solve a very old border dispute with Conquisan. Relations were so volatile that not until her father's reign did diplomatic parties once again travel between their two capitals. Back then Brierly didn't care who she had to marry—a Conquisani prince or a three-headed troll (which according to popular notion were about the same)—as long as she got Sentre Forest.

Moot point. She went back to the more entertaining pastime of prince-baiting. "Anyway, it's the squirrels you should be concerned about. Take a wrong step in a squirrel council meeting and it degenerates into a nut-flinging contest. The pointy end of an acorn can do a lot of damage. If squirrels ever master the catapult, we're all doomed."

Arpien assumed his Prince Ponders the Situation statue pose again. "Ah."

Neef took an immediate disliking to Arpien. No sense of style. Well, Arpien had reduced his clothes to sweaty rags on the briars, but that was the Thorn King's fault, not his. As they rode Brierly succumbed to her Artistic Eye and mentally designed her figment a new wardrobe of bold colors and overblown puffs. Here and there she'd stitch an uneven seam or add a frayed patch, emblems of a heroic image threatening to unravel.

In fact, it was the patches she liked best about Arpien.

Best not think on Arpien. Princes never stayed long. Luckily, Neef's ambitions filled up the next couple of hours. Unable to hear Neef's discourse, Arpien unknowingly offended the horse by interrupting with his own desperate-sounding attempt at conversation.

"So where are these dragons and electric tree eels? It's very quiet for a forest that's supposed to be rife with gryphons and catapulting squirrels."

"Oh, they're around. The animals say the road smells bad, so they avoid it."

"Human scent?"

"Fairy protection. Fairies enchanted the main roads to Estepel centuries ago so people could travel safely to the capital."

That "favor" made it so much harder to become acquainted with exotic creatures.

"The magic won't stop something from eating you if it's determined, but it does make you less appetizing."

Her rescuer eyed the immense purplish trees around them. "I can see how having one's traveling merchants and dignitaries devoured by semi-mythical beasts would tend toward an adverse impact on both politics and the economy."

An attempt at humor? A muscle twitched at the corner of her mouth. Must be a random spasm.

She waited for him to say more, but once again he seemed to be inventing something sufficiently princely in his head. It was up to Neef to fill the silence with speculation about the cuisine he could expect at Boxleyn (sweet apples, tart apples, apples and bran...) until the party came to a river. Brierly leaned forward to get a closer look at the frothing rocks.

Arpien laid his hand on her shoulder. "We'll have to go further downstream to cross. The rapids are too dangerous here."

Brierly's skin itched like a hundred years of oil and grime caked her body. It was the best evidence yet to support Arpien's impossible story that she was—at last—awake. She could take a stick and beat her pink skirts out like a rug. She rode Neef into the hard rush of the river.

"What are you doing?" Arpien said.

Pointless questions didn't deserve answers. Amazing how water could shock and soothe at the same time. Neef objected to the cold, so she dismounted. The current knocked her feet out from under her. Arpien shouted from the bank, but her head kept submerging, distorting his words. She tried to slow the water, but none of her decades of practice seizing control of her dreams made a difference. This wasn't a fully lucid dream.

The river bottom dropped sharply. Her feet found nothing to drag against.

Brierly didn't scream, not over a little thing like drowning. Whenever her head broke surface, she could see Neef swimming after her. She reached for his mane, and felt her own grabbed instead. A tangle of strong limbs, both horse and man, hauled her to the bank.

She coughed out a mouthful of water. Her lungs burned. Still, she hadn't died this time. The experience could be counted a mild success.

No one else shared her assessment. The horses complained and Arpien's voice slashed across both of theirs. "What were you thinking? Were you thinking? You could have killed yourself!"

As she'd died in thousands of other dreams. She'd been swallowed by dragons and five-headed beasts. Trapped in burning rooms. Beheaded by swords. Drowning was one of the less painful ways to die. "It doesn't matter."

"Doesn't matter? Doesn't matter?" The anger in his voice built like the rapids. "I rescue you, and the only thanks I get is you rushing off to commit suicide at the first convenient moment! Why didn't I just let you sleep another hundred years? It wouldn't have mattered to you."

It had been a long time since Brierly had been passionate about anything. Her creations tended to reflect her own mood, so she was surprised to find such ire in him.

"Your pardon for the inconvenience," she said.

Arpien wrung out his cap. "You are a perverse person, Brierly Steward. You nearly die, and you act like it's a social faux pas. Do you place so little value on your own life?"

"I wasn't trying to drown."

"Then don't take foolish risks. I might be too *inconvenienced* to save someone who cares so little for her own self-preservation." He jammed the sodden cap back on. The lumps of cloth clung to his skull like an overweight cat afraid of heights, and ruined the image of dignity.

They didn't ride any further that day. Most of the supplies would be fine after they dried before the fire Arpien built: utensils, maps, blankets, what layers of clothes they could decently remove in mixed company. The pickles survived. Most of the boiled eggs had cracked and would have to be used immediately.

The bread was the true loss. Five loaves had disintegrated into wet paste. Arpien tried to salvage it. He scooped it into his cooking pot and heated it like porridge. With a little honey or cinnamon it might have tasted like weak bread pudding. As it was it tasted like hot ceiling plaster. Brierly took one bite and scraped hers back in the pot.

"You need to eat," said the prince.

"No, I don't."

"What are you, four?" Arpien scooped some back out of the pot and extended it to her.

You could be ravenous in a dream, but you couldn't starve. She'd tried. "It's one of my fairy Gifts. I can eat whatever I want and still retain a maidenly figure."

"That's mad."

Brierly shrugged. Mad never stopped much.

He waved the bowl in front of her again. "It will at least warm you. You're rattling."

So she ate more plaster.

Over the course of the evening she watched Arpien's spine melt. The more she shivered, the softer it got, like a candle on a sweltering summer day. She asked Neef to come lay down beside her to warm her up, but Neef was holding his grudge longer than Arpien. As for Fearless, he said he was trying to stay out of it. Arpien gathered a small forest of wood for the fire. That and her almost-dry gown smothered her trembling. She never thought she'd be eager to put the accursed pink gown on again.

When Arpien spoke, it was more quietly than she'd yet heard him. "I'm sorry I yelled at you. This rescue isn't going at all how I planned. Then I saw you struggle in the water. That would have been the cruelest irony, if you died like that."

If not for her fairy Gift of a Fine Ear, she would not have been able to hear him.

"My older sister drowned in a river," he said. "I watched the current sweep her away."

Herren never told her he had a sister before. No, this was Arpien.

"I'm sorry." She'd watched her own loved ones die. It was one of Voracity's favorite themes.

"They said it wasn't my fault. How could a six-year-old drag an eleven-year-old to safety? But it was my fault."

His bare toes squeezed the sandy dirt. They were a man's toes, long and calloused and slightly fuzzy, but oddly vulnerable-looking without the protection of the stockings, which hung on a branch by the fire.

"My older brother Bo told us not to go down to the river without him. When he said he couldn't go, I cried until Kirren gave in. She doted on me. And I killed her. I stood over Kirren's grave and apologized, over and over again, that I was too weak to save her."

How well Brierly knew the special kind of torment that lay in power-lessness. She wished the figment would quit looking at her as though he could possibly understand it, too.

"For months afterward I had nightmares," the figment said. "Kirren and I would be at the river again. Only the banks weren't shallow and sandy anymore. They were high walls of rock carved by the river."

He was looking at her as though he expected her to remember the place, too.

"*Don't get too close to the edge*, Kirren would warn me. I'd run right up to it, brat that I was. She'd rush after me and slip. I'd grab her hand. The river tore her away and crushed her like some bully crushing a doll in his fist. The water would swell up, this giant foaming mouth, and swallow me down. I'd kick and scream for Kirren, for my brothers, for anyone, but no one came."

His voice was toneless, but the images he painted were so vivid that Brierly could see them before her. The dark waters roared, thousands of ravenous slobbering tongues. A six-year-old boy screamed the high pitch of terror that only the very young can achieve.

"Until you."

The scene snapped. "What do you mean?"

"The nightmares continued for half a year after my sister died. Then one night as the river swept me away, I saw a figure in white standing on the ledge above me. I yelled for help, but she didn't answer. The rapids carried me a good hundred yards downriver when—I can't explain how, it was a dream—she reached down and plucked me out of the water. I was so relieved I started crying anew. I hugged the knees of the lady in white. I thought she was my sister. She dried my tears and clothes with a touch of her hand. 'I'm sorry,' she said. 'I'm not Kirren. My name's Brierly.'"

The dream tilted, shuddered further out of her control.

"You don't even remember, do you?" A corner of his mouth tugged up in self-deprecation. "I know it was you, Brierly. I recognized you the moment I saw you asleep in that tower. Well, after I dusted you. That song you sang this morning? I've chased it in my dreams for the past twelve years." He peered into her face.

She leaned back a fraction of an inch, further from the flickering firelight.

Don't ask me for hope.

"I never imagined that once I found you, in the waking world, I'd have to convince you of what happened," Arpien said. "You can enter other people's dreams, did you realize that? My great-grandfather said he saw you in his sometimes. That night you saved me from drowning, he was the only one who believed it was anything more than a dream. Kirren would have believed me, too, but she was dead. Bo told me I was a wishful idiot. He changed after Kirren died. It changed me, too, that dream. You changed me. The nightmares eased. I went back to my sister's grave and promised her that I'd never be powerless again. I'd save anyone who needed my help. I caught snatches of you in my dreams as I grew up, your voice singing. I'd run after you to thank you, but you'd vanish. Then, when I was eleven, I saw you crossing my dream again. You were running, faster than a deer flees from hounds. I promised, with all the vehemence of an eleven-year-old, that I would save you. You patted my head and ran on."

He drew his lanky legs up and hooked one arm under his knees. "Now I suppose you'll pat my head and run on again. I envisioned a far different result when I awakened you. That you'd—"

He jabbed a stick into the fire. One fire-eaten log collapsed. Orange sparks rose into the night sky. "You never asked for my help. I'm a wishful idiot, like my brother said."

Maybe it was the sheer vulnerability of his pose. "I do remember you," Brierly whispered.

His head snapped up.

This wasn't the first time she'd dreamt of rescue. It was the first time one of her creations dredged up memories she had forgotten. He disturbed her. She needed time to put him back in his place in the dream world. Which was funny, because her life was nothing but a deep cave of time, with endless blind caverns waiting for her to fill them.

"I'm tired." She turned her back to the fire and flopped down on the ferny ground.

He was a prince—he knew a royal dismissal. For several attenuated minutes her Fine Ears picked up nothing but the crackling of the fire, the creatures gossiping in the woods. A couple squirrels bragged about the comparative sizes of their winter nut hoards. The boasting gave way to the sound of tiny claws scampering around a tree trunk and a chittering chorus of *prove it, prove it, prove it*. The night air stole away Brierly's body heat. She wished she'd thought to grab her cloak, but she was afraid that if she moved to retrieve it Arpien would resume the conversation.

She'd forgotten the little boy in the river. Once Herren/Arpien reminded her of the incident, her congested memory colored in the details he'd left out. Yes, she'd worn white that night. White to mock the innocence she'd lost. She'd just run from a dream where a childhood friend had turned on her, and Brierly had killed her to save herself. She wandered unseeing from dream to dream and came to pause above a torrential river. Which flavor of betrayal tasted the most bitter—when she murdered her friend or when her friend murdered her? It was a pointless exercise in emotional self-mutilation. Because that—abomination of a cherished one—hadn't been her friend, but another figment.

But if all the figments went away, she'd have nothing to clothe her solitude.

Then she'd heard a child's scream of utter fear.

The rush of the rapids or the incoherency of his panic made him hard to understand. But she understood the root of his plea. She resisted until he was a tiny dot sinking beneath the foam. Then her hand reached out and grabbed his.

He shivered on the bank like a brown puppy and threw small arms around her knees. Such a small thing, yet he almost knocked her down in his need to cling to something solid. She'd never met such a wet child— soaked on the outside and the inside, judging by the gallons of tears he rubbed into her skirts. Tears and whatever other fluids come out of a sobbing child. But strange to say, she felt purer in this white gown now than she did before. She dried and warmed him with a touch.

It calmed the boy enough that she was able to distinguish words. "I'm so sorry, Kirren. It's my fault you died. Don't ever go into the river again. Promise."

She stooped down and gazed into eyes that were brown and pink—no white left in them at all from his crying. "I'm sorry, I'm not Kirren. My name's Brierly." She brushed a thumb across his cheekbone and erased the puffiness left by his tears. "But I've learned this—just because people die, it doesn't mean they have to stay dead."

She'd never suspected the little boy would grow up and try to rescue her. All her other imaginary companions stayed as ageless as herself. So she hadn't recognized him a few years later when he offered to stow her up a tree until Voracity's servants passed by. The puppyish boy—how could he protect her when he wasn't even big enough to fit into his own feet? Brierly had gotten used to being her own rescuer. Although this rescuer—alarmed, skinny, and with the incongruously deep voice of a man grown—was unexpected enough to crack her resentment at rescuers for a moment. He never mentioned he was Herren.

He didn't say he was Herren now.

He looked like Herren, so he would be. While she liked the unusual, she didn't like her creations dictating the story.

I know you. I want to help you. You're safe now. Lies, all of them. Or at least perishable truths. Let Voracity see any fondness for her pet prince, and soon she'd be sending the nightmares. Herren/Arpien poisoned. Cut into pieces. He'd turn against her with that flashy oversized sword he was so proud of. She'd run across his grave as she'd run across her parents', time upon relentless time.

One of her fairy Gifts was Fleetsome Feet, good for dancing. Also good for sneaking past sleeping/brooding princes. She didn't take food or tools with her when she left. She didn't even risk taking Neef. His hooves would alert the prince. Anything she needed she could replace when the dream shifted under her control again. By necessity, she now excelled at seizing control of her dreams.

The fact that she still didn't have control of this one was either disturbing or at least, new.

4

Arpien

Arpien couldn't decide what he wanted to do most: wake Brierly up and apologize again, or wake her up and yell at her again. The consistent part of his wishes was waking her up—mostly from her accursed complacency. So after a solid hour of brooding, that was what he decided to do.

She'd wandered off. Predictable. But he'd been wide awake this time and still heard nothing. Quite the insult to his training as a warrior.

He was tempted to let her go get eaten by a bear or meander off a cliff or whatever it was her half-witted wont to do. He'd never met anyone so mule-headedly determined not to stay saved. Time to get on his horse and ride back to Conquisan.

He stuffed his toes into damp ankle boots, heaved himself up, and resaddled Fearless. "Well, you had plenty to say to her. Any words for me?"

Neef huffed. Fearless bumped Neef with his massive white shoulder.

"You don't have to say anything. I've set a crazy princess loose in the forest. It's my job to corral her again."

His princess didn't leave tracks. This time there was no singing to follow, either. Still, when he heard the commotion, he was reasonably reassured he was going the right way.

The outburst died away, but the vademecum sword kept him going in the right direction until he saw the light flickering through the trees ahead. He left the horses some three hundred feet away and crept toward a small encampment of cutpurses.

He almost burst into the camp when he saw the rough way they searched Brierly, but it was foolish to jump into their midst with nothing but a disobedient sword until he thought of a way to get back out. Arpien lifted himself silently into a tree. There were seven—no, eight men in the band. Beards that were exorbitant even by peasant standards masked the shape of their lower faces. Cloaks disguised body shape. Two men held Brierly by the arms. A third massive man questioned her. Two men guarded something by the fire—a cloth sack. Two circled the perimeter.

The eighth brigand didn't seem to have a job. He stood to the side, but was he the group's leader? Arpien had seen his brother Bo, the general of Conquisan's armies, control his men with the same imperceptible reins.

Grand. If they weren't common brigands, they were uncommon brigands.

It took Arpien a while to piece together what had the men so on edge. Brierly had wandered into the camp (past the two men keeping watch, which boosted Arpien's confidence a little) and rooted through their supplies. The cutpurses were concerned that she'd poked into that particular cloth sack. Doubtless the sack contained some jewels or treasure stolen from a passing lord or merchant. But this theory wavered as Arpien scooted closer to their debate.

"I don't like this. It was one thing to kill that peasant. But if we start killing ladies of quality, someone with means is going to take it personally."

"She's not a lady of quality. She's dressed in rags."

"Silk rags? No, she's obviously a rich merchant's daughter fallen on hard times. Maybe ran off with her sweetheart and he tired of her and dumped her in the forest."

Reword that sentence, and it might be true.

The massive man shook her by the arm. "Is that what happened, girl?"

Brierly smiled. Her eyes were as vacant as an addled kitten's. "Try again."

"She's a spy," said another. "I say we kill her."

"*That's* a spy?"

"Or she could be the distraction."

The massive man crowded her space. "Where do you come from?"

Another woman would have cowered at this menacing, bearded anvil of a man. Brierly studied the cutpurse as though he were a jester of mediocre talent. "A conundrum," Brierly said, and began singing.

I've walked a thousand miles and never budged a toe.
The longer the road is, the shorter length I go.
I left home long ago, forever and a day,
N'er to see it again, though n'er I ran away.
Today I nearly drowned, but never did get wet.
The further out I go, the deeper in I get.
I am so very weary, though I always rest.
Where am I from, you ask me? Tell me, have you guessed?

"We don't guess. You tell." The burly brigand flashed a blade under her chin.

"She's a scatter-wit. No threat to us."

"You know we can't let her go and report what she's seen."

Arpien took a second look at their horses. Quality stock. If they'd robbed a lord they'd probably stolen his horses as well. But they spoke and acted more like politicians than thieves. (*What's the difference?* went the joke in Conquisan.) Whatever was in that cloth sack must be of vital political importance. A bribe? Letters of political intrigue? Wills? Marriage records? Shouldn't highwaymen be closer to, well, the highway? Arpien would rather deal with ordinary outlaws. They could be bought with simple things—money, food. These sounded like criminals with a cause. Likely he would not have the sort of tender they'd accept.

Under him the debate continued. "She couldn't have gotten here alone."

Brierly's big toes—visible through her beheaded poulaines—tapped in beat as she sang.

A thousand folks I see, and yet I'm all alone.
All I see is mine, and still nothing I own.

"She's a fool. Driven mad by wandering alone in the forest."

"You're not threatening the right thing." The big man grabbed a fist-ful of white-gold hair and jerked her head up. "How about I improve your beauty? I'll start here"—he licked his blade and drew the flat of it in a ragged line from her temple to her lips—"and draw a line to here." He dragged it down her chin and up again to her upper lip. "Talk fast enough, I'll leave your nose attached."

Brierly sang.

A thousand truths I tell, and every one a lie.
Kill me once again, and still I'll never die.

The tip of the dagger nipped into her skin. Arpien tensed to spring, plan or no plan, but the leader pulled the other's wrist back. "If she was in her right mind, she'd have talked by now."

"What do we do with her, then?"

A few of the men had suggestions, but the leader ignored them. "Tie her up for now."

Brierly didn't struggle as they lashed her to a tree. Did she recognize it'd be useless? Or were the brigands right—she wasn't in her right mind?

Arpien whistled the cry of the night swallow. From several hundred feet away, Fearless heard him and neighed. Arpien had taught Fearless long ago to distinguish several different bird whistles. This one meant for him to provide distraction by making noise and then changing position. With luck, Neef would follow Fearless.

The distraction directed the brigands' attention to the far side of the camp. Three of the brigands slipped into the woods. Arpien slid out of the tree and crept over to Brierly. He looked down into long-lashed eyes that should be filled with relief and admiration.

"Oh. You're back," she said.

The cutpurses snapped their heads in their direction.

A smart person would have run and left her to face the consequences of her own stupidity. Not Arpien. He'd always fancied himself a rescuer.

Which was how, after a respectable battle against five men, Arpien found himself tied to the other side of Brierly's tree.

It didn't take the brigands long to figure out they would get more information from Brierly than Arpien, even if Brierly's answers didn't always make sense. "Well, look, girlie. You didn't come alone after all. Who's this?"

"Herren."

For once Arpien was delighted she'd gotten his name wrong. Who knew what they'd do if they figured out they'd captured a princess with a dowry on her head, and the brother of the Conquisani king? Of course, if Cryndien heard he was captured, he'd just as likely send assassins as help. He wouldn't risk Arpien spilling Conquisani secrets.

"Herren," the burly brigand said. "What is he to you? Brother? Fellow spy? Sweetheart?"

"Rescuer."

The men snorted. "Not very good, is he?"

"No, but he tries hard."

Arpien couldn't decide whether to be touched or offended.

"And what else does your Herren do besides rescue?"

"Chops down plants."

"Just like the old tales. A woodcutter rescues the fair damsel." The burly brigand toyed with the vademecum sword he'd taken from Arpien. "This, I suppose, is his axe?" He twirled the blade in the light of the campfire. "Looks sharp. Sharp enough to, say, chop Herren's head off his shoulders if one of you doesn't start talking."

Arpien felt the ropes stir on the other side of the tree. Brierly must have been struggling. Or shrugging.

"So one of you is mute and the other mad. I'll give you one more chance to tell me who you serve and where you come from."

There was a slight chance the brigands would let Brierly go, since she behaved like a harmless simpleton. It was unlikely they'd let her go unscathed. Arpien wished he could tell her how to use the vademecum sword, so that after they killed him, should she survive, she might find her way to Boxleyn.

When they gave the brigand no answer the man glanced at the silent leader. The leader nodded. Arpien forced himself to meet his executioner's eyes. The blade swung at his neck.

And so it was that Arpien also saw his executioner's surprise when he missed.

His companions laughed.

The burly brigand rolled his shoulders and readjusted his hands. "That one was to help him anticipate. Found your voice yet?"

Arpien did not reply, and the burly brigand swung the vademecum sword again. This time the sword missed Arpien's neck by an inch and carried through in an arc until the brigand faced away from his target.

No laughter this time. "What the combustion are you doing?" said one of his companions.

"Too much to drink, that's what," another said.

The brigand repositioned his feet and swung a third time. The vademecum sword ricocheted off an invisible wall in front of Arpien's face, turned a hundred and eighty degrees in the air, and thwacked into the trunk of a tree on the far side of the camp. The newly-budded leaves tittered with the reverberation of impact. When the vibrations ceased, the absence of sound and movement in the camp was like a solid thing.

The brigand stumbled away from Arpien. Even that shrubbery of a beard could not disguise his slack jaw. "What are you?"

Even Brierly sounded mildly surprised. "He survived? Oh, good."

Now the brigands were afraid to hold them here, and afraid to let them go. They retreated to the fire to discuss their options.

"We know well enough there are bizarre creatures in Sentre Forest. These two aren't normal humans."

"Or it's not a normal sword."

"You're talking like we're in the middle of one of the old tales."

Arpien couldn't explain why the vademecum sword hadn't lopped off his head, but he knew that had less to do with him than the sword. At last, it had done something extraordinary. If only Cryndien were here to see it.

Of course, just because the vademecum sword had saved him once, it didn't mean it would again. It tended to do what it wanted. And when it came to killing him, the brigands had many options besides the sword.

Now that the brigands were on the far side of the camp, Arpien risked speaking to Brierly. "My lady, if these are indeed our last infinitesimal moments to commingle here on Earth, I would just like you to know—"

The ropes tightened across his chest and he heard a colossal yawn from the other side of the tree. "Sorry—what?"

"You can sleep under these conditions?"

"Hm."

It was then he remembered her lack of protest when the brigands tried to kill him, how before that she'd wandered away without so much as a *thanks for your trouble*. He dug the heel of his boot into the dirt. "I hope you have a plan to get us out of here, seeing as how you sabotaged mine."

"It wasn't worth trying to escape when they were standing over us. Where are they?"

Ah. She couldn't see them from her side of the tree.

"They're all around the campfire, deciding how to dispose of us. Brierly, can you get their horses to help us?"

"Hard to untie knots with hooves."

"What about the birds?"

"It's night."

He ground his teeth. "A mountain lion."

"Have you ever tried to command a cat to do what you want?"

The tension on his chest and arms eased. Slack rope piled into his lap. "How … ?"

"Fairy Gift. I'm Handy with Needle and Thread, and therefore knots." She drifted past him to the campfire, a century-old ghost with her own agenda.

"Brierly, no!" he whispered as loudly as he dared. He extracted himself from the limp bonds and dashed after her.

Too late.

It shouldn't, by any tactic in the annals of Conquisani battle history, have worked. Brierly dusted off her skirts and strolled over to where the leader squatted by the fire with his dinner. No guile, no hurry. She might have been taking her place at her own table. The brigand leader watched her stoop before him, his expression bewildered but unalarmed. Brierly's skirts pooled around her as though she were a fair water lily. In one unextraordinary motion, she plucked the knife from the brigand leader's hand, cooked carrot still attached, and planted it in his thigh.

Even then, she didn't bother to run. If she had, the brigands might have known how to act. Only when she had strolled four or five steps away did the leader drag in a clawing gasp of pain. "Stop her!"

Arpien whistled for Fearless. Brierly seemed to have a similar idea. She meandered over to the brigands' horses. That was the last Arpien saw of her before four hulking men obscured his view. His sword was still stuck in the tree on the far side of the camp, so his only weapon was the very rope that had bound him to the tree. He tossed it overhead and looped it over a branch. He grabbed hold of both ends and swung, feet first, into the brigands. Momentum knocked down two of them. The third and fourth drew their swords, but the resistant-neck incident made them hesitate a fraction of a moment before attacking. By then Arpien had claimed a sword from one of their fallen comrades. He parried one blow with the borrowed sword. With the other hand he jerked the rope upwards. It hit the flat of the second blade and deflected the sword.

Arpien released one end of the rope, ducked two more blows, and circled around the two brigands. When he had made a complete circuit, he grabbed the other end of the rope again and yanked on both ends with his full body weight. The force of the contracting half-noose was enough to slam the men together and knock them unconscious.

At this point Fearless came pounding in, all whipping mane and glowing white flanks. The proper hero's steed. Arpien vaulted onto his back and looked for Brierly where he had last seen her by the cluster of horses. She was playing some strange game with the horses and the four remaining brigands. She bobbed and wove under arms and noses and bellies. Fleetsome Feet indeed. One of the horses kicked at Brierly and caught one of the brigands instead.

Arpien rode Fearless closer and reached down an imperative hand to Brierly. "Grab on!" Arpien swung her up sidesaddle in front of him. She weighed less than he thought, and Arpien was startled when she started to fall off the other side. But no, she was only leaning backward to grab hold of the vademecum sword as they passed. Arpien grabbed a fistful of her still slightly damp skirts and threw his weight the other direction to compensate for her gymnastics. He pulled them both upright on Fearless' back, moments before he would have brained himself on a tree.

"I got your sword for you." Brierly favored him with a sweet smile, the sort that ought to melt a man's heart but instead froze his.

If he wasn't certain before, he was now.

Something was definitely not right with his princess.

5

Arpien

Arpien spent the next few miles trying to decide whether Brierly was a genius playing the idiot, or an idiot playing the genius.

She pointed left. "Neef."

"We can't go back for him."

"I told him to meet us here. He was going to ride around the camp and set a false trail."

"When did you tell him that?"

"When you were busy with the other brigands."

"We can't afford to stop. I think we injured six of them, but that leaves two."

"It'll take them a while to figure out the knot I used to tie the reins together."

Well, that did explain the elaborate ducking and weaving around the horses. "Why didn't you just ask the horses for help?"

"Talking to animals doesn't mean I can force them to do what I say. Those horses were loyal to their humans. Fearless, go left."

Let it not be said that his horse was more the gentleman than him. They met up with Neef half a mile later. Brierly hopped down from Fearless's back and twiddled her long tapered fingers while Neef snorted and stamped at her.

Arpien patted his horse's moist neck. He was glad Fearless didn't have such a prissy attitude. "Are you ready to move on?"

"Neef isn't done scolding me."

"The brigands could still be following us."

"I don't think they are."

"What, the forest creatures told you?"

"No forest creatures to ask. I don't think the brigands are following because I don't hear them."

"Another fairy Gift?"

She nodded and undid the laces around—he squinted in the moonlight—a cloth sack.

Arpien groaned and massaged his temples. He glimpsed the bag between his fingers, as though obscuring his vision would make it disappear. "Where'd you get that?"

"The brigands."

He hid behind his hand again. If it was important enough that the brigands were ready to kill them for merely seeing it, the brigands would try to get it back.

"Should I point out that's stealing?"

"It's not stealing." She gestured her hand wide. "Everything you see is mine." True, the entire forest was her dowry. She opened the sack and eased out the top half of a mixing-bowl-sized ball of sticky opalescent bluish-white threads.

She let out a little gasp of awe. "Do you know what this is? This is an egg sac of a giant mantiz." She peered up in the trees. "I've always wanted to meet a giant mantiz."

"Mantis?"

"Mantiz. Arpien, they're beautiful. They're not true mantises, but they look a bit like them. Triangular heads. Long necks. Sleek bodies."

She bunched up her arms in front of her. "They have these powerful front arms with toothlike spikes for seizing prey. They strike so fast you can't even see them move."

She flashed an arm in and out in demonstration.

"And unlike the small mantis, they have these poisonous foot-long fangs for immobilizing their prey. A full grown one, maybe eight feet long, can take down a bear."

That didn't sound beautiful to Arpien. That sounded scary.

"The only place they've ever been spotted is in this forest, because of the hittal trees."

"I've heard that. That's why Strand is so interested in Sentre Forest. There's a bad epidemic of tree-plague in Strand."

"The trees have plague?"

"No, people catch the disease. It's called tree-plague because of the symptoms. Didn't it exist when you were growing up?"

She shook her head.

"The only treatment is the fibers of an egg sac from a giant mantiz," he said. "No wonder those brigands were this deep in Sentre Forest. You're holding in your hands a small fortune."

Brierly stroked the egg sac through the cloth, in that same motion she might tickle the tuft of fur under a kitten's chin. "Hm."

Indeed, Arpien knew Sentre Forest was full of valuable resources that could be sold to neighboring countries. Not just medicines. His brother Cryndien frothed for access to hittal trees, to build up a fleet.

Frothed was an understatement. Cryndien believed Sentre Forest was Conquisan's, due to the engagement treaty between Herren and Brierly. Nevermind that the two had never married. When the Rosarian king demanded an unreasonable price for the precious hittal wood, Cryndien sent men from Conquisan into Sentre Forest to collect their own. The thieves (patriots?) had been caught, blows exchanged, war threatened, and Rosaria had cut off all negotiations with Conquisan. That was three years ago. Within the last year the Rosarian king had promised to reconsider a contract with Conquisan for access to Sentre Forest. Those brigands might just as easily have been from Conquisan as Rosaria. Cryndien might have sent them into Sentre Forest to tag the best hittal trees.

They hadn't looked Conquisani. But then, Arpien had thought from the beginning that their beards and cloaks were excessive, almost as though they were playacting roles in a comedic performance. In fact, the only thing in the camp that might link the brigands to Conquisan was the very cloth that held the egg sac. He brushed a tentative finger across it and felt the fine twill that could only be a Conquisani weave. Strong. Soft. Durable. Near leak-proof.

Publishing this evidence would serve no one's ends, least of all his. *Hello, I just rescued your princess, and I have proof that my countrymen are raiding your forest again.*

Brierly frowned at the egg sac. "They could have been courteous enough to wait until the eggs hatched."

Arpien poked the egg sac with a cautious finger. "There are live mantizes in there?" He scanned the trees for a jealous mama or papa mantiz. Good thing, too, for he caught the movement overhead just in time to throw himself flat against Fearless' back. A pair of four-foot-long green forearms, complete with the described jagged prongs, grabbed at the air above Arpien's stomach.

"Run!"

The only one who took his advice was Fearless, who reared up at the mantiz and tossed Arpien off in his desire to obey. Seated upright Arpien might have stayed on, but in this precarious position, he slid headfirst toward the ground. He managed to tuck his knees up and flip as he fell. He landed in a squat.

The mantiz lunged for him again. No time to draw his sword. He somersaulted out of reach of the mantiz, but that put him within reach of a second one. It snatched him up by the boot. He used his free leg to kick it hard in the abdomen. The shell flexed at the impact. Arpien imagined the crunch that would follow, were this one of the mantiz's smaller relatives. But this was no underfoot beetle. The undented mantiz released him, probably out of surprise more than anything.

Arpien picked himself up and ran.

Neef had finally taken his command to heart, but Brierly still stood there.

"Will you get out of here?" he shouted.

Was she frozen in fear or fascination? Perhaps her stillness protected her. So far the mantizes hadn't attacked her.

Three mantizes dropped to the ground and closed in around Arpien. If he grabbed Brierly and pulled her out of the way, it would only draw their attention to her. So he backed away from her. He had his sword halfway out of the scabbard when the mantizes pounced. He threw himself on the ground and rolled. He dodged the three of them but a fourth mantiz dropped from a branch overhead and landed on him. The lithe insect body was not heavy, but the swift impact forced all the air from his lungs. Two daggers of ice plunged into the side of his neck.

Flashes of color covered his field of vision. Sensation flared and trickled away. He could almost hear Cryndien laughing.

Foolish little Fumbleshanks. Threw your life away on a fairy tale, and didn't even survive to see the ending.

But he hadn't thrown it away. He'd given it away. To her.

If she had sense enough to get out of here while the mantizes were distracted with him. He pushed himself up with numb limbs. Time to be a bigger distraction.

6

Brierly

Brierly's stomach clenched when the mantiz pierced Arpien's neck. Arpien pushed himself up with an inhuman cry, drew his overgrown sword, and sliced into his attacker's leg. The mantiz skittered away. Arpien smacked onto the ground. He tried to rise, once, twice, and found a drunken balance on the third. "Run, Brierly!"

She didn't run.

Something trickled through her veins, as deadly as the poison that ran through Arpien's. But this poison did not numb. Just the opposite.

She had known it for Voracity's work the whole time. Send the honorable young prince to rescue her, to promise freedom and happiness. Make him just irritating enough to seem real, so she'd start to believe. Have him tell her the lovely impossible story of how he'd known her, searched for her, for years.

Then kill him.

When he'd survived probable beheading at the brigands' camp, she'd even felt the ghost of hope. Maybe this dream would end differently. Stupid, Brierly.

He's not really in pain. It doesn't matter, doesn't matter, doesn't matter.

But for the first time in years, it did.

Arpien crashed to his knees. His listless limbs flailed like a drowning man's, as though he could not hold onto consciousness long enough to break surface.

Brierly prized the sword from Arpien's drooping hands and planted herself in front of him. She could barely lift the thing, but she knew anger would lend her strength when the mantizes attacked.

Only they didn't attack.

It was hard to tell where multifaceted eyes focused, but Brierly felt certain the mantizes looked at her, at Arpien, and at each other. Their antennae rustled.

They stared at each other long enough Brierly started to feel foolish.

vademecum sword *attack* *eggs*

Oh. It wasn't fear that made their antennae tremble. It was how they communicated. The longer she stood there, the more her sluggish Gift let her into the conversation.

save the egg sac *attack* *no attack* *it has a vademecum sword*

"I'm not an it. I'm a she."

The antennae froze. The mantizes blinked at her, as surprised as if a toadstool had broken into an aria. Well, no, they couldn't blink without eyelids. She was ascribing a human response to them.

The antennae started waving again. *did it speak* *humans not smart enough to speak* *sweep it aside* *the eggs* *belongs to a vademecum sword, no attack*

"The vademecum sword belongs to Arpien. My companion." She didn't understand all the details of mantiz life, but she thought she could guess enough to get the two of them out of there. "That means you're going to let us pass."

The mantizes kept their feet planted, but their midsections bobbed forward and back. Little swaying motions marking time. In a dog or cat it might have been prelude to a pounce. Brierly kept her own midsection tense, in case she had to throw herself out of the way.

confusion *what does it say, the sword belongs to the wounded one?* *sword belongs to the Prince*

There was no exact translation between antennae flicks and human tongue-wagging. Yet Brierly heard or felt the emphasis of the word. Not just any prince. But why would the mantizes care about the legend of the Prince of Here and There?

humans can't speak.

"It's a fairy Gift," Brierly said.

Antennae flew. There now, that made an impression.

"And because I have this sword, you're going to let me take my companion and leave."

Four pairs of claws leaned in. *can't leave* *the EGGS*

"You can have your egg sac." Brierly set the bag down with the proper care due a colony of infants. "We weren't the ones who took it. Well, we didn't take it from you." She pointed into the forest. "Back there, we found a band of criminals—humans. They stole your egg sac. I took it from them because it seemed important."

was it these humans stole the eggs? *all look the same**no, these have different colored shells* *all humans steal, can't trust* *has the sword, gave back the eggs* *wounded us* *we killed the brown-shelled one, fair trade* Antennae waved in agreement. *fair trade* *you go*

Brierly barely heard that part. She was still stuck on *we killed the brown-shelled one*. Arpien, in his muddy cloak.

"No. You go. I stay and bury my companion."

you do not wish to eat him?

"No!"

A pause, and then four sets of forearms bobbed forward and back, forward and back, like the hopeful hands of children who spy a sweet on the table. *may we eat him?*

She warded them off with a swing of the sword and a war cry. The second was more intimidating than the first. "You presume much! You weren't supposed to attack someone with a vademecum sword, were you? And now you think you deserve to eat him?"

Buggy recanting. *did not see the sword* *humans kill our young, thought you were like them* *did not mean to disobey the Prince*

"But you did, and so you are going to pay by going far away, so I can bury my companion in peace."

cannot leave our homes for long *for a short time, long enough to bury* *one day only* *yes, yes, fair trade* *what purpose, bury?*

"My kind does not eat our dead. We put them in the ground."

waste food They could not roll their multifaceted eyes, but that was a definite sneer at human stupidity. The mantizes collected their egg sac and receded into the trees. *one day* *if he's not dead by then, we return anyway.* In a few seconds she could not distinguish them from the leaves.

"Wait! What do you mean, *if?*"

Brierly dove to her knees by Arpien's side. His skin was pale and tinged with blue. She bent her ear above his mouth, and heard the whisper-soft rasp of his breath.

The relief was so great she scolded herself for it. *He's alive, but he's still not real, you great fool. He cannot save you.*

Aye, but maybe she could save him. Maybe she couldn't change things, here in this dream, where she was powerless. But in another dream …

I'm not doing this for his sake. I'm doing this to annoy Voracity.
She lay down beside her prince and closed her eyes.

The next dream world she sought was the ballroom in the royal castle in Conquisan. She heard the clock strike twelve before the scene fully materialized before her. No matter where in the sequence she landed, it was always near midnight at her engagement ball, the night she'd turned seventeen. The clock raised both hands in the air, in permanent surrender.

Brierly glanced down at her gown. Pah. The usual pink confection of lace and bows. The change of dream restored it to all its frilly splendor. She hated it for two reasons. First—it was the gown she'd worn when she pricked her finger on the spindle. Second—she'd been wearing it for decades.

Brierly smoothed the panels of her gown and sheared off bows with her hands. Blue today? She glanced at the now parti-colored gown, blue and pink. This was a dream she could control.

She pushed past the surprised herald into the red and gold-swathed ballroom. She pressed her palms together and then apart. A path opened through the gliding dancers, as though a fissure had erupted in the polished marble floor. She bounded up the eleven stairs to the royal dais in a single leap and landed in a curtsey.

The King of Conquisan was a lobster today. That was new. But not pertinent.

"Hello, I'm Brierly. I'd like to talk to Prince Herren."

The lobster in his golden crown clacked his claws together. "He's been so looking forward to meeting you."

The king was hedging. Prince Herren was so peeved about the marriage treaty with unsophisticated Rosaria that he was sulking behind the curtains. That much was historical, for it had happened before she fell asleep, at the original ball. Just like then, the queen shoved the prince onto the dais. Herren's handsome face made that familiar heart-stopping slow transformation from pout to wide-eyed wonder.

But Brierly's heart did not stop this time. It fell.

This was not the same man she had left dying in Sentre Forest.

The clock struck twelve.

She couldn't say how she knew this man was different. She had seen the original Herren only once, on that one enchanted, cursed evening. So despite her good memory, he varied from dream to dream. Taller one dream, a different shade of eyes another. The man she had left in Sentre Forest was physically enough like the one before her, they could be two versions of each other.

Only this Herren was somehow … stale. Like week-old seed buns, crusty under the pale freckles.

Prince Herren shook himself. "I'm sorry to stare. It's just that you're so—"

"Beautiful? Thanks. I'll see you later."

Herren caught up with her as she reached the bottom step. "Did I say something wrong?"

"No, you said what you always say. I just need to leave."

"Why?"

To rescue my pet figment. To pretend that I'm urgently needed and wanted.

She snapped her fingers. A mob of adoring female courtiers engulfed Herren in a rush of lace and frill. "No doubt I'll be back soon."

Brierly repaired to the balcony. Where would she find Arpien? She knew all of Herren's usual haunts in the dream world, but if Arpien was a separate entity, she had not yet had time to learn his. The only places he had yet appeared in her dreams were Estepel and Sentre Forest.

And, according to Arpien and her own distant memory, an angry river where she had saved a six-year-old boy from drowning.

She climbed up on the balcony ledge.

The clock struck twelve.

She jumped.

Her feet hit water and her skirts ballooned around her with trapped air. Rapids whipped her around, a piece of swirling blue and pink debris. She spat out a mouthful of brine. A river of salt water? It was like swimming in cold tears.

"Arpien!" No answer. Maybe the fish had seen him. She ducked underwater.

The waters were unnaturally clear, though dark. A fraction of the moonlight from above penetrated the surface. Nothing lived here. No fish, no snails, nothing to interview. All she saw were rocks and the waters welling their way to some indeterminable end. And a puffy trail of red.

She let the current shoot her forward. She crashed around a bend in the river and spotted Arpien.

He was not alone.

She backstroked and hid behind a boulder. Two merfolk—a mermaid and a merman—towed a limp Arpien behind them on a leash. They were swimming away from her, so she could only see their brilliant aquamarine scales, the iridescent glint of their long, silvery hair. She recognized the peculiar ambience of Voracity's magic—sweet and pungent, like rotting vegetables.

She imagined her gown and skin into a mottled stony grey and followed at a distance. Was Arpien alive? His skin was pale as anemic moonlight. Blood flowed from the gash in his neck where the mantiz had bitten him. In the filtered light, she could see that what she had taken for a leash was really a long vine of briars, binding his feet together and his arms at his sides. Every time the merfolk drew up the slack, the thorns pierced Arpien's flesh. Dozens of miniscule red clouds released into the water, as though Arpien were a sponge being squeezed.

Should the merfolk kill her, she would just pop into another dream. But crossing Voracity or any of her servants meant pain before escape. Once, these very merfolk had chained her to a rock and called seagulls to peck out her eyes. She'd spent fifty-one scalding days of blistering sun and fifty-one frigid nights of salty sea on that rock. If it had been real, she would have perished for lack of water in a matter of days.

Why risk herself for a figment?

Arpien's eyes drifted open. The merman punished his brief struggle with a sound smack of his whale-like tail. That seemed to knock Arpien out, but after a moment his eyes opened again, and fixed.

On her.

She broke off a beam of moonlight and ground it against the stony wall. She clenched the blade between her teeth and swam in the merfolk's wake. The moonlight blade slashed down on the briar leash.

And bounced off.

Spinning wheels.

The merfolk whipped around. Brierly snapped off a fragment of the moonlight blade and hurled it at the merman. It disintegrated before it reached him, so many grains of glimmering sand.

"The one who never wakes," the mermaid said. "So she did find a way off that island."

"We do not have time for sport." The merman brought the full force of his tail down on Brierly's wrist and shattered the bones within. The blade of moonlight spun from her grasp.

Brierly swallowed a lungful of water when she gasped in pain. The mermaid smiled at that, as though she were a pet who had done something endearingly brainless. One flash of pointed milky-blue teeth, and they were gone.

Before she could drown, Brierly modified the rules of the dream so she could breathe water. She imagined a great wave. It came a blink after she thought of it, and deposited her a few strokes in front of them.

"What have you to do with us, Sleeper?" the merman said. A fire-orange trident appeared in his hand. The prongs gave birth to hundreds of tiny bubbles, as though the water boiled around them. "Is it death you seek? Pain we can give, but not release."

The mermaid jerked on Arpien's leash. "Perhaps you seek another prize?"

"Give him to me," Brierly said, "and I will let you pass."

The merfolk raised cynical ivory brows at each other. Brierly grabbed the merman's trident with her good hand and pushed off his marble chest with all the strength in her legs. Brierly used her momentum to force the trident through the briar leash.

The trident passed through the briar chain like an oyster fork through smoke. The chain remained intact.

The mermaid lunged for Brierly. Brierly raised the trident in front of her. The prongs passed through the powerful blue-green tail without a mark, as they had the briars. Brierly let go of the trident before the mermaid could break her other wrist. Brierly hid in Arpien's shadow, willing herself flat and colorless against the river bottom.

"You think to use a trident to best the merfolk?" The mermaid flipped the trident to the merman. He stabbed the river bottom as if to fork Brierly out of shadows. The mermaid yanked Arpien closer to the surface, out of Brierly's reach.

The merfolk were too focused on the search for Brierly to notice Arpien's movements. He was turning himself upside-down, with miniscule kicks.

The merman plunged his trident into the river bottom, a scant few inches from Brierly's head. She darted from Arpien's shadow to the mermaid's. The merman grinned, lips spread around those milky-blue teeth, and raised the trident.

A flash of light ripped his attention upward as Arpien's sword fell free of its scabbard.

It drifted down through the depths, a blade of living silver that made all other shades of silver look dead. The merman reached for it. Brierly snaked along the long thin shadow of his outstretched arm.

"Don't touch it!" the mermaid shouted. "It's a—"

"Vademecum sword?" Brierly said. She erupted from the river bed and seized the sword in her left hand on her way up. She stopped even with the mermaid, the sword pointed at the creature's delicate pointed chin.

The mermaid didn't back off, as the mantizes had. "Fool. You can't destroy the briars with that. You don't know how to use it. Neither does this piece of flotsam." She jerked on Arpien's leash. Either he had passed out again, or he was playing dead. "If you did, you wouldn't belong to Voracity."

"We don't belong to Voracity."

The mermaid tossed her white-silver hair. "You both bear the brand of the thorn."

Brierly followed the mermaid's gaze to her right finger. The current teased a long thin scarlet thread from its tip. Had she punctured it on the moonlight blade?

As the merman barreled toward Brierly from below, she swung the sword at the mermaid's hand. It did not cut her, but stunned her enough to make her release the end of the briar chain. Brierly looked for the merman and then glanced over her shoulder for the mermaid. She was bent double, at least five strokes away. As soon as the mermaid let go of the briar leash, Arpien must have kicked off her to escape. He butterfly-kicked away with his bound feet.

Brierly swam toward Arpien and grabbed him by the back of his shirt. She couldn't paddle with both the sword and Arpien in tow, not with a broken wrist. So instead she called the rock wall to her.

"Close your eyes!" she shouted.

The rock wall slammed into them, through them. It flowed around them, a hundred times denser than water. When they had put about five miles of rock between them and merfolk, Brierly turned hard right, and broke into another dream.

They sailed through a world of white. No top, no bottom, only a single grey rock wall behind them. Brierly whooped aloud in relief, spent terror, and exhilaration. The sound shot out of her in red, blue, and yellow discs, each about three feet in diameter. The discs spun, shook, and bounced before her.

She sang soft low sibilants. She and Arpien skimmed the newly formed ground and came to rest on a cushion of green. It was moss, and it wasn't moss. They were lying on sheer music.

Brierly laid the sword safely to one side. She pushed herself up—a bit of work with only one functional hand—and turned toward Arpien. "You can open your eyes now."

He obeyed, but barely.

"You'll be all right now. This is a music dream. We can sing for whatever we need. Luckily for you, I have a voice so lovely it makes small forest creatures stop and sing along."

His jaw twitched in what might have been a grin, but his eyelids drooped. Just how much blood had he lost? Stubby increments of the briar vine clung to his shirt and the flesh of his arms, back, chest, and ankles. Their journey through the rock had broken the vine, but as the mermaid promised, they could not destroy it. The thorns raked deep tracks into his skin. The blood had dissipated into the water instead of soaking into his doublet. Only now that they were out of the water did she see the fresh stain spreading through the cloth. Red through midnight blue made a creeping, violent color she had no name for.

Their injuries had passed with them from dream to dream. Not all injuries did. She had known these did from the moment she tried to roll over and found her wrist still broken. This was also a good thing, for if she could heal him here, he ought to recover in the Sentre Forest dream.

She sang a song with no lyrics. Long, flexible notes to bandage their wounds. Cool pools of sounds to soothe the puckered skin at the back of his neck where the mantiz had injected her poison. Bright, airy trills to dry their sopping clothes.

After she tended to the immediate danger, Brierly closed her eyes and lost herself in the wind of harmonics. Notes stacked up to form chords that were blown apart by the next gust of melody. She built the crests higher with great trumpeting cries. She shushed the dramatic decrescendos until they were no more perceptible than the rapid fluttering of a hummingbird's wings. Because it was a dream, she was not restricted by the physical limitations of her vocal chords. So out of her mouth came a violin, a pipe, a drum, and also textures that weren't any known instrument. Higher and lower and richer and sweeter than any mortal music.

She shut her mouth and let the tide rise and fall without her. Blend and break, until all was silence.

She opened her eyes on a world of color.

Great loping trees bent overhead, with tufts of pink fluff for leaves. A purple lake extended at her feet, its surface as undisturbed as glass. Undisturbed until a flock of phoenix-geese descended and sent perfect circles of ripples across the surface of the lake. The dissonances had formed a miniature volcano that erupted in fig pudding. A long line of six-legged quarter notes carried crumbs of the volcanic rock away to their hill. Every color and texture seemed pushed beyond its natural limits. Even the red jewel in the vademecum sword surpassed its former brilliant hue.

In the noisy explosion of color, the most vibrant of all was Arpien's eyes. Strange, she'd never thought of brown as a vibrant color until now, when in a feast of visual delights he chose to gaze at her.

"You're all right," he said.

"Aye, and so are you. Or will be, if you rest a while longer. Which means," she pressed a finger firmly against his collarbone, "stop trying to sit up."

He laid his head back down on the pillow of moss. "Is this a dream? Or was the other?"

How did she it explain to him? All dreams were equally true and equally false.

She rose up on her knees. The briar chains had vanished. She reached to push his hair off his neck so she could examine the mantiz bite. The skin puckered into two raw pink circles.

His fingers closed around her wrist. "Brierly—"

She jerked away.

Concern creased his brow. "Your wrist. I forgot. Did I hurt you?"

"Sleep." An ironic command.

His eyelids drifted down and shielded her from those sympathetic brown eyes.

She unwound the strip of aria from her wrist and flexed her fingers. Whole again.

No, figment, you didn't hurt my wrist.

She could never risk herself like that again. That was how you got hurt—when you discovered your hopes were pinned on your own desperate creation, a fiction designed to ease your futility and loneliness.

Belief was a fool's comfort.

7

Arpien

In one night Arpien visited both hell and heaven.

The morning was bound to bring something more mundane, just to even things out. It did. It brought a headache and an uncomfortable horse ride.

Uncomfortable because he was lying forward, his head pressed into the warmth of Fearless's neck. He tried to sit up and found he'd been secured into the position with rope done up into a fancy bow. He blew Fearless's mane out of his field of vision and saw before him a rider with billowing fair hair.

Handy with Needle and Thread, and therefore knots.

Her keen ears detected his movement—another of her Gifts. Or maybe Fearless informed her he was awake. What would that conversation sound like? *This sack of potatoes is blowing my mane?*

Brierly halted her horse—his stopped by default—and untied Arpien with the brisk efficiency of an overqualified laundress at her bundles. "How do you feel?"

He searched her voice for concern, concern that might confirm this crazy vision of her in his dream. He detected only the polite nothings of small talk. She might have been inquiring about the weather.

"Thirsty," he said.

She nodded. "Blood loss. I'm sorry I didn't take the time to fill our water pouches, but there were pressing reasons to move on. Don't worry, the birds tell me there's a stream about three good glides south of here."

So much to say, when the only thing he could do was clamp his mouth shut for fear he'd vomit all over his princess. An effect of the mantiz venom or his pounding headache or both.

"Three good glides" translated into "endless bumpy leagues," but they did at last cross the foretold stream. Arpien lay flat on his belly at the water's edge and drank like an animal: no water skin, not even his cupped hands. When he'd forced down as much as he could without his belly rebelling, he pressed his forehead into the cool mud. It eased the pounding in his skull.

Perhaps he slept. It couldn't have been very much time before his rehydrated body began to forgive him. He pushed himself up on his elbows. For once, Brierly had not wandered away—more evidence that his patchy memory of her in the dream might be true.

And what a beautiful dream. Horrible, but then beautiful.

He watched his princess finger-comb Neef's mane. She took more care with her horse's hair than her own. Even so, her hair was stunning—long flaxen strands that captured every glint of light that struggled through the forest cover. How could he broach the subject of the beauty of her song when he couldn't even find words worthy of her travel-tangled hair?

He caught a reflection of himself in the stream. River mud streaked the center of his forehead, his nose, his chin. Hardly a face she'd take in earnest, be the subject hair or anything else. He dunked his head and upper body in the stream and hand-scrubbed the worst clods of the dirt off. Underneath the brown mud he expected to find bloodstains. Why should that be? There was nothing to substantiate his memory of deep gouges in his chest, either. Nothing he could do about the mud on his trunk hose. He was not going swimming in anything larger than a wooden tub, ever again.

He joined Brierly further up the bank, and began the inefficient process of wringing out his clothes while still wearing them.

"You cannot blame me if you're wet this time," she said.

"We escaped the mantizes." Unnecessary to say it, but narration might prompt his brain to plug the gaps.

"Yes."

"How'd we escape the mantizes?"

"I talked to them." As she'd promised she would, should the occasion arise.

"And they—deposited me onto my horse and waved us away?" There was no way she could have hefted him up on Fearless by herself.

"No. The bear helped."

You'd think he'd remember something so remarkable as that. But assistance from a bear seemed commonplace compared to his other memories of the past night.

"I dreamed—" he began. His childhood nightmare, blended with inescapable damnation. Music that rent his heart and healed his flesh. "Was it real?"

She packed her sigh with the haunting rasp of desert wind. "As real as you want it to be."

"And the mermaids?"

"One mermaid. Males are called mermen. Collectively, merfolk."

"Grammar aside, what happened?"

"You survived."

It was easy to forget how her beauty intimidated him when she was being so unhelpful. "My great-grandfather said you were eloquent."

"Brevity can be eloquent."

"So can a long, detailed story."

He got the story, though it didn't deserve the descriptor *long* or *detailed*. It was not so much that facts were missing, but color. Yet he felt too foolish to probe into her feelings after her lack of reaction to his story about their first meeting at the river. She'd rewarded that risky exposure of his soul with a plain display of boredom.

What motivated her? Not affection for him, as he'd always thought he'd find in the lady who haunted his dreams. But she had saved him from the river, hadn't she? Again. In his dream, Brierly had shown concern, cunning, spirit. In the unpoetic light of day, none of these words applied to her. He must have hallucinated.

It took them three more silent days—and uneventful days, courtesy of the gryphon repellant or whatever it was the fairies had placed on the main road—to reach Boxleyn. The closer they drew to their goal, the more reluctant Arpien grew to claim his prize.

Beautiful—Brierly was that. And brave—if you could call it brave when she didn't seem to understand the peril of her actions. He might even call her sweet of temper, as the legends said. She never raised her voice and put up with any number of inconveniences—from sleeping on the ground to being captured by brigands—with mellow poise. Unflappable.

Shouldn't she be—flapped? The sweetness of temper was really a polite indifference. Could he ever sleep beside her as her husband when he remembered the calm poise with which she buried a carroty knife in a man's leg? Self-defense was one thing. Blasé assault with a root vegetable was another.

He would drop her off at the gate of the Rosarian Palace. "Here's your long lost heir to the throne. Good luck and goodbye."

But to do that meant forfeiting his half a kingdom. He'd worked too hard to give that up.

Maybe he could still retrieve half his happy ending.

Part Two

Truth is beauty, beauty truth.
John Keats

Beauty is in the eye of the beholder.
Margaret Wolfe Hungerford

8

Nissa

If Nissa Montaine, king's ward and niece, had known she would meet a legend that day, she would have done a number of things differently. She would have changed into a fresh gown after she droobled gooseberry jam down her front while reading at the breakfast table. She would not have ridden Windried so fast or through so many mud puddles. But after last night's reception for the Strandish delegation, no one who cared a dried-up raisin what she looked like would be about yet.

Besides, who expects to meet legends in the stables?

First she met the legend's noble steed.

She rubbed Windried down and heard a *look at me* exhalation over her shoulder. She turned. A horse in the adjacent stall, his coat as sleek and deep brown as an otter's pelt, tilted his head at Nissa. She had the feeling she was being courted.

"Morrow, good sir," she said. "You're new."

The wide brown eye beckoned her closer, within reach for the horse to lip at the smear of gooseberry jam on her shoulder.

"Beggar." Nissa eased the great dark head away. "If you're exceptionally nice to me I'll see if I can bring you some sugar. But you will not snack on any of my clothes unless you yourself want to do the patching." She patted the side of the muscled neck.

"You're Nissa."

Nissa turned. A young woman about her own age—no, one hundred years older, if the tales could be believed—leaned in the entrance to the stall.

"Have we been introduced?" Nissa said, because one must say something, even to a legend.

"Never." The young woman smiled at her as though Nissa had given her an unexpected gift.

Yet there was familiarity. Although it didn't occur to the young woman to make those introductions, each seemed to know who the other was. Certainly Nissa recognized the Enchanted Princess. The Heir to the Throne. The Sleeping Beauty. Titles natural in a tower, but here, in a stable, Nissa couldn't help calling her a mental *Brierly*.

Brierly—if this was the lost princess—nodded toward the horse. "Neef approves of you."

"I approve of him. He's stunning."

"Don't make him more vain than he already is. You always groom Windried yourself."

"Who told you that?"

"Neef. He asked around the stables."

The tale always said Brierly could talk to animals.

"What else does Neef say?"

"That he has an itch on his left flank, and could someone please brush it?"

Nissa started, then took the brush from Brierly's extended hand. Neef shivered with pleasure as she tended to the offending spot.

"You were expecting something more profound?" Brierly said.

Nissa thought it over. "Most people don't say meaningful things more than once a week. It's 'Pass the bread' or 'Move your feet so I can sweep there.' Why should animals be different?"

"I think I approve of you, too." A smile blossomed on Brierly's face. She plucked it off before it could fully open. "But you'll probably turn boring soon."

Was that a compliment or an insult? Before Nissa decided, Brierly was off onto something else.

"Turtles, though, they're the talkers."

"Turtles? But they're so—slow."

"Exactly. When they can pin down someone to listen, it all has to come out. Worse, they imagine everything they say is wise."

Nissa tucked her chin and raised her shoulders. "If I were a turtle, I'd make speeches inside my shell, and they'd echo and sound very pompous and important."

"You have the Gift, too, then?"

"What gift?"

"Of Speaking to Animals."

Oh no. I mean, I do like animals, but I don't have a Gift for it, not the true fairy kind. No one's been given any Gifts, not since—" she bit her lip.

"Since me," Brierly said.

Nissa nodded and fixed her eyes on her brush.

"Honestly, some of the Gifts aren't that useful."

"Which ones do you mean?"

"Well, let me tell you mine: Fleetsome Feet, Handy with Needle and Thread, a Fine Ear, Eat-Anything-I-Want-And-Always-Retain-A-Maidenly-Figure—"

Nissa snorted. "Oh, throw away the Fine Ear and Feet thing, but keep that last. Dead useful, that one."

"Are you jesting?"

Nissa put her hands on her generous hips. "If I had that one, I'd eat a chocolate cake for breakfast every morning of my life."

"Why don't you anyway?"

"Words spoken by someone who's never had to worry about beauty." She meant it as a joke, but the tone came out lined with jealousy. She cringed.

Brierly laced her fingers and stretched upwards, as though the words might roll off her shoulders like a waterfall. "Beauty's the least useful Gift of all."

Something stirred and thumped in the loft overhead. "What's that?" Nissa said.

"Could be any number of things. A stable boy. A massive field mouse. A dragon." Brierly shrugged. "But I suspect it's Herren."

"Arpien." Scuffed boots followed the vexed voice down the ladder.

Through the hay dust, Nissa noticed two things about this Arpien. The first, that unlike his companion, this was a person who believed in introductions. Despite his slept-in-his-traveling-clothes state, he nodded a courtly bow to Nissa, a lower one to Brierly.

The second thing she noticed, by his demeanor and the wealth of what attire she could see through the travel dust, was that he was a prince. Not just the regular variety of prince. A Rescuing Prince. Only a person who has read too many folktales would think to make the distinction. Nissa herself knew a number of ordinary princes—enough not to be cowed by the title alone—but she only knew of Rescuing Princes from the old tales. Tall. Broad-shouldered and narrow-waisted. Kind eyes. Passionate, sensitive, clever, heroic, and romantic. With just the slightest hint of superiority.

"What time does your blessed king trouble himself to stir from bed and manage his kingdom?" Arpien said.

More than a slight hint.

"When we arrived last night, we were told we couldn't see the king because he was receiving special guests. More than twelve hours later, we're told he'll be so consumed with entertaining these guests that no one else can expect an audience until next week."

A noticeable dose.

"I'm sorry you find us lacking in hospitality," Nissa said. "Perhaps if I—"

"Lacking? I get the clear impression your king knows who I am and is trying to drive me away."

Actually, the longer he talked, the more he resembled a regular prince.

"Your duties may have nothing to do with accommodations, but you will understand that I was at least hoping to find better lodgings."

On that account he did have the right to complain. Who'd ever heard of a prince staying in a stable?

Brierly withstood his blast with impenetrable calm. "You're right. Who wouldn't recognize you as Prince Charming?"

Nissa wouldn't have dared provoke him like that, but Brierly's barb seemed to puncture his inflated pride. He sighed like bellows set aside after their fiery work and became an altogether different man. Nissa didn't quite abandon her notion that he might be a Rescuing Prince after all. "The king should well scorn my company, if I tongue-lash an innocent serving girl. I apologize, Maid—"

"N—Nissa." She straightened up, which given her short stature didn't make a lot of difference. "Nissa Montaine."

"You didn't mention she was nobility," Brierly said to Neef.

"The horse cares what I am?" Nissa said.

"Neef would." Indeed, Neef probably cared about royal blood more than Brierly did. Brierly didn't seem to notice that Arpien was any more extraordinary than the stable boy she suggested he might be.

Arpien. Thorns and thistles. Wasn't one of the princes of Conquisan named Arpien? She was standing, all but alone and unprotected, with the brother of Rosaria's greatest foe. A brother who was strapping on a deadly-looking sword.

It was hard to fear him when he fumbled with his sword belt. "She's nobility?" he asked the horse. He flushed and addressed Brierly. "She's nobility?"

Brierly fingered Neef's mane. "My mother was a Montaine. They rule our northernmost province."

"Well"—Nissa toed the ground—"We rule all the provinces, now."

Brierly's fingers stilled. "The kingship fell to the House of Montaine?"

Prince Arpien apologized for his mistake and performed an even deeper bow. A notorious Conquisani bow? It certainly involved a lot of feet planting and wrist rolling. The excessive recognition was worse than none at all.

Nissa bit her lip. "When the line of Steward died out, someone had to rule."

Prince Arpien arched a significant brow at her. "The line of Steward didn't die out."

"Quite right, it—fell asleep."

Welcome home, princess—you weren't expecting your kingdom back, were you?

Nissa shifted her gaze from one to the other. Arpien might turn out to be a Rescuing Prince, but he was also Conquisani, in a time when war rumbled between the two countries like warning thunder. As for Brierly—if it was Brierly—Nissa watched her scrub the walls of the stall with the brush, as if she expected it to reveal a secret passage to Elfland. When no magical portal appeared, Brierly shook off the brush and went back to grooming Neef.

Neef the talking horse.

Nissa surrendered. "I'll see if I can get you an audience with my uncle."

Boxleyn consisted of three concentric rectangles. The outer fence enclosed the royal park on the north and the town on the south. The middle wall enclosed the royal palace. Its various stables, dairies, and other support buildings clustered about its feet like downy grey chicks. Nissa made an unnecessary lap around the blocky limestone palace that was the heart of Boxleyn before deciding to lead her guests through the kitchen entrance and then up the narrow servants' stairs to reach the royal rooms on the third floor. Best let them refresh themselves before Uncle saw them.

Nissa's Uncle Emol, whatever his faults, couldn't take all the blame for the lack of hospitality Prince Arpien had endured on his arrival. Prince Arpien had only identified himself by his lesser title of Knight Obscureland, and Brierly not at all. For security reasons, he said. Nissa understood. If she sneaked into Conquisan with a rival claim to the throne, she wouldn't advertise her identity, either. But then, Arpien couldn't fault the king for failing to honor the anonymous.

To the prince's credit, he acknowledged his breech of logic with a third apology and a muttered, "This rescue isn't going at all as I planned." A phrase Prince Arpien invoked several times during his stay at Boxleyn.

Nissa outlined the steps they would take to get them their audience with the king. "First, bath. Second, clothes. Third, breakfast. When you're refreshed, I'll take you to the Reception Room." If Uncle Emol wouldn't bear an interruption from her, perhaps her cousin Timothy would listen.

There was an awkward pause while Prince Arpien showed her that his only other clothes looked like he'd run them through a cabbage-cutter. Brierly had no change of clothes at all. Nissa had three male cousins, so she imagined she could wrangle Arpien something passingly princely to wear while the laundress attacked his own attire. As for Brierly, perhaps one of the queen's ladies—

Here followed the politest spat she'd ever heard. Brierly looked forward to wearing fashions that weren't one hundred years out of date, while Prince Arpien insisted her antiquated gown would affirm her identity. Nissa deposited them in her parlor to continue the debate at their leisure while she arranged for the necessary servants and supplies. In a quarter of an hour she had Prince Arpien stowed in a guest room with a selection of servants, breads, and her cousin's second-best clothing. Not a lot of romance in organization. *(May I kiss your hand, dear organized lady?)*

Nissa glanced at Brierly, who was tweaking the nose of a stone bust of Uncle Emol. She'd better take her in hand herself.

Nissa hoped her two new friends didn't expect an eager welcome. Her own was the warmest they would receive in Boxleyn. She was predisposed to like Brierly. Nissa had been born one hundred years—to the week— after the renowned figure, and always fancied them a sort of mismatched pair of twins because of it. Very mismatched, as Brierly was wispy and fair and Nissa sturdy and dark.

Not all twins were identical. And if anyone needed a sister to look after her, it was Brierly.

Nissa examined her chambers with an eye to what a legend might expect in housing arrangements. Nissa's own bedroom and several vacant ones spidered off a central parlor used for tutoring, sewing, and warming one's toes at the hearth with a good book. Nissa was the only female member of the royal family in this generation, or she'd be sharing the space with someone besides her handmaid. It ought be have been a spacious arrangement, yet her chambers had succumbed to the universal law that any unused space will become a storage closet. Whenever Aunt Perturbance redecorated, Nissa inherited the furnishings that were too worn for the rest of the family but too good for anyone else. Her parlor was a convention of diverse chairs: wooden, upholstered, round-backed, basket-woven, all scuffed or frayed in discreet places. The demoted furnishings crowded the main room like ladies whose blossoms of youth were just starting to droop, and there was nothing for it but to pinch roses back into their cheeks and assume stately poses.

Nissa didn't care if her furniture was salvaged from the dregs of luxury. Few members of the high classes visited her, and none of her friends among the low classes were allowed to sit here. Brierly didn't seem to mind it either.

The bathing was carried off without Brierly exposing to the servants any odd behavior, other than an inordinate fascination with bubbles. Nissa lent her a clean chemise. It billowed at Brierly's sides and cut off short at the knee, which made her naked feet look like fragile bell-clappers. But she had to wear something while Nissa's favorite (well, only) handmaid Kendra begged for daywear in the wardrobes of ladies of appropriate sizes. Nissa knew none of her own gowns would fit Brierly, so she was surprised when Brierly asked to peruse her clothes chest.

"Do as you like," Nissa said. "I'm going to take advantage of the bathwater before it cools." The arrival of an unorthodox princess would annoy the queen. Nissa didn't want to provoke her fastidious aunt the more by making introductions smelling of horse sweat.

A partition blocked off the tub from the rest of the room, but Brierly's clucks and hms were enough to tell Nissa that Brierly was enjoying her introduction to modern fashion. "I'm fascinated by the cut of your clothes," Brierly said. "So square. So starched. Did you make them?"

"As few as possible. I like to embroider, though." One of the inescapable pleasures of the female nobility.

"The peacock on the sleeve is yours, right? What a clever use of color."

"I thought Beauty wasn't useful," Nissa said.

"Fashion isn't Beauty. It's Art."

Nissa didn't understand the distinction, but who was she to criticize when she distinguished regular princes from Rescuing ones?

"Oh and look—here's some of your larger work on the hoop," Brierly went on. "I recognize the stories. The Tailor and the Giant. What a puzzled expression you've captured. The Princess and the Pea. Lucky girl."

"Lucky?"

"She had insomnia."

Nissa stood up in a sudden panicked memory of what lay further down in the chest. Water sloshed everywhere. "No need to dig deeper. Kendra's coming back with some borrowed gowns." She flung a chemise about herself.

"Snow White and Rose Red. The Prince and the Serpent. The Mule and the Flea. And—"

A pungent silence. Too late Nissa burst around the partition. From here, she couldn't see what tale Brierly held frozen in her hands. But she knew.

The Sleeping Beauty.

It was her most precious work. Not the finest, for she'd worked it some years ago. But woven in every stitch was the fancy of a young girl's dream. She'd used Brierly's own portrait, before the queen ordered it thrown out in one of her fits of redecoration, to base her image of the beautiful bespelled princess. No one knew who the beauty's true love would be, so Nissa left him a faceless black silhouette in the doorway.

The rest of the scene grew worse. The princess lay on a cloud of fluffy down mattresses. Golden light streamed through the window, where a pair of bluebirds gazed on in sympathy. She'd bordered the whole in a chain of roses and thorns.

Bad enough to meet your favorite legend covered in gooseberry jam. Worse to stand here wrapped in nothing but a sideways chemise while she discovered your hero-worship for her.

Brierly tapped the corner of her mouth. "I look too peaceful. You need to place another stitch here."

"That'd make you frown."

"I have a feeling I look peevish when I sleep." The same corner of her mouth twitched. "I've been told I need dusting, too."

"Needed."

The corner pulled in further. "As you like."

Nissa laid the embroidery pieces back in the chest—difficult when one hand was occupied in holding the chemise up. "I—uh—have a fascination for the old tales. Childish really."

"Don't hide them," Brierly said. "They're superb. They deserve a better fate than to languish beneath your stockings."

"The old tales aren't in favor now. Most of the palace thinks I'm daft for wasting time and thread on them."

"I've spent time with old tales myself."

"Have you?" Nissa exhaled in relief. "I think by studying the legends we learn more about ourselves. There's truth buried in the fiction. Look at you." She flushed. "Maybe they're not all literally true, but they give us something larger than ourselves. What are we without our dreams?"

"I can't say I've ever found truth in dreams." For a moment Brierly's voice was as hard and brittle as a hundred-and-seventeen-year-old woman's ought to be.

"I hope I haven't offended."

A light smile displaced the coldness. "I'll forgive you if you let me wear this gown." Brierly pointed to a rich blue-green one on the bed. The one with the peacock on the sleeve.

"It'll never fit you."

"Fairy Gift," Brierly said. "Now go rinse the soap out of your lovely brown hair."

Lovely. The beauty called her hair lovely. Nissa took extra care in tending her hair, in the hopes that one of Brierly's Gifts was making the unremarkable remarkable with a word. Nissa was less discouraged by its commonplace color and troublesome thickness than usual.

By the time she combed and dried it, Brierly emerged in Nissa's old gown. New gown. How had Brierly made it so utterly hers in the span of an hour? Hers not in size only, but in the hang of the sleeve, the subtle readjustment of the piping, the very way the "clever use of colors" brought out the peach in her cheeks and the blue-green in her eyes. The gown would protest if Nissa ever thought to alter it back.

Fashion was Art. And Beauty. A tear trickled down Nissa's check.

"What is it?" Brierly said.

"It's just—you're so—"

"Beautiful? Thanks. Do I smell toast?"

The familiar scent of crisp yeasty toast brought Nissa back into the realm of the normal. Kendra had returned with a couple of now superfluous borrowed gowns. Now the tall thin strawberry-blond girl was warming chunks of bread over the fire for Nissa's usual post-morning-ride snack. Bless her.

As they ate, Nissa judged every aspect of Brierly as though it would help her determine whether jealousy or admiration should be her foremost reaction.

Brierly dolloped gooseberry jam on her toast. Approval.

Unlike Nissa, she nibbled it without dolloping any jam on herself. Jealousy.

Since Kendra was busy with the fire, Nissa answered the knock at her door. Another character from a fairy tale stood outside. Clean and wearing Timothy's second-best clothes, Prince Arpien did credit to his role. Well, except for the sleeves. A couple inches too short. And the waist bagged a little. But he had commandeered someone to trim that shaggy brown hair and shape the haphazard stubble into a fine line that accentuated his jaw. He made a perfectly sound secondhand hero.

"I had a servant show me to your rooms. Thank you for your graciousness, Lady Nissa Montaine." He grabbed the right corner of his borrowed cape, pressed it to his left shoulder two and a half times, and bowed. "The repast, and the garb—"

"Thank Timothy for the clothes." On second thought, perhaps he best not thank Timothy. She'd pilfered her cousin's wardrobe with the permission of Timothy's manservant, not Timothy himself.

"Yes, well, due to your generosity, I am refreshed and anxious to secure an audience with your estimable uncle the king. Are you two ready to—"

The end of his sentence was burned away by Brierly's radiance. Nissa followed his stricken gaze to the side table, where Brierly was finishing her toast. Her newly washed and combed hair glinted in the pearly light of late morning. Brierly scooped the last glob of gooseberry jam off her plate. She kissed it off her dainty finger with a tiny smack of her rosebud lips. Bad manners, plus it wasn't fair that she could look enchanting just eating. When Nissa ate she probably looked like a timid baby pig.

Brierly rose and extended the near-empty bread basket to Prince Arpien. Her skirts swirled into place like a peacock arranging his tail. Only for Brierly, it was effortless. She just stood, and perfection happened.

"Toast?" Brierly said.

"Yes. I mean, no. No, my hunger has already been satiated."

Nissa didn't have a lot of experience with male desire. She never inspired it herself. But living in a palace stuffed with courtiers gave her ample opportunity to observe it. Prince Arpien was perilously smitten. Smitten in the way poets sing about. (*Oh lady fair, but for the edge of your shadow to touch mine, I would ride my steed up a hill of glass.*) She memorized the prince's expression for future embroidery.

Prince Arpien fingered his neckband. "That gown is—most acceptable."

"It used to be one of mine," Nissa said. Nissa would have been embarrassed to witness such open adoration, were it not for three things. First, these were her own chambers. Second, Prince Arpien had forgotten she was there. Third, although the prince was gazing on his princess with a passionate glow in his eyes, Brierly proved impervious to heat. No flirtation, no rejection, just *here, have some toast.*

Nissa gathered them both out the door before Prince Arpien either noticed Brierly's indifference, spouted poetry, or set the curtains on fire.

Uncle Emol would be in the Reception Room with the Strandish delegation now. Best not interrupt. Nissa and Uncle Emol had an understanding. They kept themselves to such different circles that neither could develop affection or distaste for the other. If she wished to make an appeal, best start with her cousin Timothy.

Timothy slipped his stocky frame through the gilded Reception Room doors a few minutes later. If he noticed the stranger was dressed in his own clothes he didn't comment. Nissa began the introductions (which were not, she sensed, on par with the flourished introductions common in Conquisan). Prince Arpien performed his most elaborate bow yet, one that involved a lot of cape flicking. Perhaps it was his odd position within the Rosarian palace that made him so twitchy. He was both guest and enemy.

Nissa cleared her throat. "And this—this is the long-lost Princess Brierly of the House of Steward, recently awakened from a fairy's enchantment."

"Who?" Timothy wasn't being skeptical. There wasn't anybody else in the atrium to believe or deny.

Prince Arpien sighed. "I beg your pardon, Prince Timothy. The princess's experiences have rendered her a little—eccentric. She doesn't tend to stay where you put her."

"She exists, I promise. I wanted you to convince Uncle Emol to give her an audience," Nissa said.

"Nissa, if you ask, I will try," Timothy said. "But she cannot present her case in absentia."

Prince Arpien drew his sword.

Timothy and four nearby guards unsheathed their own in answer. "In Rosaria you'll find that we settle our differences through words, not trials of violence. But we will answer threats with a like response."

Prince Arpien lowered the sword. "No offense intended, good prince. I did not mean to threaten, but to find Princess Brierly. My sword is a rare weapon, capable of singular feats unprecedented in other arms."

"Speak plainly, sir."

"He means he can use it as a princess-detector." Nissa squeezed her cousin's arm. "That's a vademecum sword, isn't it?"

"You recognize it?" Prince Arpien said.

"From books. Is it true that when you seek the sword, the sword seeks you back?"

Prince Arpien slid the sword home in his scabbard. "Lady, I would be gratified to speak to you at length about this sword and how I obtained it. But I fear I have made a diplomatic faux pas, and must beg your good cousin's exculpation, and seek the fair Brierly using alternate methods."

Thistles, she'd heard the Conquisani were fond of speeches (even more than Uncle Emol, if it could be believed).

Prince Arpien glanced around to see the effect of his appeasing words on his audience, and rephrased himself. "I've found the easiest way to find her is to head for the commotion."

Prince Arpien evidently spoke from experience, because just then commotion reverberated from the queen's quarters upstairs.

Perhaps Nissa should have introduced Brierly to Aunt Perturbance first.

9

Brierly

Brierly wasn't trying to misplace herself. It was just that more interesting distractions kept passing by.

This interesting distraction came in the form of a couple of damp brown lapdogs. A small parade of attendants bore them across the atrium on two red fringed cushions. The hindmost dog sat alert and straight, eyes forward. The foremost barely sat at all. He twisted in circles. The servant swayed so the dog didn't topple off the cushion.

Love the bubbles, love the bubbles. Look, Bertus, a tree in a pot. I love trees. Maybe Queenie will take us outside tomorrow. Bertus, did you see how after bathtime I stood up and begged for the treat? Stood on my hind legs, too. Just like Queenie does.

The second dog bent the top half of one ear forward. *Squeezie, calm down or you'll wet the pillow again.*

No I won't, just that once.

Brierly fell into the procession.

Bertus, look! A flying thing! A flying thing, Bertus! Squeezie jumped up. The servant stumbled and cursed.

It's a bee, you fleabag. Leave it alone or it'll sting you.

I'm a hunter. Squeezie growled, then forgot all about the bee. *Bertus, who's that female-human following us?*

Brierly followed the canine convoy into the queen's parlor. The servants set the cushions down. Before Bertus could disembark, Squeezie had already darted over to sniff Brierly's extended fingers.

"I'm Brierly."

It's a brierly, Bertus. It's a brierly.

Her comment attracted the notice of more than the two dogs to which it was addressed. The servants and a handful of ladies seated further in the room turned to eye her.

That's not a word, Squeezie.

"It's better than my full name," Brierly said.

A lady in a squared-necked apple green skirt and bodice approached her. "Excuse me, are you looking for someone?"

"Just meeting the dogs." Brierly rubbed Squeezie's head for the three seconds he held it still.

Bertus gave Brierly's outstretched hand a courtesy sniff. *I say, Madam, do you understand us?*

"Of course I understand dogs," Brierly said.

The lady in green tried again. "Are you the new dog trainer?"

"Only one of these dogs needs training."

Quite right, Madam.

Like Arpien, the lady seemed unnerved without introductions, so Brierly curtseyed. "I'm Princess Brierly. May I have the pleasure … "

The lady in green made flustered introductions of herself and the rest of the queen's ladies-in-waiting. Bertus made his introductions at the same time. Albertus XII, who came from a long line of royal lapdogs. And Squeezie, a nephew with no understanding of the obligations of the family office. Said nephew was making it even harder for Brierly to hear by running around her skirts, loudly recounting the adventures of bathtime.

"Oh Squeezie, shut up!" both the lady in green and Albertus yapped in their respective languages.

Squeezie pounced. *And I caught a whole flock of bubbles. Killed them dead. I'll bring you one back, next time, if you want.*

Brierly snapped her fingers and pointed down. Squeezie plunked his rear on the floor and thumped his tail.

The lady in green stared at her. "Squeezie never obeys anyone except the queen."

Albertus raised an ear. *I say, Madam, are your services for hire?*

Silencing Squeezie earned her the immediate approval of both uncle and ladies-in-waiting. But it was Nissa's peacock gown that secured Brierly a position among the ladies as one of the admired. Brierly made a point to show interest in their own gowns, before their interest lingered on her person too long. After all, jealousy was only admiration left to fester.

Between her fairy Gifts of Sewing Skills, an Artistic Eye, and Charm, she soon had the ladies gathered around her. Brierly sat enthroned at the queen's writing desk and sketched their new fashion collaborations on the queen's fine writing paper. Albertus took command of the inkwell while Squeezie slobbered on her shoe ribbons. The ladies passed each design around the room to great communal accolade. The energy in the room so invigorated Brierly that she filled page after page.

It was on this scene that Queen Perturbance of Rosaria entered.

Squeezie shot out from under Brierly's skirts. *Queenie! Queenie! Queenie!*

The queen's thin muddy auburn hair clashed with her burgundy bodice and skirt, which was frilled with a half-inch band of lace starched into perfect fluting. She carried all her weight in her midsection. Her neck popped from her square neckline like a stem. Her thin, sharp nose and lips slashed the roundness of her face like the air slits in a pie crust.

I killed bubbles, today, Queenie. Just for you. Then I found a tree in a pot, and a brierly—

The queen tucked Squeezie under one arm like a package and sailed to the writing desk. Brierly stood and dropped her prettiest curtsey. "Your Majesty. How lovely to meet you. I've heard so much about you." She didn't mention most of it had been from the dogs.

The queen stared down at her, the sketches scattered on the floor, her diminished pile of fine paper. "Who is this . . . enchanting young person?"

The lady in green widened her eyes in alarm and whispered in the queen's ear. "Your Majesty, this is Princess Brierly of Strand."

Brierly frowned. "I never said I was from Strand."

"We thought—the Strandish delegation arrived yesterday, and you said you were a princess."

"I'm a princess of Rosaria."

All eyes flicked toward the queen.

"As Queen of Rosaria, I am in excellent position to know any princesses of Rosaria. I have three and exactly three children, none of them girls and none of them you."

"Quite right, Your Majesty. I'm your fourth cousin by marriage or somesuch. My parents were Stewards."

"The House of Steward died out over seventy years ago."

"Except me. I'm Brierly Steward."

"Brierly Steward." A flush spread from the queen's neckline up. Her cheeks and chin seemed like red apples. "If you are this legendary princess, where have you been keeping yourself for the last one hundred years?"

"A tower." Brierly gestured to the writing desk. "I'm most ungracious to keep you standing. Please, do take a seat."

The queen's nose was extraordinary. No matter how her face steamed at being offered her own chair in her own parlor, her thin nose remained a pasty white. "I suppose you'll be telling me you've come back to rule Rosaria."

"Just half of it, Arpien tells me."

"Arpien?"

"Prince of Conquisan. The kingdom part's more his idea than mine. Though it'd be diverting, to be queen for a while. That's a most unhealthy shade of red you're turning. You really should allow me to offer you a chair."

There followed an explosive silence and an even more explosive … explosion. The queen bellowed something, but Brierly couldn't make it out because Squeezie was yipping in the queen's tight grip, the ladies were running around fetching cool cloths (or maybe just running away), and the guards burst in to apprehend the danger but couldn't figure out what it was. A few moments later Nissa, Arpien, and a stout young man she didn't know crashed into the parlor.

"Oh dear." Nissa's shoulders drooped. "I see you've already met."

Since the queen wasn't going to take the chair, Brierly reclaimed it. During the commotion she inquired of Albertus the identity of the other young man.

Crown Prince Timothy.

The queen jabbed a finger at Brierly. "Now she's bothering my Poopsie!"

The diplomatic Albertus edged away from Brierly.

Brierly gave her a vague sweet smile. "He prefers 'Albertus.'"

Half the ladies gasped and half giggled. Arpien stepped between the queen and Brierly. Crown Prince Timothy led his mother to a sofa on the far side of the room. Timothy solaced her with words and the ladies solaced her with lapdogs. Albertus growled at Brierly and then apologized for the rudeness as the queen fed him treats for his good judgment. Squeezie dashed back and forth from the queen's lap to Brierly's, determined to make friends of them and unable to see the damage he was doing. The queen might forgive Brierly for winning away half her kingdom, but she would never forgive her for winning away her puppies.

In the meantime, Arpien negotiated the rollicking political waters with a great deal of dignity, bowing, and syllables. From Brierly's brief sojourn in Conquisan, she knew he was only following Conquisani custom, which suggested one's consequence was only equal to one's verbiage and the force of one's manner. Problem was, it didn't carry off well in Rosaria, and even in Conquisan Brierly had seen it done more proficiently. Arpien would meet with better success if he didn't try so hard. He was almost likeable then. Not that Brierly liked him.

If the Conquisani measure of consequence were true, in the queen's domain Nissa had no consequence at all, poor girl. Luckily Brierly didn't concern herself with truth. It wasn't worth the effort. Nor was fighting for her own right to rule an imaginary kingdom, the question that impassioned everyone else in the room.

She couldn't be the lost princess, they argued. Brierly agreed. How could she be lost when she herself was the only fixed point in the universe? Was *lost* the same thing as being forgotten or ignored because she was inconvenient? The queen, Brierly suspected from a look at both her and her parlor, was the sort of person who looked upon inconvenience as the enemy of civilization.

"Show me proof I'll believe!" the queen said.

The broad-faced crown prince, Timothy, echoed her sentiments in a more facilitating manner. "I'm not saying you're not the princess. But anyone could say she is the lost heir. Is there a single person you can bring to your defense?"

Brierly shrugged. "Nary a one."

"She means of course there is evidence," Arpien said, "just not in the form of witnesses. Everyone who remembered her has passed on. If you want evidence, send your guards to old Castle Estepel in Sentre Forest. See if the tower is empty."

"Bring pruning shears," said Brierly.

Nissa laid a couple of fingers on Brierly's shoulder and pushed down, until Brierly's ear was level with Nissa's mouth. Unnecessary but sweet.

Her whisper expanded, as though Nissa breathed into one end of a brass instrument and Brierly stuck her Fine Ear into the other.

"Brierly," Nissa said, "I know someone who would remember you. What about your godparents? Fairies live practically forever, right?"

Foolish optimism. She'd forgotten how endearing it was. And heartbreaking. "Try if you must."

Nissa bit her lip. "The old tales say that any member of the royal line can invite a fairy into their kingdom's capital." She looked at Brierly. "How do I do it?"

"Same way you'd invite anyone into your home. Just talk."

Nissa raised her hands, hesitated, and twined her fingers together in front of her. "Uh—oh honorable good fairies—uh—listen to me now—would you please stop by Boxleyn Palace, for the country is in dire peril—er—need. At your convenience."

Nissa looked at the open windows, the door, the ceiling, the curtains, as if a peck of good fairies was going to pop out any moment. Everyone else except Brierly scanned the room, too. Nissa turned a becoming shade of rose.

The eye and nostril pie-slits of the queen's face flared, as though letting out steam.

She peered down at Nissa. "I hope, young lady, you're quite finished living out your unhealthy obsession with the old tales. The fairies didn't come because they do not exist. Now start behaving like the fifteen-year-old you are."

Nissa studied the floor. "I'm seventeen."

The queen swatted the air before her nose. "Fifteen, seventeen, no one would ever guess you above seven given your childish behavior."

"Mother, must you be so harsh?" the crown prince said.

"I'm harsh because it's my duty to raise her into a useful and modest young lady, not some fluff-headed infant who dreams of ogres and enchanted swords and sleeping beauties."

How did Nissa tolerate such condescension? Brierly felt her ears grow warm. "Quite right. It is all fluff-headed dream. But I beg the queen's pardon, as I must correct her about the nature of fairies. They don't snap to do one's will. They might come tomorrow or the fifth Tuesday after a blue moon, and only if they want to. They have other things to do besides cater to human self-importance."

She said this in such a bland tone that the queen could only open and close her tight, thin lips. Nissa grabbed Brierly's peacock-embroidered sleeve and dragged her out of the room. Arpien backed out as though he expected he'd have to draw his sword in Brierly's defense.

"I can't believe you just did that," Arpien and Nissa said simultaneously.

"She's my aunt," said Nissa.

"She's the queen," said Arpien.

"Does it matter?" said Brierly. "You both wanted to see her set down, too. She's a self-absorbed tidal wave."

Arpien scowled. "That may be true, but you don't have to imply it."

"You're saying I should lie?"

"Not lie. Prevaricate."

"Ah. Make up a truth that better fits the circumstances."

Arpien gave half a nod, then assumed his Prince Ponders the Situation pose.

"I appreciate what you did for me," Nissa said, "but it really wasn't worth it."

"Because you're not a real person with feelings?" Brierly said. "I'll try not to mistake you for one again."

Nissa opened her mouth and closed it, in an unfortunate parody of her aunt.

"The point," Arpien told Brierly, "is that you've sabotaged our chances of securing an audience with the king and proving who you are."

"Maybe next time."

"You think that after you insulted the queen there will be a next time?"

Brierly sighed. "Always."

10

Nissa

There wasn't much to do but fall back on the old palace custom of hiding until the queen calmed down. Timothy would help them in that much. But beyond that? If he supported Brierly's claim, he would be giving away half his own inheritance. He was Nissa's favorite cousin, but not a martyr to philanthropy.

Nissa stowed her guests in her chambers. Brierly proclaimed it naptime and retired to Nissa's bedroom. That left Nissa alone to entertain Prince Arpien. She hesitated over which of the hodgepodge of chairs to offer him, and finally waved him into a top-heavy carved wooden one that looked particularly desperate for attention.

After their meeting in the stables, Nissa expected some arrogant protests about the queen's rejection. But Arpien just sat and looked old. "Thank you, Lady Nissa, for your aid. I see we've put you in an awkward position with your aunt."

"I'm always in an awkward position with my aunt."

A single, robust snore erupted from the next room.

"She snores?" Nissa whispered.

"She wasn't snoring when I kissed her."

The enchanted princess in her tower, bluebirds looking on, sunlight streaming across her pillow, and the loud sawing of her breath. Nissa giggled. The image, in fact the oddity of the whole day, struck Nissa as funnier the more she thought of it. Arpien rested his elbows on his knees and watched her as her giggles turned into snorts. She clapped her hands over her face.

"You remind me of my sister."

She lowered her hands and tried to make a joke of it. "Your sister is a dumpy and bookish lady then, who snorts with elegance."

"She died a long time ago."

"I'm sorry."

"You didn't know. Anyway, I meant it as a compliment. You don't look much like her, but you share some mannerisms."

Nissa squirmed under his perusal.

"That one, for instance. But I'm embarrassing you, and you're the kindest person I've met in Rosaria."

He meant except for Brierly, right? But then Brierly wasn't particularly kind to Arpien. She didn't seem to notice her prince at all. Nissa was beginning to understand Arpien's reaction to his princess, too, the odd mixture of worship and resignation. It's easy to live with a legend on a page. You open the book, study, dream, and then shut the legend safely back inside. A live legend is bound to disappoint or make a mess.

"We'll have to be patient with her," Nissa said. "Must be a shock for her, to find the world has moved on without her."

Arpien's polite smile didn't reach his eyes.

Could anything shock Brierly? Maybe if the succession skipped her and Neef was crowned Ruler of Sentre Forest instead.

Maybe.

Nissa had no wit in conversation, nor did she think Arpien would care to admire her embroidery, so she challenged him to a game of jumpstones. He was a far better strategist, and won every game up to the point Brierly rejoined them and started coaching Nissa.

Timothy entered soon after and informed them that while the King of Rosaria was too busy to grant them an audience at this time, he was willing to investigate the issue further. The first step would be questioning Brierly and Arpien separately about the details of the alleged rescue, to see if their stories matched. The two were not to speak together again until General Gapric interviewed each of them. Arpien bowed to the ladies—only one hand-circle this time—and departed.

Nissa pulled Timothy into the empty room across the hall. "Investigate the issue further? Timothy, you know that's king-speak for 'I don't care but I'll pretend I'm doing something about it.'"

Timothy massaged the wrinkle between his eyebrows with a meaty hand. "Nissa, it took two hours to knit Mother's feelings back together and convince Father to even let someone look into it. You know he's never liked that sleeping princess legend."

"He doesn't like it because it's true."

"Nissa, you're a better scholar than I am, but you're far too trusting. Have you considered this could be a Conquisani hoax?"

"Why would Conquisan send an imposter Brierly?"

"Nissa, don't ignore the danger so you can pretend in your stories."

She knew. An enemy could use Nissa's "unhealthy obsession with the old tales" to gain admittance to Boxleyn. Perhaps an enemy already had. It was a little too convenient that a Conquisani prince arrived at Boxleyn the day after negotiations opened with Strand. Both Conquisan and Strand were crazed to gain access to Sentre Forest, everyone knew that. What was not widely known, due to Uncle Emol, was that the person who rescued Brierly could claim the coveted Sentre Forest as his prize and her dowry.

"I've set guards to track each of them," Timothy said. "They won't step in unless they see a true threat to Rosarian security. By all that's reasonable, we don't need the King of Conquisan to come charging over with an army because we've thrown his little brother in the dungeon. Relations are prickly enough as it is."

"You think it'll come to that?"

"Father's made a lot of promises to both Strand and Conquisan about Sentre Forest. He's laid his strategy to play one country off the other so Rosaria can get the best price for our resources. The arrival of a Prince of Conquisan is bad timing right now."

"And the arrival of a rival claimant to Sentre Forest is worse timing," Nissa said.

"See? You are more worldly than you pretend. I've never begrudged you your interest in the old tales, Nissa. I'm just saying, look twice before you decide to take up residence there." Timothy squeezed her shoulder and left.

But she is the missing princess.

She didn't call him back and say it because the debate was growing louder in her own head. All her life she'd been hedging. Telling people she didn't really believe in the old tales, she just found useful lessons in them. But she wanted them to be true. It'd been her life's work to track, catalogue, and analyze every version of every old tale she could find, in hopes of proving them. Was her desire to be vindicated as a scholar blinding her to the mundane reality of life? That there were no Rescuing Princes in the world, no giants or quests or epic battles of good and evil, just an enclosed space of self-interested politics where she was Lady Overlooked?

If the old tales were false, then who was sitting in her chambers?

Brierly was arranging the jumpstones into intricate mosaics when Nissa returned. "Will the guards keep me here or do you think we can explore the palace?" Brierly said.

"You heard me talking to Timothy?"

Brierly flipped her earlobe. "Fairy Gift."

"Perfect." Nissa sank into the cushioned seat on the opposite side of the table. "You have to understand, they're just looking out for the interests of Rosaria."

"Certainly I understand. They're trying to decide if I'm a princess, or—like Neef—a farm horse with pretensions."

Nissa had to smile at that. "Don't you care what they decide?"

"Does what I care about make a difference in this place?"

A hint of bitterness? No, Brierly's face was serene as glass. Nissa was inclined to believe she really was the princess for that very reason. An imposter would care what people thought.

It seemed a shame to lock Brierly away when she had just escaped her tower. "We could visit the servants," Nissa said. Even supposing Brierly was a Conquisani spy, introducing her to scullery maids could hardly be considered a threat to national security.

To her surprise, Brierly said visiting the servants was a fine idea. None of the other nobles had ever supported Nissa's view of them as interesting individuals. Perhaps it was a consequence of being invisible—Nissa saw others who were invisible, too.

The servants warmed to Brierly's blind good nature and graceful manner. The women put down their ladles and pins to admire her and the men hauled around unnecessary barrels and bags of flour. How could Brierly not see the overwhelming influence of her own beauty? People gaped, and offered her samples of tonight's supper, and asked her opinion on their darning. Another day it might have been Nissa's opinion they valued, but Nissa's intelligence and rapport withered to nothing in the blistering sun of Brierly's beauty.

Worse, the servants cooed over the wretched peacock gown as if they'd never seen it before. Perhaps that was another consequence of being invisible. Anything you wore turned invisible, too. Or maybe it was the fact that Brierly had so thoroughly stripped the gown of anything that was Nissa.

Nissa felt herself shrinking. She'd almost succeeded in disappearing altogether when she noticed Brierly smiling at her. "Thank you. Nissa and I made it."

Nissa opened her mouth and shut it before a denial popped out.

She listened again. True, Brierly's unnatural beauty drew a lot of comments. But Brierly split the accolades for the gown exactly in half, as though she and Nissa were two halves of the same creative mind.

Nissa studied the peacock gown. She had been hasty to proclaim it stripped of anything that was Nissa. For there she was, in the tooling of the neckline, in the long curve of the peacock's tail. And hadn't she found the right mossy blue-green to set off the more brilliant hues of her embroidery thread? Brierly had not stolen her work. She had displayed Nissa's skill so all could better appreciate it.

In that moment Nissa forgave Brierly for being Beautiful and Gifted. She even forgave her for not living up to her expectations as her childhood heroine.

Once she allowed Brierly her imperfections and her overperfections, she was ready to look at her again and see her for who she was. She had plenty of time to observe Brierly over the next week. General Gapric questioned Arpien the very day of his arrival. But he didn't talk to Brierly for another three days and a half.

Nissa did what she could to entertain Arpien without spending much time with him. She didn't want anyone to accuse her of passing messages. She did speak with the servants to arrange for good meals and altering his clothes. Arpien seemed like an active person, so Nissa sent the armsmaster to challenge him to a good bout. There was no reason Arpien had to stay locked in his room, so long as he didn't do anything to fuel suspicions of a Conquisani conspiracy. He just couldn't talk to Brierly. Perhaps General Gapric was delaying his interview with Brierly for that precise reason.

Although Nissa spent much more time with Brierly than she did Arpien, one difference between them struck her. Arpien always asked after Brierly. Was she content, was she eating with a good appetite, how was she spending her days? Brierly never asked after Arpien. When Arpien wasn't right in front of Brierly, he passed out of all existence. Brierly seemed to view the world entirely in the present. Did she want to know when General Gapric would send for her? No. Was she preparing her case for when she finally got an audience with the king? No. Past and future only had significance in terms of Art—what she had done already, and what new directions she could take.

True to her word, Brierly sewed the collaborative designs she had sketched in the queen's parlor. Due to her fairy Gift, she churned out gowns at a rate that made Nissa's fingers ache. Once the ladies got wind that the project was still going forward, they started sneaking by Nissa's chambers with fabric in hand. The queen was still miffed—she had burned all of Brierly's original sketches. But Brierly remembered them well enough, plus the patterns changed as she got to know the individual lady each gown was meant for.

Brierly sewed personalities into her gowns. Brierly would chat with a lady in Nissa's sitting area, her needle flying through the fabric, but her eyes on the woman. Brierly was Gifted with Charm, so often the conversation flowed easily. But sometimes she'd quit talking and squint, or raise her eyebrows, or just stare at the lady in question with a vapid expression. Depending on how each lady reacted, if she squirmed, or looked away, or laughed, or got angry, Brierly would either nod and keep sewing or tear out whole seams of the garment and begin anew. It was as though Brierly drew out each person's quirks and tastes and substance and stitched them into the seams that bound the garment together.

She was, Nissa began to realize, a genius. What a ruler she'd make, if she could see so clearly into people. Yet here was the tragedy. Brierly wasn't interested in the people, not beyond the inspiration they provided. Like Arpien, the ladies existed only as long they sat in front of her.

Nissa's chambers were soon infested with gowns in progress. Gowns lay across her chest of drawers. Gowns hung over the partition. Gowns lounged in her chairs. Nissa couldn't walk into her own rooms without jumping at the invasion. Gorgeous, ingenious, hollow ladies, each half alive with the echo of a real woman.

It might have put her off, that Brierly's great passion was for clothes instead of the people who wore them. Or that she talked about the queen's lapdogs but not the man who'd rescued her. But Nissa had decided not to make another hasty conclusion about her friend.

Nissa Montaine was not cunning, but she was studious. She'd been known to read the same book over again dozens of times and comb the nuances from it. She did that with Brierly now. Not as General Gapric, who asked flat questions and got back flat answers. But by quiet observation.

Invisible people see invisible things. When Brierly used her Gift of Charm, her face glowed with animation. Yet these extremes of expression struck Nissa as the most hollow. The smallest gestures were the significant ones. A crease of weariness in her brow even as she made all the young courtiers laugh. The tiniest amused twitch of her button nose as she listened to the head gardener's lengthy discourse on which manure made the best fertilizer. It was as though there was one Brierly drifting along and another Brierly somewhere outside the action, narrating.

Perhaps Nissa and Brierly were alike after all.

General Gapric got around to questioning Brierly on the fourth day after her arrival. It only took a couple of hours. Perhaps he'd already gotten his answers from Arpien, who had been summoned four different times to talk to four different people. Did Brierly's story match Arpien's? If it did, it didn't earn Arpien and Brierly an audience with the king. Nor were the two chucked out of the palace. The one significant change was that now Arpien joined them freely. Was he a Conquisani spy? Nissa didn't think so. Let more informed people make that decision. In the meantime, she'd be a good hostess and just not say anything important about military strength. Which she didn't know a lot about anyway.

Until the crown gave Brierly an official standing within the court, there wasn't much they could do but wait. Not a skill at which Arpien excelled. Nissa could sense his annoyance building again, but he schooled it with the help of a few guards eager to test the mettle of a Conquisani swordsman. Nissa tried to give him further release by arranging for the three of them to go riding at least twice a day. Not courtly rides, either. Hard, exhilarating races across the royal park, the sort that caused unsightly perspiration. The harried guards followed them with all the subtlety of spies disguised as bushes. If Arpien saw them he didn't comment.

Neef gave Brierly an earful if they rode much past two hours. So she said. What other pastimes could two legends and a plain lady share?

The strange part was, Nissa found plenty to share with them. She didn't fully understand Brierly, but she sensed a kinship there, in more than blood. Nissa broke Arpien of the worst of his Speech Making tendencies. Perhaps because she reminded him of his sister, he quit trying to impress her and relaxed. Arpien turned out to be a collector of ballads. It was how he had tracked down the sword that led him to Brierly, he said. He even sang a few, in a shy but tolerable baritone. Nissa delighted in their talks. She'd been unable to corner a Conquisani historian or minstrel for years.

Brierly didn't contribute much to these discussions. In fact, it was during these debates that the most internal commentary seemed to bubble behind Brierly's eyes. When Brierly did voice her thoughts, they were just as often something random as something profound. Sometimes in the middle of Arpien and Nissa's scholarly discussions Brierly would crack two stones together or announce, "Thus said the frogs." Nissa and Arpien learned not to pursue these non sequiturs.

Nissa grew fonder of her new friends every day. It was the two legends who had the least to say to each other. Arpien alternated between weary resignation at Brierly's oddities, an unfortunate propensity to lecture, and overripe infatuation. The infatuation was the most interesting, but also the hardest to witness. It was rather like bracing for an impending collision of two laundresses carrying baskets of underclothes. The encounters of the prince and princess generally led to one of two verbal extremes: dumbstruck gazing or sudden inflation of Arpien's vocabulary. Words like *adulate* and *magnanimous* and *ameliorate* cropped up like clear symptoms of disease. Brierly's utter lack of reaction only inflamed the rash. She never even bothered to use her Gift of Charm on him.

Nissa knew she ought to leave them alone to address their feelings or lack thereof. But when given the opportunity for a private word, neither of them took it. He'd go off for more sword practice and she'd pick up her sewing. By some silent agreement, Arpien and Brierly had appointed Nissa facilitator. Did she understand Brierly and Arpien better than they understood each other?

It didn't bode well for True Love.

Pity. Nissa was a big proponent of True Love.

11

Arpien

Eight days. Cryndien wouldn't have stood for it.

Arpien paced the marble atrium outside the Reception Room as he waited for a response to his daily petition for an audience with King Emol. In eight days the Rosarian king hadn't found a moment to spare for the legendary sleeping princess or her rescuer. At first Arpien supposed the delay was an outgrowth of the centuries-held animosity between Conquisan and Rosaria. Now he was beginning to suspect Emol's objection wasn't to him, but to Brierly, and more specifically to her claim to Sentre Forest.

Arpien could add this to his growing list of complications he hadn't foreseen. What had he expected? A parade? After one hundred years, Brierly had no close relatives or friends to blow trumpets at her return. Everyone would have been just as happy if the beauty stayed asleep. Possibly the beauty included.

Everyone except Nissa Montaine, the soft brown rabbit of a young lady who was nibbling her bottom lip as she pondered the answer to a riddle. It had been Nissa's idea that they exchange conundrums, Arpien suspected to squelch his agitation. All three members of their strange trio were good at conundrums, Brierly frightfully so. She told several she'd made up herself. They were clever, when they made sense.

So neither Arpien nor Nissa thought much of it when Brierly said, "Gowsma."

"Is that the whole clue?" Nissa said.

"Gowsma," Brierly repeated. She pointed out the open great doors.

A hag hauled herself up the marble steps with a cane. The closer she got, the uglier she got. Balding hair. A squinty right eye. Wrinkles of brown cloth encased wrinkles of flesh. Fuchsia flowers drooped from her person. If they were meant to sweeten her appearance, they only made the rest of her uglier in contrast.

"She gave me my thirteenth christening Gift," Brierly said.

Arpien and Nissa stared at each other. "That's what a good fairy looks like?"

"That's what all fairies look like when they walk the mortal lands," Brierly said. "They're supposed to get special permission to appear in full form."

"What does she look like in full form?" Arpien said.

"I don't remember. I was a month old the last time I saw her that way. If she's consistent with other fairies, I'd say bigger and scarier."

"Scarier is hard to fathom," Nissa said. "She already looks designed to bake and eat stray children."

"Beauty is the least useful Gift of all," Brierly said. "She has to appear as a hag when she's in human form. Do you know how old she is in human years? Anyway, be nice. She's an old family friend."

Nissa bit her lip again. "She looks pretty for a hag."

"Don't tell her that. She hates fibs. I never got one past her once."

The hag rocked into the atrium. She spotted Brierly with a four-toothed grin and opened her arms wide. "Is that my little Brierly? Come here and give your old Gowsma a hug!"

Brierly floated obediently into the knobby arms. For all her words about "old family friend," Brierly tolerated the hug rather than returned it.

"It's been years, dearie. I mean, of course I knew it would be, that was the plan, but I'm so glad to see you up and about. Oh, my sweet godchild. How I have missed you."

When she had thoroughly squeezed her godchild like a cheesecloth, Gowsma took a step toward Nissa. "You're Nissa. Thanks for inviting me. It's been seventy-two years since I visited Rosarian royalty. Haven't even seen the new place yet." She squinted at the walls. "A bit self-important, isn't it?"

"Uh—"

Gowsma eased her weight off her cane and patted Nissa's hand. "Don't worry, gosling, I can see you don't fit in here."

Nissa didn't look too reassured by that.

The hag—good fairy—turned her piercing attention to Arpien. "You must be the lucky young man who kissed her. You don't look good enough for my Brierly. But the Prince picked you out himself, and he's never wrong. Even lent you a sword, I see. What's your name, lad?"

Arpien's introductions flailed a little in the wake of this disconcerting informality. He didn't know the proper bow to accord a fairy, so he settled for the *Half-Bow for Esteemed Persons of Unknown Origins but Suspected Power*. "Prince Arpien Teric Elpomp Herren Trouvel of Conquisan. I am glad to meet the"—his vocabulary floundered—"person—who saved Brierly's life."

"I'm not the expert on saving humans, but I did what I could." Gowsma turned back to Nissa. "Now, dear, was your invitation a social one or a matter of business?"

"Uh—"

Arpien came to her rescue. "We're having a little trouble with the Rosarian court—"

Gowsma batted her gnarled hand at him. "Shh, lad, the girl won't ever find her own strength if people keep trampling her."

"See, my Uncle Emol—he's the king—he doesn't believe it's her," Nissa said.

"Who's her?"

"That Brierly is ... Brierly."

"Who else would she be but herself?"

"No one in the Rosarian court believes in the old tales anymore. Not in Brierly, or the Curse, or the enchanted sleep, or fairies—"

"Not believe in fairies!" The fuchsia flowers swelled in indignation. "I suppose he thinks we'll die off if he doesn't acknowledge our existence. Where is your Uncle Emol?"

Nissa pointed to the ornate doors of the Reception Room. "In the Reception Hall. But you can't go in now, he's bargaining with Strandish dignitaries."

Gowsma was already gone. Nothing to do but follow in the wake of this tumbleweed of sharpness, humor, and warts.

Gowsma was angry enough, old enough, or ugly enough that the guards did nothing to stop her until she was already in the middle of the room. "Young man," she said.

Arpien was willing to bet no one had called King Emol *young man* like that in a long time.

"Young man, we've never met, but that doesn't mean my kind doesn't exist," said Gowsma.

"W-w-what?"

Arpien was surprised to hear King Emol sputter. Queen Perturbance seemed the one who twanged in high-bred annoyance. Everything about the king was oiled and smoothed into order, down to the tiny rows of black curls in the beard that framed his round face.

"It's like saying that your next-door neighbor doesn't exist, just because you haven't been hospitable enough to invite him over to your house," Gowsma said.

"What is this?"

"Gowsma," Brierly said.

"What's a gowsma?" King Emol said.

"Not what, who," Gowsma said. "Gowsma's my name. What I am is a fairy."

The resulting silence was amplified by the sheer number of speechless tongues. A fair dozen other nobles sat around the rectangular paneled table with the king. Their chairs were noticeably shorter than the king's. At least half the men wore well-pruned Strandish goatees.

"You'll pardon me, madam." Honey ran slowly, and could not drip quite fast enough to coat King Emol's insincerity. "No one's seen any—ah—fairies—in a very long time."

"And just because you can't see something, that gives you an excuse not to believe it's real, hmm? Humans!" Gowsma smacked the butt of her cane on the floor. "Will someone get an old woman a chair?"

The only servant brave enough to obey was one so old it looked like she could use a chair herself.

"Thank you, youngster." Gowsma sat down with a vocal creak, as though to narrate the complaints of her ancient bones. She waved her cane at the king.

He flinched.

"Easy, son, it's a cane, not a wand. See, you do believe in fairies. The children here tell me that you don't believe in the old tales anymore, and so you won't acknowledge Brierly is the same princess who fell asleep one hundred years ago. Well, here I am, a genuine fairy, and I exist. And there is Brierly, a genuine princess of Rosaria, and she exists." Gowsma sat back and crossed her brown-draped arms.

"You'll understand I need more evidence than that."

"Evidence? You have expert testimony. I, Gowsma, was at Brierly's christening. Her parents, being better schooled in manners than some other monarchs of Rosaria, invited me and eleven other good fairies to be their daughter's godparents. It was a fine celebration—good cookies, too—until an evil fairy barged in uninvited. At great personal cost, I might add. Took her decades to recover full strength. She Cursed the baby with these words: 'Before the dawning of her seventeenth birthday, the princess shall prick her finger on a spindle and die.' I was the only fairy left who hadn't given a christening Gift, so I did what I could to lessen the damage. But I was also the youngest fairy, not so powerful as the others."

It was hard to associate the word *young* with Gowsma.

"I did modify the Curse of death to one of sleep, until such time as Brierly's true love should come and wake her with a kiss. And there he stands." She waggled the cane at Arpien. "And there she stands, the same princess who pricked her finger on a spindle one hundred years ago. The same babe at that christening. I can vouch that this young lady is my own goddaughter. If you can't manage a sincere welcome for her, you'll at least be giving this lad his fair reward."

King Emol shared a look with his wife. The queen growled. Wait, that was a lapdog. The queen massaged the creature's furry head so hard folds of skin pressed in and away, in and away, from his face. Flabby cheeks, no cheeks. Flabby cheeks, no cheeks.

The king turned back to Gowsma. "What would that be?"

"Half the kingdom and her hand in marriage. The standard princess-rescuing fee. He's not who I would have picked for her, but he's who the Prince picked. That's the essential point. Brierly can refuse the match, but you cannot. You are bound by law and justice to honor the offer."

"I extended no such offer."

"Brierly's parents did." Gowsma squinted at him with her right eye. "But I can see you prefer the convenience of personalized law. New times, new rules." She glanced at an older man with a Strandish goatee. The head of Strandish delegation? "Note that well, human. He will deal no better with you than he does his own kin."

"You insult my integrity in my own home," King Emol said. The tone was cool, but the tiny black curls quivered on his jaw as he ground his teeth.

"Prove you have some, then. Honor the promise set forth by the last Stewards."

Crown Prince Timothy extended an appeasing hand. "You must agree that your story lacks plausibility. Do you know how old you'd have to be if you attended Brierly's christening?"

"I know exactly how old I'd have to be. Don't you know better than to ask a woman her age?"

"You'd have to be nearly a century and a half old." Uncle Emol wrapped his annoyed smile in condescension. The way you wrapped veal in bacon and gave it a sophisticated name. He quirked a pompous brow toward the other nobles and advisors in the room.

"At least," Gowsma said. "Look at me closely, king, and tell me I look a day younger."

"Look at her, then." The king waved a hand at Brierly. "Even supposing she could survive a century-long coma, she'd age."

"Enchanted sleep."

"Eating and drinking nothing? She'd starve."

"Fairy Gift." The hag glanced at Brierly. "Ritga's invention, wasn't it?"

Brierly nodded, as though at a bedtime story she'd heard once too often.

"Eat-Whatever-You-Want-and-Still-Retain-a-Maidenly-Figure. Which includes eating nothing. Dead useful, that Gift," said Goswana.

Nissa sighed.

"Even if it is theoretically possible, it doesn't prove either of you are who you say you are," Timothy said.

The queen spun her finger. "If you're a big powerful fairy, show us a little fairy magic."

"I can't create magic here. I can only carry magic I have created in other worlds."

"Go to some other world and fetch some back, then."

"It took me a full week to drag myself here after your niece issued her invitation. Do you think it's easy to travel in human form at my age? Besides, magic is not something to be batted around for mortal entertainment."

"How convenient."

"A long sight inconvenient at the moment. But those are the rules. I cannot create magic in my human form, and I may not transform into full form in the mortal lands unless the Prince orders it."

King Emol knitted his fingers across his belly. "So you admit, you have no way of proving who you are."

"I recognize her."

King Emol knocked a stack of papers off the table as he jerked around. It was the old servant who'd brought Gowsma her chair.

"Who the combustion are you?"

"Senesca, Your Majesty. I've had the pleasure of serving you and your father and his father before him. Before that, I served in the old castle in Estepel." Her hand trembled with fear or age.

Gowsma patted her hand. "Take my chair, dearie."

"Just how many centenarians do we have in this room?" the king said.

"I'm eighty-one, Your Majesty," Senesca said.

"Then you did not know the princess," Timothy said.

"Not when she was awake, Your Highness. But I saw her after she fell asleep. As youngest maid there, it was my job to freshen her room. The princess was a little"—she glanced at Brierly—"disturbing. But the old king and queen insisted on it. Open the windows, dust the furniture and, well, her."

"How old were you at the time, grandmother?" Timothy said.

"Nine, Your Highness."

"Nine years old. It's been what, seventy years?"

"Seventy-two, Your Highness."

"Yet you're positive this girl before you is the same one you saw in that room?"

"Yes, Your Highness. You can't, um, dust someone without getting to know them. I recognize her, too." This with a timid nod at Gowsma. "The old Stewards invited her to Castle Estepel from time to time."

"You know it's the same woman?" Timothy said.

His mother's tone was less tolerant, as though the apples in her pie had gone tart. "Don't all hags look the same to a nine-year-old?"

"You don't forget Gowsma," Senesca said.

Gowsma squared her shoulders with pride. The movement pushed the stems of the fuchsia buds out of her baggy earth-colored robes. The flowers grew half an inch. Or appeared to. Were the flowers decoration, or part of fairy physiognomy?

"Tripe," Queen Perturbance said. "The House of Montaine built Boxleyn Palace over ninety years ago. No one ruled from old Castle Estepel seventy-two years ago, so why would this creaky woman have been there dusting princesses?"

"It's true that Boxleyn has been the capital of Rosaria for ninety years." Nissa's voice sounded tight and squeaky. "The brother of the last Steward queen built the palace here. But the last Stewards lived on in Castle Estepel, years after they resigned the daily management of the kingdom to the House of Montaine."

Her family glared at her.

Nissa seemed to feel their attention as a tangible weight. Her neck retracted between her round shoulders. "I…read it…"

The Queen snorted. "In a fairy story?"

Gowsma growled. Queen Perturbance paled. Gowsma patted the old servant's shoulder. "Go on, dearie."

"Aye, the old king and queen lived there," Senesca said. "If you could call mourning living. They lingered, and dried up, like dead roses still in their vases."

Arpien stole a glance at his princess, but she had whitewashed all reactions from her face.

"The Montaines and all the courtiers moved into Boxleyn Palace. The lucky servants did, too. It was new and bright. Not like Castle Estepel. Estepel felt as Cursed with sleep as the princess. Life froze up the instant the princess fell asleep. Then there were the briars."

"Briars?" King Emol said.

"Yes, Your Majesty. They were why your great-grandfather built Boxleyn Palace in the first place. The older servants told me the briars first sprang up around the castle when the king and queen brought Princess Brierly back from Conquisan with the Curse on her. By my day the briars had taken over the whole grounds. Fifteen feet high. Moving things, like snakes. All the servants helped weed a path in and out of the castle, but every night, the briars sprouted up again. I still have the scars from pulling them out of the ground." She held up her palms, crisscrossed with faint white lines. "They were eerie, those briars. Not natural at all. Endless vines and thorns and not a single rose on the entire grounds. When the old king died, we buried him and moved out of the castle that same day."

"You abandoned the princess?" Arpien said.

Senesca studied her gnarled hands. "It was thought she'd never notice." She glanced up. "Please forgive us, Princess."

Brierly shrugged. "You were right."

"We were frightened. When the last Steward king lay dying on his bed, the briars stirred and danced as if in a great wind. We thought they'd trap us inside the castle forever the moment he died. So we set him into the ground and ran. I didn't even take my doll."

In the old woman's rheumy eyes Arpien saw the little girl mourning for her doll, for the sad but kind king, for the Cursed beauty. Whole lives choked by briars.

Gowsma stepped forward, her sauciness muted by the old servant's tale. "You see, king, what grief this Curse has brought to the line of Stewards and those who surrounded them. Grief to them, fortune to you. The Rosarian throne is now yours. Is it so much to give to Brierly half the kingdom? Sentre Forest is hers by a claim far older than your own."

"Your story grieves me." King Emol's jowls worked under his curly black beard. It was as though he told his face to droop with empathy, but his cheeks didn't understand the direction. "But moved though I be, I will need more evidence than the word of two old women, whose memories cannot be relied on."

"I have evidence."

Nissa? Why hadn't she spoken before?

"Another fairy t—" Queen Perturbance caught herself. "Something you read?"

Nissa looked at Gowsma and Arpien. "Keep them here." An unnecessary request. Who would dare leave under threat of a hag's cane?

Nissa left and returned some minutes later. She lugged a painting as tall as she was. Arpien helped her carry it the last few feet to the center of the room. Spiderwebs tickled his hands.

This portrait had to be at least a century old, yet the Brierly who peered out from the frame looked in feature and form exactly like the breathing version who stood, arms crossed, a few paces away. They only differed in subtle nuances in the arrangement of features. The artist had not only succeeded in creating an accomplished formal sitting, he'd captured the immediacy of his subject. Her tapered fingers cupped each other in her lap, yet one stuck up, unlaced, as though she might have been tapping it. Her posture was straight and correct, but she leaned a fraction of an inch forward, as though the artist would have to work quickly or his model would flit off to have adventures.

But the most striking difference was the eyes. Unguarded. Eager. Awake. Eyes that had never seen a spindle. Curiosity danced in their blue-green depths, as though portrait-Brierly yearned to slip from her world of canvas and oil and investigate her spectators.

"I ordered all those musty portraits taken down seven years ago, when I redecorated." Queen Perturbance said.

"I liked this one, so I put it in storage. As you can see, the placard reads, 'Briar Rose Steward, age sixteen.'"

"Briar Rose?" Timothy said. "This girl's name is Brierly."

"A nickname."

"My name," Brierly said. "Briar Rose is ridiculous even for a princess."

"We always called her Brierly, but she was christened Briar Rose," Gowsma said.

"Briar Rose is her legal name, too. I've read it"—Nissa eyed her Aunt Perturbance—"in the histories."

Arpien leaned toward Nissa and spoke out of the easterly half of his mouth. "Why didn't you mention this portrait before?"

"You think they would have listened, then?"

Maybe what seemed reasonable to Arpien was simply not an option Nissa's standing with the king and queen allowed. Now, with the weight of Senesca's testimony and Gowsma's personality behind it, the portrait solidified Brierly's claim. Especially with the Strandish delegates observing the proceedings. In light of Gowsma's derision of the king's integrity, King Emol had to at least appear reasonable, or lose political footing.

King Emol smiled like cracking plaster. "Brierly Steward. How good to have you back."

12

Brierly

So she was Brierly Steward. Nice to have it confirmed, she guessed. Would anyone notice if she escaped into another dream? It'd been a very trying morning.

But no, she had to wait while Nissa's oily Uncle Emol made an insincere speech. Then he blathered something about not formally extending the reward until Briar Rose and Arpien were honored at a grand ball—perhaps at the Spring Ball next month. Couldn't hand over the princess until the Crown formally reintroduced her to noble society.

Brierly yawned. Not another ball.

King Emol finally adjourned the gathering. Arpien and Nissa busied themselves hefting the portrait out the door and carrying on a hushed debate about whether it should be put under guard as vital evidence. At last, a chance to escape. Please, she couldn't stomach any more nostalgia.

But Gowsma demanded her elbow and lunch (two unassociated items, regardless of Nissa's impression of her godmother). Brierly had never been able to say no to her affectionate, feisty godmother. So she acquiesced to cold meat and cheese and a torment of broccoli florets.

"Now that that pompous clucking is over, let's have a good catch-up, shall we? Turn around and let me see how you've weathered the years. A bit thinner, are we? Eat." Gowsma shoved the plate of cheese at her.

"I can't be thinner. Ritga's Gift."

"I'll grant you that. Might have saved your life, that Gift."

There'd been times Brierly had hated that Gift. Gowsma's, too.

Still, Brierly wanted to make Gowsma happy. She stacked several slices of pungent aged cheese in the middle of her plate. She nibbled at her florets and set them upright on her plate, broccoli topiary surrounding a cheese tower, and tried to be as happy as Gowsma. She'd lost the trick of it. Could unexercised happiness atrophy? Could it go stale like bread?

"I don't suppose there are any cookies to be had? Especially that minty kind with the jam filling? I'd sell my left wing for one of those. No? No matter." Gowsma patted the seat beside her. "Move over by me, chickpea. I want to feel you close beside me. How I've missed you!"

"But not enough."

"Speak up, dear, the left ear's gone a bit deaf in the last century."

"You haven't missed me enough to seek me out, not until today. Why? All fairies have the power to walk the dream world. In their full forms, too. Voracity does. She's found me a thousand times. But not you. Not once."

"Oh, Brierly, it isn't that I didn't want to. The Prince ordered us not to interfere."

"Ah."

It was always the Prince with Gowsma. The Prince said this, the Prince said that, the Prince is so wise and good and wonderful.

The wise-good-wonderful Prince had left Voracity to torture Brierly for decades. Like Gowsma, he'd never bothered to seek her out once. Worse than Gowsma, for he didn't even bother to appear now.

Gowsma forked a slice of ham onto Brierly's plate. "You're upset."

"No."

"I can always tell when you're lying."

"I'm not lying. I'm not upset. It doesn't matter."

"False on all accounts. Do you take me for a human?" Gowsma wagged the fork. "You don't understand why we left you alone. Not truly alone, you understand. But you're right, we didn't step in and stop her. That wasn't his plan."

"Plan?" Brierly flicked over the broccoli florets, one by one. "You mean the prophecy that a Steward will bring the Prince back and defeat the evil fairy? Ingenious plan. It got me Cursed since birth and trapped in eternal sleep. You think I haven't tried to bring him back? You think I haven't fought Voracity? His plan is rotten melons."

Gowsma took Brierly's plate away from her and clanked it on the table. "I don't care if you are a hundred and seventeen—I'll stick your button nose in a corner if you slur the Prince that way."

"I don't care. He doesn't care. It doesn't matter. None of this is real."

Gowsma took Brierly's face between her liver-spotted hands and peered into it. She had a squinty right eye. Her truth eye, Gowsma called it when Brierly was a child. Brierly had loved her godmother, but she'd always been petrified of that eye. Silly.

"You believe yourself," Gowsma said.

Brierly leaned away. "You can leave now. You'll leave sooner or later. Everyone does."

"Brierly, brambleberry, listen. I know you don't understand why we didn't stop her."

"Explain it to me, then."

"That's for the Prince to tell you."

"If the Prince were real, he would have shown up a long time ago. As it is, I can't even imagine him into existence." She had tried. But a Prince of her own construct had no more power to save her than she did herself.

"Oh, child."

Brierly finished the slice of cheese in her hand, wiped her fingers on her skirts, and curtseyed. "Thanks for stopping by. Do drop in again, when you're in this part of the dream world."

13

Arpien

They'd won. Arpien wanted to share his elation with his lady, but she'd wandered off yet again. It was hard to let little things like misplacing his princess irk him when at last things were going as he planned.

He knocked on Nissa's door and inquired of Kendra if Princess Briar Rose Steward were within.

"No, but Brierly is," Brierly called from inside.

It took him a moment to find Brierly amid the flourishing population of colorful gowns that inhabited the parlor. Brierly sat on a chair, her feet tucked under her, her skirts displayed about her. Her needle sailed through the satin in her hand. It was hard to reconcile this model of domestic charm with the unpredictable adventuress who talked to animals and tamed monsters and stole the treasure of brigands. The juxtaposition was disconcerting, but also tantalizing.

He begged the pardon of one of the lifelike gowns and sat down across from her. Nissa hadn't returned, so without his facilitator he was left without much to do but heap ignorant admiration on Brierly's sewing. That subject exhausted, he turned to his favorite topic.

"After the wedding, how would you like to go on a bridal tour to meet our new subjects? I know there are populated pockets of Sentre Forest. They'd form a more favorable opinion of us if our first visit wasn't to collect taxes." He smiled at his own joke, which must have been even less funny then he thought, because Brierly just kept sewing. "Brierly, tell me what you think."

"I think it's a pretty little dream that will come to no end, because I'm not going to marry you."

"No, you misunderstood the king. He agreed you are Briar Rose Steward. He'll take a little pressuring, but he'll have to give us Sentre Forest. We can call on the Strandish delegates as witnesses to his verbal promise to us."

The needle nibbled uniform bites of the seam. "It matters not if the king honors his promise because I'm not going to marry you."

"But—but I rescued you."

"Yes, it was sweet of you to take the trouble. And yes, I heard what Gowsma said–the same as you–about the standard princess-rescuing fee. Gowsma also said I could refuse the match. And I do."

"Why?" First the hurt spoke, then the frustration. *"Why?"*

She shrugged. "There's the difference in our ages."

"One year."

"Ninety-nine."

She was both younger and older than he was. An ancient infant, trapped inside that desirable woman's body. Trapped. Was that how she felt? He would not have her exchange one prison for another.

"Would I make so hateful a husband, Brierly?"

"Hateful?" The needle choked on its tiny bite of blue silk. "I don't hate you."

"But you hate Conquisan, is that it? Like the rest of Rosaria, you believe the finger-pricking incident was some Conquisani plot."

She picked out her last stitch. "No."

"Then what? Give me a reason I can understand."

"Maybe you bore me." She yawned. "I'm going to take a nap."

Of its own volition, his body bent in the *Bow of Dignified Retreat* and deposited him in the hallway.

He'd lost her. No, he'd never had her. What he'd lost was himself. The moment he kissed her in that tower was supposed to confirm his destiny. Instead, that was the moment his destiny started to unravel.

Only when a girl with a scrubbing brush crept by him and drizzled wash water across his toes did he awaken to the fact that he had not moved for some minutes. He glanced down the hall. A couple Rosarian guards eyed him, as though they suspected his staring motionless at the neatly squared-off blocks of stone in the wall might be some kind of Conquisani reconnaissance mission.

In the privacy of his room he held the vademecum sword in front of him. "Well, this was your idea, too. What now?"

The sword had no suggestions.

He could always get another princess. There had to be at least one other fair damsel in the world in need of a rescuer. An appreciative damsel this time.

He didn't want another damsel. He wanted this one. Or at least, he wanted the one in his dreams. But then, so had Great Grandfather Herren.

The morning after Brierly plucked his six-year-old dream-self from the river, Arpien had told Great Grandfather about the lady in white. It was one of the last conversations they had together. Herren died that winter at the unbelievable age of one hundred and five. He'd outlived all of his generation, as if he'd tried to grasp on to life long enough to see his princess waken. But all mortal men, in the end, must sleep.

"She seemed so real," young Arpien had said.

"She might have been," Great Grandfather said. "For I have dreamed of the same young lady."

Young lady? From the perspective of a six-year-old she looked old, practically an adult.

Great Grandfather told Arpien the strange story of Brierly, the woman Herren was supposed to marry. They were betrothed from childhood, but they only met once. On the cusp of Brierly's seventeenth birthday, Conquisan threw a great ball to celebrate her majority and the union that would resolve the disputed territory of Sentre Forest. Oh, but Brierly was beautiful then, the aged Herren recalled. Witty. Charming. All his youth Herren had rebelled at the notion of being tied to a primitive Rosarian. Now he scarcely believed his luck.

But the next morning Brierly was missing. Angry words were exchanged—accusations about abductions. At last the guards found her collapsed in the topmost tower, unwakeable. She bore no injuries but a single puncture wound on the tip of her right index finger. A tiny drop of red stained the end of a spindle on a spinning wheel in the same room. The outraged Rosarians called it a Conquisani conspiracy to overthrow the throne of Rosaria and steal Sentre Forest. Conquisan said the unfortunate incident was Rosaria's own fault. How dare they fob off a defective princess on Herren? Herren only knew that in a single evening he had gained and lost the most enchanting creature he would ever know.

Is a single night enough to fall in love? It is enough to form an obsession. Great Grandfather willed to Arpien his private journals, to be handed over to Arpien on his tenth birthday. His journals recorded rumors about the fate of the old Stewards and their castle, half-formed plots for how Brierly might be rescued, his every memory of the enchanted princess. Arpien thought Great Grandfather meant to aid him in a rescue attempt, but perhaps he meant to warn him.

All through his long life, Brierly's image had haunted Herren. He saw her in the graceful dance steps of other ladies—never quite so fleetsome; in the banter of other courtiers—never quite so witty. He married another princess who was not half so charming but proved good-hearted enough to care for and honor. But he could never escape that terrible memory of perfection, Cursed. Once in a great while Brierly roamed the landscape of his dreams, but Herren could never catch her.

Arpien didn't understand why his great-grandfather didn't rescue Brierly. At first, said Herren, he did try. But in the post-spindle aftermath, the politics between Conquisan and Rosaria grew so hazardous that no man of Conquisan, let alone he, could cross the borders of Rosaria without starting a war. Besides, they said a thicket of magical briars guarded the princess within her castle.

"But you let—politics—keep you out," young Arpien said. Politics sounded like monsters with dozens of stick-like limbs. "You never even faced the briars."

"Someday, you'll learn that politics cut more deeply than a thicket of the sharpest briars," the old man said. "And you can't spend your whole life chasing dreams."

Like Great Grandfather, it was now time for Arpien to wake up, move on, and settle for the next best thing.

He had little enough to pack–some maps, a bedraggled cap, and some cooking ware–but Arpien couldn't bring himself to do it. Couldn't walk away from the corpse of his youthful hope without stopping to acknowledge its passing. How do you mourn the death of a dream? What dirges do you sing when the impossible arrives stillborn?

Three hard, distinct raps came at his door.

"You're thinking of leaving." Gowsma was even uglier this close. It was as if her eyebrows had shattered and fallen further down her face, where they took root as individual hairs on her chin, popping out of her warts ...

She tapped her foot. "Time is short, bones are old."

"Please sit down. May I offer you something to eat?" Perhaps a small, fat child?

That was unkind. Arpien repented by drawing up a footstool for her old bones.

"Have any mint cookies with jam filling?" Gowsma lifted a hopeful brow to him.

"Uh—no. How'd you know I was thinking of leaving?"

"Doesn't matter how. I'm asking if it's right."

Arpien gripped his knees, as though he feared his kneecaps might fall off. "Is it right to stay and force a marriage no one wants? She's completely indifferent to me."

"Only by considerable effort."

"I thought only her true love could wake her. That's what Great Grandfather Herren told me. It's what all the legends say. But you've seen her. She cares more for her horse than for me."

"Because you didn't wake her." An extra space padded each word. His childhood tutors had done the same when he failed to pay attention. "Look at her, young man. Her body moves, but her mind and soul are still asleep. She refuses to believe she's not still locked in the dream world."

"Why? She can't like it better there."

The hag squinted at him. Layers of papery flesh nearly swallowed her right eye. "You like her better there."

Arpien flinched.

"Brierly did not just sleep for one hundred years, she dreamed for one hundred years," Gowsma said. "Have you ever had a nightmare you couldn't escape?"

The icy river that had swallowed his sister a hundred times shivered down Arpien's spine.

"I see you have," Gowsma said. "As terrible as that nightmare was, in the morning, you did wake up. Brierly didn't have that option. And I know for a fact that Voracity hounded her with nightmares to try to break her."

"What sort of nightmares?"

"The sort that exploits every weakness and mutates every virtue into a flaw. Death. Torture. Desires without consequence. Pleasure without fulfillment. Futility. Voracity has been reaching into the human world this way for millennia. Brierly is her special project. Voracity wants to destroy her utterly, for fear she'll bring back the Prince. I intervened to spare Brierly's body. A clever last Gift, I thought. Not clever enough—Voracity attacked Brierly's soul instead. There's more than one way to die. You shouldn't be surprised your princess is a shell of a human being. You should be surprised she's a human being at all."

One hundred years of nightmares. Brierly's indifference seemed heroic in that light. "How do you know so much about Brierly's dreams?" he said.

"I've watched her."

"Watched her but did nothing to save her from her nightmares?"

"It was not the Prince's will that we interfere."

Arpien thought of his brother Bo. Even though Bo disapproved of the way Cryndien ran the kingdom, he refused to go against him. "Seems to me your Prince is no better than Voracity, then."

Gowsma struck his calf with her cane, with more force than any feeble old woman ought to be able to strike. "Watch yourself, young man. The Prince of Here and There is the most gentle and merciful of monarchs, but he is no weakling with knees of jelly. You may not sneer at his decisions without reprisal."

Arpien rubbed his calf. "Sorry. He was just a convenient target, because he's not here."

Gowsma mumbled something indistinct about foolish humans not understanding anything.

"If the nightmares were as bad as you say," Arpien said, "why would Brierly prefer to believe she's asleep now?"

"Two reasons, I suspect. I believe, on your journey to Boxleyn, a giant mantiz bit you and Brierly saved you from merfolk?"

How'd she know? Spying in Brierly's head again? Who knew how fairies knew things? "But that was only—"

"A dream? Yes. But didn't you notice how in that dream, Brierly had power? Most humans dream as though they were watching a puppet show. Even if they are one of the puppets, someone else is pulling the strings. Have you ever had a dream where there were no strings? Where you could dictate what happened?"

"A handful of times."

"In one hundred years, what did Brierly have to do but practice taking control of her dreams? What better incentive did she have, with Voracity hounding her with nightmares? Brierly thinks this world, what you know as reality, is nothing but a dream she cannot control. So she's just riding along, waiting until she passes into another dream where she is powerful again."

Arpien remembered his peek into Brierly's dreams. Anyone would want to do without vindictive mermaids. Merfolk. But what about the next dream, the world she shaped with her song? Color and texture and exotic genius. Brierly's dreams were a mixture of extreme cruelty and extreme beauty.

"I said there were two reasons," Gowsma said. "Each dream has its own rules. In one dream, lions may devour you, while in another, they may be your pets. What is true in one dream is not necessarily true in another. In that sense, each one is true within itself. Which collectively means most must be false."

"What?"

"Rules that contradict each other cannot be true at the same time. While each dream lasts, it appears to be the truth. But it's not Truth over them all, not reality. There can only be one of those."

"That makes sense."

"Of course it makes sense! Just because it does, you think people are going to believe it? Don't smirk—I bet you're fooled by your own notions every day. And you don't have half the excuse Brierly has." She crossed her arms and huffed. One of the fuchsia flowers at her chest huffed along with her. "You don't suppose you are the first prince to rescue her, do you?"

Arpien didn't like the idea of sharing Brierly, even with figments. "Then what can I do to convince her? Keep laying out the logic that this world is the real one?"

"Brierly might listen to logic. The past century has left her a little dazed, but she's quite brilliant, you know. But you humans think with your guts when your heads are right, and your heads when your guts are right. I didn't realize how scared and hurt Brierly was until we left the Reception Room. So lay out the case with logic, yes. But also lay it out with your Patience. With your Constancy. And with your Compassion."

He had been patient. He'd planned her rescue since that rash vow at age eleven. And constant? He never seriously pursued any other woman.

Gowsma blew her straggly hair out of her eyes. "And you think that's love? You need almost as much waking as she does. Maybe in the pursuit of one, you'll achieve the other." Gowsma glanced at the thinning spray of sunlight that spilled through the window. "My time is short. I can stay on no human ground longer than a single day."

"Nissa invited you."

"So she did, and I was pleased to come. Pleasant girl, if a bit shy. She can invite me again tomorrow, if she likes. There was a time when the Rosarian royalty invited us into their home every day. We didn't come every day. Fairies have other duties to oversee, in other places. But we did hold a high position in the court. Those days are over now." She drew her brown cloak around her shoulders and re-anchored one of the fuchsia flowers at the clasp. "There's hope those days will come again, if the Stewards once again rule the land."

"There's only one Steward left."

She poked his collarbone. "Wrong again. There are no Stewards left at all. Though they might come again, in time."

Arpien chased her down the stairs. She moved quickly for an old woman. "I still don't understand how to help Brierly," he said.

She drummed his skull with her cane. "Patience." *Rap.* "Constancy." *Rap.* "Compassion." *Rap.*

Arpien rubbed his head.

"Start with those, would-be rescuer, or logic will have no safe ground to take root. In time and with the Prince's mercy, she may wake. No promises. She may decide to sleep forever. She's still under a curse. And this one you cannot save her from, because she put her own self under it. No matter how much evidence you lay before her, if Brierly doesn't want to believe the truth, she won't. That is the human way."

Part Three

Nagging is the repetition of unpalatable truths.
Baroness Edith Summerskill

Truth is stranger than fiction
because we have made fiction to suit ourselves.
G. K. Chersterton

14

Arpien

There were knights who had to convince their ladies that their love was genuine. He must be the only man, Arpien sulked, who had to convince his lady that *he* was genuine.

He schooled himself to patience and compassion, as Gowsma recommended. Ordered. Within the hour her advice broke down his despair and resentment. If Brierly was distant, it was only because of what had been done to her. Blame it on Voracity. Blame it on her parents for being Stewards. Blame it on the Good Fairies for abandoning her for one hundred years. She was as pure and innocent as he'd believed from the beginning. Let him not be fooled by her eccentricities or even by her coldness. She was still his lady, his light.

Her Virtues glowed all the more for their forging in the one hundred years of imprisonment. All right, she was a little outlandish. It was because she was in peril (perceived or actual). So the tower was higher than he first thought. So the briars were thicker. She still deserved rescuing.

And Prince Arpien Teric Elpomp Herren Trouvel of Conquisan was a rescuer.

Destiny trumpeted through his veins again. Was he a powerless six-year-old? No! He was going to hack through those briars with his strong right arm and save her. He would woo her with an onslaught of ardor no maid could resist. He would lay siege to the tower that imprisoned her, tear the wall of her disbelief apart stone by stone.

When your hobby is rescuing princesses, you can't help but develop a taste for strategy. He delighted in the pursuit, the research, the tactics. Why, he'd spent months just tracking down the right sword. How did you win a lady's heart? For the billionth time he wished Kirren were alive, this time to unravel the female mind for him.

He went to the closest thing he had to a sister—Nissa.

The servants gave him to understand that Nissa Montaine considered the tower library an extension of her chambers, and he'd likely find her there. If not for the fact that she needed a candle to read by, Arpien might not have found her. Nissa was short and she'd turned a far desk into a nest of high stacks of books.

He peered over one such orderly fortification. "What are you reading?"

She let out a sound like a frightened hiccup and banged her elbow into a stack of books. Arpien steadied the stack with one hand and grabbed up the candle in the other before she started a conflagration.

She reclaimed the candle immediately, as though she couldn't bear to stop reading for an instant. "*Reports of the Fairies.* I've read this book a dozen times, but it's different now. They're real, Arpien. All my life, people have told me I'm a fool to hope the old tales are true. Today I have solid evidence that the fairies are real. The Sleeping Beauty is definitely real and snoring in my chambers. What if they're all true?" She bounced with excitement and gestured to the piles of books.

He'd felt a similar triumph—although he hadn't bounced—when he found the vademecum sword. The vindication of the supposed fool. "No doubt some of them are."

"The only reason Gowsma didn't show up for seventy-some years is because no one believed in her enough to invite her. I keep wondering if maybe Brierly found her way here because I've always, well, admired her. What if the only reason we can't see the truth of the old tales is because we don't believe in them?"

It sounded like a circular argument to Arpien. "You're saying I can make something true by believing in it?"

"Not exactly. But belief must be some intrinsic element of it." Nissa frowned. "Don't you think there's truth in the old tales? I mean, you rescued Brierly because of an old tale."

"Brierly is part of my family history."

"You tracked down that sword because of an old tale. That's a vademecum sword, so it belongs to the Prince of Here and There. You couldn't have found it unless you were also looking for the Prince. So you must believe in the Prince, or the sword wouldn't cooperate."

Arpien reserved his opinion on the cooperativeness of his sword. "It depends on what type of Prince you mean. A historic ruler of great power and wisdom? There's too much evidence to refute the Prince of Here and There existed. But an all-powerful Prince who knows everything and can solve all the world's problems? The Prince may turn out to be like my sword—half what the legends say and half what we made up on top of that. Oh, I'm a great admirer of the Prince, Nissa. Perhaps we're better off learning from his example and becoming strong enough to solve our own problems."

She grunted. "Clearly we need more research." She blinked at him as though she'd just noticed he was there. "But I don't suppose you came by to talk about my research."

"In a way." It humbled him to confess that he needed advice in this—sensitive area. But Nissa didn't laugh at him as he explained his need.

"Why ask me?" she said.

Arpien nodded to the shelves of books on the side walls. "You're an expert on the old romances, aren't you?"

"I've read a lot about romance, yes. But"—she blushed—"you do understand I'm an expert in theory only?"

"You're Brierly's friend. Besides, you're female. That has to count for some level of expertise."

"I think you'd be most successful if you got to know her yourself."

"She doesn't talk to me. She talks to you."

"It's not her talking that gives the most clues. Watch her. She says a lot with her body."

Arpien cleared his throat. "I've—hem—already noticed her body."

"I mean watch her expressions. I don't think she's as vapid as she pretends. She's locked deep within herself."

"Still in her tower. I know. How do I get her out of her tower?"

"I think she has to come down herself."

"What do I do in the meantime? Stand below and cry 'Rapunzel, Rapunzel, let down your hair?' Nissa, I need your help to help her. It's clear that women don't want their wooers to get to know them. They want to befuddle and irk us. Or if it's not their intention to be vague and elusive, it comes to them so naturally there's no difference."

"I resent the idea that the female mind is so inexplicable that no man can figure it out. You're talking to me, aren't you?"

"Yes, but you're not a woman."

Nissa's eyes threw spears.

"I mean, I don't think of you as a woman."

Arpien felt like he was in the river again, sinking deeper the more he paddled.

"That is to say, you make sense. You're feminine, of course. It's just your head that isn't."

Nissa thunked her head back against her chair. "Aye, you do need advice on women."

A meek "thank you" seemed the safest tactic.

She shoved the candle at him and pored over the titles on a nearby shelf. "Well, if you're looking for my advice as an expert on literary romances, let's consult the sources, shall we?" She flipped open a book. "Unless you think they are too unreliable?"

"Nissa, I didn't say the old tales are false. Just that you can't believe indiscriminately."

This seemed to appease her. "Well then. One way a suitor proves his love is by accomplishing an impossible task. How competent are you at riding up glass hills? Have you slain any fiercesome beasts lately and brought back their heads? Such as a dragon, a chimera, or a manticore?"

"I fought four giant mantizes on the way here."

"That's promising."

"Actually, Brierly wound up saving me from the mantizes. And given that she talks to animals, she might not appreciate me slaying one."

"Hmm. Well, how about obtaining a great treasure? For example, a ring that grants wishes?"

"If I had such a ring, I wouldn't have the original problem. Anyway, I have no great treasures. I'm a third son."

"You could earn one."

"Tried that. My great treasure was supposed to be half a kingdom."

"Let's look for a bargain treasure, then. The price of the treasure is not so much an issue as the difficulty in obtaining it. For example, it could be an ordinary apple, if you brought it back from all the way across the sea."

He'd brought back the vademecum sword from across the sea, but he wasn't giving that up.

"Or it could be a treasure from the palace grounds, if it took a lot of effort to find. For example, you could find a posby blossom with seven petals. Those are very rare—most have five."

"What would she do with a blossom with seven petals?"

"You're missing the point. The gift is not the flower, it's the search. You're lucky—the posby bushes are just coming into bloom."

It was a starting place. Now to plan the attack on the other front: convince Brierly this world was the real one.

15

Brierly

Brierly didn't know what to make of Arpien, recurring prince. She'd sent him away with such a slump in his back that she nearly called him back, figment or not. She even felt—what was the word? *Guilty.* Strange. One of the privileges of living in a universe without rules or meaning was a spotless conscience.

It was necessary to scare him off. She'd done it so effectively that Arpien skipped their morning ride, and she and Nissa had to go alone. Had he gone back to Conquisan? Brierly wasn't used to thinking about people who fell off the page. Characters waltzed in and out of her dreams with no guarantee of timely return, and no promise that they would remember to pick up the story where it had left off.

Nissa turned back early. Research to do in the library, she said. If Nissa had been the scheming type, Brierly might have blamed her for Arpien's sudden reappearance, just as Nissa and Windried left.

That Brierly had failed to vanquish him, did that bring her regret or pleasure? It shouldn't bring her anything, so she decided not to react at all as he and Fearless galloped closer. Fearless fell into stride beside Neef, who said something cheeky about Arpien and got into an argument with Fearless.

Arpien wasn't packed to go riding off to Conquisan. He looked—eager—vigor renewed as though he'd recently discovered a yawn was a compliment. "I want you to know that I'm real and I'm not going anywhere."

Her figment was determined to prove his own existence. "All right."

"I should have seen the problem before. You think you're still asleep."

"No, the problem is you think you're awake."

He frowned. "We can't both be right. I'm going to prove you're awake, Brierly Steward. You'll find me indefatigable."

Indefatigable? She bit the inside of her lip to keep from smiling. Curious that after she'd worked so hard to purge herself of caring too much about anything, her mind would create a character of such passionate determination.

"Why is this so important to you?" she said.

He seemed to consider several answers before saying, "Because you need saving."

"Why should you be the one to save me?"

"Why did you pull me from the river?"

Which time did he mean? When he was six or when he was captured by merfolk? Could she even explain it to herself? He wanted to believe she was good. What if her goodness was rooted in a desire to feel better about herself, a desire for revenge, or even an escape from monotony?

"A conundrum," she said. "What makes something good?"

"Is this my first test?"

"Test?" Many of the old tales centered around riddles. Whoever gave the best answer won the prize. She shrugged. "If you like."

He gave her one of his grandiose Conquisani bows—hard to accomplish from the back of a horse. "I will not fail you, my lady."

She halted Neef and watched Arpien clip away with all the ambition of a child playing hero.

"It is good to see a smile on a young person's face."

She turned to find an old man resting on a bench by a nearby statue. A copper-colored mare grazed nearby.

"I'm not smiling," she said.

"No? Why should you not smile, when you have returned home after so many years, and when you will inherit a dowry of great value?" He was not old, not truly. Careworn. He rose and bowed. Not a Conquisani bow. A small, dignified nod of the head.

She returned it.

"Princess Brierly, I know we've not been introduced, but I have great need to speak to you. I am—"

"Lord Culmney of Strand. I saw you in the Reception Room, when Gowsma visited."

Visited was an understatement, read his expression.

"I don't care much for introductions anymore," Brierly said. "Let's just talk. Hard to be formal on a horse." Although somehow Arpien managed it.

"You are wondering why I sought you here. It might not be politic for word to get back to King Emol."

Brierly slid off Neef. "All right."

The bench had been positioned so passersby could sit and admire the large stone statue. As she walked around, she recognized it as a euphemistic rendition of Nissa's Uncle Emol. Spinning wheels, how many likenesses had the man commissioned of himself? She patted the curly stone beard. "If you're not worried about him listening in."

Lord Culmney smiled. There could be no greater contrast between the stone face of the king and the lord's softened, humble one. Brierly had the feeling that if she brushed Lord Culmney's wrinkled skin it would feel like floury pastry dough, rolled thin and left in the air long enough it was just starting to crack.

She took a seat on the edge of the statue's base. Lord Culmney paced before her. "If you know my name, you perhaps know why I am here in Rosaria?"

"Access to Sentre Forest."

"Aye. Negotiations are moving too slowly for Strand. And now that you may inherit Sentre Forest, we must begin negotiations all over again. Don't misunderstand me. I am delighted you have returned to reclaim what is yours. In fact, I have hopes that you will be more agreeable to a prompt trade agreement than King Emol."

"All right."

His smile of relief was almost painful, then quickly hidden. No wonder he could not push negotiations through with King Emol, when his need was so naked on his face. "King Emol does not see that if he helps us now, our people will heal and return his investment in us sevenfold. But of course you understand that. You are a Steward. My grandfather told me it was a great pity when the Stewards passed away, for they were wise and compassionate rulers indeed."

For the second time that day, Brierly felt that mealy eggplant uneasiness in her stomach, that long-forgotten sensation of guilt. "I'm not certain I can help you."

"But you can." Lord Culmney sat now and leaned forward. "Let parties from Strand into Sentre Forest to harvest the egg sacs. Grant us the chance to save ourselves."

"What of the mantizes?"

"We will face them. There is no risk to you or your subjects."

"The mantizes are my subjects. You are killing their young."

His brow wrinkled all the more. "You cannot value human life more lightly than the spawn of those monsters."

Why was she was arguing the point? Neither the humans nor the mantizes were real. "Still, if you take all the egg sacs, no mantizes will mature, and soon there will be no egg sacs at all."

"You will forgive me for not crying over the extinction of a few man-eating bugs when my nation itself is facing extinction." He took in and released a great breath. "Pardon me, Princess Brierly. I forget that you have been asleep. Perhaps you are not aware of the devastation the tree-plague has had on my country. Nearly every family in Strand has lost someone to the disease. Some families seem particularly vulnerable and their names disappear from the Earth. Our own royal line is such a family. The king, and queen, even the crown prince contracted the disease. The youngest son alone escaped contamination, and has been fostered away in Dlindi. The other three fight to survive until the youngest is old enough to rule."

He rubbed his hands together. They faltered as though he had lost his soap.

Lord Culmney noticed her staring at his hands. "My own daughter succumbed to the disease two years ago. The disease thrives only in Strand, so you have never seen what it does to its victims. First the skin starts to harden and crack. The itch is maddening, but if the victim scratches, great calluses of her skin fall off, and she bleeds. The only relief is to bind the skin in a poultice made of the fibers of an egg sac from a giant mantiz. But the worst of the disease is how it robs the person of her soul even before the body is completely transformed. The victim falls into a trance in the middle of her daily routine. At first the spells last a few seconds, then as the disease progresses the trances can last minutes, even hours. She rots slowly, inside and out, and becomes hollow like an old tree."

"I am sorry," she said. As when Arpien told the story of his dead sister, she fought pity. Against wisdom, she imposed her own father's face on Lord Culmney. Both had lost daughters to an endless sleep. Of course she would help Lord Culmney. If he could not save his daughter, at least she could help him assuage his memory of her.

Unless he was a figment sent by Voracity to raise her sympathies, so that Voracity could destroy him.

"Strand supports your claim, of course," Lord Culmney went on, "and hopes that you will be amenable to a permanent union between our two countries."

"I see."

Lord Culmney shifted his weight. "You don't quite understand me. I—I have the highest regard for this young Prince Arpien's service to you. But when you have won your independence, I hope you will consider a"—he emphasized the words—"*permanent union* with Strand."

Ah. He wanted her to marry the ailing Strandish prince and thus secure for Strand access to Sentre Forest.

What a terrible look of hope was in Lord Culmney's face. Hope is a spark of light, a tender bud, the poets said. The poets had never considered that sometimes the death of hope is less painful than its continuation. Or that some hopes offered nothing but unending irritation, like a pinching beetle someone put down the back of your chemise.

She stood. "Your offer is most kind. But I have decided not to marry at all."

Lord Culmney rose as well. "I hope, regardless, that you will call on any service Strand may render you as you establish your new kingdom."

They were proud words, words meant to protect the fraying dignity of a nation whose people were failing. Perhaps he meant to use her, but Brierly could not help responding with a tone of respect in her voice. "Thank you."

She mounted Neef and galloped away from the old man's need before she was any more tempted to do something about it.

The conversation with Lord Culmney stuck with Brierly through the customary mid-morning toast and gooseberry jam she shared with Nissa. Nissa babbled on about Gowsma's visit and Brierly's new status. Nissa seemed to regard Brierly as an expert on the old tales, and hammered her with questions about this legend and that magical kingdom. Were the dwarves a different race or did the term just mean short humans? Did they always live communally by gender? If so, was seven a typical size for a group?

Brierly shrugged. "Why should I know?"

"But you're part of an old tale yourself. If your story is true, don't you think the others might be?"

"If you think so, I'm certain they are."

That dammed up Nissa's flow of words. Nissa's puppy-brown eyes studied her for a moment, then dropped as she toyed with her toast.

"What?" Brierly said.

Nissa shook her head and reached for the jam.

Brierly's hand got there first and pawed it out of the way. "What?"

"I didn't think you'd be patronizing."

Patronizing?

Nissa didn't sound accusatory, but apologetic. "What I mean is, we spent a lot of time yesterday arguing about who you are. No one thought to ask who you wanted to be."

"Are you asking if I'm Brierly Steward?"

"No. In fact I seem more convinced of it than you are. Or at least more excited about it. Don't you want to be the Sleeping Beauty and get your prince and kingdom? Am I being naïve again?" Nissa looked ready to duck, as though she were speaking to her Aunt Perturbance.

Patronizing?

"I do want Sentre Forest," Brierly admitted softly.

Nissa raised her eyes. "But then, that's perfect. Uncle Emol won't give in as easily as he pretended to yesterday, but I know you'll get it in the end. You deserve it. Timothy will see that it's your right to have it, and Arpien won't give it up no matter how much Uncle wheedles." Nissa tilted her glance at her. "Or is that the problem? You want the kingdom but not Arpien?"

Oh, careful. Was it a test from Voracity? Nissa had already gotten her to admit she wanted Sentre Forest. Voracity already knew this. It was why one of her recurring nightmares was the forest burning. Since the incident with the mermaids, Brierly had been very careful to prove her indifference to the recurring prince.

"Princes tend to be more trouble than they're worth." Brierly blocked her yawn with her toast instead of her hand. "Arpien's just like the rest of them."

"I don't think so," Nissa said. "He's more determined than anyone I've ever met. Half the time I believe he's the epic hero he's trying so hard to be. The other half he's a kind, sort of confused young man. Yes, he's a little stiff, but he wants so much to do good."

"You want to marry him?"

Nissa blushed rose. "That's not what I meant."

"Don't put your faith in princes, Nissa." Brierly rose and stretched. "I'm bored. Shall we visit Squeezie and Albertus?"

Nissa reminded her that the lapdogs were guarded in the lair of that protective dragon, her aunt. It didn't bother Brierly to annoy the queen, but it bothered Nissa, so for her sake Brierly put off the visit for another day. Nissa invited her to the library in the tower but Brierly declined. She'd grown to dislike books since falling asleep. Everyone knew you couldn't read in a dream. She stayed behind in Nissa's chambers with her army of gown projects. Another quarter hour of solid work would see the blue one done. She poked a listless needle at the fabric.

It was why she tended to do her artwork in a rush, riding the tide of inspiration. If she took too long, she lost the vision that had so enthralled her when she started the project. What started as a masterpiece never quite lived up to her expectations. She tied off the last thread in the blue bodice. Unsatisfactory. She tore out the sleeve and tossed it in a wad on the floor.

I'm bored.

Booooooooored.

She hadn't meant it when she used it to turn the subject with Nissa, but now she did. Not only bored, but cross. If she had to have a recurring dream, why couldn't she be stuck in the dream where she became a gryphon, fierce and intelligent and noble? Or the dream where the whole landscape was made out of chocolate?

Did it matter which dream she was stuck in? One would become just as tedious as the others.

It was Voracity's fault she was trapped here in this cycle of meaninglessness. Let the evil fairy come and face her. Put her in a dream with sword and steel and a decent body and she would show her enemy what it meant to fear. Brierly bit dents in her tongue to keep from issuing the invitation. It was tempting, and not just for vengeance.

In some dreams Voracity appeared in full form, and that was both terrifying and beautiful to behold. It tore at the borders of human comprehension, thrilling and overwhelming and generally scaring the pie filling out of her. Brierly had told Nissa that Beauty wasn't useful, but Voracity in full form was not just Beauty, but Art. The sort of art that appealed because it repulsed, that reached down and jerked your soul to a kind of writhing, wild life.

Would a few moments of devastating wonder be worth the inevitable punishment? Would it be worth the aching loneliness when Voracity had inflicted enough pain and left Brierly to better appreciate that her struggle had gotten her nowhere, that she was still imprisoned in an infinite land of nothingness? For that was the most devastating part of encountering Voracity. That just for a moment, she fulfilled a need in Brierly—for companionship, beauty, purpose, or something Brierly did not want to confess.

A knock on the door disrupted her struggle. She willed it open, remembered where she was, and walked over to answer it.

The indefatigable Arpien.

Relief hit her like a cold wave, followed by wariness. "Here to rescue me again?"

"Um, well, I was thinking we could maybe talk." Like the first time she met him, Arpien suddenly remembered his lines and started over. "I request your permission to present you with new evidence regarding your alleged somnolence."

She didn't want to hear more lies, but she didn't want to leave her mind free to focus on Voracity again. "All right."

He had brought with him a satchel and proceeded to set out a number of papers and props on the breakfast table, like a showman hawking a miracle cure at a local fair: a book, several loose sheets of paper done over in a neat, deliberate hand, and three eggs.

"Why the eggs?"

He reordered the sheets of paper. "We won't get to that until page three."

"You scripted this?"

"Yes, but I won't read my notes verbatim. I don't want to bore you."

Faint amusement turned to faint chagrin. She swatted the feeling away. Her figments had no right to make her feel guilty.

Arpien made a better prince than a merchant, that was true. But the logic behind the presentation was not shabby. People who lived entirely in the now had little use for logic, but that didn't mean Brierly couldn't appreciate the aesthetics of such thinking. It was like listening to well-crafted but outdated music. Classic.

His main argument hinged on the consistency of this world. "Think back to the rules of the world before you fell under Voracity's Curse. They're the same as now, right? Furthermore, this world follows a logical linear progression. Gowsma said the dream world does not have consequences. Well, the waking world does."

He held the eggs over the empty ash bucket and dropped them. They landed with a wet smash. "See? If this were a dream, you could imagine the eggs whole again. But this is the waking world, and here we have chronological consequences and permanence."

Brierly peered into the bucket. Yolk and shell splattered against the sides. There was something both funny and tragic about the eggs' demise. She hummed a dirge for them under her breath. *All the king's horses and all the king's men…*

"That's beautiful. What is it?" he said.

"Nothing. Proceed."

She sat through the rest of the presentation in silence. Did it amuse her, touch her, or annoy her? What made him so cocky as to think his world, this "waking world," as he called it, was the only one that counted?

While certain aspects of his world appealed to her, other bits didn't. If she accepted she was free from the Curse, she'd also have to accept that her parents were long dead. She could accept that a handsome prince had come to rescue her, but then she'd also have to give up her ability to fly, to lift mountains, to call worlds into existence with the power of her imagination and will. Was she willing to make that exchange? Did it even matter?

For the finale of his presentation he invited her to read a passage from a book, because everyone knew you couldn't read in a dream. He presented the open book to her on one knee, like a chamberlain offering a glass slipper.

Brierly leaned back in her chair. "I can't read."

"Ah, but you can. Try it."

"No, I can't."

"You mean you never learned?"

It would have been easiest to let him think her ignorant. Illiteracy was not uncommon among women, even noblewomen. "I learned, yes. But I can't read here."

"Because it's a dream."

"That's right."

"So if you can read, that proves you're awake."

What an obstinate figment. She huffed and looked down at the page. Ps and Gs danced on the page. A few whole words jumped out at her, but then skittered away under her focus like roaches withdrawing into the cracks of the floor.

"What do you see?" Arpien asked.

I see disjointedness. Language unbound by rules or meaning.

Gentle caution now replaced his eagerness. "What do you see, Brierly?"

It echoed the way he'd looked at her when she'd forced her atrophied muscles to carry her down from the tower at Estepel. Brown eyes full of admiration, concern, and encouragement. Warmth chased through her, followed by cold.

Don't believe in me, because I certainly don't believe in you.

She snapped the book shut and handed it back to him. "Thank you for the entertainment and instruction. Shall I see you tonight at dinner?"

He packed in his display and bowed an elaborate adieu. He looked disappointed, but not dejected.

She didn't know why it mattered to her if he was dejected or not, when according to his own rules he'd just proven to her that she was dreaming after all.

16

Arpien

Arpien leaned against the carved wooden door to his chambers and let out a sigh of accomplishment. "See you for dinner," sounded like a profession of undying love next to yesterday's post-fairy rejection.

He'd been up half the night preparing the discourse. He'd stayed away from poetry as too extreme a weapon to use at this point. Instead, he'd chosen a journal entry of an ancient general, praising the steadfastness of true comrades. *(Constancy!)* For most of his presentation she'd looked sleepy, but she'd listened to everything he said with only one oracular interruption. Only a few times did he see a "glint" as Nissa called it, and the only readable one came when she read the book he'd handed her. But why should it disturb her?

He flipped open the book to reread the passage. Maybe she'd read the opposite page about the torture of barbarians. Hmm, not the most propitious selection given the typical Conquisani view of Rosarians. The words of a great military mind had seemed appropriate last night, when visions of catapults bringing down towers exploded in his mind's eye.

He decided to add the seven-petaled posby blossom Nissa had mentioned to his romantic ammunition. Nissa had scribbled a sketch of one on the corner of a sheet of paper. That combined with the general location, "by the northern gate," was enough to identify the blue flowering bushes. Around the posbies lingered the sharp salty-sweet scent of anise seed and sea mist from an unexplored shore.

Arpien dismounted and surveyed the battlefield. He would attack the bush closest to the gate first and search in a counter-clockwise motion high to low around each bush. He'd even brought scraps of red cloth to tie around each bush as he finished. This would be a thorough and efficient search.

Five fruitless hours later he whistled for Fearless and the horse didn't come.

Thorns and thistles.

If something had attacked his horse, Fearless would have alerted him. Was there a mare loose? He might have asked his tailing guards, who by frequency of appearance were starting to feel like associates. He'd attempted a conversation with his Tail once, and been informed he was to disregard them completely. One guard had even exchanged a sheepish shrug with him while pretending to be invisible. Out here, he'd never get close enough to ask them any questions.

About half a mile from Boxleyn Palace, Fearless trotted up to him with the overly blithe air of a student hoping his tutor won't notice he neglected his studies. If Brierly were here she could interrogate his horse for him. But if Fearless really had gone frisking after a mare, Arpien didn't want to hear the details from Brierly.

Prince Eusar was waiting for him in his quarters with a message from the king. King Emol invited his honored guests to eat with the rest of the palace in the main dining hall. Up to this point, Arpien had taken his meals in his own rooms or Nissa's. On his arrival, General Gapric had given him to understand that the presence of a Conquisani prince of undetermined motives at table would unsettle the queen's stomach. Indeed, all the local dignitaries were "occupied elsewhere" no matter where in Boxleyn Arpien went. Or maybe everyone just hated the Conquisani. Nissa appeared to be the only noble brave enough or harmless enough to ignore the political winds.

Now at last, some courtesy. Until today Arpien had not met Eusar, the king's second son, but he recognized him. His had been the measuring eyes in the corners of the courtyard when Arpien had worked out his pent-up frustrations with the armsmaster. Eusar looked much like the rest of the Montaine bloodline—short, stocky, and dark-haired like his father and Nissa. His skin was a shade darker than Arpien's, though Arpien knew his own swarthiness was more the effect of his travels to sunny climes than a result of natural coloration. The Montaines, the armsmaster had told Arpien, much preferred the indoors. Before their rise to the monarchy, the Montaine lands were in the cold reaches of the rocky foothills. The only sport that could drive them outdoors from September to April was hunting, because, as the armsmaster remarked, the Montaines had a great respect for digestion. It was really only practical for the Montaines to prefer sports one could do indoors. Their dense build made them powerful wrestlers, and Eusar, for all his reserved manners and round face, looked as sturdy as the base of a pillar.

Prince Eusar offered Arpien full rein of his wardrobe to find clothes that would make a suitable impression. Arpien stood several inches taller than Eusar, but a velvet cape did much to cover his patched-up clothes. In lieu of a crown (Cryndien never would have neglected to pack a crown when he visited other nations) Eusar suggested a cap that was the newest symbol of trend and status in Rosaria. It was bright scarlet and accentuated with a dramatic saffron feather that swept from just behind his ear and extended back a full fourteen inches. An uncertain version of Cryndien looked back at Arpien from Eusar's mirror. Arpien returned to his own room and rehearsed the political strutting tonight would demand.

He wasn't satisfied with his performance before it was time to escort his ladies to the dining hall. Brierly wore the peacock gown again. Either boredom or an awareness of the importance of the evening had inspired her to arrange her hair in a fascinating display of loops. It took the whispers of courtiers that night to make him realize it mimicked the spread of a peacock's tail, only upside-down. Arpien only noticed that she looked strange and ravishing—two words that often fit her. He observed as much aloud. A glint in her eye sent his tongue stumbling to find better words. Nissa cut these off short with a crisp, "We're going to be late."

Now he'd offended them both, for he hadn't looked at Nissa at all, and her hair looked unusually—uh—festive—as well. He apologized by taking her elbow with the same gravity he had Brierly's and asking how her research was going. She launched into some references she'd found to the giant mantizes. It was not a topic he cared to revisit, but he wasn't going to offend Nissa further by saying so. Nissa found the poxed creatures just as fascinating as Brierly did.

The three of them barely fit abreast through the corridors. It would have been better for them if they hadn't, for then one of them might have been spared the soaking administered by King Emol's youngest son. Arpien pushed his ladies back under the cover of the atrium balcony in case a second bucket should follow. Nissa's unladylike shout of, "Cuz!" only acerbated the snorts of self-satisfied laughter from overhead.

Arpien wrung out his cap. With the now drooping feather, it would look like a bedraggled chicken had taken to roost on his head.

Nissa squeezed the soaked loops of her hair, and only succeeded in undoing half of them. "There are scarier creatures in the world perhaps, but none so trying as a twelve-year-old boy!"

Cuz's grinning head peeked out to enjoy the spectacle.

Arpien banked his own frustration in hopes he could calm Nissa. Her nose puffed the telltale red that foreshadowed tears. He'd see to Cuz, but it was not the boy who most riled his sense of injustice. If Cuz thought it was acceptable to belittle Nissa, Arpien had no doubt where he'd learned it.

He was glad her anger won out over her tears. He'd have more success combating a dragon than a maiden's tears. All he had to offer was a dry corner of his borrowed cape. It was Brierly who surprised Nissa into a laugh with a lighthearted, "Dining customs have changed in the past hundred years."

By coincidence that could only be planned, Prince Eusar opened the doors to the dining hall. "Ah, there are our intrepid heroes!" The bustle of supper came to a standstill. Eusar slid out of the way to better frame the three dripping figures in the doorway.

Arpien wondered if his face turned as red as his cap. He should have expected no better treatment from Rosarians. Poor Nissa was also crimson, though she with embarrassment. He even saw a flash in Brierly's eyes. He thought it was of anger but it must have been humor, for she dropped a grand curtsey that displayed her drenched finery to full effect.

"Good evening to you all." She rose with a smile that invited the whole company to share a joke with her. "We heard you were serving fish and dressed accordingly."

A few of the ladies tittered. It could have been in mockery or appreciation of Brierly's audacity. Brierly decided the issue for them. "May I introduce—"

Introductions? From Brierly?

"—Prince Arpien Trouvel, playing the part of the Crimson Mollusk. Your own Lady Nissa Montaine, Endearing Lady of Seaweed."

Well, Nissa's falling coiffure did look a little like seaweed.

"And I am Brierly Steward, Maiden of the Fathomless Ocean." She turned to Arpien and Nissa with a wink. "Shall we?"

She sailed forward with all the confidence of a hostess in her own household. Arpien and Nissa glanced at each other and followed her through the room to the head table. If they looked ridiculous, at least everyone believed it was intentional.

Even with a dark streak of water down the panels of her skirts, Brierly was radiant. Up to now, Arpien had assumed Great Grandfather Herren had exaggerated, or the dynamic blaze of Brierly's personality had diminished over the years. Now he realized that she had never used the full force of her Gift of Charm on him. She paused along her route to greet people. *How well you look—is the gout better? Lady Melison, I tried your suggestion for a new sleeve design and you must come by and see the result. I saw an especially fine hawk in the park today and thought I saw it return to your arm. Your rapport with the animal is uncanny. You must give me tips.*

Arpien scratched his head over what hawking advice anyone could give someone with a Gift of Animal Speech. When had she gleaned all this information? And had it come from the humans or the animals?

Even the oddities in Brierly's behavior passed for inventiveness, such as when she plucked a ribbon out of one lady's hair, tied it into a multi-tiered bow, and secured it in the woman's hair again.

The oblivious, indifferent damsel was gone. His arguments this afternoon must have been more convincing than he thought.

As neither Lord Culmney's son-in-law nor Prince Cuz had shown up yet, it left space by the Strandish delegation at the head table. It seemed Brierly already knew Lord Culmney, a man with a tepid bearing but a warm smile. He certainly favored her. Arpien was both pleased and riled by the open admiration on the faces of most of the men in the room. Even Lord Culmney's own son-in-law missed a step when he arrived at the table a few minutes later to find the striking newcomer at his table. Brierly bestowed this Sir Flatwhist with a knowing smile that would have melted Arpien's toes had it been aimed at him. He was less than pleased when Sir Flatwhist wound up seated between him and Brierly.

Nissa elbowed him and Arpien consoled himself with the platter of herbed potatoes. He scolded himself for letting his envy distract him from building political alliances in these first key moments. He forced himself to turn to Sir Flatwhist.

Flatwhist was clean-shaven but for a mere sneeze of a goatee, in the Strandish style. His answers to Arpien's polite questions were as abbreviated as his beard. Although Strand did not hate Conquisan on principle, the way Rosaria did, Conquisan and Strand had opposing interests in Sentre Forest. Conquisan wanted the hittal trees; Strand the mantiz egg sacs that could be found only in those same hittal trees.

Arpien did his best to indicate that he had no wish to be a rival to Strand's interests. But as he didn't want to make false promises either, Sir Flatwhist didn't warm to him at all. Nor did Sir Flatwhist warm to Brierly after that first staggering glance. Arpien gave himself over to the more gratifying pleasure of learning the names of key people in the room from Nissa, who sat at his right.

One name he figured out on his own. Cuz. Arpien had only caught a flash of the head grinning down on them from the balcony. But this had to be Nissa's prankster cousin, twitting this person and that for the benefit of a clump of snorting boys at the end of a table below.

Cuz was a plump boy with the queen's same muddy-auburn hair. He carried his weight with a skulk, yet he dodged several blows with athletic experience. He wasn't quite quick enough to dodge his brother Timothy, though. The crown prince snagged Cuz's wrist as he tried to filch an apple pastry from Timothy's plate. Arpien couldn't hear the words they exchanged, but they glanced his direction twice. Was Timothy scolding or praising Cuz for dousing the guests of honor?

Yes, Arpien would definitely have to deal with the boy.

King Emol signaled the end of the meal by tossing the picked-over bones of his smoked ham chops to the hunting dogs. Squeezie and Albertus, as befit their higher bloodlines, dined from the queen's plate at the same time the queen did. Only their brown ears perked above the table as they listened to the king's post-meal speech. King Emol welcomed Briar Rose Steward (without her title) and Prince Arpien Trouvel of Conquisan, then called for his Fool to entertain the company. It was a shamefully short welcome, though uttered in an unctuous tone.

Even Eusar noticed the lack. "Nay, Father, let's delay the Fool for a moment and enjoy the novelty of such company. I understand in Conquisan it is the custom for returning victors to recount their journeys. Perhaps Prince Arpien will honor us with the tale of his noble rescue?"

Arpien had half-expected the request. In Conquisan, all noblemen learned the art of boasting along with their swordplay and history. It was especially important Arpien prove himself here among antagonistic Rosarians. He sucked in a breath, put on his swagger, and stood.

He began with all the proper forms: the dramatic snap bow, the doffing of his (still wet) cap, the acknowledgement of prominent dignitaries in the room in order of rank. The earlier tutorial with Nissa proved beneficial, and he surprised a number of the nobles in the room by greeting them by name and title. Then tradition demanded a recitation of his lineage for the past ten generations. The final name in one's lineage was never an actual ancestor, but the person in history you most wished to emulate. He thought his selection impressed them. The Rosarians studied him with wide eyes.

Only then could he properly begin his story. "Many and many a year ago, the kings of our two illustrious nations thought to stave off pugnacious sentiments between us through a connubial treaty…"

He spoke of Great Grandfather Herren and the horrible Curse, and painted the tower and briars with the largest words he could find. Certain emotions demanded certain stances and hand gestures for emphasis. He confused the *Ninth Stance of Resolve* with the *Third Stance of Courage*, but the Rosarians seemed too astounded by his story to notice. He described Brierly in the tower and impressed even himself with his description of her paralyzing beauty. If the truth was more mundane and dusty than his story, well, boasting expected such liberties.

Someone giggled.

It wouldn't have distracted his brother, but it tripped Arpien. He forgot that he was going to call the beauty's hair *citrine* and fumbled for a substitute. The giggle came again. Now he couldn't even remember the word *yellow*. He glanced at Brierly's head for inspiration. She cast him a hard look, a warning clear in her blue-green eyes.

"Oh pray, Your Highness, continue," Prince Eusar said. "It's not often we hear such creative fairy tales in Rosaria."

Arpien stared at the crowd, flustered beyond recovery. For once, Arpien had been getting it right. His performance would have been lauded in Conquisan. Here in Rosaria it only earned ridicule.

Eusar had duped him.

Say something.

"So … so I kissed her and she woke up." Arpien bowed the *Double-Bow of Immense Artistic Appreciation Toward Blacksmiths, Bakers, and other*

Craftsmen. It had nothing to do with the social situation, but it allowed him to bend over far enough to hide his flushed face. He slammed into his seat.

"What an unsatisfactory ending to an awe-inspiring tale of heroism!" Eusar turned to Brierly. "Mayhaps you, beauteous one, can pick the story up from here."

"No indeed. It is much more gratifying to hear a handsome young man praise one's looks than to do it oneself, as the ladies present will agree." It was an odd response from Brierly, who proved generally immune to compliments.

A few more giggles. Were people laughing at him or with her?

"If neither of you will tell us the facts, we'll just have to make up our own." Eusar flicked a commanding finger to a man dressed in exaggerated wide trunk hose and primary colors. "Fool!"

The King's Fool took his cue to improvise a parody of Arpien's tale. No, such excruciating bumbles and affectations were prearranged. The Fool warbled and bowed in clear imitation of Arpien. He posed with his lute for effect and the crowd called out encouragement. Arpien forced himself to face the crowd with squared jaw.

Out of the corner of his eye Arpien saw Nissa mouth something to her eldest cousin. Prince Timothy silenced the Fool with a good-natured, "Stick to a song you know, Fool, so we might not suffer through the composition process."

"Very well. Since fairy tales are the order of the evening, I'll sing an old one."

Arpien recognized this new melody with trepidation. Had the whole evening been designed for Arpien's humiliation? Eusar beamed at Arpien with closed lips.

On the surface it was the classic tale of two brothers. Only one could inherit the kingdom, so their father tested their ingenuity with three challenges. On a deeper level, it was a thinly veiled political song about Sentre Forest. In the song the eldest brother, who was supposed to represent the dullard Rosarian, gave the obvious answers. The youngest brother, who stood for the quick-witted Conquisani, trumped his every answer. Only in the Rosarian version, the roles were switched.

In the first verse, the king asked his sons to fill a room with treasure. The eldest hauled in chests of gold and filled the room three feet deep in coins and jewelry. The youngest lit a candle and filled the room with light to the rafters.

Arpien listened with iron-rod spine. Even the *hey hey diddle dow days* seemed infused with insult. Through the ringing in his ears he grew aware of a second voice. It harmonized with the Fool. The dulcet voice deftly commandeered the tune, until the Fool's only recourse was to stop playing and face the singer.

"The princess is of course a better singer than I, and wishes to drown my noise with her own."

Brierly blinked innocent eyes. "Does it disturb you, to have people sing along? I guess you'll have to quit singing."

Already in high spirits, the audience oooed and applauded.

The Fool jabbed a finger into the air. "The lady challenges me to a test of musicianship and wits. Unfair to challenge a Fool to a game of wits."

"Unfair to me. For if I win, you may say, 'I am only a Fool.' If you win, I am less than a Fool."

There was no way to appease the crowd but for the Fool to agree to the singing duel.

"I will even allow you to take the part of the younger son, since you seem to favor him," Brierly said. "But I must correct you on how the eldest brother answered the King's first question."

In Brierly's version, the youngest brother's candle cast shadows around the room, and therefore failed to fill it completely. The eldest brother filled the room with laughter, also a great treasure, and it rang in every corner. The audience must know they were supposed to cheer the youngest brother, but they could not resist Brierly's expressive voice or clever lyrics. A few even applauded before they faltered under the gaze of King Emol.

In the second verse, the king sent his sons to deal with a dragon who had been menacing the countryside. The trick of the challenge was that the dragon breathed fire on any man who approached. The Fool had the youngest brother distract the dragon with gold and jewels, and deal out the killing blow from behind. This was traditionally the winning solution. It left Brierly with the second-rate solution usually tried by the first brother. Again, she simply invented a better ending.

In her version, the eldest brother noted that no man could approach the dragon without being roasted. So he dressed in women's clothes and the dragon let him near. Even then, the brother did not slay the dragon, but negotiated a treaty with him. Every shepherd in the land would set aside one sheep from his flock for the dragon. This way, no shepherd's flock was devastated, and the dragon was guaranteed a constant supply of food. In exchange, the dragon had to scare off any wolves he found near the pastures.

Coming from Brierly, negotiations with dragons sounded completely plausible. Those who might have objected to her logic had to give her credit for style. When she sang the part of the brother, she truly sounded like a man disguised as a woman. Her dragon voice was a slithery, epicurean tenor.

The Fool picked up the tune for the final task:

> *The king was very much impressed*
> *But he'd saved yet one more test.*
> *"Who answers this question, the kingdom is his.*
> *Tell me how long infinity is."*

> *The youngest said, "I once did climb*
> *A mountain much like your question of time*
> *Two miles high, and two miles through*
> *And made of diamond solid through.*

> *And when I reached the mountain's peak*
> *I saw a bird, who sharpened his beak*
> *Once on the mountain, and then flew away*
> *So when I climbed down the mountain next day*

> *I told all the people of that little bird.*
> *An old man said, 'Have you never heard*
> *How rare that bird is? How lucky is he*
> *Who sees the bird who comes once a century!'*

> *I tell you, King, all this to say*
> *When all that mountain is worn away*
> *By that little bird's beak, as time marches on,*
> *Only one second of infinity's gone."*

Again, the Fool had stolen the best answer. Undaunted, Brierly made
up another solution:

> *Said the eldest brother, "That's good, I'll own.*
> *But infinity's not measured in seconds alone.*
> *The good never lasts, the bad lasts too long."*
> *(Infinity may be the length of this song.)*
>
> *"I'll lay my case before the court.*
> *A moment is timeless, a lifetime too short.*
> *Infinity's also a dream or a fear,*
> *For instance a speech you don't want to hear.*
>
> *Marriage with a peevish spouse:*
> *That, sir, is infinity.*
> *Winter in a poor man's house:*
> *That, sir, is infinity.*
> *A single day of childhood bliss:*
> *That, sir, is infinity.*
> *The fragile instant of love's first kiss:*
> *That, sir, is infinity.*
>
> *Trying to wake from a nightmare:*
> *That, sir, is infinity.*
> *Waiting for your son to return from war:*
> *That, sir, is infinity.*
> *Wooing a maid who won't be pressed:*
> *That, sir, is infinity.*
> *Nine months from the wooing's success:*
> *Ladies, tell me, infinity?*

Some women in her audience eyed Queen Perturbance and bit their
lips, but many others laughed and nodded their concurrence. A few men
groaned their own interpretation of this particular infinity. They were
playfully nudged (and in one case, slapped) by their wives.

So we leave it with you good folk to tell
Of both these brothers who answered so well
Which one filled the room with treasure?
Which one found infinity's measure?
Which one conquered the fiercesome beast?
Who saw him murdered and who saw him fleeced?
Now that you have heard our duel
Who is the wisest? Who only the fool?

The Fool interrupted their outburst of approval with an outburst of
his own—a complicated lute solo to reclaim their attention. For all he
played the Fool, he was a master of his craft. His fingers skimmed across
the strings like a water bug darting across a pond's smooth surface. He
raised his brows at Brierly in triumph.

Brierly's eyes sparkled and she nodded in appreciation. "Well chosen,
Fool. For I brought no instrument but my own voice."

The Fool rose to accept the praise of his audience. As their applause
abated, a single strange voice came to the forefront. They were not words,
they were nonsense syllables, dits and dahs, in a rapid bouncing chain.
Brierly was imitating the instrument. Her notes exactly replicated the
Fool's, only faster.

All stared at her in silence when she finished. In one motion, the
courtiers swiveled their heads to the Fool. The Fool dropped his raised
brow and bent back over his lute.

He hurled another string of notes at Brierly, this one longer and more
elaborate. He picked great leaps in pitch, sixteenth notes that ran on for
half a minute together. Arpien was positive the man's fingertips would
start bleeding. After a three-minute cadenza he flourished to an ending
toward the high end of his range. As the pitch rose, his notes got softer
and unbelievably, faster. The audience leaned in. Somewhere in the heavens the flurry of notes vanished into a cloud.

A lady in the audience gasped.

"Hm," Brierly said. She swallowed a dainty sip of water and sucked
in a breath.

Brierly followed the Fool's example note for note. Notes zinged
through the air so quickly her voice seemed to catch up with itself and

form chords. As in the music dream, one melody washed into another. She closed her eyes, lost in the sound.

Here she departed from the Fool's example. She improvised variations even more complex. Faster and faster, until the notes came as a blur of sound, no more distinct than the flapping of a hummingbird's wings. An overriding melody floated on top of the runs. Arpien knew it was very hard to sing in tune so high without getting louder. Brierly did so while getting softer. She rose on her toes as if she might leave the ground, pulled skyward by a thousand iridescent wings.

In that moment a phoenix-bright feather flashed in Arpien's mind's eye. He had nearly forgotten that dream. Or rather, dismissed most of it as hallucination induced by sentiment and mantiz poison. Yet here she was again, the goddess who created and destroyed worlds with her unearthly music. The woman who saved him, as would he do anything to save her.

The end of her song was so soft it was more the cessation of energy than sound that indicated it. She opened those shocking blue-green eyes on her audience. They stared back. Arpien understood their awe and even fear. No mortal could produce such music.

Brierly shrugged. "Fairy Gift."

They burst into cheers.

Arpien glowed with elation and pride in her skill. There was no way to reach her through the mass of courtiers, so he turned to the Fool. The man, after all, was a master musician in his own right. He'd been acting under Eusar's orders, Arpien suspected, but maybe he could prove his goodwill. "I have never heard your like on the lute," Arpien said.

The Fool squeezed the neck of his lute, as though consoling it or choking it. "Nor will you. Throw away your sword, young prince, and use her tongue instead. An extraordinary warrior, this woman. So extraordinary she fights your battles for you."

Normally Arpien would have prickled at this insult. But Brierly had deposited him on a cupid-encrusted cloud and he still floated above everyone. "What man who has heard her would not let her sing instead of himself? I guess we know—only a Fool."

The Fool bowed and departed.

The Fool was not altogether wrong. Brierly had fought Arpien's case. But she had also fought her own. The eldest brother could represent any contender for the throne. She'd stood for both of them in a political move as artful as her music. What Arpien attempted in a stilted manner, Brierly achieved with effortless charm. What a queen she'd make.

Already his plan to spur her into her blissful destiny was working.

He shared his triumph with Nissa during their morning ride. Brierly got distracted arbitrating a dispute between squirrels. Arpien seized the moment to ride ahead with Nissa. To his surprise, Nissa didn't view his victory as clear-cut as Arpien did.

"Were you listening to her full song?" Nissa said. "Wooing a maid who won't be pressed? The good never lasts? Marriage to a peevish spouse? She was warning you."

"She also sang about the success of the wooing."

"How can you have such a good grasp of political subtext and such a bad grasp of feminine subtext?"

"Look, I followed your advice. I groped through those bothersome posby blossoms for five hours yesterday and I'm going out to look some more."

Nissa sighed skyward and rode back to meet Brierly. Arpien sank several feet off the cloud he'd been on since yesterday. Cupids sprang into the air and waved farewell as their tiny wings proved too weak to support them.

The blossoms threaded the air with the scent of mossy rocks and snuffed beeswax candles. Fearless dragged his feet as they neared the patch. Arpien dug his heels into his sides. Fearless inched closer, then sidled in an arc the opposite direction of where Arpien wanted to go.

"What's wrong with you?" Arpien forced Fearless back around.

As soon as he dismounted, Fearless tore off without him.

Arpien whistled after Fearless, but he didn't come as trained. His horse had never behaved like this in all his journeys, not until reaching Rosaria. Thistles. Now Arpien would have to walk the two miles back to Boxleyn Palace, and Eusar and the rest of Boxleyn would snicker that he couldn't control his horse.

As long as he was out here, he was going to look for the silly seven-petaled flower.

17

Nissa

Nissa didn't ride right back to meet Brierly. About a quarter mile west of northern gate, she caught the scent of freshly mixed ink and rising yeast dough. Her nose led her to the patch of posby bushes in a copse of trees. It wasn't really her job to find a seven-petaled blossom, but Arpien's wooing needed aid. Nissa would respect Brierly's wishes if she chose to reject Arpien, but only if Brierly got to know him first.

And, well, Nissa liked tales that ended in weddings.

In the ornery way of plants, the bushes had chosen to grow half inside and half outside the poles of the iron fence. Of course the most promising blossoms were on the other side. There was no one around to see her, so Nissa tucked her skirts up and climbed the ten-foot fence. She'd just started down the other side when Windried whinnied in alarm. The sound took Nissa's attention away from her footing at the wrong movement. She slipped.

Slipped or was pulled? Something grabbed her ankle. She kicked and twisted to see what had seized her, but there was nothing there. She scrambled for a foothold and lost her grip completely. Unseen beasts hauled her to the ground. On the other side of the fence, Windried bolted. Were those Windried's hooves or her own heartbeat that galloped in her eardrums?

It didn't occur to Nissa to scream. How could she when she had yet to think about breathing? She struggled against the invisible beasts and must have prevailed, because the unseen arms released her.

She scurried back against the fence. Nissa had never fought a soul in her life. Invisible people are trampled, not viewed as antagonists. She picked up a branch–unfortunately only a couple of feet long–and held the weapon like one of the knights in her embroidery.

She must not have formed an imposing picture, because one of the beasts snickered.

She jerked. Wait. That was no monster sound, that was a normal male human laugh.

"Put the branch down. No one means you any harm."

She snapped her head back to the right and found a man where there had been no man before. His build was threatening—not tall, but strongly made. His stance and tone of voice were not. They spoke of steadiness and quietness. Nissa didn't set the branch down—though what she could do against a seasoned soldier she didn't know. He wore weapons but held nothing in his hands but a small gold box with a hole in the lid.

Nissa's eyeballs tried to leap out of her head. "Where did you find an invisibilifier? The last documented use of one was in the Battle of Centaurs."

His brows flinched—in wariness? Amusement? The face seemed familiar but she couldn't read his expression. It was like reading a favorite book but with every other word altered. "What do you know of invisibili-fiers?" he said. "I did not think Rosaria held with the old tales anymore."

It occurred to Nissa that if she had failed in her part as a warrior, she had also failed in her role as a simple damsel fearful for her life. A common maid would have screamed. Failing that, as king's niece she should have tilted her chin regally and demanded his name and agenda. Nissa Montaine inquired about his magical tools.

She blushed and tried again. "If you mean no harm, I'd appreciate it if your companions turned visible as well." She hated the way her voice sounded. As though she were a timid little scullery maid asking for a second slice of cake on feast day.

He looked aside as he came to a decision, then passed the invisibili-fier to an empty piece of air who became a soldier like himself. As the invisibilifier made its way around the troop, the first man spoke again. "I am General Bothart Trouvel of Conquisan, brother to the king. You can appreciate, with the ill will between our countries, that it is wise to travel in disguise."

"Oh." Arpien's brother! No wonder he looked familiar. Familiar but Nissa could see why she'd not made the connection. He was a handful of years older, darker, and with none of Arpien's exuberance.

A diplomat would think of something better to say than "oh."

"I am Lady Nissa Montaine, king's ward and niece."

"Delightful!" said a robust new voice.

The air flickered to reveal the best embroidery fodder yet—a hero on a white horse. The hero had hair the color of gold and fire. "Here Bo was worrying if we could talk our way through the northern gate, when a royal guide arrives to escort us to the palace."

Her weight shifted to her back foot in what was not quite a stumble nor a curtsey. "You must be the—the king of Conquisan?"

He had to be the king. He was a close copy of Arpien, aged to the prime of life and burnished to a high gloss. "King Cryndien Fulgar Corussell Victor Trouvel, Heart of Conquisan, Strong Arm of her Armies, and Fire of her Soul." He gave a flourished Conquisani bow that made Arpien's look adolescent.

"Well then ... welcome," Nissa said. She bobbed the start of a curtsey, but aborted midway in case it looked like she was curtseying twice. Did two half-curtseys add up to a whole?

The Conquisani believed in decorum, and if her behavior grew any more banal she might start an international incident. So far a dozen soldiers had appeared, along with a handful of persons in richer dress who must be lesser nobles or advisors. Why was it necessary to wear such expensive attire if you were invisible? Conquisani.

Nissa was no strategist, but she wasn't an idiot, either. "Those I can see may follow me back to the palace. I'll let Arpien know you are here to see him."

"Arpien?" King Cryndien shot an expressive glance at the inexpressive general. "So the dreamer turns up at last. In Rosaria of all places. Didn't think he had the sense to survive eight months on his own."

Indignation shot through Nissa's veins. "He not only survived, he rescued the lost Princess Brierly Steward."

"Marvelous."

Nissa resisted the urge to scurry away under the king's broad feline smile. "If you're not here to see Arpien, what—uh—brings you this way?"

A party that included old women wasn't going to raid Boxleyn, was it?

"We mean to demand an audience of your king regarding his use of my forest these past one hundred years."

"I see." If someone was going to convince King Cryndien Sentre Forest wasn't his, but Brierly's, it wasn't going to be Nissa Montaine. "You'd better follow me."

If she brought back any more claimants to Sentre Forest, Uncle was going to disown her.

18

Arpien

Arpien rummaged through posby bushes until midday, then started the trek back to Boxleyn Palace. Five minutes into his walk he heard hooves behind him, but they were too light to be Fearless's. It was Windried. Only Windried. Had Nissa fallen? Arpien spoke gently to Nissa's horse and she allowed him up into the saddle.

Now would be a convenient time to have Brierly's Gift of Animal Speech. As it was, Arpien had to rely on the unreliable vademecum sword to lead him to Nissa. Contrary as usual, this time it led him to Brierly.

"Arpien, we were just talking about you." Brierly rode up on Neef. The truant Fearless trotted shamefaced alongside. "You didn't tell me it was Exchange-Your-Horse Day. I doubt Neef will want to participate."

"Nissa's not with you?"

"Should she be?"

"She said she was riding back to meet you."

Thistles. What if Nissa were lying somewhere badly hurt? "Windried, tell Brierly what happened to Nissa."

Brierly raised her brows but repeated the question for the horse. Windried reported through Brierly that strange-smelling humans attacked Nissa on the other side of the fence. They didn't hurt her, though. When Windried had seen it was safe, she was too ashamed to approach Nissa after running away. So she watched from a distance while Nissa led the strangers to Boxleyn Palace.

Arpien wanted to know what the strangers looked like.

"They looked like you," Brierly translated.

Arpien felt his blood go absolutely still. "Cryndien." Was that better or worse for Nissa than being thrown from her horse? "My brother. If you think I look like Herren, you should see the two of us."

"All humans look alike to other species," Brierly said. But Windried could describe the strangers' smell: sweat and lye soap and rotten vegetables.

"Thistles," Arpien said. "That means they brought Consulan Sitral. No wonder they were able to get this close to Boxleyn without anybody noticing."

"Who's Consulan Sitral?"

"One of Cryndien's closest advisors. She's First Consulan, although in truth she's little more than an ambitious hedge witch. Cryndien gave her the title a year ago when she helped him stamp out a rebellion. You don't have to be noble to be appointed consulan."

"You think that's wrong?"

"Not at all. Some of the best consulans in Conquisani history have been of common blood. It's Sitral herself I don't like. She can talk you into doing the most horrific things, and make it sound perfectly justified."

Now Brierly was the one whose blood seemed to stop flowing. The clear skin went pale. "What does she look like?"

"White hair, cropped close to the skull. Old, but she carries herself with a straight back. Odd yellow eyes surrounded by laugh lines. Not that she's sanguine: she smiles even when her eyes say she's annoyed."

Neef jerked a step forward.

Arpien narrowed his eyes at Brierly. "You know Consulan Sitral?"

Her hands. Was that a tremor? He couldn't tell, for Brierly busied her hands with a lock of Neef's mane. One strand, two strands, three. She started to braid. "Not by that name."

Arpien hadn't thought anything could frighten Brierly. What angered him more than anything was the strength of her mask of indifference.

There was no profanity strong enough for what he was feeling, so he spat out her name. "Voracity."

No wonder the briars hadn't vanished after he kissed Brierly awake. Voracity was still alive.

No wonder, either, that Cryndien had discouraged him from rescuing the sleeping princess. Or did Cryndien even know who his ally was?

"Windried is certain they didn't hurt Nissa?" Arpien answered his own question. "No, why would they? Nissa can gain them access to Boxleyn."

Cryndien was probably here about Sentre Forest. Unless Cryndien was prepared to wage battle here and now, it would do no good to irk King Emol by killing off his relatives.

Did Cryndien know Brierly was here, and awake? Did Voracity know? Arpien's stomach clenched. He'd traveled across oceans to save Brierly from Voracity, when Voracity had been in the Conquisani palace all along. Was he so blind?

Yet while he'd never liked Consulan Sitral, there was little to connect her to the evil fairy of the Sleeping Beauty legend besides a knack for dark magic. The tales said vanity had prompted the evil fairy to punish the House of Steward for their failure to invite her to Brierly's christening. But Consulan Sitral, vain? She had wormed her way into Cryndien's good graces by giving all the glory to him. To his face, at least. Arpien had long suspected that Sitral had no true affection for the one she served. He had said as much to Cryndien, not that Cryndien listened. Why could Arpien never save anybody from themselves?

"You think she's heard you're awake?" he said to Brierly. "She's come to Curse you again? Or maybe to guarantee you really die this time?"

"She won't bother to Curse me again."

"Let's not test that prediction."

Brierly had to hide until sunset. If Consulan Sitral was Voracity, she'd only be able to stay a single day. In the meantime Arpien would track down Nissa and investigate what Cryndien was doing here at Boxleyn.

"You really don't trust your brother, do you?" Brierly said.

"Cryndien likes to have his own way. When he finds out Sentre Forest belongs to us—you—he may—overreact. But don't worry. I know how to guard you from Cryndien. What I don't know how to do is guard you from Voracity. Can my sword kill her?"

Arpien fingered the hilt of the sword, where it stuck out of the scabbard. It was cold. Of course it was cold. Metal was cold. But it was the sort of cold that wasn't limited to temperature. It was the same sort of cold he had felt in his father's presence when Arpien tripped on the practice field. Was the vademecum sword listening? Asinine thought. But the uncompliant icicle had proven it had a mind of its own. Was it resolving to block justice, just to spite him?

"I wouldn't try to kill a fairy." Brierly voice was light but her face cool. Not cold like the sword or the specter of his father. Cool. Like the surface of a window pane on a summer night, Looking on it, you saw nothing of the shape or thickness of the glass, nothing of what lay on the other side, only a laughable reflection of yourself.

One hundred years of nightmares, Gowsma said. You should be surprised she's still human.

"She should be punished for what she did to you!"

His vehemence earned him a surprised glance from Brierly.

He took a breath and struggled to match her control. "But meting out justice could prove tricky. This is Emol's jurisdiction, and he'll claim there's no evidence. He doesn't believe the old tales. If he arrests an advisor to the Conquisani king, it could give my brother the excuse he's looking for to invade."

"Invade?'

"Cryndien is very ambitious. Even if he knows Consulan Sitral is the same Voracity who Cursed you, he won't bring her to justice."

"Let me guess. He doesn't believe in the old tales either."

"Oh, he believes them. At least, he thinks there's something behind the power and magic in them. It won't bother him that Voracity tried to kill you. He'll think he can control her."

On impulse, he reached across the gap between Neef and Fearless. Her graceful, deft hand lay in his like a dead fish, but she didn't snatch it away either. "I don't want to trigger a war, Brierly, but I won't let her hurt you again. Promise me you won't go near her."

"Only if you won't."

Arpien's pulse bounced. Was she was worried for him?

"If anyone gets to kill Voracity," she said, "it's me."

Well, maybe she wasn't worried for him, but Arpien admired bravery. "You're very strong, my lady."

She reclaimed her hand to toss her hair over her shoulder. "Hm. You still haven't agreed to stay away from Voracity."

"It may not be possible, if she's part of the Conquisani party. I must speak to my brothers. But as long as you and Nissa are safe, I will not seek her out."

Brierly appeared to be thinking it over, but instead she was listening to the horses. "Fearless says he's sorry for running off and would you please get off that dinky mare and ride him instead?"

Arpien went over to his horse and laid a hand on his side. "Tell Fearless the dinky mare is a lot faster than he is and I'm thinking about trading him for her."

Brierly's face thawed a fraction. "I'll tell him, but he won't believe me."

If Fearless didn't take Arpien's goad seriously, he did catch the urgency of his rider and flew back to the stables. They didn't have to worry about Nissa long. She was there in the stables, convincing a guard to ride out and tell Arpien his brothers were here. Nissa seemed to have no idea she'd brought an evil fairy into Boxleyn, and Arpien didn't want to tell her in public. Where would his friends be safest? Inside the palace with Voracity, or outside and unprotected? He glanced around, and his eyes fell on the guard Nissa had been talking to when he and Brierly rode up.

"I know him."

"This is Kendra's brother Gerret," Nissa said. "A good-natured soul, for letting me talk him into riding out to find you on his day off."

The guard shrugged with a sheepish smile, and Arpien placed him. He was part of his Tail—the guard who'd shrugged at him while trying to be invisible. Nissa trusted too many people, but Kendra without doubt was loyal to Nissa. Could they count Kendra's brother as an ally? Arpien glanced at Brierly and she arched a slender brow back at him.

"I think he should spend the afternoon with you," Arpien said.

Nissa blinked at him. "Huh?"

Here Brierly intervened with her expert finesse. She wanted Nissa to take her to visit the market that surrounded Boxleyn Palace, and they'd need someone to carry their things. Someone strong enough to carry multiple purchases, as one of Brierly's fairy Gifts was Shopping. (Arpien hoped this was a joke.) Gerret acquiesced with another genial shrug and the promise of a coin or two for his trouble. A man would go through great trials—even shopping—for the favor of such a woman.

His ladies as safe as they could reasonably be, Arpien went in search of his brothers.

Most of the Conquisani party was already sequestered with King Emol. Of course Cryndien had finagled an audience with the Rosarian king the moment he arrived, while it had taken Arpien over a week to manage that much. Arpien paced in a small council room while a page sent word to his brother. In a quarter hour his brother joined him. Just not the brother he expected.

"Bo."

Windried hadn't mentioned Bo, but of course Bo would be here if Cryndien was.

Arpien's stern brother unbent enough at the sight of him to grasp his upper arm and—almost—smile. "So it's true. You are here."

"You didn't come to see me, then," Arpien said.

"How could we? We haven't heard from you in eight months. It was Consulan Sitral's idea to come. 'Shanks, you didn't think to send word to your own brothers that you were alive? To your own king?"

They'd thought him a fool for undertaking this quest, and he didn't think they'd care what happened to him anyway. Their nickname for him testified that. It was also the name of an overeager, bumbling hunting dog.

Had Arpien misread them all these years?

"I would have drawn too much attention if I paid someone to carry a message across the sea. I did honor Cryndien's request that no one know I'm his brother." A hard enough delusion to carry off when they looked so much alike.

Bo shook his head. "Never did a boy try to imitate and scorn his brother as much as you."

Arpien had forgotten what it was like to have a bolt of lightning for a brother. Cryndien's flashy arrival was silent and sudden, and echoed by his booming voice. "Arpien! Little Fumbleshanks!"

Cryndien beamed at him. He was dressed entirely in white and gold, finely woven in the geometric patterns of curving flame and jagged line that characterized the Trouvelian arms. You would have thought he was attending his own coronation by the wealth of the material. He exuded brightness and strength, from the powerful calves to the embellished gold crown that sat on his orange-blond hair.

Arpien had arrived at Boxleyn scratched, dirty, and shredded like coleslaw. Cryndien arrived like an Apollonian demigod.

Perception was everything.

Cryndien's glance bounced up and down Arpien. "You don't look dead. I told you he'd survive, Bo."

Neither Bo nor Arpien pointed out that Cryndien had predicted the opposite outcome.

"The puppy's back from peril and he's not even going to greet his master? Come, Arpien, I get better treatment from my dogs."

Arpien placed his forearm on his forehead and bowed the *Double-Bow Due Reigning and Particularly Splendiferous Sovereigns of Conquisan.* It demanded perfect balance and control to execute, mainly because Cryndien would not give the signal to straighten until he was satisfied you had been down there long enough to mean it. Cryndien must have been collecting back-payments, because Arpien was down so long the blood began to rush to his head. Stars and heat filled his skull.

He was not Fumbleshanks anymore.

He did the unthinkable and stood before Cryndien gave his permission. His vision sparked from straightening too quickly. "Hello, King Cryndien." A perfectly respectful greeting, as one king might give another.

Cryndien raised his brow. "You have stayed with the Rosarian yokels a while, haven't you? I'll forgive you because I'm so glad to see you."

He embraced Arpien with a hearty series of thwacks on the back. Before Arpien could protest that he was not a drum, Cryndien released him. "So, did you ever find that weapon you were looking for? The Sword of the Prince of This and That?"

"Here and There. Yes, I did find a vademecum sword."

"Did you? Congratulations. Where did you find it? Here and There?"

In Conquisan, everyone would know to laugh. Among the three brothers, Cryndien had to laugh at his own jokes.

"May I see this unconquerable sword?"

Arpien couldn't think of a reason to refuse, so he drew the sword and extended the hilt to Cryndien. Cryndien didn't take it. Instead, he whipped out his own sword and thrust the point at Arpien's chest. Arpien rotated his wrist and the vademecum sword just in time to ward off the blow.

While his brother was still surprised, Arpien took the offensive and slashed at Cryndien's sword arm. But the vademecum sword, ever with a mind of its own, jumped from his hand and clattered to the floor. Arpien somersaulted under Cryndien's next swing, and came up with sword in hand. Their blades shook against each other as muscles strained. Slowly the pressure against Arpien's sword eased. He matched it, careful to watch for his brother to change his mind and strike at him again.

Bo watched them with his arms crossed, as though his brothers tried to kill each other on a daily basis.

It was truer than Arpien wanted to admit. A poisonous spider in Arpien's shoe. A dagger thrown at his back if he failed to back away from Cryndien with the proper referential bow.

Cryndien had always played the affronted elder brother. "When you're in our high position, lots of people will try to kill you. I'm training you to be aware. Wouldn't you rather someone try to kill you out of love than out of hate?"

Cryndien had had his entertainment for today. He sheathed his sword. "Not a bad sword you have there, if you could keep hold of it. Not unconquerable, though. Looks like you'll have to keep practicing, same as every other ordinary mortal."

Arpien returned the vademecum sword to its scabbard. It still felt cold. "You do not count yourself in our company."

"Don't be ill-spirited, brother. Of course I have to practice before I can conquer. But it is the will, not the weapon, which must be unconquerable."

Arpien wished Brierly and Nissa could be here to witness the conversation. They said Arpien liked to lecture, but if they could hear Cryndien …

"You shouldn't have brought her here," Arpien said. No one asked who he meant. His dislike of Consulan Sitral was long and well-known.

"She was invited."

"Rosarians believe in nothing but their own prowess. They wouldn't have invited her."

"Maybe you should explain that to that squat girl with the brown hair who invited my entourage into the palace. Plain little thing, but a lovely hostess."

Nissa. Arpien should have warned her. But he didn't think Cryndien would be so bold as to come here himself, let alone with an ally he could barely control.

Cryndien rolled his eyes. "Oh, don't get your morals in a bind. I'm only here to talk."

"If you want access to Sentre Forest, you'll deal with me."

"So I hear. This is unprecedented, that I must congratulate you twice in one day. Found the legendary sword and the legendary princess both. Tell me, is the one as peerless as the other?"

"My lady is without compare."

"My lady. Listen to him, Bo. Just like the day he left. Fetch me a lute so I may accompany his passionate professions."

Bo lifted his brow a fraction.

Cryndien rubbed Arpien's shoulders with over-vigorous fingers. Arpien couldn't help but remember how Queen Perturbance's fingers ploughed into the lapdog with barely repressed violence. "Relax, Arpien, you're always so stiff at my jokes. I'm delighted you found your little lady love. This will save us all a lot of time and effort. You get your princess, Conquisan gets Sentre Forest, and that'll be an end to this boundary dispute."

"Aye, because Sentre Forest will belong to Brierly and me."

"Listen, Bo, he's playing king again. Come now, Arpien, you can marry the delectable what's-her-name if you want. But don't ruin your happiness with the burden of ruling."

"A burden you would be glad to take from me."

"Of course I'd sacrifice myself for a brother."

"Brierly and I can manage Sentre Forest on our own. We will, of course, be happy to consider any reasonable trade offer you make." Ooh, that felt good.

"You are a prince of Conquisan, and your acquisitions belong to Conquisan. It's your duty. Why are you smiling?"

"We never have agreed on the definition of duty."

"Then look at it from your own self-interest. Wouldn't you rather I endure the long days and sleepless nights of toil, taxing, and administration? I could even build you a little summer home on the edge of Sentre Forest where you and Princess Peerless can be free to hole up in your fantasy land and have lots of peerless babies."

Arpien tried to find the amusement of the situation. That was how Brierly had won the battle of politics last night. "Tell you what, I'll build you a summer home on the edge of my Forest and rent it to you for a very low price."

Cryndien laughed and slapped him on the back. Arpien tensed, but not before Cryndien seized Arpien's wrist and twisted it behind his back.

"Don't cross me, little brother." Cryndien's hot breath smeared against Arpien's ear. It smelled of the sharpened mintola tree sticks he used to pick his teeth when on campaign. "You are weak. You always have been. The mighty set the rules."

It was no good looking to Bo for help. Arpien stomped on Cryndien's instep with his full weight. For one instant the pain loosened Cryndien's grip on his arm. Arpien turned, shoved Cryndien to the ground, and sprang away.

It was the only time in his life Cryndien had ever crouched down before him. Arpien wanted to savor this triumph, to remember this instant as the one in which he declared himself independent of any man's rule but his own. But he scurried from the room before he could do anything to ruin the moment.

19

Brierly

There was no need to go shopping in the dream world. You imagined what you wanted or did without. So it was probably just as well Nissa was there to handle the financial transactions. Even supposing prices were the same after one hundred years, Brierly had no interest in bargaining. She'd also forgotten, as had many young people before her, that shopping required money.

All I see is mine and still nothing I own.

Then Brierly remembered a few of the ladies had authorized her to buy whatever material she needed to complete their gowns. The magical word "credit" enabled her and Nissa to load their easy-going beast of burden to his nose. Nissa showed her own gift for color and texture as they puzzled together silk and velvet, cotton and linen. Like the good reflection she was, Nissa was eager to laugh and talk fashion, as if she too were shaken from the events of the morning and needed to release tension. All told, it would have made a pleasant afternoon if Brierly's mind were in the same location as her body.

Voracity is at Boxleyn.

As the center of her own universe, Brierly found it hard to imagine Voracity would torture her figments unless Brierly were there to watch. The surest way to put Arpien in danger was to go to him. Not that she cared what happened to such a stuffy-puffy prince.

Gerret lingered over a display of knives. Nissa made a good show of pretending to be interested as he listed the merits of each. It would be so easy to slip through the crowd, into the kitchen entrance of Boxleyn Palace. It wouldn't hurt anything for her to spy on Voracity from a distance. In this dream, Gowsma had been forced to take the form of a powerless hag. Voracity would have to as well. Probably.

You promised Arpien you wouldn't seek her out.

Not promise, exactly. He assumed. Anyway, promises to figments didn't count.

They toured the town that tried to cozy up to the blunt right corners of Boxleyn Palace's southern side. Brierly laced her elbow through Nissa's as they admired the wares of the jeweler and tinker and silversmith. Nissa squeezed her arm at this unprecedented display of easy companionship. What Brierly didn't tell her was that without Nissa's elbow to anchor her, she'd drift away. Boxleyn was a whirlpool, sucking her down, down …

By the time the sun encased the market in late-afternoon amber, Brierly was exhausted from fighting the undertow that threatened to drag her toward Voracity. Gerret deposited purchases and ladies safely in Nissa's chambers. Nissa wouldn't hear of Brierly going down to the dining hall. "I'll snatch a few pork pies and be back in a moment."

The day's last lancing fit of sunlight pierced the window and gave Brierly a headache. She gripped the polished wooden arms of her chair until the joints in her hands strained at the skin. In a few more minutes Voracity would be gone and she would be safely alone again.

Alone.

Brierly flew downstairs. Just a glimpse of what her arch-enemy was doing, to ensure—

There she was. She rested on the long marble stairs of Boxleyn Palace's grand entrance. She was old, even older than Gowsma, but her human form did not look so decrepit as Gowsma's. It was probably the straight back. The far-seeing eyes were closed to the orange and purple of the dying sun. Was she basking in the light or the dark? It was hard to believe this simple, shorn old woman had caused Brierly such pain.

Was it really her tormentor? "Hello, Voracity."

The old woman did not open her eyes. "Hello, princessling."

A battledore match whammed around in Brierly's chest. "It's been a long time."

"Too long. But doubtless you've kept me close in your thoughts."

"I hear you're serving the King of Conquisan as consulan now."

"I'll leave the word 'serving' open to interpretation."

If she could not provoke Voracity's pride, she'd match her nonchalance. Brierly lounged on the marble stairs two arms-breadths from

Voracity and hugged a knee to her chest. "Why did you bother to come?" Brierly said. "You think it matters to me that you're going to kill Arpien? I'm not a fool anymore. I know he's not real. None of it is."

Now at last the hag opened her eyes. Numinous golden eyes that spoke of secrets more ancient than the pillars of the world. "Figured that much out, have you?"

"The prince, the tower, the rescue, happily ever after? How many times do you think I'll fall for the same trick?" If there was something different about this time, this prince, now was not the time to bring it up. "You can't hurt me. Why did you come?"

"Shouldn't you be asking why you sought me out?"

"I didn't seek you out."

"Have it your way." Voracity closed her eyes again and tilted her face toward the violet-orange sky. The tacit dismissal bothered Brierly more than the attack she expected.

"Why would I want you here? What have you ever given me but pain?"

"On the contrary, that's exactly why you want me here."

"I'm not a torture-seeker."

"But you are futile. I am the last absolute in your pitiful world. If I don't exist, you won't, either."

"Of course I exist."

"You just told me you don't believe in Arpien, this world or any other. You feel nothing for anyone except me. The fact is, you seek me out because I'm the only thing that can make you feel alive. You have made me the villain so that you can play the hero. Without me, you have no meaning." She smiled. "See? You need me."

"All I've ever wanted is to be free of you."

"Then be free of me." Voracity shrugged in a parody of Brierly. It was like gazing into a distorted mirror. "If I'm not real, you follow your own rules. If I am real, you follow mine."

It so resonated with Brierly's own thoughts that she rocked backwards. A sharp right angle of stone dug into the small of her back, but she didn't move. The discomfort stabilized her. What if she had created Voracity, just as she created Neef and Arpien and every other dream? Brierly would be cut loose in the dream world forever. No enemies or friends. Herself. Free.

Alone.

Such liberty was as tantalizing and terrifying as Voracity herself.

It had to be one of Voracity's tricks.

"I made up all those nightmares on my own, is that the way of it?" Brierly said. "You're done tormenting me and now you're just going to abandon me?"

"That's what the Prince did, isn't it?"

Inside Brierly, something snapped and bled. How was it that even in her feeble hag form, Voracity could wound so deeply?

Only one sickly glimmer of sun remained above the horizon. The old woman rose on creaky knees. Her back stayed straight. With every step she descended, another withered red tendril of light shriveled up. At the bottom of the stairs Voracity glanced over her shoulder. "It's your dream, you decide what you want to believe. But remember—at least I visit."

Brierly had never felt more alone, or more repulsed at the cure.

20

Nissa

Nissa was appalled to discover she'd towed an evil fairy into Boxleyn. "You'd think after all my research I'd recognize an evil fairy when I saw one. I thought she was some minor Conquisani noble, a harmless old woman." She forced herself to quit fidgeting with the blue and green glass jumpstones and look Brierly in the face. "I could have killed you."

"No." Arpien paced Nissa's parlor, either out of nerves or the fact that Brierly's sewing projects took up every other roosting place. "I should have made the connection that Consulan Sitral was Voracity and warned you both."

"I don't understand why both of you are so eager to be guilty. Things just happen." Brierly swung her feet from her crosswise position in the blue stuffed armchair. Nissa watched them mark uneven time, two maladjusted clock pendulums in knitted stockings.

"What if Voracity comes back?" Nissa asked Brierly's feet.

"Voracity can't come back unless a member of the Rosarian royal line invites her into Boxleyn," Arpien said. "She's not the immediate threat. My brother is."

"Which brother?" Nissa said.

"It makes no difference."

"Your brothers are so alike?"

"Alike?" He shrugged his brows. "Truth be told I don't know if they even like each other. Imagine a closeness so strong it bypasses affection. Bo was bred to have one purpose and one pastime—his duty to Cryndien. Today I told Cryndien that his claims to Sentre Forest are worthless. He'll threaten and manipulate us to get it. Bo follows Cryndien's orders."

He drummed his fingers on the handle of his sword. "The vademecum sword detects princesses. Too bad it doesn't warn me when my brothers come near."

Nissa jerked upright. "Arpien, I know of such a device."

"An evil-brother-detector?"

"An ill-intention-ometer."

She dragged them both into the library—Nissa developed the strength of a small army when she was after a book—and hunted down *Fantastical and Legendary Devices: An Compendium for the Scholar of Legends and Lore.* "I read about your vademecum sword in here. There's also a page on a device that detects ill intentions. The devices were popular in Dlindi centuries ago, during their civil war."

"I've never heard of an ill-intention-ometer," Arpien said.

"They fell out of favor after the Dlindian Civil War. Maybe everyone who knew how to make them died in the war." Nissa tapped an illustration of a metal octagon, with cords attached on either side. "If anyone with malicious intent comes within five paces of you, it's supposed to warn you."

"Perfect. If we had one."

"Actually, I sort of bought one a few years ago."

Arpien grabbed her hand and planted a kiss on it. "My lady, you are beautiful."

Nissa felt her cheeks flush. "Don't make me beautiful yet. I never got it to work. It's possible the tinker who sold it to me pawned me a fake."

"It probably didn't work for you because you're not mean enough," Brierly said. "Let's see it."

Nissa retrieved it from storage. (She had holed away the hoard of a small dragon in storage.) The ill-intention-ometer had the size and appearance of an ill-made broach. Brierly held out her hand for it. It wailed the mournful groan of a lovesick ogre. It was more pathetic than alarming, but it was loud.

No one asked what Brierly was thinking that caused her such success. Instead Arpien shouted to Nissa, "How do you silence it?"

The sound ceased. Brierly blinked innocent eyes at Arpien and deposited the ill-intention-ometer in his hand.

Arpien dangled it like a smelly stocking at arm's length. "Can you imagine taking that into battle with you? It wouldn't protect you—it'd give away your position."

"There are accounts of them giving silent warnings." Nissa burrowed into her book. "Let me work on it."

Brierly stretched. "Regardless, I'd like to meet Cryndien."

"I'm not convinced that's a good idea," Arpien said.

"I'm not afraid of your brother. Are you?"

King Emol put on a much better reception for Cryndien than he had for Arpien. He opened up the Reception Room and stuffed the corners with courtiers, musicians, and appetizers. Nissa preferred to skip the evening in favor of tinkering with the ill-intention-ometer, but Aunt Perturbance claimed it would be a great affront to the Conquisani King. How could it be an affront when the fiery king didn't notice her the entire evening? Nissa stationed herself at a nearby serving table and helped the servants arrange one-inch squares of rhubarb cake onto the food platters.

King Cryndien sneered at the backwoods pretensions of the Rosarians. Still, a number of courtiers simpered and swooned around him as though he did them the greatest honor by insulting them in that booming voice of his. Perhaps one's greatest enemy was always alluring. Or maybe they wanted more fodder with which to disparage the offensive Conquisani from the back corners. Cryndien's manners were ten times as pretentious as Arpien's at his worst, but his boldness and quick tongue were irresistible. If this was the ideal of nobility in Conquisan, no wonder Arpien came across as stilted here.

But no one dared laugh at King Cryndien.

Prince Bo—he was a prince although he seemed more at home in title *General*—hovered a pace or two away from King Cryndien all night. The Trouvelian features were there, but so muted only someone as bored as Nissa would bother to compare him to Cryndien. He was shorter but powerfully built, his movements economical but purposeful. According to Arpien he followed Cryndien blindly. Was he dim-witted or lazy? He was far too watchful for Nissa to call him either.

She should have known better than to scrutinize an enemy king's bodyguard. He would be alert to any pair of staring eyes, including hers. Finally he looked straight at her. Nissa jerked around and knocked into a servant carrying a tray of candied violets. Crisp purple petals showered down on them both. They made faint dull plinking sounds against the polished wooden floor. Nissa dove on her hands and knees to clean up the mess. When she rose it was Aunt Perturbance glaring at her instead of General Bo. Nissa wiped her sticky hands on her skirts and picked a new subject for study.

In all Boxleyn, there was only one person who could match Cryndien's charisma and blazing presence. Brierly, fresh from her success at the singing duel, drew her own cadre. It included many of the ladies whose gowns she was sewing, an unprecedented number of male admirers, as well as Lord Culmney, who seemed ready to adopt her. As for physical beauty, Cryndien and Brierly were the two brightest stars in the heavens. When the two came face-to-face, it was a planetary collision.

Cryndien swept his golden cape back with his left hand and circled his right four times. He seized Brierly's hand and kissed it. "It is no wonder my baby brother abandoned the kingdom of his birth in search of you, my lady. You are exquisite."

Brierly lifted a shoulder with that flippant elegance only she could achieve. "Thanks. Same to you. Although I have seen enough versions of the Conquisani royal line I'm beginning to think there's only one pattern." She smiled at Cryndien's confusion. "You favor your great-grandfather Herren."

"Appropriate, as I will inherit the forest signed over to him one hundred years ago."

"Arpien takes after Herren even more than you do. It is interesting, is it not, what is carried from one generation to another, and what is stolen away by time? Or how sometimes what is lost suddenly reemerges?"

She was claiming Sentre Forest. At least, Nissa thought she read the political innuendo right. Brierly said it so casually she might have been commenting on field drainage or the price of potatoes.

At this point Sir Flatwhist confused Nissa for the servant she acted and asked her for more stuffed mushrooms. When Nissa returned from the kitchens, though, the Strandish knight addressed her as though he knew perfectly well who she was. "Your friend seems very astute tonight."

Nissa bristled. "Why shouldn't she? She's smart."

"And don't we all admire smart, beautiful women?" He stuck a mushroom in his mouth. For all the trouble he sent her to to get it, he seemed to barely taste it before he swallowed. It might have been a doorknob for all the culinary interest he took in it. "I don't suppose she's mentioned me? When she smiled at me last night, I thought perhaps she took an interest ..."

So even stoic Sir Flatwhist was interested in Brierly. Half the world wanted to bury her, the other half to marry her.

"No, sir. More mushrooms?" Nissa extended the platter. He shook his head no, and moved away stiffly.

It was much later in the evening that Nissa was able to talk to her friends without the Brierly proponents flapping nearby. "Your brother's not subtle about claiming Sentre Forest, is he?"

Arpien flared his nostrils at his eldest brother. "Is there anything about that you'd call subtle? But I'm glad Brierly insisted on meeting him. She was brilliant. Luminous. Virtuosic." He gave Brierly a sheepish twist of a smile. "I still feel like an idiot, but less of one with you around."

Brierly only shrugged a lovely arched eyebrow. But a few minutes after Arpien left to resume his campaign of pleasantries amongst the Rosarian nobles, Brierly said to Nissa, "That's only two grand Conquisani bows he's indulged in this evening. Impressive restraint."

She'd been watching him?

"Stop," Brierly said.

"What?"

"Embroidering us."

Nissa blushed, caught in the act of debating exactly what stitch she could use for the soft, speculative look in Brierly's young/old eyes. The Faraway Look of the Heroine was difficult to capture in life, let alone sewing. Nissa had spent hours of her childhood posed by windows as she practiced the lift of the chin, the point of focus above the horizon, the right proportions of wistfulness and determination in the brow that all baked into the recipe for the perfect Faraway Look.

On impulse Nissa squeezed Brierly's hands. "Don't worry, Brierly. Sentre Forest will go to you. It's how all the old tales end. Goodness wins out. Reward follows suffering. I know you think all princes will disappoint you, but your prince came for you."

Less than a minute later Brierly ruined every political advantage she'd gained that evening by trying to walk through the wall.

At first it looked like an accident. Nissa heard a gaggle of ladies exclaim over her friend. She wriggled through the tall crowd. Brierly looked cross-eyed. Arpien brushed her hair back from her face and examined her forehead. Brierly extracted herself from Arpien's gentle ministrations, whirled, and plucked a dessert spoon from the hand of one of her followers. She licked the spoon and traced the spaces between the stones in the wall. Then she smacked into the wall again.

She brandished the spoon in the general direction of the wall and slashed the air in the shape of a square. "I command you to open!"

Arpien disarmed her and held the squirming princess by both upper arms.

Timothy appeared at Nissa's elbow. "And that," he said, "would control the lives of thousands?"

Nissa chewed her lip.

"Are you going to help your friend or not?"

No one else was going to approach a princess in the throes of a mad fit. Nissa ran over to help Arpien escort Brierly from the room.

"Poor thing must have hit her head harder than we thought." That was the kindest of the whispers.

"What happened?" Nissa asked as soon as they were out of the Reception Room.

"I don't know." Arpien's face darkened with concern. "She behaved like a—well—normal person all night. Then she slammed into the wall."

Brierly yanked her arms from their supporting hands. "Let go of me. I want out, don't you understand?"

Nissa and Arpien glanced at each other, then released Brierly's arms in unison. They flanked her without touching her, one on each side.

"I'll just have to find another door."

"A door where, Brierly?" Nissa said.

"Doesn't matter. I'm not staying here." Her path veered sideways into the wall again. Whether she was trying to find another door or she was just dizzy, it did the same job. It knocked her out cold.

21
Brierly

Brierly spent the next few hours as a gryphon. She flew so far that the North Wind met the South Wind in a blustery dispute. Brierly reeled through the squall of their squabble. None of the sky brothers could manage a cordial conversation. She enjoyed the sensation of freefall, the paralyzing moment when she opened her eagle wings just a few yards before she would have dashed her lion's body against the rocks. She flew up six times to get caught in the storm, until the Winds huffed at her lack of manners and went their separate ways.

She thirsted for the primal and destructive. So she razed a village of gnomes. She delighted in the soft crunch of them in her powerful beak. She was strong, she was terrifying, she was animal and alien.

Most importantly, she was not human.

Her leonine body dove through the air. Her claws snagged on a cloud, and she realized she was struggling against bedsheets. She opened an eye on Nissa's bedchamber.

No, I don't want to be here.

So she dove again. She wheeled from dream to dream. She was fire. She was a giant. Anyone but Briar Rose Steward, whose prince had come for her.

Nissa was a lackwit for saying it. But Nissa was a reflection of herself, so Brierly was a lackwit for thinking it.

It wasn't just that between Arpien's moments of affectation came increasing moments of the genuine. Why, when he rode up on Windried, all worried about Nissa, he'd carried on an entire honest conversation with her without a single bow or speech. He'd been concerned and brave and passionate, but thoroughly sincere.

But no matter what Nissa said, what was Arpien but a reused dream?

But the worst was Nissa, with her talk of Goodness and Happy Endings. And the certainty that Brierly's Prince had come.

The Reception Room walls had pressed in on her like contracting heartbeats. She'd had to escape into another dream, right then. Arpien's promises were but a cruel reminder of how another Prince had abandoned her.

Spinning wheels. Voracity was right. She was the last anchor in Brierly's life. Even that anchor was slippery. Which fate was more terrifying: to cling to the fairy who Cursed her, or to have nothing to cling to at all?

The gryphon dream was gloriously elemental, the ones after it delicious but fleeting. A string octet of spiders serenaded her on tiny violas and cellos strung with their own cobwebs. They used no bows, but curled about the backs of their instruments. Four legs plucked the strings, and four legs did the fingering, if the anatomical misnomer was allowed. Such fine vibrations could only be detected by bugs and fairy-Gifted ears. How to describe the music? It was the pianissimo pizzicato of dry bones.

The first chair arachnid handed Brierly her miniscule violin. Brierly brushed her fleshy human fingers across it and broke the strings.

Then she was there again, in the recurring nightmare Arpien called the waking world.

Nissa shook her shoulder. "Brierly. Brierly, wake up."

Maybe if she ignored Nissa's urgent voice, she could avoid entering the dream. But when Nissa ordered Kendra to find the doctor, Brierly opened her eyes.

"There's a certain irony in your insistence."

"Brierly! How do you feel?"

Dismayed. Gratified. "Fine." Brierly forced a sleepy smile. "Did I miss our morning ride?"

Her status had shifted since her last visit to this dream. This was the one dream that wouldn't let her rewrite lines that had already been spoken. Ladies whispered after her in the halls. Groomsmen approached her as they might a horse they expected would kick. Even Arpien was over-careful in his attentions, a highly conscious blend of solicitous concern and studied ignorance.

Brierly slipped into deliberate obliviousness as though it were a close-fitting silk gown. Arpien and Nissa exchanged glances, as if doubtful of her regression. Brierly sprinkled the conversation with several non sequiturs about wood sprites. She'd be nobody's charming, witty princess today.

She was only half listening to the conversations around her, and nearly missed Windried's apprehensions that the army would still be outside the gate.

"What army?" Brierly said.

Windried didn't know what army, she just knew that the entourage Nissa escorted to the palace yesterday was only a portion of the soldiers she had seen.

At that point Fearless reminded them that Arpien could only understand half their conversation, but whatever he had heard had made him tense in the saddle. It was making Fearless nervous, so would Brierly please take pity on his human and translate?

Nissa chewed her lip as she listened to her horse's translated eyewitness account. "I saw maybe twenty people. Not enough to call an army," Nissa said.

"Windried is not a trained counting horse," Brierly said. "But then, maybe only a portion of them turned visible. I don't know if invisibilifiers work on animals. Not all magic does, although animals can usually sense it."

"It might explain why Fearless bolted," Arpien said. "He's a war-horse; an army alone wouldn't have bothered him. Perhaps the smell of Voracity's magic did."

Brierly snorted. "Fearless bolted because he's afraid of flowers. He told me yesterday."

Arpien frowned down at the top of his horse's white mane. "My war stallion is afraid of flowers?"

"There's some type that grows near the gate that frightens the oats out of him."

"What can a quarter-ounce blossom do to a beast that weighs hundreds of pounds?"

"Explain the logic all you want. It's not going to convince him."

"You might have said something yesterday."

"You might have listened to your horse."

Arpien's spine developed a case of broomstick. "My horse doesn't tell me what's wrong."

Brierly felt her own hackles rise. "Your horse sends you a very clear message that he doesn't want to do something, and you shove him toward it."

Nissa cleared her throat. "No doubt Arpien will apologize to Fearless later. What about the army?"

Brierly wanted to ride out to search for it now. Arpien refused to let her go unless he went, too, but he couldn't get near the gate unless Fearless cooperated. Nissa and Windried were willing to go if everyone else went, though neither seemed eager to revisit the scene of yesterday's confrontation, harmless though it had turned out to be.

"If my brother led an army here, it's my problem," Arpien said.

"It's also Rosaria's," Nissa said.

"Don't you trust me?"

"I only meant you don't have to do it alone," Nissa said.

"Nor should he," Brierly said. "If he goes to King Emol with a report about the Conquisani army, the King won't trust his word."

"It may be best to keep your uncle ignorant," Arpien said, "or he might take the initiative and confront Cryndien. My brother doesn't need much of an excuse to attack."

"So I'm to take your word that an invisible Conquisani army would be here in the Rosarian capital for—what, a pilgrimage?" Nissa said.

Arpien was relapsing into broomstick. "No, you should take my word that I can handle it."

"Are you still Conquisani, Arpien Trouvel? You left home with no plans to return. You have no love for your king. Are you a Rosarian, then? You have no love for our king, either. Whose man are you?"

"My own."

"Then, as you are neither Conquisani nor Rosarian, why are you concerning yourself in our affairs?"

Fearless sidestepped and asked Brierly to intervene in the conversation again because whatever the humans were saying was putting Arpien in battle stance.

"Because on one side are my brothers, and on the other are my friends," Arpien said.

Nissa softened. "Then, as a friend I ask you, what are you prepared to do should there be a war between Conquisan and Rosaria? Will you fight? Perhaps you shouldn't go looking for a Conquisani army until you know the answer to that question."

The swish of the horses' tails marked the time. When at last Arpien spoke, it was controlled, only a little sad. "I am not the fool you imagine, Nissa Montaine. I have asked myself these questions before. It is only since I befriended you that they grew so complicated. I do not mean to fight in a war between Conquisan and Rosaria, but to prevent one. My brother wants an empire. I've seen what he'll do to get it, because I have helped him. You think I do not know myself. But then I think you know my loyalty to you and Brierly is no act. Perhaps that's whose man I am. If the war you speak of ever comes, I will protect the two of you first."

"I am sorry if I seemed to doubt you," Nissa said, all kitten again instead of lion. "It's just—I had an odd dream last night, and it has me off-kilter this morning."

"No, it was a legitimate question," Arpien said. "You'll excuse my anger at it. I didn't sleep well myself."

By the end of their ride, Arpien announced his decision to sneak out that night to investigate Windried's claims. That way his Tail wouldn't be able to follow him.

Brierly let him believe he'd be going alone.

22

Arpien

When Arpien returned to Boxleyn Palace, one of his Tail surprised him by speaking to him. It was Gerret, Kendra's brother. And still on speaking terms after Arpien sent him on shopping duty.

"Excuse me, Your Highness, but did you remember there's a meeting in the Reception Room this morning to discuss control of Sentre Forest?"

How could Arpien remember when he'd never been invited? "Yes, thank you. What time were we meeting again?"

"They started a quarter hour ago, Your Highness."

There was no time to clean up, so he had to attend dressed as Cryndien's shabbier self. Annoyance proved a powerful fortifier. How dare they try to divvy up Sentre Forest without him? Or without Brierly, whose claims predated them all?

He was, however, only one miffed dignitary among many: King Emol, Prince Timothy, Prince Eusar, General Gapric of the Rosarian armies, Lord Culmney, Sir Flatwhist, and of course, Cryndien and Bo. So he merely nodded at King Emol, "I'm sorry I'm late," and took a seat. Even that took strategy. He didn't want to sit too close to the other delegations. Neither Conquisani nor Rosarian, Nissa had called him. But he didn't want to sit so far away that he could be discounted.

"I'm here to represent the interests of Princess Briar Rose Steward."

King Emol smirked. "She finds herself—unwell—after last night?"

"She has made a full recovery."

"Perhaps she is weary after last night's—exertions." Prince Eusar lifted a suggestive brow. "You can give us a firsthand account of her fitness. You saw her to her bedchamber last night, did you not?"

Heat rose in him. "I'm certain I do not know what you are talking about."

"I'll thank you to ease off my baby brother, Prince Eusar," Cryndien said, "as I'm also certain he doesn't know what you're talking about."

A few of the men laughed, but not so many as Arpien feared. Arpien did his best in the next hour to be worthy of their respect. Not with boasting or gestures or any of the princely arts he had been raised with. Today he chose speaking with sense over speaking with flair. Cryndien looked ashamed of his brother's barbaric manners. Even as irritated as Arpien was with his brother, it was hard to ignore Cryndien's disapproval.

The problem that arose was this: the Strandish delegation insisted they could not wait any longer to gain access to Sentre Forest. Without the mantiz egg sacs, victims in Strand died daily of the tree-plague. Their own royal line was in peril. They could not wait for a transfer of political power to seal negotiations.

Cryndien claimed Sentre Forest was his, by right of the treaty King Herren had signed one hundred years ago. If Lord Culmney meant to negotiate with anyone, it had to be him.

"It seems uncompassionate to let people perish while we discuss the paperwork," Arpien said. "One month won't matter much in the building of a fleet, Cryndien. The hittal trees will still be there. But it may matter in the lives of men. If the Strandish royal line dies, there will be political instability in the region. Of course Conquisan wants to avoid that."

His comments won him the appreciation of the Strandish, and even grudging gratitude from the Rosarians for affirming their right to handle their own lands as they saw fit, at least for the time being. But he infuriated Cryndien. Cryndien demanded King Emol withdraw all Rosarian presence from Cryndien's forest by the Spring Ball, or Conquisan would do it for him. It was an audacious claim from a king who had placed himself in the stronghold of his enemy. But perhaps not from a king who had surrounded that same stronghold with an army of his own.

Arpien had told Nissa he meant to prevent war between Conquisan and Rosaria, but he had no idea how to do it.

Mangled memories of troubled dreams left Arpien with a restless energy. He decided to burn it off at the practice fields.

In the weeks since he arrived he'd found plenty of warriors eager to put a presumptuous Conquisani in his place. It was easier to work his frustrations out on people who wished to embarrass him. There was no guilt when he trounced them. When he'd proved he had the steel to meet their challenges, he'd won a strange measure of popularity and notoriety. Soldiers brought their friends to wallop him, but when Arpien won, they seemed just as happy to have their great foe unvanquished. He hesitated to call any of them friends, but several of the regulars made a point of exchanging jovial insults with him. It was not so different from the posturing required among Conquisani nobility, only here he had the talent to redeem himself. So Arpien played their favorite villain, and in return picked up a few Rosarian sword tricks and the cautious respect of Boxleyn guard.

Today he was greeted with, "Look, it's the Crimson Mollusk! Here to terrorize us with your cap feather?"

"A feather is all I need to defend myself against your sword, Triddle," Arpien said.

The soldiers made that curious sound that was half growl, half approval.

"I'm in the mood to slide my blade into a sorry soft Rosarian gut. Who will answer?"

Enough volunteers surged up at that challenge to keep Arpien busy for the next hour. Sweaty and feeling much better about himself, Arpien threw up his hands in mock surrender. "Enough! You have dashed the wicked Conquisani into submission until tomorrow."

It was not, perhaps, the most politic thing to say, given the true threat of war. But if these Rosarian soldiers could banter with him, perhaps they'd relax their hatred against the Conquisani in general.

Arpien stretched warm muscles. Who was tampering with his doublet on the side bench? Well, not his doublet, the one he'd borrowed from Prince Timothy. Arpien was alert for an attack from Cryndien, but this conspirator was nothing so deadly. Without turning around, he said, "Put down the syrup and come here, Cuz."

Nissa's youngest cousin dragged himself over to face Arpien. "I didn't mean anything by it."

Arpien unbuckled the vademecum sword and picked up two dull metal practice swords.

"You meant to embarrass me. Now you must answer for it." He tossed one of the practice swords across the field. It embedded itself point-first in the dirt in front of Cuz's feet.

Cuz's eyes widened. "But I'm twelve."

"When you attack a man you must be prepared to fight like a man."

Cuz turned to the onlookers among the Rosarian guard. Cuz was a brat, but he was a Rosarian brat. "He'll kill me," Cuz said.

"You'll find it's hard to die by practice blade," Arpien said. "Although not altogether impossible."

The armsmaster took Arpien's measure with a hard glance. If Cuz were injured here, the armsmaster would lose his position, if not his life. Either Arpien had earned a degree of trust in the past week and a half, or the armsmaster had suffered Cuz's insolence for too many years, for he nodded. "He's right, young prince. You must answer for dishonoring a guest in your family's palace, even if he is an accursed Conquisani. But be at peace. If he kills you, I'll avenge your death."

Cuz eyed Arpien in that half-fearful, half-skeptical way, as though a groom had saddled a dragon and told Cuz to get on. As though if he stared long enough the dragon would vanish under the weight of disbelief. So Arpien brought his own blade up to attack. It was a sweeping approach, more show than speed. Cuz plucked his sword up with a shriek and parried the blow.

"Good. You didn't run."

"Of course I didn't run!" Cuz said. "You stinking Conquisani—"

Arpien took the offensive again, and Cuz parried. It was ungainly, but the boy acted on reflex, which showed he was not altogether untrained.

"Everyone knows I'm no good with a sword, so it's not fair for you to embarrass me."

"You can complain or you can fight," Arpien said.

Cuz surprised him by taking the offensive. It was a clumsy attack. His anger forecasted his moves. Arpien was impressed that he was gutsy enough to try. Stupid, but gutsy.

Arpien kept Cuz just on the cusp of his abilities. He pushed him hard enough that the boy couldn't find the wind to complain again. He was careful not to push him so far that he threw down his sword and gave up. Cuz's burst of anger was short-lived. His attacks grew smarter. Soon it was Cuz pushing himself.

When the time was right, Arpien disarmed Cuz. He nodded to the boy with the *Quarter Bow of Courteous Victory Without Intent of Boasting Much Afterward.* "Thank you for the duel, Prince Cuz."

Cuz stared at his empty hand. "Wait!" Cuz ran over to pick up his sword and assumed a fighting stance. "Are you running away?"

"Tomorrow. I'm done in for one day."

The sword sagged in Cuz's grasp. He cocked his head at Arpien. "Are you trying to make a fool of me?"

"Do you feel like a fool?"

"You're the best swordsman here. Why did you fight me?"

"I told you. You had to answer for trying to embarrass me. You paid me back, one prince to another, by doing me the honor of fighting me. You're the first noble in all Rosaria to pay me such courtesy." He picked up his syrup-lined doublet on the tip of his sword and tossed it to Cuz. "Have this cleaned, will you?"

"Wait!" Cuz ran up to Arpien and asked in a low voice, "How bad am I, really?"

Arpien shook his head. "Not bad. Your feet are like stumps and you heave that sword like an axe. But you have quick hands and good reflexes. And an eye for openings."

It was as though someone had tied a fishing line to the corner of Cuz's mouth and kept tugging it upward, trying to reel in a full smile. Then he drew himself up and scowled. "If you don't show up for our rematch tomorrow, that proves you're scared, and I win by forfeit."

He stormed off.

He took the doublet with him.

Arpien was beginning to think all Rosarian princes lurked in the corners of the practice field, because he ran into Timothy on his way out. "You could have walloped the boy, and no one would have blamed you."

"And that would have stopped the pranks?" Arpien said.

"You have an interesting way of subduing your enemies."

"The boy's not my enemy."

"He's not your friend, either. Perhaps you think to infiltrate Rosaria by earning the hero-worship of a twelve-year-old boy?"

Arpien pushed past Timothy. "If you were a third son instead of the crown prince, you would not ask me that."

"Stop, please."

Arpien turned back.

"It's just hard to believe a Conquisani would make time for my pest of a brother."

"Again, you are not a third son."

"Yes, yes, I'm trying to thank you. You have surprised me twice today, Arpien Trouvel. Before, your motives seemed—pardon me—simple enough. No doubt I show the hubris of an eldest son. I would know your mind better." He inclined his head sideways. A hank of muddy-auburn hair fell onto his brow. It ought to have diminished the dignity of his statement, but it didn't. "Would you walk with me?"

Their walk gave Arpien his first glance of the famous Gridiron Garden, reserved for the private use of the Rosarian royals. Boxleyn had plenty of spaces where nature had been intimidated into behaving itself for the enjoyment of the wealthy, but none so controlled and exclusive as this one. The same iron poles that edged the perimeter of Boxleyn, out by the posby bushes, enclosed the Gridiron. There was not a curve to be found in the garden. Every sculpture and statue incorporated a right angle, whether it sat on a square pedestal or doubled as sundial. Broad steps raised the sprouting flower boxes to different levels. Even the topiary was squared off. The archways did not arch. They stood like empty door frames, their outlines the more defined because no vine dared climb up the wrought iron poles.

When the Montaines had first moved the capital of Rosaria to Boxleyn some decades before, was the Gridiron Garden their open reaction against Estepel and its overgrowth of briars?

It was a fine location for discreet political conversation, as the burble of a meandering stream covered over moderated voices. On closer inspection, Arpien realized the stream did not have the leisure to meander. It followed channels as defined as everything else in the garden. The stream sidled under perfectly flat bridges, stairstepped down miniature stone waterfalls, then bumped its nose into sudden ninety-degree turns before it eddied dizzily and moved along. Arpien wondered if the water felt as he did, that every time he got up good momentum in one direction, the garden diverted him abruptly in another.

Arpien was honored by the crown prince's attention but careful not to answer Timothy's questions unreservedly. Most of them were casually philosophic, although Arpien had no doubt Timothy read into his answers about an ideal government. Timothy was not charismatic, nor did he try to be. But he had a calm self-assurance that invited candor.

"It is fair to deny a legitimate heir a kingdom?" Timothy said. "I say no. But I also say it's far worse to give a kingdom to an unfit ruler."

"Are you speaking of Brierly, Cryndien, or me?"

Timothy addressed his answer to a garden sculpture of a portly lady. She spouted a stream of eloquent water into a small square pool. "How contrary the Conquisani are. When you want a direct answer, they give you a show. When you'd rather be oblique, they come at you like a battering ram."

"You're very direct yourself."

Timothy's attention moved from the sculpture to Arpien. "I can at least declare I'd rather have you as my neighbor than your brother. But you cannot be king unless Brierly is your queen. As long as we're being direct, you tell me—is she capable of it?"

"Think of it as if she grew up in Rosaria and then spent years in some foreign country. It's only natural she'd pick up unusual customs during her time away."

"Such as ordering walls to open and talking to lapdogs," Timothy said.

"She can relearn your ways. I believe Brierly will make a great queen. She's brilliant, she's politically astute—"

"She talks to lapdogs," Timothy repeated.

Arpien raised his brow. "I didn't believe it at first, either. But she's told me things she never would have known unless she heard it from the animals. If she's to rule Sentre Forest, isn't it an asset that she can speak to her subjects?"

"How can I hand any of my people into the care of someone who's incapable of human attachment?"

It stopped Arpien cold. He'd complained to Gowsma himself that Brierly cared more for Neef than for him.

"Watch her with Nissa," Arpien said, "then tell me she's incapable of human attachment."

The two princes nodded to each other and parted ways. Arpien rather liked the Rosarian crown prince, his straightforwardness and quiet authority. In other circumstances, could they have become friends?

It was all the more reason to prevent a war between Conquisan and Rosaria, as it was growing harder for Arpien to pick sides.

23

Arpien

That night, before Arpien snuck outside the gate in search of an invisible army, Nissa lent him the ill-intention-ometer.

"It took some experimentation, but I figured it how to use it without it making noise." Nissa picked it up by the two cords. "You thwack it three times on the table, and it is silenced." *Wham! Wham! Wham!* "Thwack it thrice more, and it is audible again."

It was like watching one of the queen's lapdogs growl and attack. Arpien hid a smile behind a crooked finger. He caught Brierly's eye and for a moment, their amusement was shared. It was, Arpien realized, the first time he and Brierly had shared a private glimmer over anything.

Brierly turned to Nissa and asked without blinking, "And you researched this official thwacking method in your books?"

Arpien coughed into his fist.

"Well, no, I got irritated and beat it against the table. Apparently it even detects ill intentions toward itself, so I heard it go off and then stop. At first I thought I broke it. But it's designed to work this way."

"How does it warn you when it's silent?" Arpien said.

She set the device down on the table. "Brierly, think mean."

The ill-intention-ometer rattled across the table top. Brierly smiled in delight, like a child at a wind-up toy. The ill-intention-ometer went limp.

Getting past his Tail was the hardest part of sneaking out of Boxleyn, but spiriting Fearless out of the stable and past the sleeping grooms would take finesse as well. Arpien was spared the effort by Brierly. He found her some one hundred yards outside the stables. She was making lacey meshwork of Neef's mane. Windried shifted at her side. Nissa's horse looked uncomfortably overdressed in a waterfall of mane and tail braids.

Nimble fingers, silent feet, animal speech—Arpien tried to forget Brierly's fairy Gifts were equally suited to a horse thief as to a princess.

"Absolutely not," he said.

Brierly knotted Neef's brown mane. "Everything's absolute with you, isn't it?"

"We decided I would go alone this morning."

"You decided. You forgot that this is my dream."

"Exactly why you can't go. You don't take the danger seriously. This is no dream, Brierly. If you die here, you die everywhere."

"Fine. I'll take care not to die tonight." She studied her equine artwork, hands on hips. "Yes, Neef, you look every bit as stunning as Windried now. And you, Arpien, would do well to remember that if animals are the only ones who can see this invisible army, you'll need someone who can talk to animals. I'm tired of being powerless here. Let me help you."

It occurred to him, in the palest flash, that maybe she insisted on going along because she cared about him.

Then she yawned. "Besides, this is the most interesting thing going on tonight."

If he left her behind, she'd just meander off on her own. Besides, he could see the great advantage of having her along, depending on which Brierly she chose to be tonight. He conceded, on the condition she wear the ill-intention-ometer on her arm.

Luckily, tonight's Brierly was the astute one. He did not even need to speak aloud to communicate the need to leave the horses in a copse of trees. There was no way to charge through the northern gate without alerting the guards. Brierly had recovered much of her strength since she woke up three weeks ago. He was almost disappointed she didn't need more help climbing over the fence, so he'd have the excuse to catch her by the waist as she hopped down.

Windried reported—through Brierly—that the army was not here any longer. Ten minutes down the main road out of the northern gate, Arpien found a fresh trail leading into the trees. These were just the sparsest fringes of Sentre Forest—trees only five or so feet around instead of twenty—but it was still a place to travel with caution, and not just because of the human residents.

They were fortunate the leaves were only just starting to fill out, as there was little enough moonlight to filter down to the forest floor as it was. Arpien reached back for Brierly's hand so he wouldn't lose her in the dark. He snagged her sleeve instead of her fingers. As she neither tugged her sleeve away nor exchanged hand for cloth, he pushed forward in that awkward and comforting position.

Arpien was a fair tracker, but this trail had been left by someone who knew how to avoid leaving tracks. Not like a common army at all. When the trail grew cold, Brierly persuaded a curious bat to follow along and be their eyes. (Although the bat claimed he didn't need his eyes to know where things were, thank you very much.) In the end, Arpien could see their quarry fine with his own eyes.

Their quarry, however, was no army, but a single man in peasant's clothes. They tracked him to a tiny clearing, where an old woman sat by a meager fire. Her hooded cloak was dark, but not black. Green? A long pointed pin, thicker than his thumb and twice as long, gleamed under her chin.

Arpien opened his hand flat against Brierly's wrist to signal a halt. He could not see clearly from this distance, but the figure by the fire had the stature and straight posture of Consulan Sitral. Voracity.

Her face was shadowed, but certainly not invisible. But perhaps that was because she seemed to be expecting to traffick with the peasant. They exchanged a muffled greeting and the peasant sat on the opposite side of the fire.

Arpien leaned close to Brierly's ear, which was not, on consideration, necessary. "I'm moving closer. I can't hear," he said.

Now it was Brierly who grabbed his sleeve. "I can."

He expected her to let go of his sleeve, but she did not. As she tracked the conversation, he felt her grip relax. Then she dug her fingers into the cloth again.

From under his cloak the peasant produced a cloth sack similar to the one Brierly had stolen from the brigands. The man had his back to them, but his imposing size might have been the same as the brigand who'd tried to behead Arpien with the vademecum sword. Arpien had never believed them to be ordinary brigands, and here was more confirmation they were Conquisani.

The man crossed to the other side of the fire to show Voracity the contents of the sack. As the fire lit his face, Arpien saw that it was indeed the burly brigand they had met on their journey to Boxleyn. His would-be executioner. Before Arpien could think through the significance of this, Voracity snatched the laces of the bag and tossed it into the fire.

Here Brierly jerked forward, but Arpien flung his hand out to stop her. If they were mantiz eggs, there was no way Brierly could save them now. The bundle crackled and flared up for a half minute, like a heap of dried leaves. Arpien had good reason not to love mantizes, but the egg sac could have saved Strandish lives.

Voracity handed a small leather purse to the brigand. The man's voice rose in volume so that now even Arpien could hear it. This was not enough pay. His threatening tone brought other figures into the firelight. Arpien tensed. Grey Cloaks. Personal guards and assassins of the Conquisani king. The Grey Cloaks were far fewer in number than an army, but Arpien would rather deal with an army.

In Conquisan, mothers did not encourage obedience with tales of monsters under the bed. Many a noble whispered warnings to their children as they were sent off to court for the first time, "You mind yourself, and never speak a word against the king, even in the privacy of your own circle of friends. The king's men will hear, for they are the very shadows in the corners of your chambers. They will cover you with the grey cloak which no man casts off."

Arpien's position as a prince was scant protection. The Grey Cloaks answered only to the king, and too often in Conquisani history the king needed protection from his own ambitious family members. It was a mark of Bo's unquestioning loyalty and Cryndien's absolute faith in him that Bo commanded the Grey Cloaks.

For the first time Arpien began to seriously worry that the evening would end in death.

But Voracity waved the Grey Cloaks back and tossed the brigand a second purse. He dumped its contents into the palm of his hand. A shadowy shape fell to the ground as though he had dropped one of his coins. Then the brigand screamed.

It was a horrible sound, the bass tones of a warrior ripped up two octaves in pain. None of the Grey Cloaks moved. The coin itself must be the weapon. Voracity nodded to two of the Grey Cloaks. One forced the brigand to his knees before Voracity. The other grabbed the knuckle of the brigand's middle finger and held the man's hand out for Voracity's inspection. The brigand bellowed for mercy. At first all Arpien could see was the blood that gushed from the brigand's palm and coated his fingers. Voracity waggled her finger in a circle to cue the Grey Cloak to turn the brigand's hand toward the light. Arpien could see the flicker of the fire through the brigand's hand. The coin had melted a hole right through his palm.

"Still small, but already ripening." Voracity raised her voice over the man's cries. "They'll need another month or so to grow to full diameter. Perhaps less time, given what I've seen of Emol. Boxleyn is fertile soil." She nodded to the Grey Cloaks to release the brigand. He bent over double, his hand stanched against the fabric of his shirt.

One of the Grey Cloaks stirred. "Consulan Sitral, what if his shouts draw attention at the northern gate? I ask permission to silence him."

"Your sort of silence is permanent, and we may have use for him later." She nudged the cringing figure with her toe. "There're no need for this caterwauling. If you can stop the bleeding in a few minutes I imagine you'll live." She turned back to the Grey Cloak. "Search the area if you like."

Brierly's cloak slid slowly from Arpien's grasp. It was damp from the evening chill. He tightened his hold. The Grey Cloaks would hear a retreat through the brush. Arpien edged his right hand to the hilt of the vademecum sword.

A gratifying but ill-timed observation struck him. She was wearing his gift to her. The soft weave of the Conquisani woolen cloak slipped again through his fingers. He caught at it and pulled her down. He tried to send a message from his eyes to hers. *Not yet.*

But Brierly wasn't looking at him. She wasn't even watching the Grey Cloaks. Her eyes were fixed on Voracity. The straight-backed hag watched the brigand try to stanch the flow of his blood with the edge of his shirt. Brierly shifted again, and for the first time Arpien realized she was tugging toward the fire, not away from it.

Brierly's hand began to shake violently. She scowled at it as though it were a disobedient chipmunk rustling in the deadfall. Arpien grabbed hold of her hand, both for reassurance and so that she wouldn't give away their position. Only then did he understand it was not nerves that made Brierly's hand shake, but the ill-intention-ometer.

The Grey Cloaks were looking for intruders. Yes, obscure magical device, thank you for the useful report.

Arpien's hands swallowed Brierly's narrow wrist in an effort to keep it steady.

Voracity's head snapped around. "There. Search there." She pointed to their hiding spot.

Arpien seized the advantage of the sliver of time it took for the Grey Cloak to follow her finger into the shadows. "Retreat," he whispered to Brierly. If they saw him first, maybe they'd think he was the only intruder. He rolled into the Grey Cloak's ankles and knocked him to the ground. He managed to knock down another of the Grey Cloaks with a deck to the jaw. But Grey Cloaks, like mantizes, hunted in packs. In seconds they surrounded Arpien.

"You're soft, the lot of you," Arpien boomed in his best Cryndien voice. "How can I rely on you to protect me when you're too slow and cudgel-witted to stop me from getting through your circle?"

Arpien knew it would only distract them for a second. The Grey Cloaks were the king's personal guard. They would know Arpien for an imposter, even in the dark. But a second's confusion was all he needed to take out two more of the Grey Cloaks. Even that much was something to be proud of—less than a breath later four Grey Cloaks seized him by the arms. A fifth kicked him in the gut. The vademecum sword slipped from his hand. The sword was swallowed by darkness and detritus.

He had some value as a Prince of Conquisan, so the Grey Cloaks might wait on Cryndien's final orders before killing him. But Voracity— would she wait? The more successfully Arpien fought, the better Brierly's chances of escape.

Only—Thistles!—Brierly was standing by the fire, mere feet behind Voracity. Did the girl have no more sense than a pair of sugar tongs? Arpien struggled with more gusto than was warranted, to draw the enemy's attention toward himself. Brierly alone didn't look at him. Her gaze was still fixed on Voracity, a terrifying blend of hunger and revulsion.

He remembered her words. *If anyone gets to kill Voracity, it's me.*

Brierly reached out a trembling hand toward Voracity. The ill-intention-ometer was going off again.

Once again Voracity seemed to sense its magic. She whirled on Brierly. Arpien heard the smile in her voice. "So you've decided to join me."

Brierly jerked, then froze. Dark snakes slithered around the shadows of the firelight. No, not snakes. Vines.

Why didn't Brierly run? Was she caught in some spell?

"This one is no longer yours," Voracity announced. To whom? She was not looking at Arpien.

No one could have expected an attack from the wounded brigand, where he huddled in pain at Voracity's feet. Several things happened at once. The brigand lunged toward Voracity and toppled her to her knees. The vines swirled in and snagged the brigand upward. They struck so quickly that Arpien could only see the rapidly shifting bites of firelight that silhouetted flailing human limbs and serpentine vines. There was the sound of snapping and choking and the angry rasp of half-dried leaves. The vines gave the brigand one final shake, like a child coming out of a tantrum and only now realizing his toy was broken. The vines dropped his limp body with a disdainful thump.

The horror of it so repulsed Arpien that it took him a moment to realize Brierly had vanished. Voracity noticed her absence a moment later. She spun in frustration. Her golden eyes raked the dark shelter of the trees. When she found nothing, she turned to Arpien. Fury bubbled under her quiet tones. "Bring him here."

The order might have been for the Grey Cloaks, but the vines obeyed more quickly. A thorn bit into Arpien's right ankle. Even as he struggled to kick it off a second vine seized his left ankle and knocked him off-balance. Dirt and hard knobby tree roots ground against his back as the briars dragged him toward the fire.

His eyes now at ground level, Arpien spotted the glimmering red jewel in the vademecum sword, half-hidden in deadfall. He twisted, snagged the sword, and sliced at the vines. As in the half-forgotten dream about the merfolk, the vademecum sword was not sharp enough to cut through the vines. However, it was more effective now than it had been against the briar thicket surrounding Estepel. The vines shriveled when the vademecum sword touched them. Yet the instant he broke the connection with one vine to swing at another, the first grew back. The number of vines multiplied around him.

Thus ends the tale of Arpien Trouvel, felled by flora.

"My merfolk said you carried a vademecum sword," Voracity said. "Arpien Trouvel, of all humans, chosen by a vademecum sword? But you have no real idea how to wield it, do you? The little boy is no more threat to me now than when he ran away from home nearly a year ago."

Arpien was too busy battling his personal hydra to reply.

"We can all see he's not fast enough, not strong enough, to defeat my briars. Does that worry you, princessling? But no, you told me yourself you didn't care if I killed him. So I will."

She was trying to draw Brierly out. "Brierly! Stay hidden!" Arpien shouted.

It was possible, Arpien discovered, to be both relieved and dismayed that Brierly listened to his advice for once. Maybe she had already fled on those Fleetsome Feet and was halfway back to Boxleyn. There was no response from the gloom of the trees.

Until an injured—or possibly lovesick—beast bellowed from the darkness. The underbrush rustled just once, but the groaning went on and on. Arpien recognized it for what it was at once—the ill-intention-ometer. Everyone else, from the Grey Cloaks to Voracity to the briars themselves, paused in stunned reaction at this unknown threat. Their distraction gave Arpien the moment he needed to escape.

The Grey Cloaks were after him in a second, but a second's lead was all he needed. Not only was he a fast runner, but by some miraculous misfortune the two Grey Cloaks nearest him tripped over themselves at the same time.

It was not hard to guess from the ill-intention-ometer's trajectory where Brierly must have launched it. He veered left and plucked Brierly from her hiding spot behind a decaying tree trunk.

"I sewed their cloaks together," she boasted as they ran.

Handy with Thread and Needle again. "Good job."

He fended off a blow from a third Grey Cloak. Brierly, for all her remarkable recovery of stamina after a century of atrophy, was slowing. Arpien seized her hand and towed her along.

Voracity shouted something indistinguishable and the forest exploded behind them. There was a noise of sucking air. A void tugged them backwards for an instant, and then broken tree limbs pummeled them from behind. Their bodies slammed to the ground, and then Arpien dragged Brierly up by the hand again. He blinked dizzying lights from his vision as they stumbled forward.

Thorns and thistles, what kind of weapon was that?

His one consolation was that in attacking them with this strange new magic, Voracity had also eliminated the Grey Cloaks in closest pursuit. Even so, Arpien and Brierly did not stop running until they reached the fence around Boxleyn. Arpien assisted his lady over the fence with a courtly shove to the backside. Only as the horses pounded within a hundred yards of the stables did his reason catch back up with his body.

Windried leapt clean over the fence that enclosed the paddock by the Boxleyn stables. Arpien reined her in with sudden steel, determined to get control of them both. Neef landed behind him with an equine glare.

His woven mane was unraveling at the ends like a tattered fishing net. Riders and horses sweated and eyed each other. They'd narrowly escaped danger, but none fully comprehended what that danger was.

At least Arpien didn't and he doubted the horses did. Arpien had seen many of Consulan's Sitral's magical weapons, but none like that. Had Brierly? How much did she truly know about Voracity? Once again Brierly had alternately imperiled him and saved him. Would he ever fully know her motives or feelings?

He was glad for the moments he panted for breath, for it excused him from speaking. Brierly, not in as solid shape as he was, took longer to recover. Arpien watched her breathing slow and her fatigued muscles ease their shuddering.

"Back in the forest," he said at length, "Consulan Sitral said you'd told her you didn't care if she killed me."

She went still.

"Is it true?"

She tossed her windblown hair over her shoulder. "True that I don't care or true that I told her I don't care?" The blasé expression was now firmly back in place. If she had deeper emotions, he would learn nothing more of them tonight.

Better ask a factual question. She might yet answer that. "Since we met at Estepel, how many times have you spoken to Voracity?"

"Twice."

"Once tonight and once—?"

"The day the party from Conquisan arrived at Boxleyn. I found her on the front steps of the palace right before she left."

Found her? Or sought her out?

No. Brierly would never voluntarily side with the fairy who Cursed her. Voracity must emanate some kind of poisonous perfume that drew her prey in. He'd seen the same reaction often enough in Conquisan. Consulan Sitral attracted allies by filling a need in each. With Cryndien, she assured him of his power and control by pretending obedience. Not loyalty, exactly. Bo was the one person Cryndien trusted. It was the Conquisani way for loyalty to transfer to whoever currently had the most strength and power. Oh, titles were passed down according to law, but the office of king had never guaranteed its holder was the true ruler of Conquisan. Look at Great Grandfather Herren, his political influence neatly siphoned off with each passing decade. Cryndien would never be so foolish as to believe Consulan Sitral offered her services out of affection. But he would believe he could retain her as an ally so long as their partnership remained mutually beneficial.

If Arpien went to Cryndien now, would his brother rein Voracity in or encourage her further?

Brierly had aided Arpien now multiple times, both physically and politically, with her unconventional techniques. "What do you think I should do?" he said.

"Wash up. Or all Boxleyn will think you've been tromping through the forest in the middle of the night. As I suppose Sir Flatwhist does." She nodded toward a darkened figure, which paused statue-still in the doorway to the stables.

Arpien squinted. It well could be Sir Flatwhist. He had the build, even the trace of a Strandish goatee. Brierly's eyes were as sharp as her ears. Only the barest hint of dawn lightened the sky, that pale pink color of medium-rare meat.

"What's he doing here?" Arpien said.

"Might as well ride over and ask him. No doubt he wants to know the same of us."

Arpien kicked Windried forward. "Sir Flatwhist."

"I am to carry a message for Lord Culmney as far as Gunnysmith this morning," Sir Flatwhist said. "But I see I have not gotten the earliest start." The knight's watchful eyes shifted from Arpien to Brierly, who rode up behind.

Belatedly it occurred to Arpien the implication of late night adventures with an unescorted and very fair maiden. He could only hope Flatwhist would hold his tongue. "I advise you, do not ride out alone. There is danger beyond the fence."

"What kind of danger?"

"We have seen a man murdered tonight. The details I must discuss with others first."

"Who?" A tinge of alarm crept into Flatwhist's voice.

Brierly yawned. "None but a common brigand, I assure you. There is no reason you would care for the life of such a man."

Arpien had never heard Brierly actually disparage a lower class, even a criminal one. She was usually indifferent to class distinction. Sir Flatwhist stared at her.

Arpien leapt to intervene. "Even a brigand is a man, and we must investigate his death. I must speak to the king." He did not say which one. He had not decided yet.

Or had he? As they parted and Arpien and Brierly stabled the horses, Arpien realized his decision was made. They had been seen. For Brierly's reputation, as well as his own, he would have to admit the purpose of their investigations. Ironically, while Brierly had not helped him reach a decision, Sir Flatwhist had. The clear impulse of his conscience was that he could not allow the man to ride unaware into danger when a word from him might save his life. How could he do less for the Rosarians?

He saw Brierly back to Nissa's chambers, then struck out for Cryndien's.

24
Arpien

Seizing Cryndien's shoulder and shaking him awake was only slightly less dangerous than seizing an electric tree eel and shaking it by the tail. Bo warned Arpien of this. Bo had growled when Arpien woke him from his own slumber in a wooden chair in Cryndien's outer parlor. He always slept where intruders would have to pass him first to get to Cryndien. Arpien, his fear driving his anger, was in no mood to listen to caution, and Bo was cranky enough to allow Arpien to get stung.

Arpien had barely tapped Cryndien's shoulder when he found himself slammed against a bedpost. The cool flat of a blade pressed against his throat. His brother's reactions of self-defense were as lightning-like as the rest of him.

Bo brought a lit candle into the room. "Kill him for waking you if you want, Cryndien, but first wake up enough to see who you're killing."

For a moment Cryndien resembled nothing so much as an ordinary young boy roused from a bad dream. Bo's casual tone cleared the muzzy look from Cryndien's eyes. Cryndien eased the knife away, all sneering superiority and thunder again. "I told you, Bo, no puppies allowed in my chambers. They make noise and pee on the rug."

Arpien fought the urge to rub the lingering sensation of cold steel from his windpipe. "I am not surprised you tried to kill me, Cryndien. Your own men spent half the night in the attempt."

Cryndien rubbed his eyes. "If you're going to ruin my sleep, Fumbleshanks, you better say what you mean."

So he did. Admitted more than he might have about his suspicions and near-failure to escape last night, in the hope that his own indignation and horror would stir the same emotions in Cryndien. He wanted reassurance

Consulan Sitral was acting independently, wanted Cryndien to at last see her for who she was. But Cryndien's bored yawns at Arpien's predictions of danger rivaled Brierly's.

"You mean to tell me, Fumbleshanks, that you shocked me out of sleep in the middle of the night with the startling discovery that Sitral is a fairy?" Cryndien scratched the duct of his eye again. He examined a speck of morning sand on his finger, then flicked it off. "I'd have to be an idiot or a Rosarian not to have noticed. Mind, those words are virtually interchangeable."

"It's not just that she's a fairy. She's *Voracity*, Cryndien. The same fairy who Cursed Brierly, ruined the marriage treaty, and caused another century of animosity between Conquisan and Rosaria."

Cryndien slashed the air with his hand. "Never say that aloud again. 'Ruined the marriage treaty'? That treaty is our best claim to Sentre Forest. Invalidate that and we'll have to fall back on this half-a-kingdom-for-rescuing-the-princess tradition." He raked his rumpled hair. His fingers left red-gold furrows. "Although if you did marry Princess Peerless, there'd be no way Emol could claim the marriage contract was unfulfilled. What does it matter if it's you instead of Herren? You're both Conquisani princes."

"You're forgetting," Arpien said between his teeth, "I intend to rule Sentre Forest as its own kingdom, wholly apart from Conquisan or any country that would be guided by the fairy who tried to murder my future wife."

"I am not guided by Sitral any more than you are guided by a pair of fire tongs or a hammer or a sword."

"Then why did you make her a consulan? She's dangerous, Cryndien."

"You don't avoid learning to use a sword just because it's sharp. It's precisely because she's a fairy that she's useful. She has access to weaponry I could never obtain on my own."

"Then you know about the—the tornado seeds."

Cryndien ruffled Arpien's hair with a rough hand. Arpien had to steel his neck so his head didn't dunk under the force.

"Tornado seeds? Aw, Fumbleshanks, that's adorable. I ought to let you name all Sitral's weapons. I can't pronounce the fairy terms for her magic at all. She calls your tornado seeds *bishlongya* or some such word." He worked his jaw. "It seems to require anatomy besides the human tongue."

"I cannot allow you to use such an inhuman weapon against Rosaria. I will go to King Emol."

"Tell him." Cryndien flourished his right hand in the *Sideways Extension Bow of Invitation to Adjourn to Other Business or Snacks.* "Tell them all there's a nasty fairy with great nasty fairy weapons out in the woods. Like I said, idiots and Rosarians."

"You mean to start another war between Conquisan and Rosaria."

Arpien glanced at Bo for confirmation, denial, anything to help him comprehend that his fears were real. Bo stood at the doorway, in his guard's pose. His arms hung loosely at his sides in that deceptively casual way, when in reality he could draw a wide assortment of weapons hidden on his person at a breath. And he wore his guard's face, observing but not commenting.

Bo couldn't approve of this.

Could he?

But Bo had long been Cryndien's dark mirror, a blurred, unreadable reflection.

And it was Bo who commanded the Grey Cloaks.

Cryndien drew his attention back. "Only if they don't give us what's rightfully ours."

"That doesn't justify the potential loss of so many lives. It doesn't justify the Strandish you've already killed."

Cryndien rubbed his chin. The stubble rasped under his hand. "Killing Strandish? Now that one is imaginative."

"You've been paying brigands to destroy the mantiz eggs."

"I've been making Sentre Forest less lucrative to our competitors. Hardly the same thing."

"All this while I thought you were allowing Consulan Sitral to abuse her power. Now I see you've been encouraging it."

"Maybe your real issue is you're intolerant of fairies."

"I wouldn't trust her if she were a fuzzy kitten. Besides, you can't say I'm intolerant of fairies when I respect Gowsma, Brierly's godmother."

"Ah, the 'good' fairy? Gowsma's only 'good' here in Rosaria because she's on their side."

"No, she's on the Prince's side."

Cryndien rolled his eyes. "Really, Arpien. Power is power. I can't believe you, a prince of Conquisan, my own brother, are still trying to decide whose side you are on. Conquisan needs Sentre Forest. If we don't have hittal wood, we can't build ships that will reach our farthest trading partners. Our economy will suffer. We'll lose our grip on our colonies. Our enemies will see our weakness and seize our assets."

"If Strand doesn't have access to Sentre Forest, they will die of tree-plague."

"Unfortunate, but neither of us is Strandish."

"You are so selfish."

Cryndien rounded on him. "You think I never felt like abandoning the weight of my crown to go slay dragons and chase pretty women? I have put Conquisan first, my entire life. You never lived with the kind of pressure father put on me, Arpien. Perhaps if you had you wouldn't have grown up so selfish. So Strand is facing a plague. I'm sorry for them but I'm not king of Strand. I have my own people to think of. As your king I am giving you two choices. You can marry Princess Peerless and turn control of Sentre Forest over to me. Or you can go home and quit confusing negotiations with Rosaria."

"And if Emol decides not to give Sentre Forest to you?" Arpien meant the question to sound defiant. At best, it sounded hypothetical.

"Then you will stand back and let me persuade him by whatever means I deem appropriate." Cryndien beamed with sudden charisma and thumped Arpien on the back. "Come, let's be friends, brother. Why can't you be more like Bo? He always agrees with me."

No, Bo always obeys you.

Arpien left because he couldn't bring himself to argue further. Not now, when he felt like a six-year-old next to Cryndien's power and certainty. What if Cryndien were right? What if Nissa were right? What if in his attempts to become a hero, he had only managed to become a traitor to his own country?

Yet whether or not he won his lady's heart, duty would not allow him to leave now. Rescuing a fair damsel came with certain obligations. The first was that you did not leave her in worse circumstances than you found her. How easy it would be for Emol to lock her up as mad, for either king to eliminate her. Suppose Arpien convinced her to leave Boxleyn and any hope of ruling Sentre Forest. Would she be any safer outside of Boxleyn? Whatever human threat Boxleyn held, it kept Brierly safe from evil fairies, at least so long as none of the Rosarian royal line invited Voracity into the palace. Brierly was by no means helpless, but she never seemed to take any threat seriously.

His stomach churned as though he'd swallowed the ill-intention-ometer.

25

Nissa

Nissa intended to wait up with Brierly for Arpien's return. Her vigil fell pathetically short as Brierly hummed in the parlor chair opposite her. The impossibly beautiful notes wove a blanket of sleep around her. With Brierly's Fleetsome Feet, Nissa never heard her friend leave, but she woke in the early hours and noticed her absence.

Nissa threw a chunky shawl around yesterday's sleep-rumpled gown and checked the likely Brierly burrows: whistling with pigeons on the roof, holding loud conversations with Squeezie through the door to the queen's chambers (Aunt Perturbance suspected Brierly was the reason Squeezie yapped unstoppably at the door in the wee hours, but she'd never been able to catch her), or visiting the horses in the stables. Brierly wasn't in the stables, but all three horses were, which meant Arpien was back. Probably Brierly as well, for both Windried and Neef were damp with recent exertion. Nissa wasn't surprised Brierly had refused to be left out of anything dangerous, but Nissa was sheepish she'd stayed behind. She wondered if Fearless felt the same way.

Nissa returned to her own chambers to find Brierly snoozing with conviction, head buried under a down pillow. Nissa forced a few grudging and unhelpful comments from Brierly before the Sleeping Beauty reenacted her name again.

Arpien arrived, perturbed and disheveled. His back was smeared with dirt and twigs. The secondhand prince was hard on clothes. "What did Brierly tell you?" he said.

"Nothing coherent. She went right to bed."

A defiant snore from the other room reiterated the point.

Arpien guided Nissa to one of the parlor chairs, but she popped up again. "Arpien, what happened?"

"Consulan Sitral—Voracity—is outside the gate."

Only when Nissa heard the high-pitched squeak of a chair leg skidding against floorboards did she realize her knees had given out. She had flopped onto the stuffed blue armchair behind her.

The reality of swooning was nothing so graceful as her rehearsals.

"Voracity can't get in, can she? Brierly will be safe as long as she stays inside Boxleyn, right?"

"Not every threat requires an invitation." He told her about the Grey Cloaks, the murdered brigand, the thorns, and a threat she couldn't visualize, something he called tornado seeds.

Nissa worried her right hand around her left pointer finger. "We have to warn my family."

"Why would they believe me? I'm Conquisani."

"Timothy listens to me. I'll go with you."

Timothy listened to them both with a forbearance that denied his likely annoyance at being dragged outside the gate before breakfast. Breakfast was a Montaine family virtue.

Regardless of fairy involvement, a murder so close to Boxleyn called for immediate investigation. Timothy took with them a guard of two dozen men.

Though Nissa saw nothing to distinguish one trail from any other, Arpien retraced his steps to the clearing. Nothing remained but an unnaturally perfect ten-foot circle of singed woodchips. Every sapling, every fern, every fallen log within that circumference had been sawed off at exactly the same height, about a foot from the forest floor. Barren stumps and stems poked up from the scarred deadfall like boney fingers grasping their way out of their graves. Even Timothy's rationalized explanations were dented a bit by the eeriness of it.

Into the nervous silence broke an unearthly wail. Several of the guards drew their swords. One even whispered, "Prince save us." Even in Rosaria a man was allowed his superstitions when faced with the hair-raising.

It was Nissa who first stepped forward to investigate the sound.

Timothy laid a restraining hand on her shoulder.

"It's only my ill-intention-ometer," she said.

Arpien drew the vademecum sword. "Yes, but Nissa—*it's going off.*" He poked the sword into the cluster of ferns some five paces away and fished out the clunky necklace. He whacked it three times against a tree trunk. The guards rumbled low relieved laughter into the ensuing silence, like a retreating storm. Only Nissa noticed how tightly Arpien clenched the ill-intention-ometer in his hand, as though to disguise the vibrations.

Timothy kept a protective hand on her shoulder. "Nissa, what in the name of reason is that thing?"

Her explanation made the guards taunt each other. It was no supernatural thing, of course not, just one of Lady Nissa's eccentric artifacts. Arpien did not relax, nor did Timothy.

Timothy remained cordial as they returned to Boxleyn and as he dismissed the guards to their other duties. He thanked Arpien for his concern and told him he would handle it from here, but his brotherly hand kept Nissa from following Arpien. Timothy steered her into the privacy of the Reception Room.

"What are we going to do?" she said.

"Nothing."

"You saw the evidence. Voracity's back."

"Yes, let's talk about the evidence." He flicked off each item on his beefy fingers. "There was no dead body, no troop of assassins, no thorns, no fairy, nothing to support his story."

"There was the circle of destroyed woodland."

"Which any average mortal with a handsaw and a torch could have constructed."

"Why would anyone do that?"

"Maybe to draw the Rosarian royal line out of the walls of Boxleyn and into a trap?" He fixed her with a tutor's gaze. "How well do you really know Arpien Trouvel, Nissa?"

He never took that tone with her, Aunt Perturbance's tone.

"Arpien wouldn't trap us."

"You've known him for three, four weeks? How many generations of Conquisani have tried to swindle us out of Sentre Forest? Fact: Cryndien wants Sentre Forest. Fact: Arpien is his brother."

"Arpien doesn't even like his brother."

"So he told you. I've thought this could be some twisted Conquisani plot from the moment Arpien arrived with that daft beauty. Someone is exploiting your love of the old superstitions."

"Superstitions!"

"Think, Nissa. A passing blonde claims to be the Sleeping Beauty, you let her in. A bunch of Conquisani nobles claim to have a legendary magic device—the invisibility box or what have you—you let them in. Arpien claims to see fairies—you wander out blindly to meet them. If I were a Conquisani, I'd manipulate the most gullible link to the Rosarian royal line, too."

Nissa had been scolded and laughed at a hundred times before for clinging to the old tales, but never by someone she respected so much. Warmth streamed down her right cheek. Timothy wiped her cheek with a gentle thumb that belied his frown. "Nissa, you know I didn't say this to hurt you."

"You said"—her throat felt tight as a rag wrung in the hands of the laundress—"you said I'm going to bring down Boxleyn with my stupidity."

"I do not think you're stupid. Naïve, perhaps. Not the same thing at all. You're a very smart young girl."

She sniffed. "I'm not a child." How would she ever prove that if she cried like one?

Timothy produced a square of linen from inside his sleeve. "Really, you women know how to make a man feel a right scoundrel."

The linen looked less than pristine, but she needed to blow her nose. "I wasn't trying to manipulate you."

He tapped his knuckle under her chin. "I know you weren't, duck. Whatever you believe, you believe with unwavering sincerity."

"Timothy, if Voracity really is out there, isn't it just as blind to deny the old tales as to believe them blindly?"

He considered her, all red-eyed and runny-nosed as she must be, and nodded. "All right, then. Prove your argument."

That afternoon Nissa armed herself with the strongest weapons from her stockpile of books and went to convince her family. She took first aim at Uncle Emol. "The—the old tales say—"

"Speak up, girl." Uncle said. The perfect black curls of his beard were too well-oiled, too well-behaved, to even sway when he snapped his jaw shut.

"The old tales say evil fairies have great power, especially if they can trick humans into dealing with them. If Voracity is bargaining with King Cryndien, you—you have to consider that the threat she poses could be worse than any army King Cryndien could muster by himself. After all, she would have murdered Brierly if Gowsma hadn't altered the spell."

Uncle Emol's response was typical. "There are no such things as fairies."

"Then what was Gowsma?"

"An exceptionally old and ornery human. If you want to defend your country, you could use your position with the youngest Conquisani prince to learn their plot against us instead of reading fairy stories."

Nissa tried to gesture, but her fingers were caught between the pages of the book. "But these aren't made-up stories. Look, I can show you three different examples of the tale of—"

By the time she flipped to the passages, Uncle Emol was gone. Her other family members vanished just as quickly when she tried to convince them.

Eusar ruffled her hair as he left, but was "too busy for that right now, Nissa."

Aunt Perturbance took Nissa's insistence she listen to the old tales as an insult to her child-rearing skills. "You're such a child. Grow up."

It didn't aid her argument that no magical attacks came as Nissa warned. In the end the only one who was convinced of anything was Nissa. She now saw she was too small to be taken seriously. To drive the point home, she kept dreaming that she was Thumbelina—no doubt a result of her excessive exposure to the old tales. In her dreams she was no bigger than a thumb. The giants around her ignored her squeaky warnings. Uncle Emol stepped on her. Brierly watched Nissa's performance as though Nissa were an incompetent minstrel, then drifted off to sleep. Cuz caught Nissa in a mousetrap. The lapdogs, who given her reduced stature seemed like great lions, snarled and chased her around the room.

Nissa could not silence her insecurities entirely, but she found that they usually didn't follow her into the library. There she could lose herself in the wonder of the old tales and forget she was small, plain, easily-ignored Nissa Montaine. What a fearless believer she was when she faced no opposition.

She wasn't imagining it all, just swept away in a good story, was she?

If she kept researching, maybe she could find that one irrefutable passage that would win over her family and Brierly. Maybe she would find reference to a secret weapon that would protect Rosaria from Voracity.

They already had a vademecum sword and an ill-intention-ometer. Arpien claimed the vademecum sword had a mind of its own. The ill-intention-ometer seemed to work, but Brierly refused to wear it.

"If you think it's so grand, you wear it," Brierly had told Arpien in one of their many arguments about it.

"It's for your protection."

"I don't take orders from princes," she said.

Arpien threw his hands in the air and grumped in unprincely terms for Nissa to explain it to her.

The best compromise Nissa could see was that she wear it herself, and accompany Brierly whenever she left Boxleyn Palace. As a result she spent a lot of time dragging books on top of roofs and beneath trees, so she could read while Brierly visited with birds and squirrels. (The local squirrel population, Brierly insisted, was in political upheaval and needed her constant counsel to avoid any more tail-tweakings.) In fact, Brierly spent far more time addressing animal politics than human politics.

Nissa was immersed in the tale of *The Forging of the Vademecum Swords* when a long string of chittering broke her focus. Nissa was glad she didn't speak Squirrel. The tone indicated some juicy profanity. She glanced up from the book. General Bo, Arpien's brother, strolled across the lawn.

No, *strolled* wasn't the right word. *Strolled* implied *casual,* and no one planned casualness so thoroughly as the Trouvel brothers. Bo watched her as he passed. The ill-intention-ometer rattled against her leg, but the squirrels might have triggered it. Should she grab Brierly and walk away? But that was stupid; Bo wasn't attacking. So she gave him a respectful nod. The General frowned, ripped his gaze forward and walked on.

"Do you think he was carrying word to Voracity outside the gate?" Nissa asked Brierly.

"I agree. The punishment for flinging an acorn ought to be harsher than the punishment for flinging a flower seed. Acorns have pointier ends." It took Brierly a moment to come out of squirrel mediation. She blinked and turned to Nissa. "Who?"

"General Bo."

Hadn't Brierly seen him? He'd come within five yards of them.

"If he was, I don't know what we can do about it," Brierly said.

It was the opening Nissa had been waiting for. Nissa turned the pages of her book to the passage she'd carefully marked days before. "You can stop Voracity, Brierly. It's just like it predicts in the old tales."

"You know I can't read." Brierly glanced down at the book, but her eyes refused to focus. The same way Cuz managed not to see wadded-up laundry. Such things existed only for other people. Laundry for the laundress, books for Nissa.

So Nissa read it aloud. "An evil fairy will gain control over the Prince's lands. Only a Steward can stop her. Only a Steward can call the Prince back."

"I think it's talking about the Prince of Here and There," Nissa said, her eyes on Brierly's bored ones. Bored but absolutely still. "They say he once ruled all the lands. The evil fairy must be Voracity."

Brierly gave that dainty "hm" of bland fascination.

"You're the last Steward."

"I can't summon the Prince."

"You could try."

"I have tried," she snapped.

Nissa started. Brierly never snapped.

"You think I don't know that prophecy? I was raised with it. How else do you explain to a child that she's under a Curse, so she must never ever touch any spinning wheels? Of course I asked why Voracity would hate me so much as to condemn me to death at my own christening. So my parents showed me the prophecy. It didn't necessarily mean me. It could have meant one of my parents."

"You are the last Steward. It has to be you."

"Do you know how many times I've called out to the Prince to save me?" Brierly pushed down on one of the tree's lower limbs so hard it started to crack. Did she notice? "My parents and godparents were always talking about how good the Prince was, how he came to the kingdom in times of need. So after I pricked my finger, I was certain he'd come. Maybe scare me a bit as punishment for disobeying my parents about the spindle. But I knew he'd come. Then I thought, he's waiting for me to play along with Gowsma's christening Gift. I should be asking for him to send my true love to my tower. I remember the first prince who came for me. Herren, of course. I leapt up into his arms and we both cried.

Bluebirds circled overhead. Sunlight burst from behind the clouds." Brierly shook her head. "At the gate of Estepel a dragon ate him."

The limb made a snapping sound and Brierly released it. "My rescuers didn't all look like Herren. But they did all fail. Geoffrey was trampled by his horse. Hubert fell into a moat of lava. Kendar lost all his skin and bled to death. A few of them rescued me and then killed me. Or worse."

Nissa didn't ask what *or worse* was. "Brierly, I'm so sorry."

She rolled a shoulder. "It doesn't matter. I'm only bringing it up to point out that the Prince is no use to us. Either those rescuers were from Voracity, and the Prince was too weak to stop them, or the Prince sent them himself, which makes him just as bad as Voracity. And our final option—the Prince doesn't exist at all."

"But Brierly, the Prince did send a rescuer to wake you."

"Arpien?" Brierly sighed. Nissa didn't know whether to read it as disappointment or affection.

"You still don't want to believe you're awake."

"I believe in self-reliance. You're sweet, Nissa, but you're going to disappear, too. It will be as though we never had this conversation. Which maybe we aren't." A faraway, fierce look blazed in her eye. "There are only two of us."

Did she mean Voracity? Nissa had never been overlooked in quite this way. She could tell Brierly liked her. But as long as Brierly believed she was dreaming, the bonds of friendship were nothing compared to the power Voracity had over Brierly. In this moment Brierly was once more a figure of legend. The artist in Nissa wanted to capture that image of the heroine gazing to the horizon, to that inevitable, final confrontation with her doom. She was beautiful and brave and impossibly larger than life.

"You're going to go after her, aren't you?" Nissa said.

Brierly was silent a long time. "Why would I do that?" She fingered a tendril of hair back behind her ear.

That tiny, childlike gesture shrank Brierly back down to just somebody in need of a friend. *Because you're so lonely hatred resembles love. Because in some strange way you need her, or at least you think you do.*

"You sought Voracity out last week," Nissa said.

Brierly turned to Nissa, as though the comment brought Nissa into existence again. "That was the first time I'd seen her in—I don't know—decades."

"Doesn't that prove that something's different? If she's scared enough to come here in person, maybe that means you're awake."

"It means she's playing with me."

"Try just one more time, Brierly. Call the Prince back."

Brierly studied Nissa with grey eyes, the color of an empty sea. "Whose voice are you? The Prince's? Voracity's? My own? Or are they all three the same?"

"I am my own voice," Nissa said. "But I don't know how to convince you of that."

Still, this was the longest speech Nissa had ever heard Brierly give. She tried to draw encouragement from that, even as her heart ached for her friend.

Nissa closed the book. "Let's go riding."

26

Arpien

As Arpien expected, Cryndien's deadly pranks started within a few days of their confrontation with Voracity in the woods. Arpien had been on edge since his brother appeared, which Cryndien would enjoy as much as the trap itself.

The purpose of Cryndien's games, he always claimed, was not to kill, but to teach.

And Arpien had to learn his place.

The first was a wire stretched across his doorway went he went to bed. Only the tiny gleam of reflected candlelight against the thread-thin wire saved him from cutting his own leg off at the ankle. He stopped his forward momentum by shoving against the doorframe. His Tail would think him paranoid, but Arpien knew what razor wire could do. Cryndien's Grey Cloaks could behead a man with a quick jerk of a noose made of the wire.

He didn't sleep well that night. What little sleep he did catch was tortured by the same nightmare he'd been having since his brothers arrived. The characters and setting varied, but the plot was always the same. Someone was in trouble—Brierly, Nissa, Kirren, Cuz, even Fearless. It was up to Arpien to save them, but something always went wrong with his rescue. His sword turned into a fish. His rope wasn't long enough. The scent of flowers paralyzed him. He heard people laughing at him— Brierly, Cryndien, a woman whose rich laughter sounded familiar but he never saw. Consulan Sitral?

You're powerless. You play the hero but that's all you're doing—playing.

Failure in his dreams made him all the more resolute to be the hero when he was awake. But it was hard to be a hero when his damsel didn't want to be saved. She said she was fond of Sentre Forest, but she didn't seem to care enough to do the politicking necessary to defend her interests. She said she'd rather take etiquette lessons from Queen Perturbance than wear the ill-intention-ometer.

Short on sleep and with visions of loss upbraiding his nerves, he snarled at Brierly with a vocabulary wider in scope than even Nissa had guessed. Why couldn't Brierly listen to reason?

Nissa's expressive brow told him this was not a method the old romances recommended for winning the heart of a fair maid. It was hard to schedule time to properly woo a lady in between political maneuverings and assassination attempts. It was more than a week after his brothers arrived at Boxleyn that Arpien found time to complete any more romantic objectives.

He found Brierly on the open-air fifth floor of Boxleyn Palace. Boxleyn Palace was a pretentious building, large but squat, much like its rulers. It had been built during a transition of architectural fashion, so while it was blocky and wide, according to modern tastes, it also sported two old-fashioned towers that perked from the flat roof like donkey's ears. The towers were too ornamental to be a true sign of the past. They also were squat and square, with too many corners to survive a siege. But then, sieges were out of vogue as well. To discourage her guests from visiting the roof for a closer look at the unsightly towers, Queen Perturbance remodeled them from centerpieces to storage areas. The east tower housed the secondary library, where inconvenient books and nieces were stowed.

The real deterrent to visitors, Arpien thought, was the statues perched on the hip-height wall that enclosed the perimeter of the roof. Not gods or gargoyles, these, but important Montaines. They, too, were square, squat, and pretentious. Arpien couldn't decide if the artist had done his job poorly or too accurately. The Montaines had never been great adventurers or generals, but rather speakers, traders, and hunters. The hunters inspired exciting poses, but men with money in their hands or women with their mouths hanging open did not.

Brierly sat cross-legged on the roof ledge, a spotted pigeon perched on each knee. The birds flapped and fussed at each other. Brierly interfered with an occasional, "She does have a point." The birds jerked their heads sideways and took in her interjections with round eyes.

"What are they saying?" Arpien said.

His approach hadn't taken her by surprise, but his comment seemed to. "Home décor."

"What?"

"They're arguing about their nest. She says they won't have enough room for a three-egg family. He says she should have thought of that when they moved in, and she'll just have to wait until next spring if she wants more space."

A grin worked at the side of his mouth. "Sounds like an argument my old nurse and her husband would have."

A tiny grin tugged at her own mouth. "You don't believe me? Now there's a twist."

Arpien had been the subject of enough mockery in his life that it took a moment to define this as teasing, not insult, and a further moment to appreciate the irony of her statement. He wanted so badly for her to believe she was awake that it didn't occur to him how pushy he must seem to her. Three reactions flashed through him. The first was defensive. He was only pushing her toward truth. The second was chagrin. Had he imagined she had nothing of value to teach him? What finally burst out of his mouth, triggered by her own wry amusement, was a long chain of chuckles. Brierly's eyes widened a fraction and that small grin fought harder at the corners of those sweet lips.

Arpien leaned against the ledge on the opposite side of the atrocious statue of some long dead Montaine. "What else do animals talk about?"

Brierly's explanations were sometimes funny, sometimes profound, and he asked all manner of questions about the minutiae of animal life he'd never thought to consider. Brierly wasn't so hard to talk to as he thought.

Brierly's understanding of animal relations was comprehensive. It was possible to forget she was talking about animals, and hear her instead as a brilliant diplomat. At least until she interjected clearly animal issues like prey/predator relations into the conversation. Brierly spoke not with her Charm, but not her usual blasé manner either. She was … sincere. Arpien had long imagined the discussions they'd share about their forest. This was just as pleasant as he'd dreamed, but different. Her love of Sentre Forest opened his eyes to a world both alien and wild.

"I was right. You are destined to be the perfect Queen of Sentre Forest."

The spark in her eye snuffed out.

Thistles. Arpien tried to recapture the moment of connection by doing what he'd come up here to do in the first place.

"I have the answer to your conundrum," he said.

She arched one lovely brow.

"What makes something good?"

"Ah."

"Time," he said. "Only time can tell if a decision was a good one or bad one. If by lowering taxes you aided the people or left the public coffers empty in a time of need. That's why it's important to study history, so you can tell what steps made the tyrant the tyrant, and avoid those mistakes. It's why heroic epics are important, to lift up what was glorious from the past as a beacon for our future. Whatever the present cost, does a choice bring more happiness or suffering in the end? Only time can tell."

This time both her eyebrows raised, in what was either a shrug or approval.

He drew another of Cupid's arrows from his quiver. "I would be honored—nay, exalted—if you would accept a humble token of my radiant admiration for—"

He thought of Nissa's advice, paused mid-flourish, and thrust his hand out instead.

"This is for you."

"Oh. Thank you." She tucked his offering behind her ear, like a scribe would his quill.

"Did you see what it is?"

"A posby blossom."

"Count how many petals it has."

Brierly plucked the blossom from behind her ear. "Seven."

"Seven," Arpien repeated in triumph. He held up the appropriate number of fingers, like a child who had just learned to count so high.

"It's lovely."

"Most posby blossoms have five petals."

"I didn't realize you were a botanist."

"A bot—no, I just thought you'd like it."

Brierly stuck it back behind her ear. "It's lovely. Thank you."

Well, if that didn't squish the pits out of his roasted plums. How did you impress someone who habitually fought merfolk and swam through solid rock? She could open her mouth and sing exotic landscapes into existence. What was a seven-petaled flower compared to that?

27

Brierly

Huh. A rare flower and the answer to a riddle. Arpien had been talking to Nissa. Her innocent little friend was a scheming matchmaker.

Brierly didn't like playing to other people's scripts, even her favored figments'.

But that long conversation about animals hadn't seemed scripted. The Arpien she'd gotten to know was an odd mixture of pride and need for approval. Until today she'd never heard him laugh at himself. Scold himself, defend himself, boast about himself, yes, but not laugh. She had been both disappointed and relieved when he slipped back into his hero persona.

Brierly twirled the flower stem through her fingers and whistled a lilting tune. Her nurse Daertha had always said a seven-petaled posby blossom would grant you a wish. Brierly had found only two such blossoms in her life. The first time she had wished to travel outside Rosaria. Her over-protective parents seemed intent that she'd live out her life within ten miles of Estepel. That wish had taken until the age of nearly seventeen to come true.

Her second wish had been that her parents would let her have a pet gryphon.

It was that wish that proved the substandard success rate of seven-petaled posby blossoms.

She rose, and the movement sent the pigeons flapping back to their much-debated nest. Her Fleetsome Feet ensured she didn't need to watch her footing. She meandered down the ledge. If she fell, she'd just pop into another dream. Smashing into the stone walkway five stories below would be painful and inconvenient, but not irreversible.

She watched the posby flower circle end over end from pointer finger to pinky, and back again. An appropriate gift for her: pretty and useless. She windmilled her arms and twirled on the ledge. The flower baton slipped. She caught it, one inch of the stem jammed between her last two fingers. The blossom head quivered in the spring breeze. The scent of fresh posbies filled her nose, watered-down essence of lavender mixed with thyme.

She leapt down onto the roof and crossed to the tower she normally avoided: Nissa's library. She dug out the dustiest book she could find, pressed the flower into the center, and refiled it on the highest shelf. Let no one imagine she was keeping the flower for *his* sake.

She meant to lecture Nissa for playing matchmaker, but never got around to it. Scolding Nissa was like kicking a lapdog. Anyway, she and Nissa had better things to talk about. Not the Prince of Here and There. You couldn't stopper Nissa's excitement about her research for long, but wander off enough times during that topic and anyone would catch the hint. Almost anyone. Nor did they talk about Arpien. Nor Voracity, nor the prophecy. Brierly was not going to risk such exposure again.

Instead they spoke of fascinating nothings. What they would do if a star fell from the sky and they were to find it on the grounds of Boxleyn. Funny things that had happened at social functions. Brierly's ear for voices made her a lively imitator of people. Nissa was one of Brierly's sanest and most down-to-earth creations, but she had the most girlish giggle. To inspire it felt like some kind of personal reward. They invented a great number of ridiculous stories. Brierly guided the outlandish scenario with a serious expression, and Nissa interjected with clever improvements of her own.

Being with Nissa was comfortable and safe. Being with Arpien was the opposite. He attracted a series of increasingly nasty pranks. A missing step in a dimly lit stairway. A shard of broken glass in his water after sword practice. A rusty nail under Fearless' saddle. Luckily Fearless did not bolt, only winced and complained to Brierly, and the nail was quickly removed. That incident angered Arpien more than the other tricks, and Brierly liked him the better for coming to the defense of his horse.

At first she suspected Cuz, but Cuz's arsenal, though wet, sticky, and sometimes crawling, was not harmful. Besides, she had let Cuz know that he was not the only person in Boxleyn capable of mischief. In the days that followed their soaking, Brierly had arranged for Cuz to meet water buckets at three different doors. In the future he'd consider carefully whether it was worth embarrassing Nissa.

When the dangerous pranks started, she investigated to see if Cuz needed another lesson. She tracked him to the practice fields. Cuz swung a sword at Arpien with all the vigor in his sulky body. Until now she'd at least given the brat some credit for cunning, but to attack Arpien outright? To her surprise, Arpien allowed the attack to continue for some time before disarming the lad. Then he reviewed the bout with Cuz blow by blow, praising here, correcting there. Arpien dunked the boy's head for an impudent remark, and Cuz came up beaming.

Males made little sense in any world.

It was more than gender differences that baffled Brierly. Arpien had narrowly escaped humiliation the night of the singing duel, starting with Cuz's prank. Why then befriend the boy? Cuz was a Rosarian prince, but too young and too far down the line of succession to help Arpien advance in society. Why put aside that formidable pride to mentor a pest?

Some of the men on the practice field called out cheerful insults to Arpien, and he bantered back. But these were common soldiers. Brierly could see no political strategy in earning their goodwill. Gerret might have the highest connections of them all, and his only claim to power was that his sister Kendra served the king's niece.

The conundrum so puzzled Brierly that she observed Arpien unseen from a window above the practice yard the next day, and the next. When Arpien fought Cuz, he let Cuz know who was master, but he neither pampered nor humiliated the boy. When Cuz tired, the guards vied to see who would test Arpien's mettle. Brierly studied Arpien's form as he dueled (all for the sake of research), supple and muscular and confident. He was good. Too good to waste his time on a twelve-year-old of mediocre talent.

It was unlikely that a Conquisani prince should enjoy popularity in the middle of Boxleyn Palace. But she could see now why the guards and Cuz admired him. Skill with a blade was only part of it.

She spent four most satisfactory mornings watching her recurring prince exert himself on the practice field. Then Cryndien visited.

It was almost as bad as the night of the singing duel. Cryndien did not need to raise a sword to fight his younger brother (though that would have been a battle to keep the ladies talking for a month). One or two well-selected goads on Cryndien's part, laced with that booming charismatic laughter, were enough to turn the confident young warrior into a stilted young boy groping to prove himself. Arpien did not respond to his brother in words, but he steamed liked a salted boiled cabbage. Once he even dropped his sword. Yet there was a strange parallel here to Cuz. If Cryndien would have praised or even corrected Arpien with that same sincerity, would Arpien have glowed with the adulation of a twelve-year-old boy?

It was only when Cryndien strolled away that Brierly saw Bo trailing him. Why hadn't Bo intervened? Perhaps for the same reason Brierly hadn't. It was, in the end, Arpien's battle.

It also stirred her back to her senses. If she lingered over the practice field like a moony girl, Voracity would notice. If Brierly wanted to keep her pet figment intact, she had to stay away from him.

Yet it grew harder to do so. Every day he came by with more "evidence" to convince her she was really awake. She found myriad ways to interrupt the discourse. She arranged the furniture in a circle and played leapfrog around the room. She answered his arguments in rhyme. She trained a housefly to land on Arpien's nose every time he used the word "real."

"Pesky fly, that," she said.

After a month, Arpien still couldn't settle on whether to worship, rescue, or lecture her. Their relationship seemed built around a pedestal, and he constantly shifted which of the pair of them belonged atop it.

The easy companionship between Arpien and Nissa was unlucky, for it meant that when he came to visit Nissa, Brierly couldn't turn him out of the room. The couple of times she tried to wander off alone, Arpien rose with gentlemanly insistence that he escort her. Whoever was attacking him now increasingly turned to her. She'd acquired a number of self-appointed guard dogs: Arpien, Nissa, Kendra, Kendra's brother. Even with her Fleetsome Feet, it wasn't always easy to slip away. So Brierly stayed and lingered at the corners of their conversation, and more times than she liked to admit let it draw her in.

When Arpien forgot to act like a Rescuing Prince, Brierly forgot to treat him like one. Sometimes Brierly was well engaged in conversation with Arpien before she realized she had let her indifference slip. The moment either of them grew aware of the rapport, the spell was broken. She rearranged her indifference, and he rearranged his courtly rescuer demeanor. And Nissa leaned her chin on her fist and studied the pair of them as the reader speculates about the likelihood of a happy ending.

Brierly gave up telling her there would be no happy ending. Anyway, this "waking world" had profound drawbacks. She'd long ago given up any expectation of a reunion with her parents, but she liked to imagine that they were still out there ruling wisely, still loving her. In this dream they had wilted away in passive despair. Their country had all but forgotten their vision of friendship between Conquisan and Rosaria. Perturbance seemed to view Brierly as some baked-on scrap of food that required further soaking before she scoured the palace clean of the line of Stewards forever. Brierly didn't waste much time on Perturbance, other than purloining her lapdogs. But she resented this version of events, in which her parents had spent their whole lives in service to Rosaria, and their people didn't even acknowledge the gift.

Besides that, she had so little control over this dream. It was a depressing regression after years of torturous practice learning to create and destroy worlds with a thought. When others in Boxleyn Palace complained of disturbing dreams, Brierly looked forward to nighttime as a chance to experience that power again. She was a falling star. She was the number seven. She was abstract and mighty.

Yet when each dawn trapped Brierly back in Boxleyn Palace, her first thought wasn't always escape. More and more, her first thought was of how she could spend another day making Nissa giggle and flummoxing Arpien.

She didn't realize how disgustingly sentimental she was getting until the dream altered one of her mementos without her permission. There was a breath of frost in the spring air that day, so she grabbed the Conquisani cloak as she and Nissa left to go riding. Out of habit she didn't know she had developed, her fingers sought the frayed edges of the tear created the day she and Arpien had escaped Estepel.

Only the tear had been mended. She shook off a silly pang of disappointment and turned to Nissa with a tiny smile.

"Thank you, but you didn't have to do that. I kind of liked it the way it was."

Nissa cocked her head at her. Like Squeezie.

"My cloak. You mended it."

"No, I didn't."

Brierly widened her grin. "It's a magic cloak, that mends itself."

Nissa grinned back without belief. "Kendra must have done it. She'd mean it as a kindness." She touched the healed tear. "Although these don't look like her stitches."

Brierly was not acquainted with Kendra's handwork, but on closer inspection she had to agree. There was nothing wrong with the work—it was precise and sturdy—but it was also large and basic. A seamstress or tailor prided themselves on how many stitches would fit into an inch. Brierly's keen eyes caught tiny holes where the needle had punctured the wrong spots.

"Kendra," Nissa called into the next room, "Did you fix Princess Brierly's cloak for her?"

"No, my lady. Was I supposed to? I'm sorry."

"You did nothing wrong. Do you know who did mend it?"

Kendra's strawberry-blond head popped into the doorway. "You might ask Prince Arpien. He came by earlier to deliver it. Said Princess Brierly left it in the stables."

It was easy to picture the well-made, strong hands on the handle of a sword. But to picture those large fingers grasping a much smaller blade, a slender needle? Brierly arched an eyebrow at Nissa. "Another weapon from your romantic arsenal?"

It was as close as she came to a reprimand about Nissa's matchmaking, and even at such a mild scolding Nissa blushed. "Not this one. Where would he learn to sew?"

"All soldiers learn basic patching skills, in case they must repair a saddle or clothing out in the field."

Brierly traced the little holes and imagined the scene: Arpien frowned in concentration, aimed the needle, missed, aimed again. Such a picture of quiet patience did not fit at all with her notion of Arpien.

Nissa eyed her. Brierly flung the cloak around her shoulders. "Boredom is the mother of invention. Let's go."

During the trio's morning ride, Brierly studied Arpien from the corner of her eye whenever she thought she could get away with it. Arpien did resemble Herren. Or was her memory of Herren starting to resemble Arpien? You'd think that if Arpien wanted to repair clothing he'd start with his own. His only outfits were his midnight blue doublet and trunk hose and the ill-fitting formal attire he'd cobbled together from the Rosarian princes. She waited all morning for him to say something about her cloak, for some flourish and bow and sweeping presentation, but it never came.

Her fingers toyed with the new stitches. He knew she could fix her own clothes. She had left it undone because—because it was part of their story. She was glad these stitches were large. It would leave a neatly made-over scar in the cloak.

Only when her friend–the scheming matchmaker–tucked Brierly safely away in her chambers and left for the library did Brierly put her question to Kendra. "What ever happened to the set of blue clothes Arpien brought with him to Boxleyn?"

"Those poor things? They were beyond repair. Shredded in dozens of places. Such a shame. It's expensive material. Prince Arpien was kind enough to let me save it for trimming."

"Kendra, would you mind if—if I had a look at them?"

"For the gowns you're sewing for the Spring Ball? Certainly, Your Highness. That's just the sort of thing they ought to be used for."

Brierly spent the next half hour practicing her spider dialect with the resident of a web in Nissa's bedroom. They were interrupted by the arrival of dinner in the far corner of the web. As the spider wasn't much for mealtime conversation, Brierly wandered back to the sitting room.

Kendra had come and gone again. She'd left the requested items on a chair in the lap of one of Brierly's incomplete gowns. Brierly's Fine Ears picked up Kendra's slightly out-of-tune love song as she dusted the room across the hall. Brierly was never left completely without a nursemaid. As there was little theoretical difference between being alone and being minded by figments, she didn't bother to resent it this time.

So. Alone with Arpien's clothes. Strange, she felt shier at this moment than any she had spent with the man himself. She reprimanded herself: she had created both Arpien and his clothes. Shyness, like guilt, was an old and mildewed emotion. She snatched the clothes up and spread them across her lap for dispassionate examination.

One of Brierly's Gifts was the language of animals, but she also spoke the language of clothes. Oh, she did not talk to clothes (except in that one particularly odd dream a few decades back) but she could hear them whisper unspoken secrets. What young maid had lowered the neckline of her bodice a few stitches before going to the fair, then whipstitched it back up before returning home. The merchant's wife who dressed in finery to wait on patrons but underneath her skirts wore broken-in, scuffed shoes, since she'd be on her feet all day. Ugly clothes often had more character than sublime ones. Beauty of form and face was, at least in part, accident. But clothes were complete artifice. Every story they told was manmade.

Even in the days before the Cursed sleep took away her power to read and write, Brierly hadn't been one to record her thoughts in words. Oh, the improvised song here and there, yes, but her instrument of expression was not a pen, but a pin. What essence of character others might capture in quill and ink, she preserved in needle and thread. You never truly understood someone until you understood their clothes.

Which was perhaps why she'd never sewn anything for Arpien. She literally couldn't pin him down. She sewed hours for the ladies in the palace. Those designs were conceived in a burst of inspiration, and the ladies, like the designs, were as yet broad sketches, initial insights pushed to innovative extremes. It was when she got to know someone's complexities that she had to rip out seams and alter silhouettes to fit her changing perception.

Who or what was Arpien Trouvel?

Her fingers trailed across the folds and tears in Arpien's sleeves. She hadn't paid much attention to Arpien's rescuing outfit at the time of the rescue. After all, even given the interesting fashion implications, she had seen much weirder versions of Herren. She bit her lip on a smile as she remembered her first glimpse of Arpien in that outfit. The doffing of the cap, that ridiculous bow, starting his speech all over again. It was very Arpien to think to drag formal attire on an eight-month quest for the calculated purpose of looking the part when he finally reached its culmination.

It was also very Arpien to have his carefully laid plans thwarted. Look at the pitiful outfit now. Snags and rips up to eight inches long criss-crossed the deep blue material. Even as scrap, the fabric was valuable. But even after the servants had laundered it, here and there Brierly found the faintest stain of blood.

She retrieved her cloak from the peg by the door and laid the garments side by side. Her one rip, his dozens. Unsettling, long-forgotten feelings stirred in her veins yet again that day. Memories flashed before her of the race through the vicious thicket, interspersed with memories of that stupid egg breaking in the bucket. Did his body still bear scars from the thorns? She'd check next time she saw him. Um, then again no. That image unsettled her in an entirely different way.

He'd fixed her cloak; she supposed she ought to return the favor. With her unnatural Gift of being Handy with Needle and Thread, she could mend the doublet and trunk hose with stitches that would barely show. But rather than hide the damage to the garments, she opted to magnify it. She'd long thought that the patches were the most interesting part of Arpien.

From the scraps of fine material from other projects, she sorted out every shade of yellow she could find: the glossy color she thought of as Cryndien gold, but also burnished gold, old gold, saffron, sun yellow; and of all types of material—velvet, cotton, silk, linen. She folded back the frayed edges of each tear and finished the edges, then patched the opening from underneath with one of the yellow scraps. An array of golds shone from every scar of the midnight blue garments. The sleeves were especially dramatic, having taken the worst of the damage.

What were the slashes? Marks of the unraveling hero? Badges of honor? Hints of treasure under the exterior? Sometimes Art is best unexplained. Certainly she didn't want to explain it to Arpien or Nissa. Best let everyone think the outfit was still in the bottom of some scrap basket.

Which was, in the end, where she left it.

28

Arpien

If Cryndien ever truly resolved to see Arpien dead, only a miracle of quick reaction would save Arpien from the Grey Cloaks. The more stubborn Arpien's refusal to hand Sentre Forest over to Cryndien, the more serious the attacks grew. What could Arpien do, complain to King Emol? What did the Rosarian king care if the competitors for Sentre Forest killed each other off, so long as it didn't lower the profit he could get from Sentre Forest or get blood on the rugs?

Eusar promoted the rumors around Boxleyn that Arpien and Brierly were unfit to rule Sentre Forest. She was shallow and daft, he obsessive and paranoid. Some days Brierly fulfilled this description, and others she was as astute as she had been the night of the singing duel. Brierly's refusal to play by anyone's rules but her own meant that it was harder for Arpien to protect her when she too was targeted. How was Arpien to stop it? He was one man against a palace.

The Rosarians—save Nissa—seemed just as oblivious to danger as Brierly was. Arpien spent hours every day trying to win the favor of the old lords of Rosaria with his plans for Sentre Forest. He seemed to make some progress in that regard, but little in warning them about Voracity.

"There are no such things as evil fairies," most said.

Arpien couldn't tell if it was the concept of fairies or evil they found more objectionable.

"What about the Prince? What about Gowsma? You saw her yourself," he said.

"Exaggerations of natural phenomena."

His discussions did gain some supporters. What Arpien lacked in charisma he made up for in deliberation. His dual childhood hobbies had been planning princess-rescue-attempts and the management of Sentre Forest. He listened closely to the suggestions of the Rosarians who had experience living there. Some of the lords and ladies tired of the Montaines' obstinate incredulity. Those who lived in and around Sentre Forest had seen too many strange and marvelous creatures to dismiss the notion of fairies out of hand.

"It'd be nice to have this issue of Sentre Forest settled," one of the boldest of the lords admitted, well away from Emol's ears. "Things were always best when a Steward controlled Sentre Forest."

Emol's handling of Sentre Forest was the only major grudge the lords and ladies of Rosaria held against him. For all its self-importance and double-dealing, the House of Montaine had provided Rosaria with nearly a century of slow economic growth. Some of the Montaines were downright admirable. Timothy and Nissa had picked up the better traits of the line. But reliability and practicality rarely inspire ballads. It was Brierly who captured the underfed imagination of Boxleyn.

Brierly's bizarre Beauty attracted attention wherever she went. Her Charm gave her entrance into almost any part of Boxleyn society. More than one evening found Brierly hosting an illicit gathering of young nobles tired of the Boxleyn Box. Brierly entertained them with an array of jongleur's tricks. She finished couplets with amusing lines. She repeated back extensive musical selections. She imitated voices and mannerisms of people from Boxleyn. King Emol's Fool muttered that she made a better fool than he did. Even when Brierly tried to walk up a wall or wore shoes on her hands or dumped out a salt cellar to scrub her elbows in salt, only half of Boxleyn questioned her fitness to rule. The other half lauded her innovation. Even Arpien could not always tell when her eccentric behavior was incisive social commentary, and when it was a random spasm of a creative mind.

This, however, led him to the other thing that troubled him. When Brierly was at her most Charming and exuberant, he could sometimes read a hint of desperation in her exertions to entertain the crowd. She grew bored of herself before they did, and when she announced it, she was considered hilarious and witty. Brierly thrived on social events, yet sometimes Arpien saw an overlay of soul-weariness on Brierly's dazzling smile that chilled him. The face of indifference that she often wore with him and the face of Charm that she wore with the courtiers seemed equally cold. Was either the real Brierly?

She laughed at such questions. There was no one real Brierly any more than there was one real world. She developed a number of tricks to distract him when he presented his evidence that she was awake. That she adopted the simpleton act during his arguments he took as encouragement. She wouldn't try so hard to avoid the discussion unless she was worried it might persuade her.

He continued to seek out Brierly's company daily. She seemed immune to his compliments, but here and there she joined in a discussion with a sincerity that surprised and pleased him. While her insistence on living in the moment could be frustrating, it was also freeing. From the age of six, Arpien had spent his life trying to prove himself. The constant calculating fight to meet expectations was exhausting. Brierly didn't give a dried-up raisin what anyone else expected of her. It was not altogether a good trait—when one expected nothing of life it could hold neither disappointment nor hope. But for brief moments when they spoke together, they seemed to reach some middle ground. A place where her refusal to take things too seriously made him laugh at himself, and his intensity and drive sparked a rediscovery of her own lost sense of conviction. The comfortable rapport that flowed between them then was just enough to keep him from giving up on winning her, for he saw a glimpse of just how good they might be for each other. But he always managed to say something to ruin the moment.

Not that there was time for very many moments. Cryndien's attacks were coming daily now. There were a few guards within Boxleyn whom Arpien trusted to watch after Brierly when he wasn't there, Kendra's brother Gerret among them. A few traps Arpien didn't see until they sprang. More than once he had to push Brierly out of the path of a blade or grab her before she fell through a missing stair. Brierly never thanked him.

At least Nissa was willing to wear the ill-intention-ometer. Thank the Prince for Nissa in general. He quickly learned that while Nissa was fond of Brierly, she didn't want to hear Arpien praise Brierly's beauty endlessly. Nor did she show particular interest in hearing the details of Squalian naval tactics or Gibreltan wrestling matches he had observed in his travels. But Nissa was a useful source of information about magical devices and old tales. She roused in him an affection and protectiveness. It would be a lot less stressful to fall in love with Nissa than Brierly, but perhaps such easy company was only possible because they were not attracted to each other. She was more like a sister. And he was not the only one in Boxleyn to regard her as such.

Only for the other person the parallel was not so kind.

It was Nissa who drew his attention to it one night at supper. "Is your brother staring at you or me?"

Arpien turned to Cryndien, but Cryndien was absorbed in retelling some brave feat to his dinner partner. Oh. She meant Bo. It was easy to lose Bo in the edges of Cryndien's radiance.

Bo turned away when he saw them studying him, but not before Arpien saw his face. Bo was hard to read. It was one of the things that made him an effective bodyguard to the king. But Arpien knew his brother well enough to recognize that haunted look.

"You, I think," Arpien said to Nissa. "I imagine you remind him of Kirren."

"Kirren?"

"Our sister. She drowned when I was six. Bo was twelve and blamed himself for it. They were very close—only a year apart in age."

"Yes, I'm sorry, I remember now. You mentioned her the day you and Brierly arrived." She squirmed, which again increased her resemblance to his sister. "But you don't look at me like that."

"Like what?"

"Like—like I'm going to do something horrible to you personally."

"Well, I've had time to get to know you. I look at you, I see Nissa. He looks at you, he sees a ghost of Kirren."

"I thought you said I didn't look much like her."

"You don't, except for the dark hair. It's the mannerisms. And Kirren loved books too. She used to read to me by the hour. Bo would do the dragon voices." He had forgotten that, until now.

He nearly missed the trace of poison in his wine. An acridity so faint you didn't taste it; you felt it smirk in the back of your throat. If he hadn't tasted it before, his mouth would not have been sensitized to detect it. Cryndien had toasted him with poisoned wine on his seventeenth birthday, to celebrate his majority. Not enough to kill, but enough to make him vomit for hours. The palace blamed his illness on too much celebration. At least publicly.

Arpien spat his mouthful of wine across the table. He knocked Brierly's cup out of her hand and it too splattered the table, the floor, even a few passersby. The courtiers exclaimed in protest. So did the head laundress, from a low servants' table.

"The wine's poisoned," Arpien sputtered.

The king's taste-tester, had Emol been disposed to loan him or Arpien disposed to let him die, couldn't drink from empty glasses. No one was falling insensate into their herbed potatoes and roast meat. Once again Arpien looked like a paranoid idiot.

Across the room, Eusar silently toasted Arpien with his own goblet. That unnerved Arpien more than the attack itself. Hadn't Cryndien planned the poisoning? It was, after all, something Cryndien had done before. But then why was Eusar smiling? And who, come to think of it, would have had access to Arpien's glass that night? Far easier for Eusar to speak to the servers than Cryndien.

They'd have to start watching for threats on both fronts.

29

Brierly

Although it wasn't officially a fairy Gift, Rumor Gathering had always been effortless for Brierly. Fleetsome Feet were excellent tools for investigation. Even when she wasn't actively Charming secrets from people, her cadre of admiring young nobles blurted out plenty of juicy revelations in an effort to win her attention. And Animal Speech gave her a literal fly-on-the-wall perspective that would make spies drool. Animals were her favorite informants. Some animals might have vicious teeth and claws, but their tongues weren't so vicious as humans', and their motives were easier to track.

Brierly learned more than she wanted to know about the queen from the royal lapdogs. Albertus loved reciting pedigrees, both human and canine. He had the queen's down to a stately cadence, and moved his tiny brown paws back and forth as though he were marching to his own performance. Squeezie raved about his Queenie as he raved about anyone who fed him, including "Flash-Boom Man."

"Who?" Brierly said.

He means His Royal Majesty King Cryndien Trouvel of Conquisan. Albertus sniffed at his nephew, who was stalking bubbles. *Squeezie, use your titles.*

Brierly had offered to give the dogs their weekly bath, and the Royal Dog Attendant was glad to surrender the Royal Canine Scrub Brush. Squeezie in a tub was a hurricane. Which was why Nissa was reading her book in the dry safety of the hallway as she waited for Brierly.

Flash-Boom Man scratches the spot that makes my foot thump. And he feeds me treats if I catch the flying things. Squeezie wiggled his hindquarters and pounced. Water slopped over the rim of the washtub. *He calls me a ferocious hunter.*

Funny. Brierly had heard Cryndien refer to the lapdogs as "useless rats."

I wish you wouldn't be quite so forthright with your enthusiasm for the Conquisani king. It isn't politic.

You eat his treats, too, Bertus.

Albertus dog-paddled his hundredth lap around the wooden tub, head held high. The fur on his head was not even wet. *Yes, well, only as a diplomatic duty. And only when the Queen is otherwise occupied.*

Squeezie looked up from his latest kill. *So we do like Flash-Boom Man or not?*

The point, dear fleabrain, is not whether we like him, but how the thing is perceived.

Squeezie cocked his head. Suds slid off his ear.

It depends on the situation

Squeezie cocked his head the other way. *Do I still get my treats?*

Yes, my little cat-bait. Albertus nodded toward the bubbles. *You missed one.*

Even with Fleetsome Feet, it was difficult to dodge the queen long enough to hold a substantial conversation with the lapdogs. Luckily, compared to briar-ridden, barren Estepel, Boxleyn was infested with animals to talk to. Brierly took an immediate liking to a pair of spotted pigeons for building their nest in the open mouth of Nissa's Great Great Aunt Zalia, whom Brierly had known and disliked. The statue consisted of a boulder-sized head and a six-foot-long arm that extended over the ledge of the roof and pointed to the horizon. Brierly climbed up on the arm to fully appreciate how the twigs made the statue look like it was foaming at the mouth. Even Nissa had allowed herself to laugh at her relative's expense, though she was not brave enough to inspect the statue from Brierly's vantage point. In fact, Nissa objected when Brierly made her own roost on top of the statue's hand. It might have had something to do with the five-story drop, but how else was Brierly to properly converse with the birds?

She took to visiting the birds at dawn, when birdkind was most talkative, and any other time she felt like dodging well-meaning people who lectured her about wearing the ill-intention-ometer. Today she'd managed the slip during the bustle before the evening meal, by telling Arpien she was eating upstairs with Nissa, and Nissa that she was eating downstairs with Arpien. The dying sun was a corpulent ruby in the sky.

She didn't turn around when her Fine Ears detected human footsteps. Not Nissa's. Male. Not Arpien's, either. Not even Cuz's, who she could easily imagine trying to sneak up on her.

"Not hungry, Eusar?"

She turned then and saw she'd guessed right. Nissa's cousin Eusar jumped as though he had not noticed her fifteen feet away. "Princess Brierly. You startled me. Out enjoying the sunset?"

"As are you and your friends." Two of them, she noted as she turned further.

Eusar smiled. "I heard you talking to your—friends—as well." He glanced at the nest.

"Actually, they were doing most of the talking."

"Careful, Princess. People will think you're daft if you say such things. Some would say you're daft to sit so high up, in such a precarious position." He smiled and extended a courtly hand. "May I help you down?"

If there was anything more tiresome than death in the dream world, it was death accompanied by bad puns.

"Thank you, no."

He climbed onto the ledge. "Please take my hand, princess. How could I bear it if you were to fall?"

Her eyes were fixed on Eusar, so she did not see the attacker behind her. Nor did she need to, with her Fine Ear. But it would have been helpful if she'd been prepared for the broomstick that jabbed her in between her shoulder blades.

She barely had time to hook her arms around the statue's chubby one. She dangled there for a moment. The ground looked miles beneath her. Eusar cursed.

It took the broom smashing down on her knuckles for her to realize she was not afraid, but annoyed. This was her dream. She was in charge.

She swung forward and caught her toes in the stone gutter. She walked her hands forward until she stood upright. Then she was ducking again, as both broomstick and scabbarded blade reached for her. Fleetsome Feet gave her excellent balance, and she scrambled along the gutter to the next statue. The gutter ran the perimeter of the building, several feet beneath the wall that outlined the roof. It was hard for her attackers to coordinate a deadly attack around the unwieldy stone limbs of pompous Montaines. If Brierly somehow swung herself up to the ledge of the wall, she couldn't make it up and over before they caught her. The route down appealed even less.

As quickly as she dodged and scurried, there were still three of them and one of her. Eusar and one of his companions caught her between statues. The third could now leisurely beat at her unsheltered back until she fell.

"Grab hold, little bird." The broom dangled close to her where she crouched on the ledge. Bristles teased her hair. "I'll pull you to safety."

He leaned over the wall. She tore the broom from his grasp and knocked his head with the other end of the broom.

He fell.

He grabbed a fistful of her skirts in an effort to save himself. Her right elbow smacked the ledge with a jarring sting that reverberated through her entire skeleton. The rough grit of the stone gutter grated burning ridges into her left palm as it took the entire weight of his flailing body. She could not will her tingling arm to grab the gutter overhead.

The cloth tore free.

She decided she was more attached to this particular dream than she thought.

A cry of pain from overhead called her attention upward. Steel rang against steel. She heard Eusar's shout. "Quit attacking, idiot! We were trying to help her! She thought she could fly off the building."

The clash of swords ceased. "Then get out of my way."

Arpien's head jutted over the ledge. For a moment Brierly couldn't determine if she was more afraid of what lay above or below her. For now Eusar would push him from behind, or stab him ...

Arpien's head gave her some inane advice to hold on, disappeared from view, and demanded sword and cloaks of Eusar and his companion. Their swords Arpien chucked over the wall. The cloaks he knotted together with his own cloak and doublet to form a makeshift rope. It was not quite long enough for Brierly to reach it. Moments later she heard a sound she'd never heard before—the pumice-melon sound of metal slicing through rock. He'd sunk the vademecum sword into the ledge.

Arpien anchored the rope of cloaks to the sword, climbed down, and reached his hand out to her.

If she took his hand, would she be saving herself or condemning him?

Arpien flashed her a shaky grin that reoriented gravity. "Do you want me to save you now or does later fit better into your schedule?"

A grunt drew her attention once more to the roof. "Eusar, stop!" she shouted.

Too late. Eusar pried the vademecum sword loose and both Arpien and Brierly fell in a tangle of limbs down the side of the palace.

Suddenly the vademecum sword bit into stone again. The makeshift rope jerked taut. Brierly and Arpien crashed through the Reception Room window. Arpien struck it feet-first and rolled on top of her so that he sheltered her from the worst of the falling glass. When the shattering stopped, they both sat up.

"Careful. There's glass in your hair." He brushed a shard from her tresses, which was funny given the myriad tiny shards that glinted in his own hair. She looked her recurring prince over in wonder. How was he intact?

"How did you know?" she asked.

"A bird told me."

"You can talk to animals now?"

"Not in words, but why else would two pigeons grab me by the scruff of the neck, unless they came from you?"

A few weeks ago he never would have taken advice from birds.

He glanced down at the blond lock of her hair still between his fingers. He released it and stood. He extended a hand to help her up, and this time she took it. It was warm and strong and—she wasn't imagining it—it shook the slightest bit. She noted as much aloud in surprise. He flushed.

As soon as he lifted her upright he tried to extract his hand, but she wouldn't let him. They both stared at their joined hands, as though they'd been glued together by some mysterious prank of Cuz's, and then up at each other. Brierly didn't name what she read in his face, but it had something to do with the tremor in his hand. Only the tremor was in her own hand, and spread to unlikely places throughout her body. His brown eyes had gotten much closer to her own. She leaned in too, pulled in by the same inexplicable force that glued their hands together. One of the birds had broken into her ribcage and was now frantically trying to beat its way back out.

She hauled back and slapped Arpien.

If she'd done the slapping, why did her own ears ring?

She picked her way through the shards.

"Oh, no. Eusar just tried to kill you, and you think I'm letting you go anywhere on your own?"

She'd never heard that edge in Arpien's voice before—jagged as the glass that littered the ground.

Heat surged through her again. Didn't he understand? She was in no danger. He was. Hadn't that been Voracity's plan all along? Send him to rescue her, with that brave intensity and endearing vulnerability? Then when Voracity had proof that Brierly had fallen in love with her own figment, she'd destroy him.

Don't let her see. Don't let anyone see.

Brierly turned and shrugged. "If you like."

Servants rushed in from the lower level to investigate the great crash. Even Eusar appeared. His surprise to find them alive was likely not entirely feigned. "Thorns. Arpien, my friend, are you all right? And dear Cousin Brierly? What happened?"

Pointless questions didn't deserve answers. If they accused Eusar of causing their fall, he would simply tell another version of the story, perhaps the one where the crazy princess who talked to birds tried to fly like one. The bystanders might suspect Eusar capable of removing his competition—her Fine Ears had picked up plenty of gossip about Eusar's envy of Timothy's royal inheritance—but in the end they'd profess whatever was in their best political interest.

Arpien's fingers whitened as they clamped the handle of the vademecum sword. Brierly hadn't considered that her recurring prince might die as punishment for dueling Eusar in the middle of the atrium. She caught Arpien's eye and shook her head slightly. He would not ignore her unspoken advice. Still, it was no gentlemanly arm that hauled her to the safety of Nissa's chambers.

Arpien ranted and paced, Nissa tried to piece together what had happened in concerned confusion, Kendra listened in while she pretended to sweep the hearth, and Brierly retreated to the bedroom to collect the rags of her indifference. Eusar's lackey had torn a whole panel from the peacock gown when he fell. Brierly could not rub out the memory of his wide eyes as the last threads snapped. His fingers groped and scrambled like fleshy, desperate spiders. Her own fairy-Gifted fingers felt sluggish, bloodless, detached. It took them five minutes to hook up the fastenings of her new gown.

So he was dead. What did it matter? He was a figment. A nasty figment. It wasn't the first time she'd had to kill.

Why then did she keep thinking of eggs splattering into a bucket?

Through the door she could hear Arpien's fury. "It's unendurable. Am I supposed to sit on my thumbs when they attack her? I'm not proving my morality, but my cowardice."

"What Eusar did is inexcusable," Nissa said. "But he's my cousin. Please remember that before you threaten his life."

"He threatened mine first. Mine and your closest friend's. Who will make him answer for it? Your uncle? He probably asked him to do it. Timothy? He might disapprove, but he won't embarrass the Rosarian royal line with such scandal. Cryndien would pretend to be outraged if he knew, but only because it'd make a glorious excuse to start a war, and Bo always sides with Cryndien. No, Nissa, in the end no one cares about right and wrong, because the mighty make the rules."

Brierly took a breath and strolled into Nissa's sitting room. "Don't take your anger at me out on Nissa."

"I'm not mad at either of you. I'm mad at Eusar."

"Fine. Be mad at Eusar." Brierly shrugged. "Seems like a great deal of effort for something that doesn't really matter, though."

"You almost died today." Despite his claim that he wasn't angry at her, Arpien whacked the cushioned back of one of the mismatched parlor chairs. "Someone else did die. A real, flawed human being. Will you never get the truth through your head? You're awake. This world is the real one. Listen to reason!"

Arpien's fingers indented the surface of the blue velvet. Perfect pools of cushion supported the legs of a water bug.

Fingers grooming a shard of glass from her hair. Fingers glued to her own. Fingers motionless on Kendra's broom handle. Fingers groping for a handhold in aquamarine fabric.

"Reason?" Brierly flopped onto a stuffed chair in a philosophic pose copied from one of the statues on the roof. She furrowed her brow and supported her chin on her fist. "Believe in this world because its rules are consistent. Horseradish. People determine their own truth, you said it yourself."

"I never said that."

"You just said the mighty make the rules."

That silenced him for a moment, but only a moment. "I believe in the Greater Good. Whatever serves society is right."

"Which society? If Emol keeps Sentre Forest, Cryndien can't have his hittal trees for ships for Conquisan and your economy suffers. If Cryndien gets his trees, Lord Culmney can't get his egg sacs and people die in Strand. If Lord Culmney gets his egg sacs, the mantizes die. Greater Good? Squirrel nubbins. Everyone's in this for himself. Your 'waking world' is no different from the rest of the dream world. So I might as well be there, if it's all the same to you."

His tone gentled. "It's not all the same to me."

Couldn't the man have the decency to stay self-righteous?

"You're just confused because of this horrible Curse Voracity laid on you. In your heart, I know you are good and pure."

"That's sweet of you." She swung her feet over the arms of the stuffed chair and yawned to cover her mistake. "But there are as many versions of good as there are politicians. And as many truths as there are dreams. Speaking of which, all this prancing about gutters has worn me out."

"Of course. I shouldn't be here." Arpien looked down at his uncovered shirt. For the first time he seemed to notice that he was most improperly dressed for an unmarried man in private rooms with unmarried young women. His cloak and doublet still flew like a banner from the walls of Boxleyn. "I can't be seen leaving your rooms dressed like this."

"You were seen entering them like this."

"That was unavoidable." Arpien whirled on Nissa. "And I'll not have you begging for your cousins' clothes or my brothers' or anyone else who's tried to murder me lately."

Nissa chewed her bottom lip. "Arpien, are you expecting Brierly to sew you an outfit here and now?"

Kendra's eyes widened. "Princess Brierly, have you cut up Prince Arpien's old doublet and trunk hose yet?"

Spinning wheels. Brierly's heels banged a soft hollow *thwump thwump thwump* against the plush upholstery. "They might still be wearable. Now where did I leave them?"

She tried not to let her eyes catch on the scrap basket too quickly. "Ah yes."

She dumped the basket upside down. Fabric bits went flying like colorful butterflies. The incriminating doublet and trunk hose plopped onto the floor. She displayed the riot of gold and yellow gashes to Arpien.

If she hadn't been fighting embarrassment, Brierly might have laughed at the parade of expressions that marched across Arpien's face and finally finished with the same furious indignation he'd shown when she rescued the pickles from Estepel.

"WHAT DID YOU DO TO MY CLOTHES?"

"I was experimenting with a new fashion technique."

"You had no right to mutilate my clothes."

"They were already mutilated, and they aren't your clothes. You gave them to Kendra and she gave them to me. Don't fuss when it seems I've helped you."

"I DON'T NEED ANY HELP LOOKING LIKE A FOOL!"

In the background Nissa bit her lip again. Brierly couldn't tell if she was scandalized or amused.

"Thistles, Brierly, is this what your Gift says about me?" Arpien said. "That I'm weak? Incompetent? Sloppy? Vain? Mawkish?"

"Slashed sleeves could become the new fashion, Herren."

"My. Name. Is. Arpien." He kicked a limp sleeve over with his toe, as if to see if it were alive. "What are you trying to say about me?"

That was the last question Brierly could answer. "Art speaks for itself, or not at all."

"So that's the verdict? I revere you and you feel nothing for me. I'm a rag doll you can dress up and then discard in a dusty corner until you feel like playing again."

In his righteous rage he was the very image of Cryndien, not Herren.

She yawned. "Will you leave now, please? I'm tired."

"You're not tired. You're running away." He snatched up the doublet and trunk hose. "And another thing—if you're really asleep, how can you be tired?" He slammed the door behind him.

But she'd been tired for years.

She stared at the heavy wooden door and dug a cold knuckle into her lips.

What if you let him kiss you?

Voracity would kill him.

He's a figment. You could just imagine him back to life later.

Could she? Was Arpien Voracity's creation or hers?

She'd forgotten Nissa was still there, analyzing every flicker her face revealed. "Do you think I'm running away, too?" Brierly said.

"I didn't say that," Nissa said.

"You never say anything." What was this? She scolded Arpien for taking his anger out on Nissa but it was fine for her to?

"You're right. I never say what I should be saying." Nissa shoved aside a green brocade and sat opposite Brierly. "The person keeping you imprisoned isn't Voracity or the Prince, it's you. You refuse to see that you're awake. Listen, Brierly, everything I've researched indicates the prophecy is true. Please, please, just try calling the Prince back one more time."

"I don't want to hear it."

Nissa toed the floor. "That's why I never say anything."

Heat wormed through Brierly's veins. "I'm going to go lie down. Not because I'm running away. Because—because there are dreams out there more interesting than this one."

"Then why are you still here?"

"The opportunity for an easy exit hasn't presented itself."

"What would you call Eusar chucking you off the roof?"

"Maybe I don't like taking orders from figments."

Nissa lowered her eyes again. "You say this dream is just like the others, but you don't act like it."

"You shouldn't say things like that." What if Voracity was listening? "If you think I'm so attached to this place, why did you and Arpien both accuse me of running away?"

"Because you know what you want, but you don't want to pay the price to get it."

"What do you know of what I want?"

Nissa flinched.

Brierly had a brief mental flash of Queen Perturbance's face overlaid with hers, towering over Nissa. "I'm sorry—I—"

Brierly went to bed without another word. Emaciated rays of sunlight still winked through the window. Her listless young supporters among the Boxleyn nobles would be expecting her to provide mutual entertainment and distraction well into the night. It was far too early to go to sleep. What was she thinking? She was already asleep. She compromised by shutting one eye and leaving the other open to stare at the wall.

She felt guilty for getting angry with Nissa. She felt angry because Nissa made her feel guilty. She shouldn't be feeling anything. Lying here remembering the texture of Arpien's hand—calloused and strong and gentle—was dangerous. Envisioning the warmth of that unexpected nervous smile as he dangled five stories above the ground—that was deadly.

She'd had plenty of time to mould dream-Herren into the perfect man. But she'd never been able to finish the job of falling in love with him. It wasn't just that Voracity periodically destroyed her favorite figment. It was that Herren, like the rag doll, had no choice in his actions. If she told him to capture the moon for her, he got a net and fished it out of the sky. If she wanted him to kiss her, he pressed his lips to hers as gently or urgently as she preferred. But it was a kiss without a spark, as self-referential as kissing a pillow. She could create her figments with any appearance, but she could not give them wills of their own. Without that, love was only the fondness the artist had for her favorite sketch.

So when Arpien didn't behave how she expected, it made him seem like he might have that spark all the other Herrens lacked. The notion made her veins run with molten ice.

You say this dream is just like the others, but you don't act like it.

How long could she maintain indifference? A year? A century? Perhaps it was best to let Voracity finish him off before she grew any more attached to him.

She sat up in bed. That was an unexpected solution. Take the small cut now to avoid the gaping wound later. The way to finally escape this recurring dream was not for her to die, but for Arpien to die. He had started this dream, hadn't he? To end it she need only follow him to a dream where he was in danger, wait until Voracity knew she was watching, and bite her tongue while he perished.

The thought made her head pound with nausea, which only convinced her she was right. If she was silly enough to care about a figment now, how much worse would it be later?

If she was lucky, maybe he'd die without ever knowing she was there. She didn't want to see the disenchantment in his face as he realized his "good" and "pure" princess was no such thing.

Spinning wheels. She really had been around Arpien too long. What were such words doing in her vocabulary?

How long did it take an efficient surgeon to amputate a limb? Five minutes? Better get it over with all at once. She burrowed back into the scratchy linens in search of a landscape in which to kill her prince.

30

Arpien

That night Arpien played more the ineffectual rescuer than ever in his nightmares. This time the victim was Cuz. He and Arpien fought back-to-back on dream practice fields while warrior after warrior attacked them, deadlier and more massive than they had ever been in real life. Cryndien. Eusar. Bo. Timothy. Emol. Gerret. They attacked in irrepressible waves, until it was more like fighting a thicket of blades than individuals. Arpien thrust and parried with his dull practice blade. His arms weakened and thinned into paper.

A woman watched him from a window above the practice fields, but he could not identify her. Behind him, Cuz gasped for breath, a whimper in each exhalation. "Courage, Cuz," Arpien said, as much for his own sake as the boy's. Arpien's body was completely flat now, and his paper sword flapped. If only he had the vademecum sword.

A blade reached past his guard and took Cuz in the back. Arpien caught the dying boy as he fell. Blood trickled in stairsteps from the corner of Cuz's mouth. "Why didn't you save me? You were my hero." His glassy eyes closed.

Arpien shook Cuz's shoulders. "Don't close your eyes, Cuz!"

Cuz obeyed, but the fiery gold eyes that opened were not his own. "You should leave Rosaria, paper prince. No one wants you here. You couldn't rescue a slice of cheese from a mouse."

Voracity. Was she controlling Cuz's body? Arpien leapt to his feet, paper sword in hand, and whirled toward the window where he'd seen the shadowy woman looking on. It was empty.

An incalculable pain took him between his shoulder blades, and he folded to his knees. He looked down at his chest and saw the tip of a dull practice blade. Cuz's face, distorted into Voracity's expression, leered at him. "Spare yourself any more pain. Run away."

Arpien tried to insist that Arpien Trouvel did not run, but he couldn't pump the words past the pain. Cryndien impaled him with another sword. With ceremonious deliberation, each warrior stepped forward to reach past his weakening guard and skewer him.

Someone jerked a blade from his body and the world went a blinding white. He heard someone cry out, but it was not his own voice. The pain diminished as someone yanked the blades free one by one. He pressed his hand to his chest, wet and sticky with the horror of—

—glue?

He wiped glue from his eyes. Where a vengeful Cuz had been a moment before stood a snowman. Glueman. White sludge began to melt off the figure in a rumble of rage. More glue gushed down on top of it. Underneath he could see spinning flashes of color, something alive and beautiful and inhuman. Was he about to fight a fairy in full form?

Arpien seized his gloopy paper sword in his right hand. Another hand grabbed his left and yanked him away. It was a slender hand, surprisingly strong, and the moment it gripped his he felt himself turn to flesh and blood again.

"Sometimes," Brierly said, "running away is smart."

She tossed a long green knitted scarf at the glueman. It entangled the glueman's neck and arms long enough for them to escape. Brierly dove into the sticky liquid surface of the practice field and pulled Arpien after her.

Drowning in glue reminded him far too much of his nightmares of drowning in Kirren's river. But this was Brierly's hand, and he let it pull him down to the very bottom of the opaque white ocean. They hit the ocean floor. Up became down and down up, and Arpien found himself standing in the middle of Sentre Forest, clean and whole.

Free of the glue, he at last got a good look at his companion. It *was* Brierly, wasn't it? Not a dream about Brierly, but Brierly herself walking the dream world? The expression on her face was too naked to be feigned. Had it been Brierly or Voracity watching from the window?

Did it matter?

Their hands clung together as though she had not been able to erase all traces of the previous dream. It brought back a similar scene from yesterday's waking hours. Brierly must have remembered it, too, for she blanched and let go of his hand.

For the first time since they'd met, Brierly babbled. "I couldn't— you're not—I didn't mean—"

"Shh ..." Her lips were silk under his calloused fingertips. "It's all right."

She didn't slap him, that was promising. Her lips parted just enough that he could feel the wavering air stream as she exhaled. But she said nothing. She looked at him as though she were drowning, or he was. Arpien held his own breath, as though they were two shipwrecked victims tossed into an uncertain sea, and neither knew the way to the surface.

She backed through the woods and the trees closed in around her.

He ran after her—

—smack into a tree.

He sat up and rubbed his head. The last month had brought more trauma to his skull than the rest of his life combined. Was he so clumsy, or had Brierly, with her control over the dreamscape, shunted the trees into his path?

It was their recurring dream together. He chased his lady in white. She eluded him. Yet how could he give up on her when she kept giving him reason to hope?

He wished again for the vademecum sword. His princess-detector. In the way of dreams, the hilt of the practice sword lengthened and changed shape in his fist. He drew the vademecum sword and closed his eyes. It needled northward. The walls of the forest? his mind? rippled and parted at the touch of the blade.

He stepped through the rift and into the unknown.

Part Four

Is not general incivility the very essence of love?
Jane Austen

I am by no means of opinion that a ball of this kind,
given to respectable people, can have any evil tendency.
Jane Austen

31

Arpien

He wasn't in the unknown. He was home.

It wasn't home as Arpien remembered it. This was the Conquisani palace, but the red and gold banners were smaller. The stone bust of Great Great Uncle Nedferin, the very one he'd broken as a boy, had his beaky nose again.

A pair of gentlemen in antiquated parti-colored hose passed by. One gestured grandly, in the throes of a traditional Conquisani boasting story.

Arpien sheathed the vademecum sword and stepped into their path. He tucked his right arm behind his back and extended his left to his side, pointer finger up, and bowed the *Half-Bow of Mannerly and Slightly Urgent Interruption*. "Three thousand and three pardons, my lords—"

They walked straight through him.

Arpien's spine tingled. Ghosts? If so, who was the ghost?

No, no, it was a dream. Brierly's dream, not his, judging by the strains of old-fashioned string ensemble music drifting from the ballroom. He'd cut into the scene enough to see and hear and smell the ball, but not enough to take part in it.

He headed toward the noise—always a good place to look for Brierly. He spotted his princess in the middle of the ballroom floor, where a long line of ladies danced with a long line of gentlemen. Must be a style of dancing popular from Brierly's memories. Arpien couldn't remember ever seeing it in his own time. She'd exchanged her white gown for the pink one he'd first found her wearing in the tower, on Kissing Day. Then it had been dingy and sleep-rumpled. Now it was so pink it gave him a toothache.

He had full view of her face, so he saw her yawn so wide as to drink up the sea in one gulp. He'd pity Brierly's partner if the gentleman were real. Good luck trying to impress her.

The line of men reached across to the line of ladies. Partners spun and crossed in a neat drill of collapsing geometric figures. Only when the row of ladies and gentlemen switched positions did he get a good look at Brierly's dance partner.

It was he himself.

He squeezed through the crowd to get a better vantage point, and clutched a column.

No, wait. It was Great Grandfather Herren.

No wonder Brierly insisted on calling Arpien *Herren*. Arpien was only a pale copy of her first love.

But look at her face. Arpien had seen the same expression on the faces of his childhood friends, when he rambled on too long about the comparative merits of hedge clippers versus pruning shears.

She'd had one hundred years to shape Herren into the literal man of her dreams. He still wasn't enough.

Most of the night was an endless cycle of the same dance to the same music. Midnight trumpeted Brierly's birthday in with red and gold fireworks. Herren beamed at his betrothed. Brierly yawned. How many times had she turned seventeen?

Brierly brushed through Arpien on her way from the ballroom. He followed. The moment her foot hit the first step of the tower, the whole tenor of the dream sharpened. Arpien squeezed the handle of the vademecum sword.

Arpien compared the Conquisani version of the crime with Brierly's dream-memory of it. Herren recorded that the Rosarians only agreed to let Brierly travel with them to the Conquisani palace if she were quartered in the highest tower. It would be easier to guard, Brierly's father said.

Arpien trailed Brierly up the tower stairs, past a dozen guards in Rosarian green and a dozen in Conquisani red and gold. They nodded to the princess but didn't spare Arpien a glance. Even the arrow slits they passed in ascent had been blocked up, but for an inch or two where a chatty bird might squeeze through to loiter with the visiting princess.

Herren's mother, the queen, must have taken extra care to transform the drafty tower into guest quarters worthy of her future daughter-in-law: silk bed curtains, plush velvet floor coverings to guard royal toes from the chill stone floor, a mirror set in a purple ferrus wood frame. A middle-aged handmaid circled the room and lit candles, tall molded candles that stood straight in their metal holders like honey-brown soldiers ready to see service for the first time.

The growing candlelight revealed a pile of packages against the wall. "What's this?" Brierly said.

The handmaid winked. "As if you weren't expecting presents, Your Highness. Your parents didn't want to risk another public gift-giving ceremony, so they had them brought here." She put her hands on her hips. "You may open your presents at dawn and not before. Your mother's orders."

Dawn. No doubt Brierly's mother set that deadline because she knew the terms of Voracity's Curse as well as Arpien.

Before the dawning of her seventeenth birthday, the princess shall prick her finger on a spindle and die.

A few more hours, and Brierly would be safe.

"I'm too tired to open them now, anyway." Brierly stretched. The motion shifted the lines of her body as a deft artist might sweep two pure and fluid strokes of a brush against the canvas.

"No, wait," Brierly said. "Where's that one from the old woman we met on the road?"

"It can't be more than a bit of woven wool or a gypsy trinket."

"She told me it was exactly what I wanted." Brierly yawned. "Nevermind, Daertha. You're tired, too. I'll open everything in the morning, I promise."

"I'll help you undress."

Arpien's pulse rabbited. It was less than honorable to watch this, even in a dream.

But Brierly said, "Don't bother. I'm never taking this dress off. I want to remember exactly how happy I am right now." She spoke as if she were reciting lines.

Daertha rolled her eyes and smiled. "Good night, Princess Brierly."

Brierly hummed a dance tune under her breath. Her reflection in the glass twirled and flirted on its own. Arpien couldn't imagine the Brierly he knew ever behaving in such an immature but endearing way. It was too—young. While her reflection preened, the other Brierly scanned the pile of presents. Her absent humming formed an eerie counterpoint to the song her reflection sang.

Despite her words of "in the morning," Brierly knelt down on the floor and retrieved a misshapen bundle of brown paper. She grasped it between two fingers, the way you might an exotic beetle, and unwrapped the present.

She stopped humming. The reflection stopped singing, too, and turned its eyes to the other Brierly's hands.

A spindle.

Was one of the palace clocks slow, or did it just strike midnight again?

Had Brierly recognized the spindle for what it was, that night one hundred years ago? The old woman on the road, that had to have been Voracity in hag form. How had Brierly ever fallen into so obvious a trap?

It must have been ignorance. Her parents had made the mistake of burning every spinning wheel in Rosaria. How would she recognize a spindle?

Brierly stared at the strange present. "I wish that old woman were here to show me what it's for."

Thistles. For one hundred years Rosaria had accused Conquisan of inviting Voracity into the Conquisani castle to attack their beloved princess. Brierly had invited Voracity herself. As the betrothed of a Conquisani prince, she had the authority.

She set the spindle on her dressing table, touching it only by the paper, and set about pinching out the candles. After she snuffed each candle, she turned back to glance at the spindle. Her feet moved to her own music as she circled the room. Finally one candle remained, the one on her dressing table.

Her wretched reflection picked up the song again. Arpien tried to turn the mirror around to no effect. The other Brierly approached the dressing table with her fingers twined behind her back. She unlaced one hand and reached out—

"*Don't touch it!*" Arpien cried.

—and picked up the candle.

She jerked around and marched herself across the room. The trapped fabric of her skirts made a dim red smear against the wall as she slid down. Her eyes were dark and wide in her pale face. The candle guttered.

Her reflection clenched her fists at her sides. "I won't, I won't."

Brierly's breath came in shallow pants, as though she stood at the edge of a great height.

Arpien squatted down in front her. "Brierly. Wake up. You don't have to relive this."

Her reflection laughed out loud, as if trying to break the tension. Might as well cut a taut rope with a spoon. Brierly stood and walked through Arpien.

"Such a small thing," her reflection said.

The clock struck midnight.

Brierly grabbed the spindle.

Arpien chased her to the uppermost room in the tower, the one immediately under the roof. Brierly set the spindle and candle on the floor. She opened a door to a slanting storage room wedged under the curve of the winding stairs. Arpien glimpsed a wooden hoop set on four stubby legs. A spinning wheel. She inched it from the closet with the same care you would move an elderly relative.

Once she placed it in the middle of the room, Arpien understood. The spinning wheel was missing a part. Only then did he recall that part of the Conquisani accounts. In the blame exchanged in the aftermath of the spindle disaster, the Conquisani testified they had ordered all spindles locked up until after the royal wedding. Textiles were a vital Conquisani export—they weren't about to burn all their spinning wheels as extremists had done in Rosaria. Rosaria had always accused the Conquisan authorities of faulty collection techniques, if not outright sabotage. Here again, the blame seemed misplaced. Brierly had brought the spindle into the Conquisani palace herself.

It took Brierly several attempts to fit the spindle in place, like a child piecing together a puzzle of an unfamiliar beast. "I'm not spinning. I'm just seeing how it fits together."

An elderly servant toddled into the room. Brierly sprang back from the wheel and dropped the candle. The light drowned in its own wax. At first the intrusion seemed Brierly's salvation. Then the figure raised her own candle. Shadows traced a face with ancient yellow eyes. "Oh, excuse me, pretty lady. Please, forgive a doddering old woman."

Arpien waved his hands. *"That's Voracity! Run, Brierly."*

Brierly jerked away. "I'm not. I mean, I'm not doing anything. I'm leaving."

"I didn't mean to disturb your spinning."

"I'm not spinning." Her protests came too fast. "I don't even know how to spin."

"How does a young woman reach such an age without learning? Are your parents trying to keep you a child forever?"

"No. In fact I'm to be wed within the week."

"Congratulations. At least they allow you the liberty of your own choice of husband."

"We've been betrothed since childhood."

"What? Don't your parents trust you to make your own decisions at all?"

"They're doing what's best for the kingdom."

"Best for themselves. They're controlling you."

Brierly's thin-soled dancing slippers rasped on the stone floor as she turned. "I think I'll go to bed now."

"Forgive me, lady. Old women say what's on their minds. Fetch me that basket of wool?"

Brierly hesitated, then brought the old woman the basket. She hovered as the old woman carded the wool with two wooden boards dotted with stubby metal spikes.

"You have to get the fibers straight, before you spin. Try." The old woman extended the cards.

"I shouldn't."

"It's not spinning, it's carding. Help an old woman with arthritic joints."

So Brierly carded the wool. The hag peeled the wool from the cards and started on the wheel. Brierly's eyes followed the spindle, the magical transformation of wool into yarn.

What more could Arpien do? Brierly knew the danger and deliberately ignored it.

The hag smiled and reached a liver-spotted hand for Brierly's. "Here, try it."

"My parents say that if I prick my finger on a spindle, I'll die."

The hag snorted. "That's the sort of tale you tell a child to scare it into doing what you want." Brierly watched the spinning wheel, and the old woman watched her. "Do you know what spinning is? Twisting fibers. The same as twirling your hair around your finger."

"I really don't want to know."

"A young woman who would be queen should not be afraid of knowledge."

It wasn't knowledge the hag was offering.

Brierly reached out a long, tapered finger.

"Don't touch it! Brierly!" Arpien grabbed her wrist, but his hand passed through hers.

He couldn't stop Brierly, so Arpien drew the vademecum sword and sliced through the hag. Voracity dissipated into smoke.

He'd been expecting a battle. But this was only a dream image of Voracity, not Voracity in the dream world.

His dramatic attack did have the effect of making Brierly aware of him. "How'd you get here? Get out!"

The vademecum sword must have finally cut the rest of the way into her dream. Brierly swelled up, half damsel, half dragon, and shoved him into the wall. Stone and mortar caved at his back. The impact knocked the wind from him.

Arpien thought he'd prefer battle with Voracity.

Brierly's face flamed, and in more ways than one. Fire shot from her nostrils. She wouldn't meet his eyes, and suddenly he couldn't meet hers. This was more embarrassing than if he had watched her undress. He'd seen her soul naked. All these years he'd thought of her as an innocent victim, when she'd pricked her own finger willingly.

She picked up a stone half her own weight and hurled it at him. "Get out!"

Arpien didn't know how to get out of her dream. So instead he froze the stone in its trajectory. The stone vibrated in midair, caught between the force of their wills. It emitted a high-pitched wail, turned red, and crumbled to dust.

How had he done that? Crimson dragon scales flaked from Brierly's face and neck, revealing cheeks gone as pale as death lilies.

He extended a hand toward her.

Don't fear me. Never fear me.

She vanished.

Perfect. He'd either scared her into another dream or scared her awake. Either way, he didn't follow, because he couldn't find words adequate to deal with the occasion. He could only find Gowsma's words.

She's still under a curse. And this one you cannot save her from, because she put her own self under it.

32
Brierly

Run.

Brierly leaned forward and whispered it again in Neef's whipping mane. Run.

None of that should have happened. She'd promised herself never to rescue Arpien from Voracity or her minions again.

In an effort to purge him from her system, she'd relived the Conquisani ball. She'd even worn the tooth-rotting pink gown again, to rub her face in every tedious aspect. Then she danced round after mind-numbing round with her betrothed.

See? He's just another banal copy of Herren.

She hadn't intended to see the memory out to its end. Why could she never resist the spindle? She felt caught in some sort of private obscenity. So she chased him away with rocks. Rocks which he plucked from her control.

If figments had wills of their own, were they really figments?

Why did it bother her so much to have him see her like that? So what if she had a spindle obsession? When there were no lasting consequences, there could be no guilt.

He scared her. Just as she'd predicted he'd wound her, he had. He slew her imaginary enemies. He answered attacks with kindness. Paper princes she could control. She couldn't control Arpien.

And if there was one good thing about being alone, it was that she got to be queen.

Nissa and Windried were already out for their morning ride. Neef detoured to meet them. Brierly kicked him back on route. He obeyed with a petulant whicker.

It didn't make any difference. Nissa was a fine horsewoman, and Windried could circle Boxleyn twice before Neef exerted himself enough to muss his mane.

"Brierly! Wait for us."

Windried fell into step alongside Neef and struck up a companionable conversation about Neef, Neef's favorite topic. The humans rode in silence for a few minutes. In that mysterious way of hers, Nissa seemed to understand what Brierly did not say. More evidence that Nissa was an extension of her own self.

"You're leaving," Nissa said.

"Hm."

"Are you running from the assassins? I don't think you'll be any safer out there alone in Sentre Forest," Nissa said.

She was always safer alone. Bored, but safer.

"If you want to go, I won't stop you. In fact, I'll go with you."

Which would defeat the point of being alone. Dear Nissa. Imagine the pair of them camping in the wilderness. *Here, you read up on edible wildflowers while I sew us a tent out of bark.*

"Couldn't we just stay through the ball?" Nissa said.

"I've seen enough balls."

"But it's my first. Well, first since I reached my majority. You know, now that I'm—"

"Marketable?"

Nissa fidgeted. "I wanted to go through this with a friend. You know, someone to do my hair—"

"Kendra can do your hair."

"It's not the same. Kendra is very dear to me, but it's another thing to talk about a ball with someone's who's actually going, someone who knows what it's like to have people speculating and politicking. Please, Brierly? I'm braver when you're there."

Did Nissa really care about the ball, or was she just grabbing an excuse to keep Brierly at Boxleyn? Brierly dug through the endless piles of ballroom scenes, heaped like rotten potato peelings in her memory. Somewhere under here was the unspoiled memory of the ball to celebrate her own majority. Not the dreams, the original. Ignore what happened afterward. Think of everything up to midnight. The nerves. The music. The all-important dress. The fretting over the prince.

Brierly wavered. She told herself it was because Nissa's naiveté would make the ball diverting. She didn't care a dried-up raisin about anyone else who might attend the monotonous ball.

There was another reason to give in to Nissa's request. Arpien had slashed his way from this dream into the other. Brierly had to convince him not to follow her. Or convince herself she didn't want to be followed.

Brierly relented. "I'll stay through the ball."

Nissa rewarded her with a smile of relief.

"But I'm not wearing that detestable pink gown. I'll never make a pink dress again."

"All right." Nissa led the way back.

33

Arpien

When Arpien finally woke up, he had second thoughts about chasing Brierly. First, she wasn't likely to appreciate conversation about what he'd witnessed. At least in the waking world she couldn't chuck boulders at him.

Second …

For years he'd held before him the image of his lady in white. It was for that image he'd climbed mountains and gotten lost in caves and ruined his favorite shirt. Perhaps she'd turned out to be odd and distant, but he'd told himself that was not her fault. It hadn't crushed the image of a maiden of surpassing virtue. Even her flaws were heroic flaws. She was unearthly, ingenious, insane, radiant. A goddess.

Brierly wasn't the only one who could create figments.

He felt like a pounded steak. He rolled stiff neck and shoulder muscles and snuck out to retrieve his sword and doublet before it was light enough for anyone to notice him. Here in the waking world, both were still stuck in the side of Boxleyn Palace. He had to bow his way into Lord Culmney's chambers and lean out the window to get close enough to snag them. Arpien couldn't tell if the Strandish Lord had believed his explanation of how he'd gotten his sword stuck in the wall—or his testimony of the vademecum sword's other astounding properties. But Lord Culmney's worn face had creased in a diplomatic smile, and now Arpien had his belongings in hand.

Along with a written reprimand from Queen Perturbance and a bill from King Emol for smashing a hole in the signature Montaine stained glass window.

The brown doublet he'd borrowed from Timothy on his arrival had once come two inches too short on his wrists. The fall had stretched it out like taffy. Now his sleeves hung a full two inches past the tips of his fingers. He flapped his arms inside his sleeves like bell clappers.

Rescuing princesses was hard on clothes.

His eyes fell to where he'd tossed the wadded midnight blue doublet, the one Brierly had "repaired" with slashes of gold fabric. He put it on and hesitantly faced the mirror. He looked foolish and noble and vulnerable and battled-hardened all at once. As though every wound, every mistake, had been healed but not erased. Brierly had immortalized every scar in gold.

Was that how she saw him? If so, how could he do less than return the courtesy?

When people fall off their pedestals, you have two options. Either you can hate them for letting you down, or you can look at them eye to eye and sympathize, *you're just like me.*

At his core, when he wasn't playing the hero, didn't he struggle with failure and vulnerability, too? Couldn't they resonate in their own frail, human way?

Women who wanted to resonate probably didn't throw boulders. Suppose he loved her despite, even because of her flaws. She still hated him for seeing them.

You couldn't save people who didn't want to be saved from themselves. First, they never stayed saved. Second, rescue pressed too deep turned into violation. If Brierly stood ready to throw herself from her tower, of course he'd yank her back. It would be another thing to tie her to a chair so she didn't get too close to the edge again.

What was love? Letting her have her own way, even if it killed her? Or demanding his?

Thorns and thistles.

He spoke of the spindle dream to no one, not even Nissa. That glimpse of Brierly was too personal. It was not his to share.

He didn't bring it up with Brierly, either. With the Spring Ball only a week away, Brierly found ample excuse to barricade herself in dresses and fittings for half the palace ladies. Such a barrage of femininity Arpien didn't dare challenge, so any hopes of a one-on-one discussion with Brierly were delayed until the Spring Ball.

If they had spoken of the spindle dream, Arpien felt certain they would have said the same thing. *It doesn't matter.* But they would not have meant the same thing.

Arpien had plenty of his own preparations for the ball, mainly in the realm of politics. Several of the lords and ladies whose fiefs bordered Sentre Forest visited him quietly to discuss how he meant to rule it. They hinted that the Montaines had never understood the complexity of the situation. Many of the younger generation also threw in their exuberant support for their favorite fantasy couple. Lord Culmney of the Strandish delegation made it widely known how he admired Brierly, although as an ambassador of a weak and plague-riddled nation, his support counted for little. Timothy favored Arpien over Cryndien, and King Emol gave the lost princess lip service, but by no means did Arpien trust the transfer of Sentre Forest to go smoothly. King Emol might well cave to Cryndien's threats. Cryndien had no power to invite Voracity into the grounds of Boxleyn; only the Rosarian royals could do that. But could Cryndien bring some of Voracity's magic inside Boxleyn? Arpien still had no idea how to defend Boxleyn from Voracity.

Or even how to convince the Rosarians to defend themselves.

34

Nissa

Four days to the Spring Ball. The confectioners spun colored sugar into candy blossoms, the butchers slaughtered the most tender of the spring lambs, the musicians argued over tempo. Certain ladies of the palace, more concerned with the perils of apparel than assassination attempts, once again took up residence in Nissa's chambers to ensure that Brierly finished their dresses in time for the ball.

Also here by Brierly's invitation were the spotted pigeons from the roof and a nest of mice from beneath the floorboards. Unfortunately the rodents and ladies did not associate well, and the birds, with eyes situated on opposite sides of their heads, proved indifferent seamstresses. So Brierly assigned the sympathetic forest creatures to Special Acquisitions of Accessories.

It took Nissa and the ladies several days to figure out this meant stealing odds and ends of ribbons, lace, and beads from all over Boxleyn. Brierly still had trouble with the concept of private property. She believed everything she encountered originated from her own mind. The ladies resigned themselves to a little petty thievery as a minor cost of finishing their gowns. Brierly said she just wished the birds had eyes better suited to color-matching.

All the chatter and gossip annoyed Nissa. How could she read with half the birds and noblewomen in Boxleyn roosting in her sitting chamber? The ill-intention-ometer kept going off whenever Brierly did a final fitting. Each gown was innovative, exquisitely sewn, and captured some essence of its wearer. By and large Brierly had chosen to accentuate the positive traits of her models. Once or twice she'd emphasized a less flattering character trait, but luckily those women were blind to the commentary.

Watching Brierly work was both a pleasure and a frustration. At first Nissa took advantage of her captive audience to try to warn them about Voracity. But as no one wanted to add evil fairies to their growing lists of things to fret about, Nissa gave up after a sentence or two. Like the other women, Nissa oohed with admiration whenever a lady tried on one of Brierly's creations. Nissa couldn't help but bite back a wish that her own legs were so long, her own waist so narrow, or long for whatever particular beauty each woman displayed. Nissa stuck her nose back in her book and reminded herself that Beauty was not useful. Still, it was hard to concentrate on vengeful fairies in the flurry of silk, lace, and ribbon.

Whatever each woman thought of Brierly as a person or potential ruler, she was indispensable as a seamstress. Her popularity soared as the ball drew near. Even the assassination attempts tapered off, perhaps for the simple reason that Brierly was constantly surrounded by a bevy of sharp-eyed witnesses who had a vested interest in her survival.

Nissa wasn't about to leave Brierly unattended after Eusar had tried to push her off the roof. Arpien couldn't visit with all the dress fittings underway. But—there was a certain passage Nissa wanted to look up in the library, and if she could just sneak away for a few minutes … She handed the ill-intention-ometer to Kendra and promised to be back in a quarter of an hour.

The book was not where she remembered shelving it, so Nissa took longer than the quarter hour she had promised Kendra. As she searched, her worries about beauty and dresses faded in comparison to the larger troubles that threatened her friends and Rosaria. Even if Uncle Emol did honor his promise to give Sentre Forest to Brierly at the Spring Ball, how would Brierly defend it against Cryndien? Sentre Forest had no standing army; Conquisan had one of the strongest on the continent.

If only Brierly would try to bring back the Prince. Nissa didn't blame her friend for her skepticism—Nissa couldn't explain why Brierly's previous efforts hadn't brought back the Prince. But the more Nissa read, the more she was convinced that the Prince was the key to protecting Rosaria. He was a warrior of enormous power.

Nissa had pieced together a great deal in the past week about the Stewards' relationship with the Prince. How the Prince of Here and There had once ruled the land, and he left it in the care of his Stewards. It didn't say where the Prince of Here and There had gone. It didn't even decisively say he had gone anywhere. No one had seen him for centuries, although the rulers of Rosaria supposedly turned to him for protection.

He is both here and there. He is not lost, though many never find him. They are too busy looking in the wrong places, at the wrong time, with the wrong motives and the wrong tools.

How could people be looking in the wrong places if he was "both here and there?" In fact, many of the old tales about the Prince seemed to contradict each other. Some of the old tales said the Prince of Here and There was human, and by some accounts he wasn't human at all. Some accounts called him immortal, like a fairy, but others said he had died a long time ago. A conundrum: How can the Prince be both present and absent, frail and mighty, human and not-human, immortal and dead, ruler and subject, hero and victim?

"Because he's a part of the dream world," Brierly had said when Nissa mused over the riddle aloud. "You can make him anything you want."

If that were true, why did Brierly complain that he'd never come to her in the dream world?

"What did you lose?"

Nissa straightened up so quickly she banged her elbow on the ladder. Prince Bo was watching her from some paces away.

She rubbed her tingling funny bone and frowned at him. How did she keep winding up alone and unprotected with Conquisani princes? It seemed foolish to imagine the general of an enemy nation would view her as a threat or a valuable captive. He must have seen that if he wanted a hostage, he'd gain more leverage by abducting the lapdogs? He couldn't be here because of her.

"A book," she said.

"And you decided to search for it in a library?"

Was Prince Bo being funny? No, how could such a grim man be joking?

"I could help you find it," he said.

Nissa didn't want him to see her research and laugh at her. "You must have your own work to pursue."

He nodded and turned to a bookshelf at the far end of the room.

Should the general invade Rosaria with his army, Nissa would be appalled; his invasion of her library was disturbing enough. If he demanded none of her attention, how was it that all her attention was on him? On the methodical fingers that brushed across the words on the page, a dozen or so even sweeps, then slotted the book away and invited down the next in line for inspection. Did he move with this same—pragmatic stealth—when his brother ordered him to assassinate people? If she actually believed him an assassin, shouldn't she be frightened? Instead, she found herself trying to imagine a young Bo with his sister Kirren.

Let him get what he wanted and leave her to her work. "I organized this library myself. I can probably help you get what you want," she said.

He raised his brow a fraction. She persisted. "What are you looking for?"

"A book."

Flat sarcasm? Another glimmer of a joke? Nissa let her response reflect both.

"In a library?"

He grimaced and turned away.

She'd come to the library in part for seclusion, but she was not going to get it. At least the next visitor was a welcome one. Arpien nosed his way into the library, sword first.

From the way he held his sword before him, not in a fighting stance, but the way you might give your hunting dog his head, he was taking Nissa's latest advice on weaponry. She had pointed out some passages from *Fantastical and Legendary Devices: An Appendium for the Scholar of Legends and Lore.* Between the assassination attempts and threat of war, Arpien was eager to learn better control of his sword.

Arpien let his sword arm drop to his side as soon as he spotted Nissa and Bo. The move was sudden, sheepish, as though he were a little boy caught out in some mischief. The fact that the sleeves of his doublet had somehow grown too long for his arms only added to the image.

Bo left as soon as Arpien entered. So that was the way of things.

"What was Bo doing here?" Arpien said.

"Practicing looking dour." She stepped another rung higher on the wooden ladder and scanned the top shelf. "Why can't people ever put books back where they're supposed to go?"

Her irritation bounced off Arpien unnoticed. "You'll be interested to know, the vademecum sword is no better at finding the Prince than it is at finding princesses."

It had been Nissa's idea that Arpien's sword could find the Prince if Brierly was unwilling. "Did you try concentrating on one of the old tales about the Prince, like the book recommends?"

"Yes. The sword did what it normally does. Pointed where it wanted instead of where I wanted. But I found an interesting side effect."

He plucked a stone paperweight from Nissa's desk and tossed it in the air. Before it hit the ground he zinged the sword through the air and cleaved the rock in two. He picked up one half and showed her how smooth the cut was—as if the rock were a neatly pared apple.

"The sword gets sharper when I concentrate on the Prince. The Prince made it, so maybe it works best for those loyal to him. So if I think of him, the sword believes I'm one of the Prince's men. It fits with what happened the morning Eusar tried to throw Brierly off the roof. I used the sword to lead me to Brierly. Anytime you use the sword as a compass, you have to seek the sword."

"Seek it?"

"Communicate with it. I don't know how to describe it—I barely do it right half the time myself. Maybe in seeking the sword, I'm also somehow seeking the man who forged it. So I could use the sword as a compass because I was thinking of the Prince, and I could cut into the rock ledge because I was thinking about the Prince."

"Then why could Eusar pull it loose?"

"Because I'd found Brierly and quit actively using the sword as a compass? Because the sword knew we'd be safer if we fell? I told you, it's ornery." He patted the handle as though it were the head of his favorite hunting dog.

"Arpien, if the sword works best for people who are loyal to the Prince, maybe all you have to do is declare your loyalty to unlock all its properties."

"Nissa, you know I'm a great admirer of the Prince."

"Is that the same thing?" She let out a squeal. "Here it is! *The History of Squalian Whale Fishery.*"

"That's something to be excited about?"

The spine of the book was so broad that she couldn't carry it down in one hand. Arpien reached up before she toppled off the ladder. She handed the book to him.

He pretended to stagger. "Thistles, is there a real whale in here?"

"Ha. You joke now, but if I remember right, this passage will verify everything I've been telling Timothy about the Great Storm."

"Why have you been telling Timothy about the Great Storm?"

"Because if I can convince him the Prince caused it, he'll have the proof he needs to believe me about the rest of the old tales and the danger Voracity poses." She scrambled down the ladder. "I'll take it back now."

Arpien arranged himself in a studious pose against the desk and thumbed through the pages. "Oh no, I'm not relinquishing such an entrancing find. Ah. Statistics on the trends of blubber thickness in the past fifty years. With illustrations."

She elbowed him.

He flipped to the next chapter. "And here's—"

He froze. Something was caught within the pages, near the book's spine. A very dead something—she could smell it rotting from here. A posby blossom.

Nissa scraped it off the page with her fingernail. It had been fresh when it was shut in here, moist enough to mildew. The page would bear the mark forever, if she didn't have to rip it out completely to spare the rest of the book from molding. Arpien exchanged her the injured book for the injured flower and counted petals.

"Seven."

She kept it.

True, Brierly let it molder in the depths of blubber diagrams. But why had she saved it, and then lied about throwing it out?

The object of their unspoken speculation floated into the room. "Nissa, Kendra is beside herself with hair ribbons. Could you—"

Arpien and Nissa broke apart. Nissa snapped the book shut, and Arpien closed his fist around the blossom. Brierly raised her brow.

Nissa hugged the book to her chest. Maybe her sleeves would disguise it. "Kendra wanted me?"

"If it's convenient, she says, but she'd order you there if she could. I'll tell her you're busy with Arpien."

"I'm not busy. Certainly not with Arpien. I just came to look for a book, and I found it, and I'm done."

"Ah."

Nissa wedged the book into the bottom of a stack. "So let's go."

"Aren't you going to bring the book?"

"What book?"

Brierly pointed. "The book you came here to find."

"Oh, that one. No, Arpien, you wanted to look in it a while longer, right?"

"He wants to look in the book you didn't find together?"

"He doesn't. Didn't. I talked him into it. Revealing stuff within."

Arpien cringed, but not nearly as much as Nissa did.

A Gift of Eloquence would really help right now, but Nissa opted for the more solid escape technique of grabbing Brierly's hand and charging out the door. "Let's save Kendra."

35

Nissa

The day of the ball came at last, and with it the tedious and delightful rituals of femininity. Nissa thought Brierly's ice-green dress with the jagged asymmetrical trimming was one of the strangest of her creations, but she wasn't going to say so. Instead she planted the spiky silver pins in Brierly's hair as prompted, then switched places so she could have her own scalp tugged in unnatural directions. Nissa picked at her hair, using her hands to visualize how Brierly dressed it. Brierly whapped her hand with the back of a tortoise shell hair comb.

"Worry with that if you need to occupy your hands." Brierly dangled a green silk ribbon in front of Nissa's nose. "Or you could chew on it. Squeezie tells me he finds that a great comfort."

"I wouldn't be tempted to poke my hair if you'd let me look in the mirror."

"My dream, my rules."

"Aren't you nervous about tonight?"

Brierly anchored one last pin in Nissa's hair. "People who ask such questions do it because they are nervous themselves."

"Why should I be nervous? Voracity can't enter the palace unless a member of the Rosarian royal line invites her, and no one would try to hurt you or Arpien among so many witnesses."

Brierly flipped up the lid of Nissa's wooden clothes chest. Why was Kendra grinning? On top of her usual clothes lay a pink garment Nissa had never seen before. Nissa shook the folds free. Yards of lightweight silk unfurled like a flower blossoming. Forest green piping twined over one shoulder and diagonally down the bodice and skirt. Here and there Brierly had carefully basted Nissa's own embroidered roses. Like the peacock dress, Brierly had not merely designed a stunning gown, but displayed Nissa's work to best advantage.

"Guaranteed to restore calm," Brierly said.

"B-but ... you hate pink. You swore you'd never sew another pink dress again."

Brierly petted the dress, as if to soothe an offended cat. "It's not pink. It's rose. Just right to bring out your glow."

Brierly and Kendra helped Nissa perform a slow dive into the dress, to preserve her hair. Only then would they allow Nissa to look in the mirror.

The lovely young lady in the mirror was not a stranger, nor was she Lady Overlooked. Once again, Brierly had found some essential core of her model and designed the whole dress around it. Brierly had gathered Nissa's brown hair in a loose pile on top of her head, with a curl spilling over here and there. The comb secured a single rose just verging on full bloom. Nissa still looked short and sturdy but—endearingly so. A friendly elf. Youthful, but not childish. The dress flattered and concealed the correct curves. Not even Aunt Perturbance would mistake her for fifteen tonight. Nissa blushed–ith pleasure at her appearance, yes–but mainly that her childhood heroine would think so highly of her as to craft such a masterpiece. That she would know her so well as to reflect the true Nissa, but love her so well as to reflect the best possible Nissa.

And this gift from the girl who claimed not to care for anyone.

Brierly's reflection joined her own in the mirror, not quite brushing against her arm. "Twins," Brierly said.

Nissa laughed. "Aye, identical."

"Not all twins are identical. Some twins complement each other." Brierly pointed to the mirror. "See the joke? I am the briar and you the rose."

"You have the roles reversed."

"No, you get to be the rose because you are warm and beautiful and tender. And I am the vine of thorns, for I am prickly and cold."

Was she teasing? To air the mood, Nissa posed as a statue. "I'm not beautiful. I'm Art."

"No, Nissa, you are beautiful. But it has nothing to do with what I see." Brierly tugged on her friend's sleeve. "The rest of you can be Art."

Did Brierly's fairy Gift allow her to sew magic into the seams of her garments? Nissa felt invincible as she and Brierly entered the ballroom.

Eager dance partners soon snatched Brierly away. The servers, many of them Nissa's friends, scowled at Nissa for hiding behind the pyramid of cream puffs. It was Cuz who flushed Nissa out into the open. He staked a position on the balcony, armed with a slingshot and chicken croquettes. Nissa only witnessed the aftermath of his failed attempt to splatter her—a boyish squeak and the firm hand of General Bo disarming her cousin. Nissa shifted to the edge of the dance floor, away from all overhead hazards.

Growing up, Nissa had always wanted a fairy godmother. Yet it was Brierly who gave her the magic gown to wear to the ball. Whether it made her beautiful or not, it certainly made her visible. Both Timothy and Arpien claimed dances out of brotherly affection, but three lesser lords and a landless knight also asked her to dance. True *You-Seem-Like-A-Desirable-Partner* dances.

She was not the most graceful dancer on the floor. The ill-intention-ometer kept buzzing and making her lose counts. Two rival jousters. Jealous maids and suitors. Every way she turned she jabbed into the pointy corner of a love triangle. Disheartening to see how many ill intentions stewed behind the poised smiles. But as long as her friends were safe, nothing could fully dishearten Nissa this evening. If she wasn't the most lithe of form or elegant of foot, she was at least having the most fun.

Still, she was knocked completely off-center when Prince Bo crossed over to her and extended his hand. "I'd like to dance with you."

(May I take your hand, dear organized lady?)

He might have been discussing the day's drills with his men. Certainly he didn't look as though her acceptance would bring him pleasure. She couldn't read him at all.

Nissa Montaine read things until she understood them. She closed her mouth and gave him her hand. "All right."

Bo nodded gravely and led her to the dance floor just as the first notes made their deliberate procession from the recorder. Had he picked the *pavane* because of its dignity or its simplicity? It didn't require any complicated footwork. Just *step, step, step step step* in slow, mind-numbing repetition. It left the tongue free to be nimble as the other parts of the body were not.

Although she'd hardly call his tongue nimble. It took him several turns to dredge up anything to say.

"Thank you for accepting. I know you don't like me."

No, she felt nothing that strong for or against him. She couldn't categorize him, and it troubled her. Rescuing Prince or Regular? Enemy or Sympathizer?

"I do owe you a thank you for rescuing my dress. Aye, I saw. Cuz looked as cowed as I've ever seen him. What did you say?"

"What you normally say to a twelve-year-old idiot."

Nissa swallowed a chortle. Who'd have imagined Bo would make her laugh?

"Cuz isn't so bad. I used to look after him when he was younger. It's only recently that he's—"

"An idiot," he completed. "All twelve-year-old boys are. I was one. Once." He spoke as Brierly did, as though he had to chisel through a century of bedrock to find a glimmer of childhood.

That's what he reminded her of. Rock. She could see the Conquisani line in him, though his features were not so well-crafted as Cryndien's or Arpien's. He was not so tall, either. Broader. More muscle. A boulder. His eyes were set deep in his face, his stern brow set over them like a guard to discourage anyone from searching within. He reminded Nissa of a half-finished granite statue. Or a slightly depressed brown bear.

He didn't dance like a brown bear, though. *(Have you danced with a bear of any kind, Nissa?)* She had plenty of time to analyze his manner, as they completed the next few turns in silence. His movements were precise. If he weren't an enemy general she'd even call them graceful.

It was a stately dance, the motions honey-thick and weighted. Nissa pictured herself as a small, elegant elephant, trunk arched just so in the air. It made her smile, to think of the brown bear and the elephant, dancing the *pachyderm pavane*. But still, why did he want to dance with her? Her pride in her dress did not extend so far as to make her imagine the maneuver wasn't calculated.

"So other than brilliant conversation, what did you want from this dance?"

His brow lifted slightly.

"Come now, I don't have enough political clout to make you seek my favor, and by the end of the *pavane* I'll have exhausted my witty repartee. So what interests you in me? And don't make small talk about my appearance. I'm plain, not stupid."

What had gotten into her tonight? The observations she was never brave enough to say aloud came prancing off her tongue like she was a—a person worth reckoning with.

"I would not dare call you either," Bo said. "I wanted to talk to you about the Prince of Here and There."

"You—you did?" She'd sooner believe he'd sought her out for witty conversation.

"You are fond of the old tales."

"Yes ..." Had he glimpsed the titles in her stack of research?

"Do you believe them?"

She searched his tone for condescension. "Some of them."

"Which ones?"

Ah, now she understood why he had invaded her library. "You want to know about the prophecy that the Prince will return, so Conquisan can circumvent it."

"No. I already know that prophecy. I know all the tales of the Prince."

"From dancing with other scholars?"

"No. I read them when I was a boy."

The general, curled up with a book of the old tales?

His interest seemed sincere, so she found herself answering sincerely. "I think there's truth in a number of those concerning the Prince. Brierly's real. The fairies are real. Who knows what else we once considered legend will in fact turn out to be truth? Some of the tales can be documented. I've traced the tale of the Prince and the Serpent back over two thousand years. I personally own four different accounts of the tale of the Prince and the Storm, from four different countries. The stories share a remarkable number of details."

"Does that make them true? What if someone made up a single story and it spread to four countries?"

"Not these four countries. Too far apart. Travel between them would have been rare at the time they were first written down. No one had a boat strong enough to reach the island of Squali."

"You're convinced your Prince sent this storm?"

"Who else would have been powerful enough to create a storm that big?"

"Who would want to believe in a Prince cruel enough to send a storm that big?"

She'd been hoping for a sincere intellectual inquiry. This was a skeptic listening to himself talk. "I wonder why you debate with me. You've obviously already made up your mind that the old tales are false."

"I grew up."

Brierly was ancient compared to Bo's twenty-odd years, but she never made Nissa feel infantile. "Aye. And now you say what you normally say to a seventeen-year-old idiot."

"Do not let your faith in the imaginary mercy of an unseen Prince blind you to reality," Bo said.

"As if it's not possible to have a clear mind and believe in the old tales. Are you certain you're not a Rosarian?"

"I don't mean to insult you—"

"I suppose the fact that Grey Cloaks are camped in the woods outside our gate is not considered an insult?"

"—but to warn you."

Warn. It could mean threaten, it could mean something else entirely. She looked up—it seemed a long way—into his eyes. "Why?"

His voice was deep, growly, like the bear she pictured earlier. "You remind me of—someone I once cared for dearly. She died before she ever had the chance to grow up."

His sister. Sweet. But a seventeen-year-old in a gorgeous new dress does not want to be told by any sort of prince, Rescuing or Regular, that she reminds him of his eleven-year-old sister. Nor does she want to be lectured.

The moment the musicians found their last note, she gave him her most dignified and *adult* curtsey.

"Thank you for the dance and the warning. But I'll take my chances with the Prince."

36

Brierly

All told, Brierly had clothed seventeen of the guests at the Spring Ball. That they proudly displayed their novel Sleeping Princess designs was in itself a visual badge of alliance. Brierly scanned the ballroom and sorted the guests into factions. The Strandish with their goatees and faded blues. The blazing reds, golds, and whites of the haughty Conquisani. The squared and starched silhouettes of those loyal to the rule of the Montaines. And the "audaciously fresh" flowing style of those who supported Brierly and Arpien. Dancers wove around the dance floor in a complex pattern of textiles and politics.

If clothes told stories about their wearers, she who controlled fashion controlled the story. Which didn't explain why seeing Arpien in the slashed doublet and breeches made her feel less in control of the story.

He'd been insulted by her repairs, hadn't he? Was he trying to unnerve her? Compliment her? Perhaps it was as practical as this: he had no other clothes of his own to wear to a ball.

Whatever the cause of his choice, he had no right to look so handsome. The palace maidens mooned over him, but otherwise public opinion on whether the outfit made Arpien look daring or ridiculous depended largely on whether the viewer sided with Arpien's politics. Arpien had gained his fair portion of supporters—enough that slashed sleeves and breeches might actually become the next Rosarian high style, as she'd predicted.

With Arpien in the midnight blue and Cryndien in his overstated sun hues, they looked like night and day versions of the Trouvelian line. It was hard to say which brother outsplendored the other. Many commented on the brothers' striking resemblance, but Brierly thought putting them side by side only accentuated the differences. Everything about Cryndien radiated outward—booming voice, dramatic gestures, jovial goading. Arpien seemed intent on containing himself. He no longer swaggered like a proper Conquisani, but he was still too much a Conquisani to dismiss Cryndien's boisterous insults. Brierly could see Arpien's jaw tense up whenever Cryndien cornered him for a brotherly chat.

She had little doubt what the brothers discussed. Brierly didn't always understand her recurring prince, but Cryndien knew him even less than she did if he thought he could bully Arpien into handing Sentre Forest over to Conquisan. Not that it was Arpien's to hand over. Even should King Emol give the forest to Brierly as promised, there was no way Brierly could allow herself to marry Arpien. Her own muddy wishes on the matter were a non-issue when their engagement would prove his death sentence, signed by Voracity.

Nissa whirled by, self-assured and innocently happy. Several people were taking note of Nissa Montaine tonight.

Brierly didn't know whether to be annoyed or gratified that Arpien wasn't one of these. Oh, Arpien danced with Nissa, all right, and Brierly's Fine Ears caught the due compliments he paid. Brierly detected no other symptom of love. Certainly nothing as indicative as their flustered response when Brierly interrupted the pair in the library last week.

At first the suspicion that Arpien's affections had started to turn to Nissa had stunned her. On closer inspection, it might at last provide her a way out of the unhappy ending that was certain to come sooner or later. All princes died or abandoned her or disappeared or turned on her in the end. If she had to lose Arpien, wasn't it best that she lose him to Nissa? It was the only ending without death or betrayal. The only ending where the people she wasn't supposed to care about wound up happy.

She couldn't explain to herself why the happiness of figments mattered to her. Nor could she explain why, after playing matchmaker with her friends, she should be relieved that they didn't take her hint.

She wasn't going to let Voracity seduce her into a fragile fantasy life with Arpien. So Brierly spent most of the evening avoiding the man everyone expected her to be wildly in love with.

She'd modeled her own gown on the briar to send the clear signal, *touch me and I'll hurt you.* But her very nature, while it could allow her to create something eccentric, couldn't allow her to create something inartistic. She wanted her bizarre dress to say *go away*. Instead it said *I am exotic and mysterious and forbidden*. Endless suitors sought her hand for a dance. It didn't help that her dowry added to her attractions. Still, dancing with them meant she couldn't be dancing with Arpien. And adapting to one hundred years' worth of new dances was simple enough when Gifted with Music and Fleetsome Feet.

It became a game. When he drew too close she picked another man and focused all her Charm on him. False sparkling laughter. A back turned, an arm laced. If there was no convenient man to grab, she just whirled in the opposite direction. It was easy when her Fine Ear was attuned to Arpien's footstep, his voice. There were a few narrow escapes when the music swelled, and she suddenly found him only a few steps away. She got away each time, her heart beating faster but intact. It had all the traits of flirtation except the most vital. She didn't want a thing to do with him.

She even, in an attempt to outmaneuver Arpien, accepted a dance with Sir Flatwhist, the perpetually sober-faced knight from Strand.

"You pay little attention to Prince Arpien," Sir Flatwhist said. "One might conclude you do not wish to marry him."

She arched a careless eyebrow. "It's all the same to me."

"Then why not marry where you would do the most good?"

They shifted right and left, kicking vigorously. "You, you mean?"

His chin tightened under that Strandish goatee. "I meant you could marry the Strandish prince. Our countries have always been on better terms than Conquisan and Rosaria. Your dowry could heal my land."

"Why do you need my dowry? To add legitimacy to what you are already taking illegitimately?"

He stuttered a little in the dance.

"The wound in your thigh has healed well," she said. "You only favored it a little in the galliard. If you'd chosen a dance with fewer kicks, I might have never known you'd been injured last month."

Here the women stood a pace back while the men danced solo. Brierly could almost see Sir Flatwhist's feet scrambling to catch up with his brain. She so enjoyed this expression, when people who took her for a butterfly realized she was as cunning as a fox.

He stilled, and now it was the women's turn for a solo.

"I should never have asked you to dance," he said.

"Don't fash yourself. I've guessed since Lord Culmney introduced us."

"How?" They circled each other.

"I have a good ear for voices. Besides, you winced when you saw me on the night of the singing duel. I still had doubts until the night we ran into you in the stable yard. I told you a brigand was dead. You couldn't mask that that meant something to you. Mind, I don't think you miss him much. You suspected one of your companions was stealing the mantiz egg sacs you had stolen from Sentre Forest. That's why you were out so early, wasn't it? You wanted to catch him in the act of treachery. Voracity probably spared you getting blood on your hands."

"That's an intricate accusation based on very little evidence."

Brierly sighed. "And it's unlikely anyone will want the testimony of your horses. None of whom have forgiven me for tying them together the night Arpien and I escaped from a troop of brigands in the woods."

There were times, Brierly admitted, she truly relished the role of wise fool. She dazzled Sir Flatwhist with her most Charming smile, and clapped her hand against his for another turn. "Don't be so stiff, Sir Flatwhist. It makes you an awkward dance partner. I've told no one so far, why bother now?"

"Why haven't you?"

"I told you, it's all the same to me. What does it matter that a minor Strandish knight spends his spare time posing as a Conquisani brigand with a remarkably false beard?"

There had been no need to reveal what she knew to everyone in Boxleyn and embarrass Lord Culmney, that figment who reminded her of some frayed version of her father. If she chose to twit Sir Flatwhist with the information now—well, she could be forgiven for trying to relieve her annoyance at this constant insistence she go marry a figment and live happily ever after.

Sir Flatwhist glanced around to see if they'd been overheard. "You truly are as unfeeling as you look," he said.

"Much like you, I imagine."

The afterglow of smugness when they parted was short-lived. She'd saved the knowledge of Sir Flatwhist's identity up like a child saving up copper coins for a sweetcake. Now she'd spent her thin coins on a mouthful and was left picking at the crumbs.

No, it wasn't the fleeting distraction of playing with Sir Flatwhist that left her unguarded. It was Nissa's fault she got caught.

Brierly saw Bo extend his hand to her surprised friend. It was gratifying to see that Nissa in her new dress was fully capable of captivating a prince, even if it wasn't the prince Brierly had intended.

Nissa sought Brierly out immediately after to report. Brierly didn't have any good explanations why Bo would be interested in the Prince of Here and There, either, but the point of ballroom conversation is rarely to reach any actual solutions.

"You're taking up more space than usual," Brierly told Nissa.

"I've stayed away from the refreshment table nearly all night."

"Not that sort of space, Lady Oversensitive. I mean you're taller. Inside. It showed on the ballroom floor."

"It did?"

"You set that prince down with great panache."

Nissa chortled and lifted her nose in the air. "Aye, who needs princes?"

"Away with princes!" Brierly agreed.

Nissa glanced over Brierly's shoulder and blushed. "Well, then, I'll just, um—"

Oh please, don't let Bo be behind her. Nissa would be horrified at the idea that she'd insulted someone's feelings.

It was Arpien. Not any better.

"This sounds like an unfortunate time to be a prince," he said.

"Most unfortunate." Brierly turned to stalk off with Nissa, but Nissa had vanished on feet as fleetsome as Brierly's. No excuse to leave now, or he'd see it was her own desire to flee that motivated her, instead of Nissa's. So she faced him with a bland smile.

He returned it. "You've been avoiding me."

"We just haven't crossed paths."

"An intricate dance in itself."

"If I haven't sought you out, it's because you're not as interesting as the other men in the room."

"Yes, you seemed most interested in them."

Had she? No, he was being facetious. "Well, here's your chance to outdo them all. Amuse me, Herren."

His face tightened, then relaxed. "You know who I am. You're just trying to vex me so I'll go away."

"I don't care what you do."

"Then you won't care if I partner you in the *allemande*."

"Not a whit."

He cocked an eyebrow.

"You seem to think you deserve some kind of special consideration, good or bad. You're not special, Arpien. You're one of a thousand replaceable copies."

"All right. Let's dance." He grinned at her.

What? Spinning wheels, she'd called him Arpien.

She meant to undo the damage—or do more, depending on how you looked at it—by responding to his every comment with a yawn. This proved impossible. Arpien seemed content to hold her and let the music do whatever speaking was necessary. Her Fleetsome Feet made her the better dancer, but she could find in him no deficiency to mock.

When she couldn't stand his serenity any longer, she prodded it with an amiable comment. "No lectures?"

"Lectures?"

"You always have a lecture for me. I just wanted to give you enough time to complete this one before this set ends."

"I'm sorry I've been arrogant. No more lectures. I've decided for every one I give, I deserve two myself. Do you forgive me?"

She shrugged—an impressive feat with their hands arranged for promenading. They faced the same direction as they stepped in time. One joined pair of hands brushed their stomachs. The other pair joined up high, so that she felt the warmth of Arpien's fingers graze the space between her shoulder blades.

"It never mattered," she said.

But it did matter.

"What do you want then?"

"I want to dance with you."

"Come now, we're all here to benefit ourselves. Is my Charming presence compensation enough? Or were you planning one last plea for my dowry, oh noble rescuer?"

"All right, I wouldn't object to being a king. But that's never been the whole story and you know it."

"The other half would be your search for vindication." She rammed a thorn into his most vulnerable spot. "Poor little Arpien, helpless as his sister drowns. Now go save the world, prove you aren't a weak little boy anymore."

His hand tensed against her back, but he didn't back away. Stupid man, to cling to a briar. How many times did she have to cut him before he let her go?

"You're trying to make me angry."

She lifted innocent blue-green eyes. "Why would I do that?"

"You tell me, if you are so indifferent to me."

How could she answer that?

"Then I'll tell you." His voice was as quiet as that day he'd pulled her out of the river and told her about his sister. "You're scared. Better to push me away now. Brierly Steward, you may not believe me yet, but I will never abandon you."

You can't promise such things. How dare he respond to cruelty with kindness? He was supposed to be noticing she was a thorn and Nissa a rose. She felt her spine soften. His strong, gentle hand melted vertebrae made of ancient ice. But what a horror, for if he succeeded she could not stand at all.

The musicians accelerandoed into the second dance of the set.

"I know this tune." Arpien hummed along. "Now that's funny. Back home, this is a tavern song."

She refused to be pulled into his amusement. "That's nice."

"Actually, for a tavern song, it is nice. By which I mean there are no murders or deflowered maids in it."

"Virtue triumphs. Huzzah."

"I don't know if I'd say that." He leaned in—easy when the dance required the couples to constantly sway two steps in and two steps out in locked pairs—and sang softly. He didn't remember all the words and had to fill in lines with da diddly deeing. Which stupidly made the song more endearing.

"You're off-key," Brierly said.

"No doubt." Arpien kept singing.

She glanced at the other couple in their group of eight. "People are watching. Don't you care that you sound like a keening dog?"

This was impossible. If not for her Fine Ear, she wouldn't have been able to hear him over the swishing of her own skirts against the side of his leg.

"Do you care?"

"Not at all."

So she had to endure his breath on her ear, the private concert, the concluding line that startled a laugh out of her.

He looked down at her in surprise. "You laughed."

"It's foolish song."

"Very foolish," he agreed gravely.

Foolish song, foolish to stare up into his tender eyes, foolish to—

The clock struck midnight.

She should have run away days ago. Could still run away now, before the coach turned into a pumpkin and Neef into a mouse and Arpien into a wizened copy of Herren, or worse. But it was too late. Midnight's past mending, the old saying went.

So she drifted up to the dais, where the King of Rosaria had told them all to report at twelve o'clock for formal speeches. So the crown could welcome the lost princess and announce the reward for her brave rescuer—her hand in marriage.

In the tales and in her own experience, midnight meant inescapable doom.

37

Arpien

Arpien grasped Nissa's elbow on the way to the dais. "Well? Any ill intentions?"

"In a ballroom? Every time a woman walks by with a prettier hair arrangement, or a thinner waist, or a more attentive dance partner, someone glares at her and that thing goes off."

"You must be misinterpreting it."

"You really don't understand women, do you? I had Kendra take it back to my room. That incessant vibrating kept distracting me from my surroundings. Doubtless it's a fine tool when you're on a quest in the Unpopulated Unknown. But in a room full of politicians?" She shook her head.

Any further lecture was cut short by the queen, who was arranging the royal family—and guest—on the dais. She ordered Arpien next to Brierly on the far left, and Nissa at the very end of the order of ascension on the far right. Nissa poked Cuz for letting out a yawn as expansive as one of Brierly's best. Cuz didn't poke back. He must be tired.

Arpien wished someone would poke him, as King Emol acknowledged two and a half pages of nobles without the least artistry or Conquisani flair. *(That, sir, is infinity.)* Arpien entertained himself by scanning the ballroom for threats, but the most interesting thing in the room was watching throats of the nobles flex like bullfrogs as they swallowed their yawns.

Finally King Emol introduced the guests of honor. Anticlimactic introductions, even by Rosarian standards. Emol's speech of gratitude was even more anticlimactic. It was as if this princess legend featured a glass valley instead of glass hill. Once he started the tale, the excitement of the story just kept sliding down.

"Some time ago, this young woman contracted an unusual affliction which caused her to spend some years in a coma. Only recently was anyone able to find a cure. For our dear girl's recovery, we acknowledge our debt to Prince Arpien Trouvel of Conquisan. By this act of charity, he initiates a new era of friendship between our two great nations."

What? Where were the fairies, the spinning wheel, the century of elapsed time?

"Sentre Forest is Brierly's dowry, hers on the day she marries. As she is well past her majority"—the king paused for delayed laughter—"her selection of husband—or no husband—is hers alone. Let her choose who makes her happy. We will delight to approve her choice when she has had a chance to acclimate to modern society."

Translation: Should Brierly ever present a man she wished to marry, Emol would tell her to "acclimate to modern society" a while longer.

They'd lost Sentre Forest. Together or separately.

Brierly's eyes had the fixed, glazed look of boredom or terror. Arpien reached over and squeezed her hand in a wordless promise. He'd see to it she got her forest.

She didn't react, but Cryndien did. His brother looked ready to ignite into a thin blade of fire at the announcement. When King Emol stepped back to allow Queen Perturbance to speak, Cryndien slashed a path through the audience and out of the ballroom. Even Bo seemed affronted. He fixed a stone-hard glance on the dais, then turned and followed Cryndien.

Arpien glanced at the queen to see how she was taking this insult. Queen Perturbance was impersonating an apple, as usual. A red steamed one. But—interesting—Nissa also flushed rose. She matched her dress.

And then Nissa—Nissa of all people—stumbled forward and interrupted the queen's speech. "Stop!"

The queen caught a word on her tongue and sucked it back in as a frog would a fly.

"Voracity's going to attack," Nissa said. "We're all in danger up here. We've got to spread out, move, get the guards. Something."

Nissa wasn't wearing the ill-intention-ometer. It couldn't have warned her. Then what—?

Bo hadn't directed that stone-hard glance at the queen or Emol. Arpien knew it hadn't been directed toward him, though he'd seen that expression on Bo's face often enough, warning him to tread carefully.

Bo had been glaring at *Nissa*.

"Nissa, you're interrupting." Aunt Perturbance narrowed her apple-pie-slit eyes. "We've tolerated your childish fascination with the old tales well past your childhood. There are no such things as evil fairies."

Nissa stared the queen down—quite a feat given Nissa was a foot shorter. "You're in danger. Move!"

Arpien grabbed Brierly's hand and towed her down the stairs. He heard footsteps behind him. He turned. Cuz had followed Nissa's command? And behind Cuz, Arpien saw the danger.

The whole Rosarian line ... gathered neatly together on the dais so an enemy could destroy them with one blow. Once they were dead, the killer would be de facto king of Rosaria, giving him the authority to invite Voracity into Boxleyn.

Arpien drew the vademecum sword with his right hand. He still held on to Brierly with his left. Nissa started down the steps, then paused to look over her shoulder at her family. Weren't the rest of them coming? Timothy, at least? No, they just stared at Nissa as though she were a tame pet bunny gone rabid.

Then the dais splintered into a million flying shards.

Part Five

Faith is not bereft of reason.
Ravi Zacharias

I'll not listen to reason ...
reason always means what someone else has got to say.
Elizabeth Gaskell

38

Brierly

"Move!" Nissa ordered in a tone Brierly had never heard her gentle companion use before. Seconds later a perfect forty-foot circle of the roof crashed in.

Brierly smelled it before it happened—a sweet stench of decaying plants. Arpien must have smelled it too, or felt her hand turn in his as she twisted back toward the dais. He shoved her to the marble floor belly-first and threw himself on top of her. Between Arpien's gold-slashed sleeves she saw a rotating whirl of lights and patterns. Saw—or sensed—because the mess of disorienting lights was both *there* and *not there,* as though she were trying to perceive the color red with a hound's eyes.

The paper-thin tornado slammed downward. It decimated everything from the floor of the dais up. Nissa, standing halfway down the steps, was barely short enough to escape beheading. The wheel of lights flung debris of wood, rock, and upholstery across the ballroom. One of the heavy carved legs of the oaken throne slammed Nissa backwards. She bashed her head against the dais steps. Arpien shifted forward to better cover Brierly's head. Her senses took in nothing but a meaningless roar and the warm dome of his body.

Brierly didn't care if the whirl of incomprehensible lights killed her, but suddenly she minded very much that she was sheltered under Arpien's body while he bore the brunt of the destruction. Despite her best efforts of indifference, Voracity had seen, and known. Now, more than ever before, Brierly strained to seize control of the dream. *My dream, my rules. My dream, my rules—*

The roar faded, yet it transmuted, became internal, went on and on in her ears. She caught the belated screams and shouts of people only now able to express their horror. Arpien's chest expanded against her back. The roar in her head pulsed a duet of frantic heartbeats: one rhythm hers, one his. Her doomed prince was unhurt. She barely had time to consider what that meant to her before the warmth of his body lifted from hers.

The deadly whirl of lights had disappeared, but it had ripped into the ballroom with such destructive force she might have been looking on the landscape of another dream altogether. From the colorful factions of fashion to the pyramids of cream puffs, everything was now jumbled together and coated in a fog of pale grey plaster dust.

"Get to the guards," Arpien said, and ran toward the rubble of the dais. A memory flashed before her of Arpien facing the giant mantizes, vademecum sword in hand, moving toward the danger so she could get away from it.

No, come back.

The window for running away had closed days ago, and locked on the stroke of midnight. Her feet were bound by her own heart.

Through the falling dust she glimpsed a swatch of rose-colored fabric poking out from under the fallen rubble.

Nissa.

It was not her friend's body, no, no, just a rose blossom, plucked and trampled into the ground. A wealth of images overlaid the horror before her, and Brierly saw the past month from a gut-wrenching new perspective. She'd been so careful to distance herself from Arpien, so careful to root the weeds of romance out of her heart. She hadn't noticed the danger of the slower, gentler kind love that was friendship.

It was her fault Nissa lay dead under the debris.

Why had she sewn Nissa that dress? Might as well hire heralds to trumpet *Look! Brierly's closest friend. Come get her.* As if the dress weren't enough, she'd stood in front of a mirror and called her *twin.*

Twin. Evil fairy bait. The same thing.

When Arpien had neared death, she'd found him in another dream and saved him there. In the midst of the chaos and screams, Brierly laid her head back down in the dust and debris and closed her eyes.

By cunning or subconscious urge, Brierly found herself in a library. Ha. Of course. "Nissa!"

No answer.

Brierly plucked a book at random from the towering shelves and threw it into the air. The pages flapped awkwardly and struggled upward. It turned upside down and latched onto the ornate ceiling.

She had control of the dream. Perhaps the rules of this dream said she could not create things, only transform them. She threw another book into the air. It landed with a thunk, spine up, several pages bent underneath it.

A moment later Nissa sprawled on the ground, skirts tangled beneath her. "You shouldn't treat books like that."

Brierly couldn't suppress a grin as she offered her friend a hand up. Their hands met and Brierly shrugged off a flash of distortion.

"Should we go riding?" Nissa threw two more books in the air, one marbled red, one deep brown, and there stood Windried and Neef.

"Later," Brierly said.

Nissa grabbed hold of Neef's mane and tail and pulled them together. Neef folded neatly down the middle, and in his place stood the brown book. The book looked indignant. Nissa put a gentle hand on Windried's head and thrust her fingers in the horse's nostrils. Windried stood complacently as Nissa dragged the horse's nostrils up, between her eyes and ears, and then planted them in the middle of her mane. Windried snorted out of her newly formed blowhole. Now a roan whale lounged in the middle of the library.

Brierly frowned. Nissa would never let a whale into her library, crushing book spines with its massive weight, getting pages wet …

"You're not the real Nissa." What was she saying? All Nissas were equally real and unreal.

"Maybe you can't see I'm real because you don't believe in me."

Nissa folded the whale in half just as she had Neef.

"This will help." She reopened the book and extended it to Brierly.

Brierly picked up the object nested in the center of the book. A seven-petaled posby blossom. It smelled tangy and sweet, yet somehow *off.* It was as though a careless cook had dumped in too much or too little of a key ingredient in gooseberry jam, and the recipe refused to congeal.

"Make a wish," Nissa said.

In Brierly's cupped hands the posby bloomed. Arpien had given her such a flower, with earnestness written on his face. But she'd known then that the posby couldn't give her what she wanted.

Nissa tapped the blossom. "Why should anything be denied you, if you are queen of your own fate? Use the blossom and make your own truth."

So Brierly rewrote the ending of the ball. The roof never collapsed. Nissa never died, for here she was. But the Nissa who stood before her in the library with the vague smile of a sage, spouting posby blossom philosophy, this was not the Nissa she'd came to regard as a friend. The flower withered.

Brierly erased the dream and tried again.

The dream world was infinite. It was not possible to search every dream, as though Nissa were an improperly shelved book. As long as Brierly was in a dream she could control, she ought to be able bring Nissa to her. Again and again Brierly dreamed up Nissa, but every version lacked some essential spark. Left to themselves, the imitation Nissas didn't behave like Nissa. If Brierly dictated their words and actions, they seemed flat. Like a great artist trying to duplicate her own masterpiece, Brierly was only able to churn out hundreds of inferior copies.

If Nissa were Brierly's creation, why couldn't she recreate her? There her mind stuck, like a dog on a tether.

Something was tugging her shoulder into another world. Brierly opened her eyes. For a moment, she thought she was back in her tower at Estepel. Dust covered her face. Arpien hovered over her. No, it was the concerned, creased face of Lord Culmney above her. Grey plaster dust covered his skin and turned him into a ghost.

She felt like a ghost herself.

"Are you hurt?" he said.

Pointless questions did not deserve answers, but she didn't have it in her to resent the gentle Strandish lord.

"I saw you faint, but I couldn't tell if it was from shock or injury," he said.

One of the green jeweled spikes was gouging her scalp. She sat up on her elbow and ripped it out of her crumbling coiffure. "I can't find Nissa."

"She's—" Lord Culmney's watery gaze shifted to the ruined dais, where people in rattled finery struggled to haul away the debris. "Don't worry about that now. I'm going to take you someplace safe."

Safety reminded her of Arpien. Spinning wheels, where was he? Either he'd left the ballroom or he was indistinguishable from all the other powder-covered specters who labored to free the victims from the rubble.

No, Brierly would know him anywhere, should he appear with an extra arm or blue hair or caked in dust.

She let Lord Culmney tuck her arm in his and lead her away. Her filmy skirts wafted the dust into the air again. Motes churned softly in the ballroom air. Now she saw that while together they made a grey fog, the individual particles were brown, blue, red, every color that had been painted onto the plaster ceiling. She was just one unanchored ice-green speck among millions.

The ache inside her decimated her insides, like the whirl of lights Voracity had sent to destroy the Rosarian line. It slammed from her head down to the soles of her feet, until all that was left of her was a paper-thin shell of skin. The shell drifted alongside Lord Culmney, sat demurely in the chair he offered, sipped at the wine meant to calm her nerves.

Her hands were steady, but the distorting inner roar returned to her head. She could see her reflection in the wine in perfect clarity. For the moment she set aside the question of whether or not she was awake. What seemed clear was that the people of this world were irreproducible. Voracity had destroyed Nissa for the joy of proving her own power over Brierly.

That was it. Voracity had taken Nissa from her. Brierly would force her to give Nissa back, just as she'd once stolen Arpien back from the merfolk.

Everything in the dream world sprang from with Brierly's own mind or Voracity's. Could it be possible that Voracity had created Nissa? Her soul rebelled at the notion. But rejecting that meant Nissa and Arpien had been right all along. If Nissa was dead in the only real world, she would be—

No. I won't let that be true.

She didn't have a plan, but when had she ever? Like Voracity, she would become a single driving purpose—obliterate the other, and herself if necessary. That had been her fate since the day she'd been christened Briar Rose.

Only there could be no roses in her now. No softness. Only thorns.

Lord Culmney must have been saying something, because his sudden silence rang in her ears. Her words were not for him. "I am Brierly, cold and sharp as my namesake. I have been your victim. I will now be the thorn in your heel."

To Lord Culmney it must have looked like she fainted again. But she was plunging into battle.

39

Arpien

By the time Arpien noticed Nissa still on the steps of the dais, it was too late to do anything about it. He tackled Brierly to the ground. Then, for the second time in his life, Arpien watched as a girl who was a sister to him was swept to her destruction.

The old feeling of helplessness rose up in a wave to swallow Arpien. He held Brierly more tightly. *No*, every muscle in his body screamed. *Brierly will not lose everything again. You will not kill a harmless girl and her family without repercussions.*

The moment the strange magic wheel was gone, Arpien was off after his brothers. He heard Cryndien in the atrium, barking Voracity's name and cursing.

Arpien burst around the corner, the vademecum sword drawn. *You tried to kill me!* But Cryndien was always trying to kill him. So he said, "You killed Nissa."

"A lot of good it did me." Cryndien clawed the air with a grand dismissive sweep. "One of the Rosarian line is still alive. Princess Peerless? I don't see why you're complaining, then."

How did he—?

Then he realized. "You can't invite Voracity into Boxleyn," Arpien said.

"No doubt it's your fault she's still alive, you treacherous whelp." Cryndien drew his sword and advanced on him, Bo at his flank. Arpien was a fair match for either brother, but both of them at once?

Bo halted Cryndien with a warning hand to his arm. "I hear the Rosarians coming. If you mean to take this country, best withdraw and return with a full army."

"Yes," Arpien said, "because that's what you do when your charisma fails, isn't it? Overpower, destroy, and take what you want." Arpien's blade rang against Cryndien's.

After a few thrusts and parries, Bo shoved Cryndien out of the way. "Go!" Now it was Bo's steel that met Arpien's.

In the moment of distraction Sir Flatwhist of Strand rushed in, along with half the Rosarian guard. All Arpien's attention went toward warding off the attack of the Rosarian guards while trying to persuade them their true enemy was escaping down the front steps. Did Cryndien and Bo have the invisibilifier with them? Or were the Rosarians thirsty for Conquisani blood, and Arpien's would do just as well as any?

In a final desperate bid to get the attention of the Rosarians, Arpien flung aside his sword. "Just listen, will you?"

The gamble made them pause. Sir Flatwhist stepped forward. "I overheard him talking to his brother. His job is to stay behind and finish off the rest of the Rosarian line. Then Conquisan can seize control of Boxleyn."

Arpien stared. "That's ludicrous. If I meant to kill the royal line, I would have left Brierly up there on the dais with the rest of them."

Sir Flatwhist circled him, the point of his blade aimed at his chest. "Everyone knows you're besotted with Princess Brierly."

"And Nissa is my friend!"

"Maybe you offered her her own safety in exchange for Sentre Forest. If everyone else died, she'd be Queen of Rosaria. Only at the last moment Lady Nissa couldn't stomach the deaths of her family, so she warned everyone."

"Nissa Montaine, an ambitious conspirator?"

"Then maybe you meant to kill her as well, only she discerned your intentions in time to warn her family."

At least in this version of events Nissa got to be a hero instead of traitor. "I don't suppose you've noticed that I was up on the dais, too."

Sir Flatwhist had an answer for everything. "Strategy. You aimed the attack—perhaps planted some magical device yourself—and then got out of range."

Arpien scanned the tense faces of the Rosarian guard. He'd gone from honored guest to subversive enemy in three minutes. The Rosarians had seen their government demolished in the very heart of Boxleyn, right where they felt safest. People so eager to find a culprit will usually find one.

What really goaded was the realization that he was just as prejudiced as these Rosarians. Arpien had assumed the Strandish delegates were toothless victims, because their nation was riddled with plague. He'd never paid much attention to Sir Flatwhist, and so never until this moment studied the sharp features long enough to notice a certain resemblance to a Conquisani brigand. A brigand who might not be Conquisani after all.

What chances Arpien had of talking his way out of this were ruined by his own temper. "I got out of the way because Nissa warned us all. How could I have known?"

General Gapric ordered the guard to take him to the dungeon. Arpien fought their restraining arms, more out of frustration than an actual attempt to escape. He was outnumbered and swordless.

As the guard bullied him down to the dungeon, two things caught his eye. The first was Sir Flatwhist picking up the vademecum sword. The second was Cuz watching the humiliating procession from the entrance to the ballroom, his eyes wide and spiritless in pudgy, powdery cheeks.

Arpien had never felt more a failure.

40
Brierly

You didn't summon Voracity to you, the way you did other dreams. Brierly prided herself in her own ability to hide in the dream world. Fairies, she knew from experience, innately excelled at doing what she had taken decades of trial and agonizing error to learn. Not all of Voracity's minions had this skill. Brierly could locate one of them and insist they take her to Voracity. Not the merfolk, preferably. The memories of starving blind on a blistering reef were too vivid. She imagined herself into a dream with Voracity's most inept follower.

Brierly stared at the familiar narrow-throated tower. "I never thought I'd come back here of my own volition." But of course, this was only a dream of Castle Estepel. She'd left it and returned in countless other dreams.

The thorns stirred and parted for her former guard. The Thorn King limped to the gates. "Brierly." His voice was less raspy than before. His cloak was a stiff fading maroon, as though he had not bled as much lately. His ankle, however, had been pierced clear through with a thorn. It jutted seven-inches out the side. The skin around the puncture swelled and festered.

"You've come to see me." His smile was heartwrenchingly sincere. What a poor lonely simpleton.

"I've come to see Voracity. Take me to her."

"Why?"

"I need Nissa back."

"Why?"

"Because she's my"—she stumbled over the unaccustomed word—"friend."

"You know Voracity has her?"

"I don't have time for your fool's performance." What else did she have but time? "If it is a performance. But I suspect you're like me—you pretend not to know things for the sheer joy of annoying people. This is not the time for that. Take me to Voracity."

"No."

"No?"

She blinked. What, was this dream not lucid either?

She increased her height by two or three feet. "Do you know who I am?"

"You are Briar Rose Steward."

"Brierly. Briar Rose is stupid even for a princess. And I have better control of the dream world than probably any human ever to walk it. I've been practicing night and day for one hundred years. Don't cross me."

He didn't wince. "I am not afraid of you."

Brierly sprouted a few rows of dragon fangs to inspire him.

"I pity you," he said.

Her fangs retracted an inch. "Why?"

"You're like a sheep without a shepherd."

"As much as I appreciate animal analogies in general, I must tell you, it's impossible to hold an intelligent conversation with a sheep. They are the most stubborn creatures alive, except possibly for adolescent drummers, and just as distracted and wayward in groups. I don't find the comparison very flattering."

"I don't mean to flatter you."

"Why pity me? Look at you, a slave to Voracity, and so mutilated by her thorns you can barely walk."

"I wear these thorns for one I love."

Brierly wrinkled her nose. She couldn't bring herself to take a swipe at the already wounded Thorn King, so she huffed smoke out her nostrils and went to find the merfolk instead.

She imagined herself into the vast ocean, vademecum sword in hand. It only made the merfolk laugh, when Brierly found them.

The mermaid swam in a sinuous circle around her, never quite within reach. "You still don't know how to use that sword, do you, little sleeper?"

One good thing came of having the sword. It put the merfolk in the mood to mock rather than fight. They jibed at her expense all the way to Voracity, but at least they brought her.

Brierly heaved herself onto shore. Her sodden skirts twisted about the vademecum sword like so much kelp round an anchor. She dried and hardened the jagged edges of her dress into porcupine quills. The mermaid patted Brierly's head and flipped out of range before Brierly could pull the sword out from under her knees.

"I look forward to seeing you try to best Voracity with that overgrown sewing needle." The mermaid blew her a kiss.

So Brierly abandoned the vademecum sword at the gates to Voracity's stone fortress.

Only in a dream could such a structure stand. Its base was a thin arching neck. Why so thin? Perhaps to hold the bulk of the palace out of reach of the hungry briars. As she drew closer, though, Brierly saw that the whole structure was held together with vines. Crushed thorns poked out of the very mortar that glued the soot-colored stones together.

She had taken only two steps through the gates when, in the right corner of her peripheral vision, Brierly detected the spin of jagged lines that were both *there* and *not there*. Voracity's exquisitely sculpted form thrust through the lights. Her body, though it towered several feet over her, was generally human in shape. Bits did not materialize fully even here in the dream world: the jagged lines that formed her wings, smoky feet and hair. Brierly might as well have been a child playing dress-up, a gooseberry bush at a costume ball, compared to the breathtaking beauty of this fairy who grew foot-long thorns from her smoky hair.

"Brierly. What would your parents think of such behavior, barging into my home without a proper invitation?"

A fairy, even one you hated, was stunning in full form. Brierly's brain felt numb and foggy, as though she was a child who had gorged on too many sweets and was caught now between coma and stomachache. Brierly clutched her hatred as though it were a fiery brand that could help keep her alert.

"I haven't come to debate my parents' christening etiquette. I came for Nissa," Brierly said.

"Nissa?" Voracity's surprise was not even well-feigned. "That sugary creampuff Prince-slavering bookmole?"

"I know you have her. Give her back!"

"A contest of queens. Are you certain you want that? If I am queen, you have no power here. You are mine to rule. If you are queen, then you made me, you made Nissa, you made your own reality. You're alone in all the worlds. What will it be, Brierly? Solitary freedom? Or eternity with me?"

"You're a liar."

"Do you not yet know what that word means? A lie is simply an option you'd rather not consider."

Brierly opened her mouth and let loose a banshee aria of swooping pitches. One of these pitches would resonate with the stone and mortar behind Voracity. The fortress would rattle apart.

Voracity tore a swatch off each sleeve, rolled them between her long fingers, and inserted the tubes in her pointed ears.

Brierly scooped her pitch high then low, like a plunging hawk, and up again. There! The glass on the side of the fortress shattered. Shards rained down like jagged diamonds. Brierly leapt out of the way, but the shards turned abruptly in midair and embedded in the mortar. The stones shifted, chewed the glass, and resettled like a giant after a feast.

Voracity applauded, each clap spaced well apart like the ticking of a metronome set on *Adagio*. "Is your concert over?"

"Don't applaud between movements," Brierly said.

Brierly launched a series of running sixteenth notes, faster than any she had sung during her singing duel with the King's Fool. She aimed them at the base of the fortress, where the vines of thorns twisted up the fortress's spindly neck. The sharp points of the double flags on the sixteenth notes blurred as they whirled through the air and whacked into the vines.

Voracity cupped her hand, palm up, by her shoulder. A tar-black crow grew out of the spikes of her left wing and perched on her shoulder. It shook its plumage, and Brierly saw that each of its shaggy feathers was a musical note. She could not count the frizzy pinions, but they must be thirty-second notes, or sixty-fourth, notes so fast she could not separate them into distinct pitches. It beat its wings, each beat a rip of sound.

The crow hurled itself into the air so quickly that Brierly could not track its movements. It let loose a hoarse caw, like a bat seeking insects. The slower-moving sixteenth notes were no match for the crow's speed. The crow spiraled around the throat of the fortress and swallowed up the sixteenth notes. The heavy stories of stone groaned and swayed, but the vines caught them up and held them firm. Frantic sixteenth notes skittered away, a confused swarm of plinking dissonances. The crow's beak snapped them into staccato silence.

The terrifying cacophony covered over the formation of Brierly's whole note. She sang it out in a slow controlled exhale, as she might blow a giant bubble, until her diaphragm burned. The whole note floated, slow-moving, translucent, and low in the air. The crow plunged at it, into it. The whole note swallowed, swelled blue-black, and burped mangled feathers.

Then the whole note popped with a sound like the belch of bruised harp.

Voracity flashed to Brierly's side in a motion more rapid than her pet crow. "That was unnecessary."

Voracity yanked Brierly up by her hair. Her other hand closed on Brierly's windpipe. Her icy strong fingers paused, half crushing, half considering.

"Kill me, then," Brierly forced through her bruised throat.

Voracity released her neck and tweaked her nose with barely suppressed violence. "Do you promise to stay dead this time?" Her fingers squeezed the sides of Brierly's nostrils and cut off her air. "All I can offer you is pain. Is that what you want, suicidal little princessling?"

Voracity twisted Brierly's nose and it came off in her hand. Brierly gasped and snorted blood into her throat.

"Does pain offer you confirmation of your own paltry existence?" Voracity said.

What if, Brierly thought with a pang, she was just as self-destructive as the Thorn King? But she hadn't come for that this time. She grew her nose back, as well as twenty feet of hair. She imagined a pair of sewing scissors and cropped her Rapunzel coiffure. Voracity was left holding the slack end.

Brierly wielded the four-inch sewing scissors before her. "I want Nissa back."

"You demand Nissa of me yet offer nothing in return."

"What can I possibly have that you can't get by your own power?"

"The spindle."

Brierly imagined a spindle into the dream and hurtled it toward Voracity like a javelin. It turned to dry pine needles mid-trajectory and scattered to the wind.

"Not just any spindle, princessling. If you want to save Nissa, bring me the spindle from the world where you first met her."

"I don't even know where the spindle is."

Voracity arched a single brow. "Estepel. Didn't you know your darling mama brought it back from Conquisan? She thought she could destroy it, the silly little dear. Ah, but you slept right through that. Just go to Estepel and I'm sure you'll be able to find it from there. It is your spindle, after all."

"Why do you want it?"

Voracity looked at her with a small smile.

Brierly crouched like a wary cat. "I don't trust you."

"That doesn't mean we can't be useful to each other. I can't—won't bring Nissa back unless you go fetch that spindle. Besides, what could the spindle do to you at this point? You're already asleep."

Still Brierly hesitated.

"You see, little briar girl, in your heart you are a coward. I offer you a solution to your quandary, but you would rather play my victim. Because without me, who are you?"

"I am Brierly Steward!" Brierly hurled another fleet of spindles at Voracity. They paused midair, then clattered together in a heap, but not before everything had vanished of Voracity but her mocking laughter.

A jolt knocked Brierly into another dream. The scent of horse filled her nostrils, and muscled flesh moved beneath her. Another jolt as the horse's hoof found a root in the road and jarred her well into awareness.

She was riding through the green depths of her beloved Sentre Forest. Now that she was fully in this dream her legs tightened out of reflex into proper sitting posture. A masculine arm at her waist kept her from moving too far. Had she fled Boxleyn with Arpien? Dreams didn't always bother filling in gaps. She twisted around to ask her riding partner what happened.

It was Sir Flatwhist of Strand.

41

Arpien

The dungeons of Boxleyn were pristine, as dungeons went. The Montaines' policy toward troublemakers tended toward either negotiating with them or quietly whisking them off the playing board. Neither option lent for lengthy dungeon stays. Yet the vacant cells carried the vinegary scent of recent scrubbing, no doubt by the order of the fastidious Queen Perturbance. Everything was spartan but in perfect order, down to the regulation dungeon swill and the heirloom torture devices displayed on the wall opposite Arpien's cell. They were intimidating, but so clean Arpien doubted they'd ever been used. Which might be nothing but his own wishful thinking.

There was plenty of time for thinking, both the wishful and the hopeless kind. Enough time to deduce that Sir Flatwhist must have falsely accused him to gain two things: Brierly and the vademecum sword. Both would help him get the mantiz egg sacs Strand so badly needed as a cure to plague. Arpien had heard the rumors of Strand's marriage counterproposal, but never heeded them. Brierly was no more likely to wed a prince she had never seen than she was to wed him.

Arpien banged his forehead softly against the bars. Softly because the guard looked ready to chain him to the wall if Arpien hit his cage with any real force. The guard eyed him as though Arpien might be casting some magical escape spell on loan from the rest of the Conquisani. Or as though he could headbutt his way out of his cell.

Arpien cursed himself with each thunk.

Fool. Fool to tell Lord Culmney anything about the vademecum sword's unusual properties. Though he hadn't gone out of his way to keep his sword a secret. He'd bragged to his brother, set Nissa to researching it, and practiced letting it drag him about the grounds. Of course Sir Flatwhist had found out about its powers, mantiz-taming and otherwise.

Fool.

Arpien tried to send warning to Brierly through the dungeon guard. At first the guard refused to pass along any message from a Conquisani conspirator. When the guard finally gave way, he returned shame-faced to admit that Princess Brierly was nowhere to be found. Arpien sent a plea to Cuz to find her, without much hope that his message would be heard in the confusion after the roof collapse. After several more indeterminable hours, the guard reported that the entire Strandish delegation had vacated Boxleyn after the tragedy at the ball. One groom had spotted an unconscious fair-haired young woman among them. Half her face was wrapped in bandages, so he'd assumed she was one of the Strandish delegation who'd been wounded when the roof collapsed. The Rosarians insisted they did not have the men to go after her.

Arpien kicked the walls of his tidy dungeon cell. He was as helpless to save Brierly as he was to help Nissa. As helpless as he'd been to save Kirren.

Brierly had meant to hurt him with that barb, and she had. He did not blame her. Her own desperation had made her lash out at him, but what made it effective was that the end of the whip was soaked in truth. He'd told her himself of the vow spoken on his sister's grave. Every step he'd taken away from that river bank had been to forge himself into the undefeatable hero. Arpien's earliest memories were of Kirren reading a finger-loved copy of *Tales of the Prince*, while Arpien dashed about the room on chubby legs and reenacted the scenes. Did he attempt mighty deeds because he was brave, or because he was terrified? Was he eighteen years old, or had he been six for twelve extra years?

He hurled his swill bowl against the immaculate stone wall. The only effect this had was startling the guard and the few lean rats who tried to scrounge a living in the rarely inhabited cells. The rats decided he was mostly bluster and tricked in for the leftover swill he'd spattered across the room.

Was this what Brierly felt like? Trapped in the prison of her mind, no one to care if she screamed or begged or wrote sonnets? A single day had brought him to this, and she'd faced imprisonment for 36,525 days.

He wouldn't be in prison that long. Admit it, unless someone in Rosaria grew a brain, they were likely to kill him in a matter of days. He might last longer if they tortured Conquisani military secrets from him first. Cheerful thought.

A conundrum: What does the rescuer do when he himself needs rescuing?

Perhaps from these months of practice it was natural that he sought the vademecum sword without fully realizing what he did. The waves of anger and helplessness did not ebb, but by slow bits he realized they no longer ripped him here and there at their capricious will. He'd latched on to some solid reef, a reef that took on a shape remarkably like the vademecum sword.

It was not possible. Sir Flatwhist had stolen the sword. Arpien moved the fluid hands of his mind around his anchor, testing its stability. The sword itself felt miles away, but its personality felt closer than ever before. Alive and wild. Calling him to action.

It infused him with strength that could bend bars of iron. He clenched the bars of his cell and sucked in a deep breath. He was a rescuer, was he not? He strained against the bars.

Nothing happened.

The power drained out of him long before he quit trying to bend the bars. He really was powerless without his sword.

No, he was powerless without the one who forged it.

"I give up," he said aloud. "I don't have what it takes. He does. So tell me what I'm supposed to do."

There was no flash of insight. Still, drop by slow drop, a white peace dripped into Arpien's soul. For the first time in months, perhaps his whole life, Arpien Trouvel quit trying to save the world. That choice was in the hands of someone else. In those hands Arpien found security he hadn't known since before Kirren died.

Four hours later, Cuz trudged down to the dungeon. His eyes were sunken like an old man's. In less than a day his childhood had been scathed from him with a paring knife.

"Is it true, what they're saying?" Cuz said.

"It is true Conquisan is behind the attack at the ball. But I had nothing to do with it."

Arpien reached through the bars as if to touch Cuz's shoulder. The guard took a step forward, and Arpien curled his hand around a bar of the door instead. "Cuz, are you all right?"

"What a stupid question." Here the familiar childish petulance emerged. "My family's been murdered by a fictitious creature, they say your brother's gone back to muster an army, and everyone's expecting me to know what to do about it."

Cuz was in charge? Then the rest of the royal line really was dead. Oh, Nissa.

"What will you do about it?" Arpien said.

"General Gapric says we should keep you as a hostage and try to bargain with you."

Arpien barked a humorless laugh. "I'd fetch a poor price. Cryndien tried to kill me, too."

"Can you stop him?"

"Not by myself. But I can go after Brierly. There's a prophecy that says she can bring back the Prince, and he can stop Voracity."

"Sleepyhead can do that?" Cuz scrunched up his nose in an expression of adolescent skepticism, but said, "Go on and get her, if you can. I don't care. I just don't want you here, because they say I should torture you. Maybe I even want to."

At Cuz's signal, which he had to give twice, a guard unlocked Arpien's cell. Now Arpien did touch the boy's shoulder. "Cuz—"

Cuz shrugged him off and stormed up the stairs. "Get out of here." His voice sounded like he had a sudden violent cold.

Arpien ran straight for the stables. Rather than risk Fearless dumping him when he reached the posby bushes by the northern gate, he saddled Windried. Windried was the fastest of the three horses, and Nissa would not have minded him stealing her horse if she knew it was to save Brierly.

There were two routes to Strand. Brierly's captors might catch a ship at the southern port of Selkeh. Or perhaps they'd battle their way through one of the rough passes through the mountains that separated Strand from Rosaria. But which one?

If only he had the vademecum sword. He could use it as a princess detector.

Wait. As long as the Strandish had both Brierly and the sword, he need only locate one to find both. And he knew how to find the sword, even from a distance. Months ago, he'd called to the sword in the Teardrop Mountains, far overseas, and it had called back. And hadn't he just felt the sword's presence, even in his dungeon cell?

You seek the sword and the sword seeks you.

His soul spun and latched onto a point in the middle of Sentre Forest, just as though he held the sword in his hand.

He wheeled Windried around north.

42
Brierly

Not the most comfortable position in the world, to ride crammed against the pommel of a jostling saddle, neck craned about like a stork. Sir Flatwhist's stubby brown goatee jutted forward, a caterpillar flexing its muscles. After a good ten-second stare, Brierly gave her favorite bland "hm" and faced front. Sir Flatwhist's sinewy arm tensed around her as though he expected her to leap off the horse. In another mood she might have grinned at the heavy iron manacles that clanked between her limp wrists. Sir Flatwhist clearly remembered her propensity for undoing rope knots. But Brierly was in no mood for amusement. She rode without protest, until Sir Flatwhist broke the silence.

"You're surprisingly devoid of curiosity."

Pointless statements didn't require answers.

"I don't mean to harm you, if that's what's keeping you silent. Of course, if you try to skewer me like last time, I may have to harm you."

"It doesn't matter." She tried to yawn, but her heart wasn't in it. She'd seen better acting than hers in an amateur Punch and Judy show.

"So you always say," Sir Flatwhist said. "Since that's the case, we're going to do something that matters to me. Heal my land."

"I don't want to heal, I want to wound."

"Aye, wounding Strandishmen seems to give you pleasure."

"Not Strand."

"Then who? The Conquisani? Aye, you'd be most effective in battle. Perhaps you could faint again."

She flipped her head so her hair smacked him in the face like a horse's tail. She hoped it tickled. Or itched. Or both. "You understand nothing."

"I understand better than you think. Someone dear to you dies, and you must utterly destroy the destroyer. Until then, no bread will fill you, no water quench your thirst, no sun warm you." His tone was bland. Bland as the bread that did not fill.

"Your wife." She trampled a pang of understanding. It was almost the first thing Lord Culmney had told her, all those weeks ago when she arrived at Boxleyn. Culmney had lost his only daughter to the tree-plague. Sir Flatwhist was his son-in-law.

His fist clenched. It pressed into her stomach, as though she had run into an iron doorknob.

"You were right, woman of briars. We are much alike. Rather than waste you in your own fruitless attempt for justice, you will help me in mine, and live the longer for it. In Rosaria, how many times did someone try to assassinate you? How long would you last in a battle with Conquisan? An extraordinary number of people wish you ill, Your Highness. In my country, everyone will place your life ahead of his own."

"Until you force me to marry your prince, get my dowry, and have no further use for me."

"How long we can use you will be up to you. Wouldn't you like to be the banner of a resurrected nation? In Strand people will revere you as the compassionate princess who restored their kingdom. Musicians will sing songs about you. The poor will name their children after you. The rich will commission statues of you."

Another pedestal from which to fall.

"All you have to do to get it," he said, "is keep your mouth closed."

She shifted, and something cold and hard rammed into her hip. She glanced down. Strapped to the saddle were three bags of fine Conquisani weave. She wasn't surprised the Strandish were stealing mantiz egg sacs again. No, what drew her eyes like a magnet to ferrus wood was the handle jutting from a familiar scabbard.

"You have the vademecum sword."

"Prince Arpien didn't need it anymore."

Her vivid imagination offered her an array of images of Arpien skewered on his brother's sword, disintegrated into dust motes by Voracity, fricasseed by dragon's flame—all the traditional endings for her rescuing princes.

I don't care. I don't care.

"Why not?" she said.

"He's been arrested for the assassination of the Rosarian royal line."

It was sick humor. She twisted around. "That's not true. He had nothing to do with it."

"Truth is a matter of perception. Besides, you told me yourself of your indifference to him. Or were you hoping he'd rescue you again? Don't you see that only I can save you now?"

If everyone defined his own right and wrong, as she'd been saying for years, then she had no way to tell him he was wrong now.

"I should warn you, then, what becomes of my rescuers." She turned her back to him and didn't speak again until nightfall.

The next two silent days of the abduction proved a trying ordeal for Brierly. Sir Flatwhist didn't abuse her. Other than keeping her in iron manacles, he was no worse than a brusque bodyguard. What anger she felt toward the Strandish knight for kidnapping her was negated by a reluctant pity for his loss. What little they spoke to each other was matter-of-fact. *We're stopping here for the night. Eat this. I need to relieve myself.*

No, the trying part of her abduction was how much time it left her to think. They spent hour after hour galloping through Sentre Forest. No forest creatures appeared to talk to. Sir Flatwhist's horse refused to speak to her because she had tied his tether in an impossible tangle when she escaped the brigands. There were no courtiers to amuse with her ditties and tricks. Just as desperately as they had turned to the charming young princess for distraction, she craved distraction herself. Otherwise her mind went back to Nissa, the young rose crushed under a falling roof. It went back to Arpien, humming a soft ballad in her ear while they swept across the ballroom floor. Arpien, vulnerable without his vademecum sword, in the dungeons below Boxleyn. Were both Arpien and Nissa lost to her, as were her parents, her childhood friends, her fairy godparents, the Prince himself? Was Voracity right—she was the only constant in Brierly's life?

The hours Brierly rode like a gunnysack through the endless forest become a symbol for her entire existence. Tedious. Chaffing. Always in motion, but running toward something? Away from something?

For the time being she let the dream tug her toward Estepel, because that's where Voracity had said she would find the spindle. But once Voracity had what she wanted, why would she honor her promise? Better yet, why did Voracity want the spindle? If Brierly controlled the spindle, could she use Voracity's own power against her? Or if she could destroy the spindle, could she destroy the Curse? Even destroy Voracity herself, if the link between the evil fairy and the spindle were strong enough?

Before she could solve any of these issues, she had to get away from Sir Flatwhist. And soon, because they were fast approaching Estepel. Brierly recognized the landmarks: the purple bark of the ferrus trees that flourished just south of Estepel, the crisp snaps of lightning sparks in their foliage as the electric tree eels leaped from branch to branch.

Her opportunity came on the third morning after the ruinous Spring Ball. She'd slept chained between Sir Flatwhist and the horse. It wasn't as uncomfortable as it sounded. Sir Flatwhist was not cruel—he just took thorough precautions against the woman who had once stabbed him in the thigh with a root vegetable. He'd left enough slack in the chain that she could lie down with hands pillowed under her cheek. However, he distanced himself from the horse such that Brierly, suspended between the two, would be unable to reach either should she decide to attack them while they slept.

After a short night, Sir Flatwhist demanded they press on. Brierly yawned as Sir Flatwhist hoisted her into the saddle. She was full well capable of mounting on her own, but it had become a matter of stubbornness to inconvenience the knight by making him drag her around like a limp doll.

As he posed to spring up behind her in the saddle, she let herself start to slide drowsily toward the ground. He growled at her and pushed her back upright by her shoulders. As he did, there came the slow scrape of metal against metal.

Brierly let the sound register with him before pressing the cold, hard tip of the vademecum sword against his breastbone. She'd grabbed the handle while pretending to fall off the horse, and he'd been so annoyed pushing her back upright that he hadn't realized she was drawing the sword from his scabbard.

Brierly smiled sleepily down at him. "Mother-May-I says, take one giant step back." She dug deeper with the sword to encourage his participation in the childhood game. Oh, the frustration on his face as he obeyed was the most entertaining thing she'd seen for days. She jerked the vademecum sword away from his chest and up through the chain that linked him to her. At the same time she kicked her heels against the horse's sides with a cry to spur him into motion.

Several things went wrong at once. She had overdone the war cry and startled the horse into a full gallop. The bothersome vademecum sword, the very sword she'd seen Arpien drive into the rock walls of Boxleyn Palace, glanced off the chain like a butter knife. The intact chain jerked Sir Flatwhist forward and dragged him full tilt behind the horse.

Brierly groaned. She didn't like this figment, but she didn't mean to drag him to shreds like Hector around the walls of Troy. The chain that bound her to Sir Flatwhist went completely taut as he skidded behind them. The tension nearly jerked her shoulder out of socket. She clenched her legs with all her strength to try to remain in the saddle, which the horse took as further encouragement to run faster. She had to stop or be ripped apart.

With one hand wrenched behind her and the other clinging to the pommel of the saddle, she couldn't even lift her hands to grab the reins. She had managed to keep hold of the vademecum sword, but it was in the hand that was currently being stretched to twice its normal length behind her. She couldn't swing it at an angle that might have cut the chain.

Behind her Sir Flatwhist pulled himself up the chain arm-over-arm. His leather riding armor protected his skin from being chaffed clean off his flesh. Brierly entwined her feet in the stirrups and wound the slack chain that tied her right arm to the saddle around the pommel. She reached her left hand across her body to grab the vademecum sword from her right, and sliced through the leather strap that held the saddle on the horse.

Brierly flung the vademecum sword to one side as she tumbled off the horse. She slammed to the ground and rolled in a tangle of leather, metal links, and trampling hooves. The fall tried to accomplish what the chains hadn't and knock her right shoulder out of socket.

Spindles, that hurt.

She might have screamed, if she had any wind left in her lungs. She lay paralyzed on the ground, and listened to the roiled duet of her rapid pulse and the horse's retreating hoofbeats.

Sir Flatwhist glowered down at her. The reclaimed vademecum sword quivered from anger or muscle fatigue in his clenched fist.

With her left arm wrapped up tightly in the chain, and her right spasming as though pulled out of its socket, Brierly couldn't even raise a hand to defend herself. Her focus fixed on Sir Flatwhist's trembling fist. Was he going to kill her? Her heartbeat accelerated with anticipation. Yet she wasn't afraid. Perhaps it was because twigs jutted from the knight's hair and clothes like he was an unkempt porcupine. Perhaps it was the flash of insight that he hated the plague more than he hated her. Her dowry could save his country, and thus it could save her.

"I wasn't trying to kill you." It was hard to form the wheezy words. Her lungs were flat bellows.

The hint of pity set him off. He grabbed the chain and jerked her up by her injured shoulder. Painful specks of light swarmed from the back of her head to her eyes and nose. It momentarily cut off both sight and breath. Then, as though through a thick blanket, she heard a voice.

"If you hurt her I will run you through where you stand."

Her recurring prince.

Her vision cleared a little, but she didn't trust it. Arpien rode into her line of sight, sword drawn. Both sword and horse were the wrong shape and color. Wait. Windried?

Her heartbeat was a galloping horse, and she doubted even Windried could go faster.

"If you try to run me through, I will hurt her first," Sir Flatwhist said.

Brierly sagged from her abused right arm and swam back toward the dream with Arpien in it. "He won't kill me, Arpien. He needs my dowry."

"I said hurt, not kill," Sir Flatwhist said. "Though I will do both if necessary."

"You will do neither while I have breath," Arpien said.

Even smeared in her fuzzy vision, her recurring prince made a dashing silhouette.

"The best way to ensure that is to let us proceed into Strand. She will be honored there as queen."

"This is your idea of honor? Look at her!"

"Her injuries are entirely her own doing. Ask her."

Even in the fog of pain, the one thought that became clear to her was that Arpien must remain intact. If it had hurt so much to lose Nissa, how could she bear to lose Arpien, too?

If she agreed to go to Strand, would Arpien stand down? But the spindle would not be in Strand. What did she want more—to preserve her pet figment or avenge herself against Voracity?

As the two warriors faced off, her Fine Ears picked up a faint whinny of terror. The men were too engaged in taking each other's measure to notice. The hittal trees rustled above her.

She might not have to go to Strand after all.

With a grunt she foisted the saddle, bags, and chains into the air. "Look!" she shouted. "I have your egg sacs!"

She couldn't raise her right arm even halfway, and the strength of her left wasn't great enough to hold everything aloft more than a few breaths. Luckily, the mantizes didn't take much convincing. Six beautifully sleek and dangerous insects leapt from the branches and encircled the humans on the ground. Windried sidestepped nervously, but this time Arpien was forewarned to keep tight rein on his horse.

Her fairy Gift was quicker, this time, to let her in on the mantizes' conversation.

why is it here again with our eggs? *not our eggs, but of our kind* *our agreement for one day only* *expired* *expired*

Antennae rustled in agreement.

it has stolen eggs twice *danger* *kill it*

"No." Brierly pointed at Sir Flatwhist. The chains rendered the gesture only partially effective. "This is the one who's been taking your egg sacs."

all humans look alike *kill them all. danger to eggs* *waste to kill only human smart enough to talk* *hungry* *you ate whole horse*

"For the last time, you may not eat Arpien!" Brierly said.

The other two humans might not understand Mantiz, but it hardly needed translation for them to understand that Brierly was losing the debate. The mantizes tightened their circle. Arpien and Sir Flatwhist raised their swords.

It was then that the mantizes noticed a complication Brierly had forgotten. *it has the Prince's sword!*

Every creature tensed in nervous anticipation, but only Brierly fully understood the joke of their improbable standoff. Sir Flatwhist wanted to attack Brierly but was held off by his need for her dowry. Arpien wanted to attack Sir Flatwhist but was held back by the threat to Brierly. The mantizes wanted to attack them all but were held back by the vademecum sword.

"Then you aren't a madwoman. You do have the Gift of Animal Speech," Sir Flatwhist said. "Tell them to back away."

When Brierly remained silent, he shook the vademecum sword at the encroaching insects. "Do it!"

The mantizes sat back without her command.

"What you bragged about was true, young prince. The mantizes obey the sword." Sir Flatwhist ran his thumb across the tiny gleaming teardrop-shaped ruby inlaid in the blade near the sword's hilt. "Do you know what this could mean to Strand? Princess, tell them to retrieve their egg sacs and bring them here."

"You're asking them to sacrifice their children."

"They're just bugs."

"They're my subjects!"

The mantizes understood only half of the conversation, but it was enough to set their antennae waving in agitation. *it wants more eggs?* *will not give it our offspring* *it has a Prince's sword, must obey* *it is a false wielder. Prince would not ask this* *you claim you know Prince's orders?*

Sir Flatwhist held the vademecum sword like a banner in front of him. "Eat him." He nodded toward Arpien. "Then go fetch your eggs. Tell them, Princess."

"No."

"Tell them!" He jerked her arm. Her vision flickered with specks of light again, as though pixies danced before her.

"Don't hurt her!" Arpien lunged toward Sir Flatwhist, but one of the mantizes plucked Arpien from Windried's back. Windried tore off with a flash of strawberry-red tail.

Arpien started to plunge his sword at the mantiz, but Brierly stopped him. "Arpien, it only wants to examine you."

Triangular heads and multifaceted eyes peered at Arpien. He dangled upside-down by one leg. *same one as last time. Blood smells same* *brown-shelled one had sword last time* *then why does blue-shelled one have Prince's sword now?*

"Arpien," Brierly said, "they want you to prove you own the sword."

Arpien's face was turning an impressive radish red from either frustration or the blood rushing to his head. "That bossy butter knife only listens to me half the time!"

Sir Flatwhist smothered Brierly's next suggestion with his scraped-up hand. The grit on his hand grated against her lips as she tried to speak.

"That's enough from you, Princess," Sir Flatwhist said. "I think they understand the basics well enough without you and your fairy Gift." With the sword's tip he pointed to the mantizes and then to Arpien. "Eat him."

Arpien closed his eyes and went limp. The mantiz holding him dropped him. Arpien landed with an *oof* and rolled to his feet.

brown-shelled one is the true wielder *kill the false.*

The air around Brierly blurred with green saw-toothed limbs. The justice of mantizes was swift. Sir Flatwhist screamed. His grip on Brierly contracted, then released. The mantizes dragged Sir Flatwhist's body overhead into the trees. Brierly, still chained to Sir Flatwhist, gasped as she was wrenched upward after him.

But here was Arpien. He seized the vademecum sword where it had fallen from Sir Flatwhist's numb grasp. The sword, which refused to slice the chain for Brierly, had no scruples about doing so for Arpien. It bit a good five inches into the bark of the hittal tree. Arpien caught Brierly as she fell. He set her down only long enough to pry the vademecum sword from the tree and slice through the other chain that bound her to the saddle. He scooped her up again and dashed them both away from the feeding mantizes.

It was entirely too nice to ride in those strong arms, but nothing affected her more than the faint tremor in his hands.

"You can set me down," she said. "My legs work fine. I don't think the mantizes will attack us now."

He obeyed and attempted that shaky smile of his that made gravity switch direction. Her knees were warm candle wax. Maybe her legs didn't work as well as she thought.

"Only now do I fully appreciate what fate I might have met a month ago, had you not talked the mantizes out of it," he said.

She hadn't talked them out of it this time. Sir Flatwhist had brought about his own fate by trying to steal the mantizes' young, but Brierly understood why he had. Another figment blotted out, and by her doing.

"You convinced that mantiz to release you. How?" she asked.

"I concentrated on the sword. That's how I found you, too. I've been following you for two days and nights."

Brierly examined her recurring prince for alterations, and found him scruffy but relatively undamaged. Indeed, he looked much as he had the first time she'd met him, outfitted in bedraggled midnight blue doublet and breeches, minus the cap and the stage fright. Why then did he look entirely new to her? The only thing she could name that was different was the short brown stubble on his face, which made him look troublesomely, ruggedly handsome. The pesky bird was flapping around in her ribcage again.

She shifted away from him and winced as it added pressure to her arm. She cupped her left palm under her right forearm to lift some of the weight off her shoulder.

"Uh-oh. I've seen soldiers hold their arms like that before."

He reached out a tentative hand, waited for permission she neither gave nor denied, then probed her shoulder, fingers as light as a lithe cat skimming a rooftop. No doubt he was as careful as he could be, but by the time he pulled away Brierly had discovered her vocabulary was in some respects broader than even Arpien's. She managed to swallow most of it back down, as well as making a fair attempt to swallow her own tongue.

Arpien shook his head. "If you knocked it partially out of socket earlier, it snapped back on its own. Shoulder joints do that sometimes. It'll swell as big and red as Cryndien's head for a day or two, but it will heal. Faster if you can keep from moving it." He glanced around. "We should make you a sling."

Out of what? They had nothing but a couple of swords and the clothes on their backs, and Brierly would rather keep material on her back than on her arm.

But the sturdy, broad greenwax ferns made for a good substitute. Arpien hacked down the thin trailing end of a pliable vine and tied her cradled arm up in a half-bend. It tickled when he scooped fallen locks of her hair out of the way and over her opposite shoulder, like an awkward chamberlain drawing a curtain to one side. But her giggles died stillborn when he tied the ends of the vine together and his warm knuckles brushed her nape.

Her vision started to blur, and she was surprised to find that it was not from lightheadedness but from an excess of moisture in her eyes. She needed a distraction, now. She grabbed onto the physical pain as though it were a solid thing.

Arpien glanced at her profile, but if he noticed the stupid sheen, he was too tactful to mention it—or as much out of his element with tears as she was.

She didn't tell him she bit her bottom lip not to ward against pain but to ward against his gentleness.

She knew she ought to run away from Arpien. Their very proximity was an invitation to Voracity. Yet Arpien didn't appear to need the vademecum sword in his hand to use it as a princess-detector. And, she finally admitted, she didn't want to run from Arpien.

"Finished," he said, but his fingers kept smoothing imaginary hairs from the vine knot. She knew they were imaginary, because she felt no corresponding prickle on her scalp. At least not the unpleasurable kind.

Brierly's Fine Ears picked up the ticking of a clock approaching midnight.

She sighed. "Well, there's nothing for it. You better come with me so I can keep an eye on you."

"I thought I was keeping an eye on you."

"Well, it can't hurt if I look back."

What was this silly rush of warmth in her cheeks? She tossed her hair so some of the loose locks hid her face from him. She felt the heat of his touch lift away, like a feverish moth taking flight.

"Even without Windried, we can't be more than half a day from Estepel," she said.

"Estepel? I thought you'd want to go to Boxleyn."

"The spindle's at Estepel. Voracity said that if I brought her the spindle, she'd give back Nissa."

Through ragged blond draperies Brierly saw Arpien's brown eyes soften. "Brierly, Nissa was my friend, too, but I don't think even a fairy has the power—"

Brierly waved his objection aside. The gesture sent spiky tingles across her collarbone and down her sore arm. "Just because people die, it doesn't mean they have to stay dead."

"We know Voracity's a liar. And the spindle has proven rather, uh, unbeneficial to your health in the past."

"You're the strategist. Why would Voracity ask for the spindle unless it gives her power? Gowsma told me that Voracity invested a lot of her power in the spindle. If we have it, we can use it against it her."

"No offense, but when did you become proficient in spindle-wielding?"

He must be remembering her hunger for the spindle in the embarrassing dream of her seventeenth birthday ball. Too bad she couldn't grow dragon fangs here. Luckily, dragon fangs weren't necessary to persuade him; Arpien consulted the vademecum sword as a tiebreaker. It too pointed toward Estepel.

Outvoted, Arpien slammed the sword back into his scabbard. "Fine, you blunt piece of tin. But if we're going to prune hedges again, you better be more helpful this time."

The blade vibrated at Arpien's side, as though it were snickering at him.

"And to think how badly I wanted this bossy fire poker back," he said.

Brierly didn't believe a word of his fussing. But she did note that for the first time, she and the overrated pig-sticker agreed on something.

43
Nissa

Nissa Montaine woke from her long sleep to find a prince hovering by her bedside. It would have been a scene fit for embroidery but for two things. First, her right eye had swollen shut. Second, the prince slumped in a chair at her bedside was chubby, sullen, and wore mismatched stockings.

He poked her arm until she came fully awake. "I thought you were going to sleep forever."

Nissa pushed herself up on her elbows. "Cuz, what happened? Did everyone get out safely?"

He shook his head no.

Dead? *Oh, Brierly. Oh, Arpien and Timothy, who were both kind to me.* She even mourned Uncle Emol and Aunt Perturbance. Perhaps they hadn't been affectionate, but they had seen she had a bed and food and a passing education. They'd been family. All of them gone, now. Except this one bratty boy before her, thrust suddenly into adulthood.

His eyes widened. "I'm king now."

If he were older, she would have encouraged him with her solemn fealty. If he were younger, she would have hugged him. But he was twelve. Combustible, fragile twelve.

Cuz swung his foot back and forth. His toe rammed against the bed. "How did you know about the attack?"

"Prince Bo warned me. I think."

"Why would he warn you and then kill everybody?"

"I don't think it was Bo, but Voracity."

"General Gapric says there's no such person as Voracity. He says this garble about evil fairies is a tactic to make Conquisan seem more powerful."

"Some things are real, whether we like it or not."

"If Bo was on our side, he wouldn't be preparing the Conquisani army to attack Boxleyn right now."

Thorns and thistles. "He isn't. They aren't."

"Some things are real, whether we like it or not," he shot back at her. "General Gapric says they could reach Boxleyn in less than two weeks."

"We've got to ride out to stop them. Cuz, did you send troops to meet them?"

"Of course. I'm not stupid. No one can find them. It's like they're invisible."

And Nissa knew they possessed an invisibilifier.

"How do you know they're coming?" she asked.

"Because they're leaving a big swath through Sentre Forest. And they're stealing things from the holdings they pass. Hams. Chickens."

"How can you believe in magic but not in Voracity?"

"I never said that. I said General Gapric thinks there's no such person."

"What do you think, Cuz?"

Cuz kicked the bed frame harder. "I wish people would quit asking me what I think!" he said.

You're king.

Cuz must know how much rested on him. He was a pest, not an idiot. But it must be hard to lead a country against invasion when you had never expected to inherit the throne, when you had no battle experience, and when you had just lost everyone you loved.

"I'm so sorry, Cuz," she said. "I lost my parents, too. I wasn't old enough to remember much about it, but I remember that horrible distortion. As if ceilings were floors and floors were ceilings."

"I'm not a little boy." Cuz crossed his arms and scowled, which negated the effect of his statement. "Don't pretend you're sad. You never loved my parents and they never loved you."

Each little jolt of Cuz' foot banging against the bed seemed to intensify as it traveled through the frame, the ropes, the down mattresses, into Nissa's very skin. For a stupid moment Nissa felt like the princess in the old tale, tormented by a small dried pea under her mattress. Battered by the un-ignorable, compressed ball of pain.

As though in comparison to Cuz, the tiny bruises she felt only proved that she was never a true member of the royal family.

"Your friends are still alive," said Cuz. "So how could you know what I feel?"

Nissa sat up the rest of the way. "You said they were all dead."

"You're as bad as General Gapric. You hear things I never said."

"Brierly and Arpien survived? Where are they?"

Cuz glanced away like he'd been caught in some mischief. "Uh, well, I don't really know. Brierly disappeared less than a day after the ball. We think the Strandish kidnapped her."

"Send someone after her!"

"I can't. There's an army coming, Nissa."

She knew that, but still …

"Arpien rode after them to get his sword back. Maybe he'll get her back, too," Cuz said.

"I'll help you defend Boxleyn." Nissa swung her feet out of bed. Where were her stockings? She teetered on feet made tingly from being bedridden too long.

Cuz leaned forward, but sank back down when she found her balance. "Thanks, but what can you do, Nissa? Organize a sewing circle?"

"I'll invite Gowsma back," she said, her head buried in the chest at the foot of her bed.

"That ugly hag?"

"Good fairy." Nissa chucked a stocking at him. "You saw what power Voracity had. Think what another fairy could do against her. You really should send someone after Brierly. She's the last Steward. The prophecy says—"

"An evil fairy will take over, only a Steward can stop her and bring back the Prince." Cuz retrieved the stocking from the bed—she had missed him by a yard—and balled the sock in his hands. "If you believe all that."

"You believed me at the ball."

"I felt guilty for firing croquettes at you earlier." He launched the balled-up sock at her, but this attack, too, fell short.

"Oh. Well, believe me now. Our best chance is to bring the Prince back, and we can't do that unless we get Brierly back."

"I told you, Nissa, there's an army coming. Besides, the Strandish are a two-day ride ahead of us, and we don't know exactly where they are."

"I was asleep so long?"

"Yeah." There was a knock on the door. A messenger entered and murmured in Cuz's ear. Cuz stood up. "Sorry, got to go run my kingdom now." His voice wasn't quite brave enough to give the line its proper flippancy.

Kendra wasn't here, so Nissa stuffed her bruised limbs into her loosest dress without assistance. The rose-colored dress, the one Brierly had sewn for her with her Gift, had slipped to the floor when she threw open her trunk. One sleeve reached up, like a collapsed supplicant denied entry.

Thinking of Brierly brought a pang of hurt.

Nissa spoke aloud. "Prince, look after Brierly and Arpien. And come back to Rosaria. I know we haven't been very … loyal lately. But please, please come back." She started to leave the room, then paused again. "Gowsma, if you can come, we need you. In a the-kingdom's-in-dire-peril kind of way. Please."

If they had only days left until the Conquisani army arrived at their gate, Nissa could not waste a single one in inaction. Boxleyn needed her. Cuz needed her. Was she supposed to play mother to him or vassal? Maybe … advisor?

Lady Nissa Montaine, Advisor to the King sounded far too overwhelming. So by rote she turned left to reach the servants' stairway instead of right, which would have taken her to the apartments of the nobles.

She so startled a scullery maid that the poor girl dropped an entire tray. Sweetbreads cartwheeled down the stairs at her heels. Nissa could not pass without helping her clean the mess first, which flustered the apologetic maid all the more. A gruff female voice from below demanded explanation for the noise. Nissa accompanied the maid to the kitchens to defuse the blame, and was greeted by more shattering. Her excuse died on her lips, killed by the shocked silence that filled the room. Finally Dorothy the cheesewife clamped Nissa in a hug without a by-your-leave.

"Nissa! Lady Nissa, you gave us a fright, clattering in here like one of the very dead. They did say you would never leave your bed again. I told them they were wrong, that no gnaggered skull is going to finish off our Nissa Montaine. And see, you prove me right, child. Lady. Though I should be offering sympathy for your family, but you'll not mind, it's just such a wonder to see you."

Dorothy produced a chair and the latest palace gossip as Nissa choked down soggy bread-in-milk. Perhaps it was being fussed over that made

Nissa feel so uncomfortable. Everyone was either staring or trying to avoid her gaze. Was she so astonishing an apparition?

As soon as she decently could, she ducked into the queen's chambers to find a mirror. Squeezie charged her ankles hopefully when she cracked open the door. His tiny furry body bounced off her skirts, and he went to sulk under the couch. Albertus for his part stood on the edge of the bed, where he had no right to be, but Nissa had no heart to order him down. He barked, a single, formal bark.

It might have been anything, but Nissa replied, "I'm sorry, too."

He settled back into covers that bore the trails of many treading paws.

She shouldn't have come here at all, but Aunt Perturbance kept the smoothest, clearest mirror.

Nissa's own reflection frightened her. The swelling distorted the flesh at her eyebrow. It pushed the lid of her right eye out and down. She poked the purple-green mass as if her own body were a monster's. Now she was surprised she had woken at all.

Her mismatched eyes reminded her of nothing so much as a squinty gnome she had embroidered years ago. Perhaps even a little of—she laughed—Gowsma. There would be no retreat into Lady Overlooked now.

Beauty's the least useful Gift of all.

Were the bruise gone, were her face delicate and her form graceful, would the Conquisani army turn around and go home? What she understood she finally accepted.

It was time to use the gifts she had instead of worrying about the ones she didn't.

44

Arpien

Arpien understood Brierly's motives for returning to Estepel, but what were the vademecum sword's? Something to do with the prophecy? If only a Steward could bring back the Prince and defeat the evil fairy, perhaps Brierly's parents or great-great-grandparents had left some kind of clue within the walls of Estepel. He'd search for it as she went spindle-hunting.

None of the horses had returned, and he wasn't about to seek out the mantizes to inquire about the extent of their menu. The mantizes might have saved Brierly yesterday, they might even be on the Prince's side, but their manner of justice gave him nightmares.

Nothing for it but to walk.

Brierly managed it even still shod in her dancing slippers. Her Fleetsome Feet skipped over the roots and puddles his clunky feet found. Yet he could tell from the stiff way Brierly held her upper body that her shoulder bothered her. He'd gladly carry her to Estepel, but as she pointed out, there was nothing wrong with her legs. Besides, toting a fair damsel around in one's arms was probably only romantic until you started perspiring.

The best he could do when her body language reflected her soreness was feign unbearable hunger and insist they stop to eat. Since their last journey through the forest, a month's worth of spring vegetables had lined the road. He brought back an armful of mushrooms.

Brierly piled them on her lap, sorted through them with her left hand, and chucked a few into the ferns. "Poisonous. Shrinking. Causes growth of ear hair." She nibbled on a purple cap. "Bland, but filling,"

"Too bad we don't have any grandmother pickles," Arpien said.

Brierly made an odd coughing noise.

His lady, so melodic in every other sound she made, laughed like a rusty door hinge. He'd rather listen to her unCharming laughter than a thousand ballads.

Arpien laughed, too, and felt a handle dig into his gut. It was awkward, arranging two scabbards at an easy angle for sitting. He shifted the belts about his waist.

"Whose sword did you steal?"

It was an unusual question coming from Brierly, who believed neither in private property nor logic. Why shouldn't a sword just pop into existence out of nowhere, if this were a dream?

But Arpien just answered the question. "Lord Culmney donated it to the cause. I caught up with the Strandish delegation the first day out of Boxleyn. They'd sent Flatwhist ahead, to scuttle you out of country the sooner."

"But Lord Culmney is the one who drugged me. Why would he help you?"

"Your choice of the word *steal* was perhaps more accurate than *donate.*"

They shared a smile at that. It helped bank his lingering fury at the Strandish. The harmless-looking Lord Culmney had looked sheepish at Arpien's accusations, but not repentant; just as Arpien could understand his motivations for abducting Brierly, although he didn't think they justified the act. Brierly ought to have a choice in who she married.

But what if in the end, she still didn't choose him?

The potential price of losing her was growing steeper all the time.

Their eyes locked too long, or perhaps Brierly was just too restless to sit still.

"I don't really have to eat, anyway. Fairy Gift." She swept suddenly to her feet. Only a slight hitch as she rose marked her injury.

Arpien scrambled after her with the rest of the mushrooms. He discussed their next move between bites. How would they find the spindle?

"Voracity said the spindle belongs to me," Brierly said. "Maybe I'll be able to feel where it is."

This sounded like dream-logic to Arpien. Wish for something, and there it was. But he had no better plan.

He drew the vademecum sword as soon as they approached the wrought-iron and sandstone gates of Estepel. "All right, here we are, sword. Happy? Take us to the spindle."

The vademecum sword ignored him.

He flashed Brierly a rueful grin. "Looks like we'll have to be our own hunting dogs. Do you sense anything?"

She raised her head like a deer reading the wind, then shrugged with one arm. "Thorns."

"Then where do we start looking?"

"Inside the gates is better than outside."

"That's not much incentive." Arpien had bad memories—both of mind and muscle—of being trapped inside the rapidly regenerating vines.

"Incentive?" Her voice was soft and very, very close.

Instantly every hair on his arm stood on end, and not because she had startled him. Nor because he was cold, because he very much wasn't that, either.

"But you already have incentive."

She couldn't possibly mean—?

"You were just saying earlier today that you were hungry for grandmother pickles."

All the heat building up in his body went straight to his ears. He disguised his flaming ears by raising his arms overhead and bringing down the vademecum sword against the briars. He cut halfway through a couple briars, and snapped a small dried vine the thickness of his thumb clean in two.

So the vademecum sword had decided to cooperate. Somewhat. When Arpien remembered to concentrate on the sword's owner, the sword behaved like a well-mannered woodsman's axe.

Brierly borrowed Arpien's boot knife (the spare Strandish sword proved too heavy for her to handle with one arm) and made her own attempt at pruning hedges. Arpien reclaimed it before Brierly completely nicked and dulled the blade hacking at the thorns. Brierly settled for clearing away the cut vines.

About twenty minutes and as many feet into the thicket, Brierly drew his attention by tilting her head so those Fine Ears could pick up some noise his couldn't.

"Him again?" he said.

Brierly nodded.

There was nowhere to run. The vines at the gates scabbed over the hole where Arpien and Brierly had entered the thicket. Arpien handed his boot knife back to her. He didn't ask if she knew how to use it to defend herself. A lady who wielded other eating utensils so memorably could figure it out.

Arpien recoiled anew as the vines shifted to reveal the Thorn King. He limped to meet them at the gates. Most of his wounds had puckered closed, but one new and particularly ghastly thorn, as thick and hard-looking as a bull's horn, jutted out from his right ankle. For all he might be an enemy, Arpien cringed for him with every step.

The Thorn King steadied himself against the open gates. He smiled. "Brierly, Arpien. You've come back."

Had the lonely man *missed* them? Did this strange man stay here of his own volition or because Voracity had condemned him with some Curse? Was this new thorn an accident, an attack, or worse, self-inflicted?

Amid all his visceral reactions, the only thought Arpien could articulate was, "How do you know my name?"

"The same way I know hers." The Thorn King nodded at Brierly.

Had Voracity told him? Had he overheard them talking to each other last time?

"The question is, do you yet know who I am?" The Thorn King's voice reminded Arpien of a dozen yellowed papers rustling together.

"You're—"

"You're the gardener," Brierly interrupted.

Arpien turned to her with eyebrow lifted, and she glanced back, as though she had surprised even herself.

"He looked different then. No thorns. But there was something in his expression just now—"

The Thorn King smiled again. "I see you remember something of me."

"Not a lot. I remember that the rabbits were worried you'd be upset at them for nibbling on the ornamental cabbage. I remember my mother liked to help you prune the rose hedges."

"Do you remember the gloves I gave you so you could help her one spring?"

Brierly tasted the words slowly. "I was six. I gave it up because I got scratched."

The Thorn King laughed, and it was now the sound of the wings of old geese taking flight. "You gave it up because you got distracted talking to a caterpillar. And you didn't like digging around in the dirt in case your spade disturbed an earthworm. You were a warm-hearted girl."

"Earthworms complain too much."

Her brow iced over, yet Arpien felt himself smiling.

"What?" she said to Arpien.

"I would have liked to meet you as a child."

"Yes." The Thorn King was looking at him now. "But it would have driven any adult who had charge of you to distraction, had the pair of you ever joined forces at that age. For both of you were bright children with a great sense of adventure and no sense of self-preservation."

How would he know that?

"And this one," the Thorn King glanced at Brierly and crossed his arms in mock severity, "should have been reined in for her mischief far more than she was. Only Gowsma could resist her Gift of Charm."

"Just because I remember you doesn't mean I trust you," Brierly said. "Yes, people from my Pre-Sleep life appear in my dreams. This is the first time you've told me anything of yourself."

"This is the first time you've asked."

"You might be a misbehaving figment." She glanced sidelong at Arpien, then back to the Thorn King. "And if you didn't come out of my head, you're some creature of Voracity's. You can control her thorns, you live in her thorns, you wear her thorns."

"I wear these thorns for one I love."

Ugh. Was he in love with Voracity? Better love a wayward enchanted princess than a vindictive fairy.

"We need to get to that castle," Arpien said. "I have no quarrel with you as long as you don't try to stop us."

"I'll lead you there myself if that's what you want. But if you want my help, you have to give me something."

"A fine Strandish sword?"

They had no use for two swords. In all these weeks Brierly had revealed no talent for swordsmanship, though he wouldn't put it past her once her shoulder healed.

The Thorn King's eyes fell to Arpien's hand. Arpien felt his grip tighten. "Your other sword is more valuable, but I have no interest in taking either off your hands."

Arpien hoped the Thorn King asked for his money pouch, because there was nothing in it but wool. He wore it in plain sight at his waist because it was the fashion, in Rosaria, to wear ornamental money pouches on formal occasions. The plumpness of the pouch advertised your fortune. The geese or grain or family crest embroidered on the finger-sized pouch advertised the wearer's family, region, or skill. Arpien's had a sword with a red dot at the hilt.

Brierly, in typical fashion, refused to wear a money pouch at all.

So they had no money to offer the Thorn King. Not that he had to know that.

"What would you have of us?" Arpien said.

"Your thorns."

Brierly shook her head. "We told you, we don't have any—"

Arpien laid a hand on Brierly's left arm. "We'll give you all the thorns we have after you get us through this thicket. And out again."

"You think to dupe a fool with clever words, Arpien Trouvel. But hear me truly. Carry out your promise, or I won't be able to give you the help you most desperately need."

He turned, and the briars parted like a curtain before him.

Arpien and Brierly glanced at each other, then followed.

If Arpien hadn't known that the briars had scared away the animals in Estepel, he would have sworn he saw a turtle pass them through the underbrush. It hardly seemed chivalrous to hurry the Thorn King along when the man had such a pronounced limp. Yet Arpien wondered if the solitary man was dragging the journey out on purpose, because he enjoyed his captive audience. As the Thorn King hobbled along, he told stories. "Did you ever hear the story about the Prince and the Whale?"

Well, if humoring him helped them reach the castle …

When the Thorn King finished one story, he launched into another. Midway through his third story, he paused to rub his ankle. "Do you mind if we sit for a minute?"

That terrible thorn must pain him. What could it hurt to let the poor man rest for a few minutes?

A few minutes stretched into twenty, then thirty. Arpien found himself leaning in to catch every word. The rasp gave his voice a texture and depth, by turns gritty and gentle. He used it to good effect, coloring phrases without ever making a production of it. The Thorn King would never be a success in Conquisan, but his conversational style suited this intimate setting: just three people huddled in a cozy bramble, trading stories.

Well, two people trading stories and a third there under duress. Around the fourth tale Brierly purloined the vademecum sword and attempted to hack her own way through the briars. She couldn't even dent them, certainly not with one arm. Arpien was so engaged in the stories that he didn't notice Brierly's struggles until she glowered over him, a heaving, scratched-up tower of green dress and sweaty hair.

"Oh, sweet prince ..." she said in a sing-song voice that told him he was in trouble.

Arpien batted her wrist down—she was leaning over him with sword in hand, and Arpien was in danger of a shave. "Brierly, come listen to this."

"Arpien, there're just the same old tales."

"When he tells them, they're new."

"How?"

Arpien couldn't say. They were to the point, most no longer than a few minutes. Arpien's own vocabulary was far more extensive, yet somehow less effective. The stories used commonplace imagery yet painted vivid pictures in Arpien's mind. Vivid, yet tantalizingly out of reach. It was like looking at a painting but only being able to see half the colors. Yet the more stories Arpien listened to, the more colors he was able to see.

"Arpien." Brierly shook his shoulder. From the way she said his name, he guessed it must have been the third or fourth time she'd tried to get his attention.

Arpien tugged at her wrist. "Brierly, come sit down. You've got to hear these stories."

Brierly resisted his pull. "I doubt that's healthy."

"Healthy?"

"Have you forgotten what we're here for? All you do is sit there like you're under a spell."

Her concern for him did more to startle him out of his mood of contentment than anything else could have. Arpien stood. His legs stung from the pins and needles of sitting too long on the hard ground. "You're right."

Arpien pointed the vademecum sword at the Thorn King's nose. "What spell are you casting? You said you'd lead us to the castle."

The Thorn King pushed himself to his feet. He wobbled so much on the pierced foot that Arpien put out a hand to brace him without thinking. The Thorn King grasped his hand. His feet might be unsteady but his handclasp was firmer than Arpien expected. He would have expected it to disgust him, too, for all the scabbed-over wounds. It just felt warm and rough.

The Thorn King clasped him lightly on the shoulder. "Thank you, son." He turned and limped forward.

No one, not his brothers or tutors or the Conquisani armsmaster, had ever called him *son*. Not even his father.

The word landed on Arpien and sank into his skin. Arpien felt the imprint of the Thorn King's hand on his shoulder all the way to the castle door.

"I will wait here until you are ready to pass back through the briars. Remember your promise to me. Bring me your thorns." The Thorn King looked first at one, then the other. "Be careful."

"Yes. Er … thank you." Arpien's body started to bend out of habit. Which Conquisani bow would be appropriate? He tried to remember the one for *Flower-Arrangers, Foresters, and Other Professions Having to Do With Plants*. It started with the right hand spiraling upward, and then—

Brierly laid a hand on his arm. "Don't let him fool you."

Arpien's spine snapped straight as a maypole. He wasn't naïve. In Conquisan you bowed to friend and foe alike. Indeed, some of the most fun bows were reserved for enemies. The Thorn King might just be helping them so they could bring Voracity the spindle. But why would a servant of Voracity tell stories about the Prince?

Maybe Arpien's confusion really was the result of a spell.

At least now that they'd crossed the threshold into the atrium, the Thorn King remained outside, uninvited. He couldn't get in now unless Brierly asked him, and she seemed more than disinclined.

Arpien had not sheathed the vademecum sword since they arrived at Estepel. "So where do we start looking?" he asked.

The sword had no opinion, but Brierly did. "The most secure place in Estepel is the vault. If my parents wanted to ensure that no one stole the spindle, that would be the place."

"What secures it?"

"Father always stationed two guards there, but they'll be long gone."

"Human guards?" This was Sentre Forest.

Brierly tapped the side of her cheek. "Well, there is Snowball, too."

"Snowball?"

"Our fire-breathing dragon."

Arpien swallowed.

He caught a grin on her face, a small one, but the first softening of her features since they reached Estepel.

"Liar," he said.

She dropped the grin and blinked innocent eyes. "Every dragon needs a hoard, and every hoard needs a dragon. This way."

She led him through the castle to a long winding down staircase. Estepel had towers both above and below ground. Within fifteen steps they lost daylight, which forced them to come back up for flint and steel. They found some in the kitchens, and Arpien lit a torch from the staircase wall. Brierly carried it downstairs, so Arpien could walk in front, sword at the ready. His feet force-marched his shadow further and further down the stairwell.

"If there is a dragon, that will be your assignment, since you're the one with the fairy Gift," he said.

"Oh, Snowball's as tame as an oyster. He's only fricasseed a couple of people."

She was teasing.

She was.

But the only barrier between them and the vault was a series of nine iron locks. "Where are the keys?" Arpien said.

"Does it matter?" Brierly extracted one of the last five spiky hairpins remaining in her unraveling ball coiffure and picked the locks, one by one.

Handy with Needles again.

The hinges had rusted shut. Arpien handed the sword to Brierly, took several steps back, and hurled himself at the door. It opened with the groan of architectural indigestion that only ancient buildings can produce. Arpien whisked the sword away from Brierly and brought it to the ready.

He counted a dozen heartbeats. "Still no dragon."

Brierly poked him from behind. Arpien yelped, whirled, and landed some three paces away.

He lowered the sword. "That wasn't funny. I might have sliced your head off."

"It was a little funny." Her mood had certainly improved since they shed the Thorn King at the castle door.

No self-respecting dragon would have chosen this as a hoard, anyway. There was little gold, silver, or jewelry. The few coins in the room were scattered on a high shelf, as though someone short had missed them when he swept stacks of coins into bags and carried them away. As there was no sign of forced entry, Arpien could only guess that the Montaines had taken the nation's wealth with them when they moved the capital to Boxleyn.

What there was, was plenty of rough-hewn wooden shelving, cobwebs, and scrolls. Arpien's heart leapt at the sight of the scrolls. One of them might contain information about where to find the Prince. As expected, Brierly drifted right past the scrolls. She still insisted that she couldn't read in a dream. Arpien started to call her back with the light, but his words disintegrated when he saw what the torchlight illuminated further in.

Relics of the old tales.

A row of worn-out dancing slippers. A translucent brown and yellow marbled tortoise shell hair comb, labeled POISONOUS. DO NOT TOUCH. Seven mirrors of various sizes and shapes. One of them spouted half a sonnet before falling back asleep. When Arpien found that out, he tapped the surface of each mirror in the room. Some reflected landscapes, some faces. One sang.

Brierly raised a finger. "You'll want to leave that one asleep. It only speaks in dirty limericks."

He withdrew his finger and picked up a ring. Inset was a round, opaque, green stone.

"Brierly, what's this one?"

"The pea that kept the princess awake, even when it was buried under twenty-seven mattresses."

Now that Brierly had moved closer with the light, Arpien could see the wrinkles where the pea had shriveled over the years.

"So that's why someone took the rest of the jewelry but not this piece."

"Yes, that and it causes bruising. But keep it. We might get hungry."

"I am not going to eat evidence for the old tales." For that must be the other reason these treasures were left behind. They had no value outside the old tales, and too much if you wanted to squelch them.

"Good thing you're so fond of grandmother pickles, then."

Brierly hitched up her muddy skirts above the ankles—she had lovely ankles—and put her own feet beside the row of dancing slippers, as though checking for size. It was hard to tell whose slippers were in worse condition.

"Wait 'til we tell Nissa about this place," said Arpien.

It was a stupid thing to say, but regret doesn't unsay things.

"Yes, well, we'd better find the spindle then." Brierly dropped her skirts and moved further into the vault.

"Brierly, maybe it's best that the spindle stay lost."

"It's the only way to bring Nissa back."

"If it means risking you or empowering Voracity, would Nissa want to be brought back? Even supposing Voracity means to carry out her promise, which I doubt."

"Then I'll use the spindle to avenge her."

"The spindle's poison to you."

"It might have been one hundred years ago. I've had one hundred years of battle experience since then. And we have no other choice."

"What about the Pr—"

She held up a hand. "He doesn't exist."

"You can stand here in this room and say that? Brierly, this is the best repository of Prince artifacts I've ever seen."

"Then I dreamed them up."

"You've been in the vault before, or you wouldn't know so much. Tell me you didn't come here as a child."

"Arpien, please. Let's not argue. You go look for your Prince of Here and There if that's what makes you happy. Leave me alone to fight Voracity my own way."

She took the light with her further into the vault. Arpien didn't even bother to try to wheedle her back to the front room with the torch so he could read the scrolls. He loaded his arms to the nose and went back upstairs to the atrium to read by the light that spilled through the open doorway.

The scrolls might have been safe from intruders down in the vault, but not from mildew. The damp of the underground room had left several of the scrolls stained with age, and a few completely unreadable.

Arpien tried to ignore the Thorn King, where he sat huddled against the door frame. But he had to move close to the door to obtain the best light.

Arpien unrolled a scroll, inch by inch. A genealogy. He picked up the next. An inventory of livestock. The next dozen were almost identical except for slight variation in numbers. He snorted.

"What?" the Thorn King said.

What could it hurt to tell him? "Tax records."

"If it weren't for tax records, no one would learn to read and write."

Arpien wanted to smile, so he grunted instead. He picked up the next scroll. "What is this? 1 lb butter, 1 lb flour, 1 oz essence of mint, 40 candied mint leaves—"

"Mint jam cookies!"

Evil minions liked cookies?

The Thorn King extended his hand for the scroll. Arpien handed it over. He couldn't imagine the forces of evil conquering humanity with a surfeit of baked goods.

"Why would the Stewards lock up their recipes in a treasure vault?" Arpien said.

"They were Very. Good. Cookies." The Thorn King's eyes swept across the lines. He chuckled and smacked his lips.

Where did a gardener learn to read?

"You're not really a gardener, are you?"

The Thorn King looked up from the scroll. "But I am."

"And what else?"

"A friend, if you'll accept one."

Debatable.

Arpien opened the next scroll in the pile. He squinted at the mildewed text.

"What about that one?" The Thorn King asked.

"The first sentence mentions the Prince, but the paper's as liver-spotted as a hag's hands."

"Read what you can aloud. Maybe I can help."

"In the days of the fairy wars, the Prince walked his lands and—something something—cabin in the woods—something—three bears."

"Oh, yes, I know that one." The Thorn King picked up the story. Arpien was familiar with the general outline, but as before, the story sounded different coming from the Thorn King's lips.

"I learned it like this." Arpien compared it aloud to his own version. "I wonder which version is correct."

"Mine."

It was so simply said, without hesitation. Like a child. Arpien laughed. "How do you know? Where you there?"

"The Prince was there."

"And he told you? You bide company with the Prince of Here and There?"

"I know him better than anyone else does."

"All right, then explain why in one story a particular thing happens, and in another, the opposite happens."

"Simple. One of the tales never occurred. It doesn't mean they're all false."

"Then which ones are true?"

"The ones the Prince told about himself."

That led to a knee-numbing debate on historical context and the verification of truth. They peeled the skin from story after story, heaping them up like apples for saucing. The discussion so engrossed Arpien that he didn't notice the sky outside darkening until the stone floor freckled with raindrops. He shoved the scrolls back. A cold wind finished the task of scattering them out of order. He'd have to start all over.

The rain angled and beat against the side of the castle. The Thorn King turned in the doorway, and looked out to where the briars heaved and bobbed under the press of the rain. His cloak had no hood, but he pulled the neckline up to cover his head.

How ungallant would that be, to leave a wounded man waiting for them in a cold downpour? "If I were convinced you'd do us no harm I'd let you in."

"Thank you," said the Thorn King, and stepped inside.

Arpien took a step back. He'd meant to ease his own conscience, not invite him in. "I thought you couldn't enter a home unless you were invited by the owner."

"No, I was just being polite." The Thorn King lowered his cloak back to his shoulders. His head popped out like a turtle.

"But Voracity and Gowsma couldn't."

The Thorn King flapped the edges of his cloak. "Do you see wings?"

Arpien flushed. "No, but Gowmsa and Voracity didn't have them either."

"Oh, they have them. But I'm as human as you, Arpien Trouvel."

"You've been living in this thicket for a hundred years."

"So did Brierly."

"Without anything to eat?"

"So did Brierly."

"She wasn't so"—it seemed impolitic to point it out—"wounded."

The Thorn King raised a swollen eyebrow. "All curses leave their marks."

"Is that why you stay here? You're Cursed like Brierly?"

"I stay here of my own free will."

"That makes no sense. These thorns are killing you."

"Yes. But Arpien, when you love someone enough, you bear more than mere sense dictates."

"That doesn't justify following someone so cruel."

The Thorn King furrowed his brow. It turned to a wince as the thorn crown scratched his forehead. "What do you mean?"

"You're Voracity's servant."

"Where did you get that?"

"But—aren't you? You can command the thorns."

"I hate the thorns." Once again, the straightforward purity of the Thorn King's tone reminded Arpien of a child. Not in intelligence or maturity. But his hatred was unalloyed with defensiveness or guilt or anger. Just *I hate the thorns* the same unarguable way you might point out *acorns don't sprout maple trees.* The ideas were indisputable.

"But you're always asking for thorns," said Arpien.

"I have no thorns but those I am given. But I would rid the world of thorns if it allowed. They are a canker."

"You commanded them to attack us when I first brought Brierly out of her tower."

"I wanted her out of her tower as much as you did. Why else did I cut a path for you to the gate?"

Arpien revisited the scene from all those weeks ago. Yes, the vines had snapped at their heels, raked their sleeves, but on the Thorn King's orders? And the Thorn King could have led them deeper into the bramble. Why head toward the gate unless he meant for them to escape?

"You just said you loved Voracity," Arpien said.

"I have never followed Voracity and never will. Though I did love her, and she loved me once. But she has since gone her own way."

Unrequited love. "I can relate."

The Thorn King raised a brow. "Can you?"

"Brierly. Though sometimes I think she might feel as I do, but she's just scared." There was something about the Thorn King that invited honesty, as though even the clumsiest secrets wouldn't shock him.

"Love isn't a set of saddlebags," said the Thorn King. "It's not as though you load one side up and not the other, and the horse tips over. Love doesn't have to be even. Sometimes it shows its true presence when you feel anything but love, but you act for the good of the other person anyway."

Courtship advice from Uncle Thorny.

"Sometimes I think nothing I do will make her love me," Arpien said. "I could bring back the distilled birdsong juice of the water-nightingale and she'd just shrug."

"Very likely. Love may be an action, but it's not a recipe. You can't mix certain ingredients and poof here's a cake. Love is always a choice, or it is not love. But it's a little early for despair, Arpien. You do not yet know what lies in her heart."

But more and more, he did. Brierly might be the bravest person he knew, when it came to rivers, fairies, assassins, merfolk, social functions, overgrown bugs, brigands, heights, and singing solos in public. All the things that made his guts quiver like cherry pudding, the things he tried to forget by playing the part of rescuer.

"But she's afraid of posby blossoms," Arpien said.

"Posby blossoms?" The Thorn King wrinkled his forehead. "But she used to pick them as a child. I planted some by the gate."

So that's why Fearless had wandered off during their first visit to Estepel.

"It's—figurative. Are you really the gardener?"

The Thorn King nodded.

"Why didn't you leave with all the others?"

The Thorn King gestured around him. "I don't know if you've noticed, Arpien, but this garden needs help."

"What was it like here, one hundred years ago?" Arpien had studied enough sleeping princess legends, he'd know if the man was lying.

He wanted to know about the Curse, but the man seemed to take it as a job inquiry. "I'd wake up to the sound of birds calling and a little girl chatting with them. Dawn's the best time for gardening. The dew softens the ground so it's easier to pull weeds. Then I'd pick whatever cook wanted for the day's meals. That woman was queen of the kitchen." He grinned. "The scullery maids and cook's assistants and I never dared be late, or she'd shake her spoon at us like a scepter. Oh, but it was worth it. She made a brambleberry tart you'd sell your own house for."

"No, no, I mean after that."

"Well, after that I'd do the ornamentals. I'm quite the artist with topiary. And then the flowers, but I always saved the roses for last, for Golda."

Golda? He called Brierly's mother by first name alone, no titles? But come to think of it, the Thorn King hadn't called Arpien and Brierly by their titles.

"They were as much her roses as mine. Oh, I carted in the manure, but she didn't hesitate to get her hands dirty. Golda loved those roses like children. In a way, Brierly was simply the best and brightest bloom in her bouquet. Golda named her for them."

"Briar Rose."

The Thorn King nodded. "Though poor Golda, the name wouldn't stick, even if that's what was declared at the christening. Golda insisted on calling her Briar Rose for years, but it was like stuffing a child into shoes she doesn't want to wear. As soon as she was out of sight, Brierly shed the name." He shook his head. "A shame, really, to lose the rose."

"Why do some of the legends call her Aurora?"

"Oh, that? A nickname. Aurora, Princess of the Dawn, because she made as much racket as the birds in the morning. I think it was a courtier from Strand who first said it. He stayed up into the wee hours celebrating, only to be woken a few hours later by a chirpy seven-year-old in a tree outside his window."

Arpien smiled at the image. "You speak as though you know her well."

"As well as I know you."

"Yes, you hinted at that earlier. But why should you know my name, or what I was like as a child? You've never been to Conquisan."

"Perhaps the Prince told me."

"I don't remember ever meeting the Prince, either. If I had, it'd be a lot easier to find him now."

"Oh, but he knows everything about you."

"That's a little—" *Nerve-wracking? Improbable?* "Embarrassing."

"Why?"

Arpien studied his boots. "I had a very awkward childhood."

"The Prince adored you as a child. He loved your sense of adventure. Your thirst for excellence."

"Then he must have a taste for comedy, because I failed at just about everything." Then as now.

"Is that as important as why you made the effort? The Prince sees the heart, Arpien. He cried with you for six months after Kirren drowned."

"The Prince knew about Kirren?"

The Thorn King nodded. "He loved her, too."

"Then why didn't he rescue her? Or Brierly?"

"That's not for me to say. One day you may ask him."

Arpien rubbed the space between his eyes. "You're as frustrating as Gowsma."

The Thorn King's eyes twinkled. "Ah, the cookie-eater." He sobered. "Arpien, people don't die or get hurt because the Prince hates them or is indifferent. He loves them."

"Then he should prove it."

"What proof would you accept?"

"He could come back now, for one thing."

"Perhaps he wants to. I think he's told you under what conditions he'll come."

"What, if we prove ourselves worthy?"

"No, the prophesy."

"He'll come if a Steward calls him back."

"That's all it takes."

Arpien shook his head. "Brierly won't do it. The Prince let her down too many times."

"Do not mistake timing for failure. The Prince cares for her, Arpien, believe me."

Arpien stood. It was time to see how Brierly was getting on, anyway. "Stay here. I'll do what I can. But like I said, she needs proof."

45

The Thorn King

After Arpien left, the Thorn King massaged his ankle again, careful not to probe too close to the wound. The inflamed skin puckered like a swollen and cracked mouth choking upon the thorn. No medicine in the world would cure the infection. He would have to bear it.

But for how much longer? There wasn't much time.

Arpien was coming along nicely. The young prince half trusted him already. It was the other who concerned him.

He heard the susurrus of leather on stone. A pale green ribbon whipped around the corner of the hallway that led to the lower staircase.

The scars on his face pulled the skin into tight knots that ached when he smiled. He might have guessed she'd spy on them. Her Fleetsome Feet and Fine Ears made it easy enough.

He did not chase after her, to catch her out. His ankle would not support the impact. Already the thorn ate away the bone. It shot out roots through his muscles like veins. What flesh the thorn did not rot it transformed into its own substance.

He need only be patient. She would return. Oh, he knew her well, understood the danger she posed better than she did. Gifted beyond any of her own generation or this current one. Willful. If she resisted him, he could not overcome her.

Yes, he knew she would return. But when she did, what could he possibly say to convince her? All this hostility—it wasn't because she thought he was on Voracity's side. It was because she thought he was on the Prince's.

This was going to take drastic measures.

46

Arpien

The vault door gaped open, wide as one of Brierly's best yawns.

Arpien took the lit torch from the holder on the wall. "Brierly?"

He held the torch higher. Shadows lay prone on the ground. Arpien strode past the shelves of scrolls. If she'd found the spindle, she would have fetched him, right?

"Brierly!"

"You don't have to shout. I have Fine Ears."

He spun around. She stood by a row of seven reduced-scale pickaxes.

He heaved a sigh of relief. "You're all right."

Was it the torchlight, or did her face soften?

"Did you find anything?" he asked.

"Lots of anything, too much anything. But no spindle. I'm ready to give up on the vault and search upstairs."

"Let me grab some scrolls and I'll go with you." He doubted the spindle would be of any real help to them, but he wanted her in his sight for a while.

She gave a one-armed shrug, but she waited for him.

On his first trip to Estepel, Arpien had only visited the upper tower and the kitchens. Now he realized just how extensive the old castle was. His home in the Conquisani capital was more spacious, perhaps, but in Conquisan space was valued for its own sake. You needed high ceilings with acoustics for proper boasting.

Estepel coiled in on itself, nooks within nooks. Small rooms budded off central ones as though they had grown wherever nature took her whim. Hallways branched in unpredictable directions and vined up and down tiny flights of steps for the sheer fun of it.

"You must have had a million hiding places here," Arpien said.

"Yes. I loved playing tag."

"Because no one could catch you. That's practically cheating, with your Fleetsome Feet."

"I was accused of cheating many times."

"And did you?"

"There was no need to. Mostly. What about you?"

He broke through another cobweb and brushed it from his ear. "What?"

She poked him. That made twice in one day. "Oh, Arpien Trouvel was too upstanding even as a child to cheat at tag."

"We weren't allowed to run in the palace."

Arpien knew Brierly was one hundred and seventeen years old, but as they made their way room to room, she was many ages all at once. The ghost of her lost childhood scampered before them. It picked up stray memories that lay abandoned in the corners. It caressed one, cringed at another, and then tossed them back into the dust.

At first she told him stories about Estepel as it was. It was as though, in opening drawers and cabinets and chests in search of the spindle, moths of her old life fluttered out. As Arpien and Brierly probed deeper into Estepel, Brierly's graceful hands would snag on a sheet of music, or a painting, or some other object that dried the stories up in her throat. They searched those rooms in silence, but for the occasional sneeze or creak of hinges.

Brierly unearthed a stringed instrument. She set it on her lap and strummed an out-of-tune chord. Clumps of dust flaked from the strings and fell like soft grey snow.

"What's it like for you, being here?" he said.

Her fingers plucked out a dissonant arpeggio. She set the instrument back down into its exact dustprint. "Like eating the rind."

She rubbed her shoulder. In the dim light, she looked and sounded again like a hundred-and-seventeen-year-old woman.

Arpien faked a yawn for her sake, but a real one followed it, as though inspired by example. He'd slept but a handful of hours since the night before the Spring Ball. "We should think about resting."

"Not here. I can't breathe."

He didn't know if it was memories or dust that choked her, but he didn't want to sleep here, either. Nor did he suggest she head for her tower bedroom. In the end they pulled the bottom layers of the bed-clothes from several beds and hauled them to the atrium where the cool outside breeze could reach them.

It was full night now. Arpien saw no silhouette of the Thorn King either inside the atrium or in the doorway. Brierly set about making her-self a nest with all the proficiency of one who has received architectural advice from birds for years. Arpien laid his own bed near the threshold, where any intruder would have to trip on him to reach her.

She was already snoring, dainty faint snores, when he settled himself down on the floor. No wonder she had respiratory troubles, after spend-ing a century in this mess. But she must have been faking, because a moment later she said, "Arpien?"

The day was already swirling, sucking him into sleep. "What?"

"Thank you for coming for me."

Gratitude from Brierly? The shock woke him up. It made him wish he had something else to hug tonight other than the vademecum sword.

He heard her roll over. Her next words were muffled. "It was a foolish thing to do, but thank you."

Ah, that was more like it. He relaxed and a moment later was asleep.

47

Nissa

The fatal power of the magical weapon at the Spring Ball shook even the most pragmatic of the Rosarian nobles. It also left them with a loophole to escape standing with their king. They had sworn fealty to Uncle Emol. Cuz was a childish prankster, neither fit nor of age to take the crown. General Gapric threw together a slipshod coronation for young King Cuzzar. The playacting stifled open objection to Cuz's rule. Everyone assumed General Gapric would act as leader during the hostilities with Conquisan. Those who left Boxleyn now did so in the least-advertised moments of bleak pre-dawn.

It surprised Nissa how many stayed, or at least left a presence in Boxleyn. After seeing most of the royal line decimated in a single attack, many nobles sent their heirs home while they themselves remained. Those heirs sent back troops in the form of local guards, prisoners promised acquittal for service, and peasants who knew little of warfare but risked death at the promise of reward. Some warriors charged into Boxleyn with righteous fury, vowing to avenge their old enemy's wrongful attack on their homeland. Where hope is in short supply, fury will serve as a cheap substitute intoxicant. The arrival of a knight worked into a good upright lather always drew a crowd. King Emol's Fool, who had been out of favor ever since Brierly trounced him in the singing duel, now found audiences eager to suck up even the most cobbled-together of epic ballads and valorous platitudes.

If Nissa had Brierly's Gift of Music, she might have countered the Fool's enterprising vapidity with a tale of more substance. But Nissa was not musical, she was organized. After a week, there were more people flowing into Boxleyn than sneaking out. Few in Boxleyn had lived through a siege, and even such unglamorous necessities such as—*where will we empty all the chamber pots?*—required a plan and a planner.

Nissa fell into the role without question. It gave her a sense of tangible accomplishment to roll bandages and count bags of grain and settle disputes over which kitchen maids had to share blankets. The servants already respected her abilities. Some treated her as a good luck charm. Had she not predicted the danger at the Spring Ball and survived the attack of an evil fairy?

Nissa had never been more uncertain about her future, yet never had she been more fulfilled. There was a state worse than being overlooked, and that was being superfluous. On previous occasions in her life, the servants had allowed her to be useful. But she was useful in the way a shoehorn is useful—she eased tasks but was not absolutely necessary. For the first time in her life, people needed her—*truly* needed her. She worked herself into exhaustion, and what few hours she did snatch for slumber were thick as ham gravy and undisturbed by dreams.

About a week and a half after the Spring Ball, Nissa was awakened by someone trying to beat her door down with a piece of furniture. A chair leg, maybe.

Nissa slid the book off her face. She'd fallen asleep rereading the old tales, and her nose had served as a bookmark all night. Where was Kendra? Hiding under her own blankets on the floor at the side of Nissa's bed. Well, not fair to send Kendra as the sacrificial lamb.

Nissa hovered by the door with a hearth shovel and pretended to be intimidating. "Do you know what time it is?"

"Do *you* know what time it is? Foolish human, I wouldn't be here if I didn't know how important the time is. Get over here and open this door, young legs!"

Nissa threw open the bolt to reveal the most beautiful sight she'd seen in days.

"You came!" Nissa threw her arms around the wrinkles, warts, and fuchsia flowers.

"Yes, and I responded a sight faster than you bothered to issue your invitation. Waiting for an invitation from Rosarian royalty these days is like waiting for cookies to bake in a cold oven."

Gowsma's hug belied her chiding words. Hags gave the best hugs.

"I rearranged a very busy schedule to accommodate you. But I can only stay a quarter of an hour."

The sun was setting even as it rose. "Why?"

"Fairy business. And you'll mind your own, it's all you can handle for now. Let an old woman sit, will you, I'll talk faster." Gowsma kept speaking as Nissa scrambled for a chair. "The Prince is pleased with you."

"With me?"

"Aye, quit making obvious interjections. Of this generation, you are first in Rosaria to join his side."

Nissa chewed her lip as she thought back. "All I said was, 'I'll take my chances with the Prince.'"

"It doesn't take fancy words, it takes loyalty. The reward for work well done is more work, so I hope you got a good night's sleep."

Gowsma didn't seem to notice her own hand in Nissa's interrupted slumber.

"What work?"

"The Prince's work. That knot on your noggin didn't addle your wits, did it? Think, child."

"Voracity's coming, just like the prophecy said she would. So then the next step would be bringing the Prince back. I don't see how either work can be mine." She thought of the passage she'd fallen asleep rereading. "Gowsma, the prophecy says that only a Steward can call the Prince back. But Brierly was abducted, and—"

"Don't fuss, Nissa Montaine. Brierly and Arpien are free of the Strandish knight."

"They are?" Nissa grabbed Gowsma's wrinkly sleeve. "They're all right? Where are they?"

"Estepel. And yes, they're all right for the moment. The help they need is right in Estepel with them, if they could figure out where to look. Not that anyone will be all right by week's end. War is coming, and duckling, yanking around a poor old woman's arm isn't going to help."

Nissa released Gowsma's sleeve. "Sorry."

"I'll forgive you if you have cookies."

Kendra and Nissa exchanged glances. "Uh—maybe down in the kitchen."

"The best human food and no human ever has them at hand. Where are their priorities?"

"The war, Gowsma, can we stop it?"

"No. Nor can you hope to win without the Prince. It will be a war fought with swords, and magic, and terrible beasts. But it will also be a war fought with spindles, and needles, and thread."

It sounded like another prophecy out of a book. "What does that mean?"

"It means what it says. Humans!" Gowsma looked at Nissa and relented. "It means not to undervalue the smallest weapons the Prince puts in the hands of his most underrated servants."

Nissa pictured herself brandishing a two-inch needle at a four-foot sword. *En garde!* No, that would look asinine even in embroidery.

Embroidery.

"Wait there." Nissa ran to her bedroom.

"Time is short, bones are old."

"I'll just be a minute." Nissa opened her chest. Dresses flew through the air and Kendra tried to collect them before they hit the ground.

There, languishing beneath her stockings, was the answer.

She grabbed up the pile and ran back to Gowsma.

"Here. This is what you meant, right?"

Gowsma groused through the stack of embroidered scenes. "I don't make the prophesies, I just repeat them." But a slow smile curved her wrinkles upward. "Not a bad interpretation, child. Ideas are the sharpest weapons of all."

"I'll make them into standards. Most of the soldiers can't read, but they can understand these."

"And which ones will you use?"

"Not—all of them?"

"Wouldn't it be best to use the true ones?"

"Which ones are those?"

"Come now, child. For a good two minutes you were as wise as any human I've seen. Now tell me, what makes something true?"

"Uh—belief?"

"Nissa Montaine!" Gowsma smacked her cane on the floor.

Nissa jumped.

"Why must humans get everything backwards?" Gowsma humphed at the sun. "My time has passed." She shoved old bones into a standing position with a groan.

"Can't you give me another hint?" Nissa said.

"The Prince has given you all the hints you need. But here, take another hint, my gift to you. You don't have to see everything to believe it, but nor is faith absent of reason."

Gowsma paused at the door. Her wrinkles softened. "The Prince be with you, Nissa Montaine."

Nissa didn't feel as grateful as she thought she should be. She wanted clear answers. Gowsma told her she already knew them.

Kendra finished tidying the bedroom right after Gowsma left (by coincidence, she claimed). Together they spread Nissa's embroidery pieces on the floor like a gigantic quilt. Over the years, she'd sewn over a hundred scenes from the old tales. How was she supposed to find the true ones? Gowsma hadn't even given her a number to work with.

A conundrum: What makes something true?

Not belief. That was backwards, according to Gowsma.

Things aren't true because you believe them. You should believe them because they are true.

Nissa Montaine was an organizer. She rearranged the stories by country of origin. Then by age of first written documentation. Then by chronological order. Then by number of recurrences. And lastly by theme. It took most of the morning, so she sent Kendra off to help inventory the stockrooms.

No one criterion gave her a complete answer. But the same pieces kept drawing her notice time after time. The Prince and the Storm. The Prince and the Serpent. The Thorn King. And a few dozen others.

Most of them were the oldest tales in her collection. They came from a variety of sources, but all ones Nissa could track back hundreds of years. Many of them were corroborated by other tales and known facts. Not ten years ago, some questing knight had found the Lost Valley of Unicorns, exactly where the story purported it to be. And then there was the Sleeping Beauty. She was a firsthand witness to that one. This was different from picking and choosing which bits of truth she happened to prefer. This was testing each tale rigorously, to see if it stood up intellectually, historically, morally, and emotionally. She had to lay a few of her favorite tales aside. Good entertainment, but not verifiable.

But here was the strangest part. She pulled aside the few dozen stories that met her stringent criteria. When she rearranged the pieces on the floor in chronological order, a larger pattern started to emerge. A love story. Loss and reunion. The early tales pointed to the later tales, and the later tales confirmed the earlier ones. How could several dozen tales, written over a span of hundreds of years and by numerous authors, tell the same cohesive tale?

Nissa slid the last tale into place and read her embroidery from start to finish. This was more than a fairy tale to amuse undiscerning babes. In fact, bits of it were so dark, they made her cringe even as an adult. But Nissa didn't gloss over the ugly parts. Especially not now that she saw them in context. Taken together, they formed a bold tale, of Heroes and Daring Rescues and Battles. It was a romantic tale, of Brides and Love Lost and Regained. It was a tragic tale, of Betrayal and Death and Sacrifice. Wise, deep, and true.

And it most definitely pointed to a happy ending.

Tears streamed down Nissa's face. It was the best story she'd ever read (so to speak), and she'd missed it until this moment. And she'd hidden it underneath her socks, too embarrassed to really *see*.

Nissa blew her nose and ran to find Kendra. Stories this good were meant to be shared.

48

Arpien

There was no chance of reenacting their former wake-up scene the next morning. Despite the shortage of birds to talk to, Brierly was up long before Arpien. Her shoulder must be feeling better, for she had discarded the homemade plant sling. It lay on the floor like a wilted salad. Arpien found Brierly in the kitchen, where she persuaded him to lug another thirty-pound crock out of the larder.

If love was not a powerful enough motivator to make him face the inflammable grandmother pickles, hunger was.

He found the Thorn King huddled against the walls of the castle just outside the doorway. Arpien hesitated to touch the red-stained cloak, then shook his shoulder lightly. "Are you hungry?"

Perhaps the Thorn King did not need to eat, like Brierly with her fairy Gift of Eat-Whatever-I-Want-And-Always-Retain-A-Maidenly-Figure. But the Thorn King accepted his offer and started to push himself up. Arpien offered his hand.

"Why did you sleep outside? The cool air must have made your leg stiffen overnight."

"I was guarding the castle."

Behind him Brierly sucked in her breath. Arpien turned.

Brierly arched her spine like a hissing cat. "Arpien, how can you invite him in? He admits himself he was guarding us. Just as he guarded me for a hundred years."

Morning made the Thorn King's voice hoarser than ever. "Yes, I did. But you seem to think I guarded it to keep you *in.*"

Arpien pulled Brierly aside. "If he meant to harm us, he could have done so while we were asleep."

"Not until you invited him in."

"He doesn't need an invitation. If he did, you alone could issue it since Estepel's your home. I'll make him leave if you're uncomfortable, but he's done nothing but help us so far. I wish you'd hear him out, Brierly."

"I'm not gullible."

"Neither am I. I'm just taking his words under consideration. I'll keep an eye on him, Brierly. You needn't worry for your safety."

Brierly eyed the Thorn King, on edge like a wolf.

"Brierly, I want to make it clear I am not one of Voracity's creations, nor her servant. I side with the Prince. If that means you'd rather I stay away, I will. It's your choice," the Thorn King said.

Brierly's shoulders eased back to their normal position. Arpien watched her eyes sink back behind her mask of indifference. "It doesn't matter."

"Are you certain?" Arpien said. Understanding women generally required multiple clarifications, and even then they didn't always say what they meant.

She waved an airy hand and consoled herself with a pickle.

They dined on tension and vegetables. Arpien garnished their breakfast with the rest of the roadside mushrooms. They were slightly mashed from traveling in his cap. He went through a great many mushrooms before daring a pickle.

Arpien stared down the dripping slice of cucumber on the end of his knife. "I have faced tornado seeds and giant mantizes. I will not be cowed by a gherkin."

He held his breath, stuffed it into his mouth, and swallowed it whole.

Brierly's blue-green eyes watched him as though he were a sword-swallower. Or more literally, a fire-eater. "Well?"

A smug corner of his mouth tipped up.

Then a slow bubble of lava spread up the lining of his throat, singed his tonsils, cut off the air in his nose, and spilled out his eyes.

"Water." Were he not driven mad by the flames, he would remember that he'd fled Boxleyn without a water pouch to his name. But he flung out his hand, and a cold cast iron pot handle pressed into it. He spilled half the water onto his chest rather than into his mouth, but it tasted of the very spring of eternal life. The sweet coolness coated his throat in blessed relief.

"That was no Rosarian delicacy," he gasped. "That was death by incineration."

Through the blur of his watery eyes he could see his lady trying to suppress a grin. The Thorn King didn't even try to suppress his.

Rosarians.

Brierly handed him a towel and he mopped himself. He'd seen her filch it from the back of a drawer in the kitchens, protected from dust. "But where did you get the water?" he asked.

"I made myself useful during the storm and collected the rainwater," the Thorn King said. Now Arpien saw the two dozen pots and pans that sat outside the atrium door. Behind them the briars still wept a few last raindrops. How many trips back and forth to the kitchens had the Thorn King made on that wounded foot?

The Thorn King extended a smaller pot to Brierly.

"I'm not thirsty," she said.

Impossible. Arpien had just seen her eat five whole grandmother pickles herself. "What is your mouth made of? Tin? Steel?"

She crunched another pickle. "I told you there were fire-breathing dragons at Estepel."

Arpien and Brierly spent the morning and well into the afternoon combing the servants' quarters for the spindle. Brierly didn't tell many stories today, but she did make him talk about his childhood in Conquisan. Was she actually interested or did she just need distraction?

"Why do your brothers call you Fumbleshanks?" she asked as she climbed up on a chair beside a cabinet.

"It's the name of a hunting dog."

She shifted aside gardening tools on the top shelf. "So, because you track enchanted princesses and swords?"

He tugged at the neckline of his doublet. "Ah, no, because Fumbleshanks was inept."

Those blue-green eyes studied him in that unnerving way she had of giving away nothing. Please, he didn't want her pity.

After a moment she shrugged with one arm. "Well, you are like a puppy. And it's not such a bad thing to be compared to a dog." From anyone but Brierly it would have been an insult. "They're loyal."

"They have bad breath."

She scratched the back of her mussed head. "Well …"

Arpien cupped his hand over his mouth and nose, exhaled, and inhaled.

Brierly snorted again. Her hand seemed to be trying to squish a smile off her face.

"I took the bait. Again."

She nodded.

He found he liked her teasing. "Perhaps you should reassess." On impulse he scooped her off the chair. She shrieked in surprise as she fell into his arms.

The impact changed the tenor of her shriek and cut it short.

"Brierly?" He immediately set her down on the chair and knelt at her side.

She rubbed her shoulder.

Thistles. Thistles. Thistles. How could he have been so stupid as to forget?

"I'm sorry." His voice was as hoarse as the Thorn King's.

"It doesn't matter."

He glimpsed a dark bruise at the edge of her collarbone, where her fingers probed under her neckline. He sucked in a sympathetic breath.

"We're taking a break."

"Arpien, stop it. It's only pain."

"I need a break. I'm thirsty."

She let him escort her back to the atrium.

There was no point in entertaining his companions by eating the grandmother pickles again. Whatever sustenance they provided probably burned away before it reached his stomach. He sipped on some cider that had gone very very hard in the last century. Brierly nibbled on half a pickle and left the rest. She had a fairy Gift, she'd be fine. What worried Arpien was her shoulder. She held her breath every time she shifted position. He held it with her.

The Thorn King passed Brierly a pot of water.

"No, thank you. I'm not thirsty."

He nodded at the pot. "For your arm."

How did he know? But it must be obvious from the stiff way she moved.

She took the pot and fished out a heart-shaped leaf, broad as her hand. "Easemint."

"It grows by the gate. Wrap your shoulder in it and it'll numb the pain."

She dropped the leaf back into the pot and tried to hand it back. "I'm numb enough. Why don't you use it?"

"No medicine can aid me."

She set the pot down and regarded him. "What happened to you? Did Voracity Curse you, as she did me?"

"I wear these thorns for one I love."

"So you let yourself get injured on purpose?"

"Yes."

She wrinkled her nose. "And you think something's wrong with me?"

"Brierly, there is more to life than pain and numbness."

"To be sure. There are taxes."

"Will you let me help you?"

"I don't want your easemint."

"I know where the spindle is."

They stared.

"Oh come, it wasn't hard to figure out," the Thorn King said. "It's clear from Arpien's interest in the old tales that he's searching for the Prince. But you, Brierly, you're searching for something else. What else could draw you back to Estepel?"

"Tell me where it is."

"What do you plan to do with the spindle, Brierly?"

She hesitated. Did she still believe there was any hope Voracity would give Nissa back? But she said, "Use it against Voracity."

"You cannot. You can turn a dagger against your enemy, but not a cancer. The only thing to be done is to destroy it."

"Fine." She started to shrug, then switched to playing with her hair with her good arm. "I'll destroy it."

"Your mother also thought that if she destroyed the spindle she could destroy the Curse. When your parents brought you home from Conquisan in your enchanted sleep, your mother insisted they also bring the spinning wheel. Your father believed that only the promise laid out by Gowsma's Gift could wake you, but he didn't have the heart to forbid your mother to try. First she tried to burn it in a blacksmith's forge. The wooden wheel burned, but the spindle didn't. She ordered the blacksmith to beat the spindle shapeless. It shattered his anvil. She soaked the spindle in the strongest potions alchemy could brew. It became plain to her that nothing she could do could break the spindle's power over you. She feared what might happen if another were to gain control of the spindle. Would that person then gain control over you? In secret one night she hid the spindle on the grounds of Estepel. But hiding something does not destroy it. If you do find the spindle, you must not touch it. Come tell me right away. Please, Brierly."

"You want to give it to Voracity yourself."

"No. I told you I do not serve Voracity."

"Then you want it for yourself."

"I want to keep you from harm."

"Why do you care what happens to me?"

"Because the Prince does."

"Thank you, but I don't need help from figments. From you or the Prince." She rose to leave.

"Brierly," Arpien said, "you really ought to—"

She looked over her shoulder at Arpien. Her gaze pinned him like a beetle. "From anyone."

Arpien started to follow her, but the Thorn King gestured for him to sit. "She has said no."

"What if she finds the spindle? I don't trust her alone with it."

"She's not walking in the right direction to find it."

"I should to least talk to her."

"What would you say that she's ready to hear? No, Arpien, love always leaves a choice. But if one day she is ready to listen, give her this." He handed Arpien a square of paper, folded multiple times.

"What is it?"

"Tell her it will explain the meaning of life." In his scar-puckered face, the Thorn King's eyes flickered with mischief.

"Are you jesting?" Arpien started to unfold the paper.

The Thorn King held up his palm to stop him. "It will only make sense to her. And don't you have a quest of your own?"

Arpien tucked the enigmatic message into his boot. Was it good procedure to store the meaning of life next to one's feet? "Find the Prince. Right. Do you know where he is?"

"He is both here and there."

"Thanks for the tip."

Arpien walked a few paces away from the Thorn King. He shook out his muscles, as he might before a long run. Roll the neck, twist the torso. He drew the vademecum sword and held it double-fisted in the front of him.

"All right, sword. Here's your chance to earn your wages. Take me to the Prince."

The sword did nothing.

Long inhale, exhale. Think about the Prince.

"Take me to the Prince."

Nothing.

"The Prince the Prince the Prince, you cantankerous gate-pole."

His arms were getting tired. He dropped them and turned to the Thorn King. "All right, why isn't it working?"

"Maybe you're not really looking for him."

"The sword's the one with the problem. What kind of compass only points where and when it wants?"

"The kind of sword that points where you ought to go. That's not always the same as where you want to go."

"Why wouldn't it want me to find the Prince? That's a reasonable enough order."

The Thorn King shook his head. "The vademecum sword doesn't take orders, only requests."

"Then it's a reasonable request. And the compass issue is only the beginning. This sword is supposed to be the sharpest in the world. That's the whole reason I crossed an ocean to find it, so I could cut through the briars. And you see how that went."

"Whose sword is it?"

"Mine. Well, the Prince's. Look, I already know that if I think about the Prince the blade gets sharper. That's not enough for the thrice-contrary sausage roaster."

"Hmmm. Or perhaps you simply need to get to know the Prince?"

Arpien bristled. "I've been researching the Prince for years. My first memory is my sister reading me *Tales of the Prince*. I sought out and memorized three thousand and three ballads about the Prince in order to track down his sword." Actually, he had no idea how many ballads he'd memorized. That was just the number you always gave in Conquisan when you meant *a lot*.

"All excellent things, Arpien. But that's knowing *about* the Prince. I said *knowing* the Prince."

Introduce him to the Prince of Here and There? Could he? Arpien tried to imagine the proper Conquisani bow. Would he take the *Fifth Stance of Resolve* or the *Seventh Stance of Admiration*?

"Do you know who he is as a person? Are you loyal to him?"

"Are you?" Arpien shot back.

"I know the Prince better than anyone. I could no more turn against him than I could draw a square circle."

"Well, I'm loyal, too."

The Thorn King raised an eyebrow. "Why?"

"If we don't find the Prince, my brother will take over Rosaria."

"So you are loyal because you want to defeat your brother."

"And Voracity, of course."

"Of course."

"You don't think she should be punished for what she did to Brierly?"

"I told you, I am no servant of Voracity's. But I'm not certain you're a servant of the Prince, either."

"My objectives are exactly the same as the Prince's."

"Are they? What if the Prince doesn't want to do what you want? Let's say the Prince has decided you'll never be king of any kingdom. Your brother will breach the walls of Boxleyn Palace, and Brierly will die before Cryndien crowns himself king."

There was a weight to the prediction that made it more than hypothetical. Did this strange, wounded man know what the future held?

"All these stories you've been telling have been about how compassionate and powerful the Prince is. Yet you tell me he's decided Brierly will die?" Arpien's voice sounded frail in his own ears, a six-year-old's voice.

The Thorn King nodded. "We all die, Arpien."

His mind crashed with ways the prediction could be fulfilled. "Could I have some clarification on how and when this happens?"

"The Prince does not accept conditional fealty. And that is why you have not yet unleashed half the sword's power."

Arpien scowled. "I'm just trying to make an informed decision."

"Then make it starting with the Prince's character."

"How can I do that? I've never met the man."

The Thorn King gave an unexpected smile. "Let me tell you another story."

49
Brierly

Searching for the spindle was no fun without Arpien. Well, fun wasn't the word. He stabilized her. But some memories, even the good ones, especially the good ones, twanged and cut like a lute strings snapping under her fingers.

They were gone. Her mother, father, nurse, tutors, friends. The groom's son who helped her ride amuck through Estepel. The horses they'd rode amuck on. Her fairy godparents. She even wondered what had happened to the people she hadn't gotten along with. Even with the aid of Charm, some people found her overdose of fairy Gifts too bizarre for polite company. She missed them all. What kind of lives had they led, the ones who fled the castle? If not for the Curse, how might have their lives intertwined with hers, like pole bean vines dancing and shoving against each other for sunlight?

She commanded the dream to bring everyone back. But even in her imagination, she could not fill Estepel with bustle, the music of concerts, the tweeting, barking, braying jabber of animals. Silence clogged her Fine Ears. She couldn't even hear the ticking of the clock that had haunted her since the Spring Ball. Here, the clock had stopped, and she didn't know how to restart it.

She rubbed her shoulder, but it wasn't just her shoulder that felt sore and dislocated.

Brierly finished her search of the servants' quarters. No spindle. Well, that left nothing but the family rooms. Brierly had no desire to see her tower again. Her parents would not have stored the spindle within so easy a reach any more than you would decorate an injured knight's sickroom with the blade that defeated him.

Back to the vault, then. Maybe she'd missed something.

She had to pass through the atrium to get to the vault. Her Gifts had made her a natural spy since her christening day. She crept through the feasting hall and sat on one of the long benches, just out of the sightlines of the open door.

Oh. Arpien and the Thorn King were going on about the Prince again. Spinning wheels, the Thorn King talked like Gowsma.

Well, she could usurp the subject the moment she stepped into the room. She was the queen of distraction. What non sequitur would she use this time?

Come see the lovely sonnet the spiders spelled out in their cobwebs. Ode to the Wriggling Fly.

No, no, if Arpien believed her he'd be elated she could read and start *that* argument over. And spiders never wrote sonnets. Arachnids had no grasp of a rhyme scheme. They preferred blank verse, specifically iambic octameter.

Sometimes simply walking into the room was enough to distract Arpien. But letting her Gift of Beauty manipulate a reaction from him felt like cheating. Manufactured affection was about as filling as a stale dream-cream-puff. If Arpien looked on her with admiration, let it be for something she had actually done for him, like finding his horse or helping him dodge Voracity or—

She shook her head. Was she actually trying to figure out how to impress a figment?

The shocking idea froze her feet inches from the doorway.

She cared what Arpien thought.

Spinning wheels.

So she paused at the door, just out of sight, and lingered in the fringes of the conversation in the atrium. Arpien was right—the Thorn King was a good storyteller. Not a dramatic one, but compelling. Her parents and fairy godparents had told her the old tales time enough, yet Brierly did feel like she was hearing them for the first time. She wished they were true, that the Prince really would come back if she called.

Why couldn't the old tales be true, in some other dream? She'd manipulated the rules of the various dream worlds often enough.

It wasn't enough. Not after all she'd been through. If she was going to trust the Prince, he needed to be reliable all the time, both here and there.

She'd wait for some ludicrous line and fly into the atrium then with a good retort.

But as yesterday, that moment didn't come. Oh, there were ludicrous parts of the stories, but she kept waiting. Maybe the Thorn King could explain them. She willed Arpien to ask the questions she voiced in her own mind, and he anticipated a number of them. But her disobedient figment fixated on logistics that would keep no one but Arpien awake at night. Time, place, and physical technicalities didn't matter nearly as much to Brierly. After all her practice in the dream world, wasn't she queen of them?

No. Not quite. But she would be once she found the spindle and destroyed it.

Or used it. Which one?

She realized she was still standing and walked back to her bench.

She plunked herself down in her own dustprint and continued her spy work. With her good arm she drew spirals on the table. Only when she reached the very end of the row of benches and looked back at the labyrinth spread across five tables did she realize how long she had been listening.

When it was too dark to sketch she crooked her good arm on the last table and pillowed her brow against her elbow. The words of her recurring prince and the Thorn King lapped against her. Perhaps it was natural then that the next dream landed her in a boat in the middle of a placid turquoise ocean.

For some lovely hours she baited her fishing string with worms, old slippers, clocks, bells. Each brought a different catch to the surface: an urchin, a whale, a singing teapot. She always threw her catch back after a brief conversation. The whale would have sunk the boat anyway. And the matronly teapot was altogether too chipper.

A persistent east wind tugged her back into *that* dream. Her skin was warm with imprints of body parts not meant to squish together. Wool brushed against her chin. What was this—a cloak? So Arpien had caught her spying after all.

Her sore shoulder had stiffened overnight. She crept into the atrium, though she'd known from the slow depth of his breathing that Arpien was asleep. In the not-quite-light of dawn she could see that the rest of the room was empty. The Thorn King must have slept outside again. Was he really protecting them from the thorns?

As the light strengthened, color seeped into the monochromatic world. She could see now that the cloak she wore was mottled red.

She yanked it off. But it did not feel wet or disgusting. It just felt like a warm cloak.

She couldn't bring herself to leave it wadded on the floor, not when the mysterious man had doubtless meant it as a kindness. Had he been cold out there in the night air without it? She picked it up, folded it, and set it by the door for the Thorn King to find when he woke.

She tilted her head. What was that? Three low notes in the distance, a pause, and the same three notes again. Birds? But there were no birds in Estepel, not since the briars had scared them off.

She waited, but the notes didn't come again.

Unwitnessed, she allowed herself to hover over Arpien. He slept sprawled half in and half out of his blankets, fully dressed but for his boots and stockings. The back of one wrist lay across the scabbard of the vademecum sword, as though it were a favorite toy. One long bare toe twitched in his sleep. She ignored both the wave of protectiveness and laughter that welled up in her. She might reverse their waking scene, right now.

Mad princess.

Then there they were again. The narrow throat of the tower exhaled three low notes. She held her breath for the next two notes that should follow, but her Fine Ears picked up nothing. So she hummed them herself. The next five pitches danced down the stairs.

Brierly should have learned, long since, not to follow mysterious compulsions to investigate towers. But she placed a slippered foot on the first stone step and hummed an ascending line as she crept upward. One note for each step. Then a pause for the answer to drift down. It was a man's voice, she could hear now.

She hummed another three notes up the stairs. She barely heard herself over the whooshing in her head.

It couldn't be.

But they had played this game over a century ago, when Brierly was a tiny chirping soprano. He did it to draw her out of hiding when it was time for bed.

If it was him, he'd only be a memory.

Brierly's voice was tinny and tight against her eardrums. This was the first time in a century of dreaming that she'd voluntarily reentered her tower. She stepped through the dusty doorframe into the room that served as her childhood bedroom, current prison, and future tomb.

Semi-transparent pink bed curtains shrouded the bed. She half expected to see herself there, snoring away. But the sheets were half-pulled off the bed like taffy. It was the way she'd always left them for her maids, even as a child, when she bounded out of bed to chat with birds. It was also the way she'd left them the day Arpien came with his speech and feathered cap.

Even though the bed was not occupied, the chair drawn up bedside it was. A man sat posed as though he sang a lullaby to his feverish daughter. His back was to her, but even so, she could see now that it wasn't *him*.

It wasn't her father.

She braced herself for the disappointment that always hammered her down when dream memories betrayed her. But it was impossible to resent anyone who could sing as this man did. In his next phrase he painted the curve of longing and home. Actually, his raspy baritone was not so very like her father's solid bass, except in the way the melody cuddled around her like a blanket.

She'd stopped singing the moment she entered the tower room, and he'd carried on solo. Now she hummed a tentative pitch over his. It harmonized. Of course it did. She knew this song better than she knew any other.

The question was, how did *he?*

How did the Thorn King know the song she herself had made up about her beloved Sentre Forest, over one hundred years ago?

The logical answer was that the Thorn King was a figment born of her own mind, as the song itself was. For she would not allow that a creature of Voracity could breathe the scope of her mind into such intimate shape.

Her throat shifted from the closed posture of humming to open vowel sounds, and finally, words. She had plenty: one hundred twenty-six verses.

The Thorn King knew every word.

They sang at first with the simplicity of her early childhood: singsong melody, rhymes and meter approximate, with unabashed affection for twigs and bugs and trees. The lyrics grew more clever, the counterpoint more playful. Here the song preened itself on its own wit. Then followed a richer harmony, passionate and full of such open expectations for life, she felt exposed to sing with such sincerity. The Thorn King supplied her with missing lines where her memory failed.

From a soaring major they crashed into a stormy minor. Even the Thorn King's dissonance against her melody was perfect. When the lyrics dried up in her throat, the Thorn King carried the song on solo, singing out her pain and loss with low notes that were more groans than words. The Forest gone, her parents gone, her childhood gone. The melody subsided into long eerie quarter tones, notes that refused to settle on one pitch or another. Her eyes and throat clamped shut like metal traps.

His voice creaked like the wood of a ship's hull. Rising and sinking, rising and sinking, grey tides of a sea after a storm. Softly now, gentle waves lapping the shoals. The aching muscles of her throat began to loosen.

She hummed a monotone accompaniment, intermittent and having no real relation to the Thorn King's melody. It lacked the energy for either harmony or dissonance. Just notes. Washing her up on shore.

Silence.

Her lashes clung to each other, sealed with sand and dried salt water. Beyond the final measure, was this lack of sound and feeling peace?

Then a coda.

Brierly knew there was no more to the song. They had wrung out the music like a wet towel until it couldn't squeeze another drop. But the Thorn King was humming again. The same tune as before, her Sentre Forest tune, but altered.

How dare he commandeer her song? But she couldn't muster resentment. Anyone afflicted with a fairy Gift of Music would know it was impossible to resist a duet with a musician whose style both matched and challenged yours. Brierly heard herself improvising a frail obbligato over his gravelly baritone. He crescendoed, *poco a poco*, as did she. Stronger, clearer.

Here was a one hundred twenty-seventh verse, and one hundred twenty-eighth. What? There was no more to be said about Sentre Forest. Yet she found herself saying it, matching the Thorn King word for word. Verse one hundred twenty-nine. It held all the ancient weight of Sentre Forest, green and deep, but now budding with new branches of melody.

Their voices rose in the air, flying close together then shifting formation like two of the birds from the very forest of which they sang. It was like her favorite music dream, where she could sing worlds into existence. Only there, she sang duets with her own echoes. Now, her singing partner did not merely echo her melody, he shaped it in his turn. He read the flow of her melody so quickly she wasn't sure whose song it was anymore.

If the Thorn King was born of Brierly's own mind, how could he sing of a future she was too empty to imagine on her own?

She broke off the melody. The resulting caesura stung the air like a snapped slingshot.

She whirled around to retreat downstairs and sucked in a breath when she found Arpien leaning in the doorway. Her Fine Ears rarely allowed anyone to approach without warning. The blood drained from her head then rushed back. For Arpien's wonderful eyes held that same expression they had when she had healed him with her music, after the mantizes bit him. She was struck again by the unlikely vibrancy of the color brown.

Arpien's brown eyes flicked from Brierly to the Thorn King and back. He cleared his throat. Hoarseness must be catching. "He knows your song."

"I wrote the song," the Thorn King said, "but she chose to sing it."

Brierly marched herself down the tower stairs. When she reached the bottom she discovered she had Arpien in tow. Her hand must have snagged his sleeve as she brushed past him.

She released the midnight blue fabric and paced away, walked back and gripped his sleeve again between her first two knuckles, and repeated the process. On her third round of grabbing and releasing Arpien's sleeve, his calloused fingers clasped hers to his forearm before she could come unanchored again.

"Brierly, are you feeling all right?"

"A little discomposed." She laughed at her own pun.

Arpien raised his eyebrows in alarm. The hairs had kinked into separate directions in his sleep.

Brierly sobered, so she didn't distress her figment more. "Who is he, Arpien?"

Asking a figment about a figment.

"I think he's who he says he is," he said.

Not Voracity's creation. Not hers.

"You think he really knows the Prince."

"His stories, Brierly—it's like someone filling in the blanks of a larger story you were told as a child and long since forgot. I wonder, was he sent to mislead us with half-truths? And yet, yes, I find myself believing him." He studied her face. "But you don't."

"Hm."

Arpien opened his mouth, but swallowed back whatever argument he was about to present. He took her wrist very lightly. "I wish I could make everything all right for you."

She blinked as though she had some foreign object in her eye.

"It's all right, Arpien. You don't have to rescue me. I shouldn't have said—at the ball—"

"But you were right. I can't." His eyes rested on the stairway that led up the tower, and Brierly read his unstated, *but ...*

Was she ready for that?

"Please. I need some time," she said.

Arpien squeezed her hand once and released it. His retreating boots were the ticking of a clock.

Her own mud-spotted dancing slippers made almost no sound on the floor. She really should find some more solid shoes. The cold seeped through the thinning pads, and the grungy fraying ribbons would put off even such a connoisseur as Squeezie. She remembered a sturdy pair of leather shoes she had worn Pre-Sleep, but wasn't about to go back into the tower to look for them. Perhaps in her mother's room?

Queen Golda, who didn't care one way or another for the company of birds, lived on the first floor. Brierly rammed her shoulder—the one that wasn't sore—into the heavy door and forced the age-swollen wood to give way. She tested the air for the scent of her mother, but only caught stale air.

Wait—here was a glass vial of the rosewater her mother had worn on special occasions. Brierly wriggled the stopper until it came out. All the liquid had evaporated, but the stopper trapped a pale echo of her mother's favorite flower.

Shoes, shoes. She made quick work of the lock with a hairpin.

The dry hinges creaked a protest when she opened the lid. Linen, linen, velvet. Her hand brushed against something long and sharp.

She froze, then eased her hand out of the chest.

No. Her mother wouldn't have hidden it here.

The only light in the room spilled in from the open door. It took Brierly a full five minutes to empty the chest, layer by layer, so that she wouldn't touch it by accident again. What she finally unveiled at the bottom of the chest was the broken spike of a tortoise shell hair comb.

Not a spindle.

She brushed the cobwebby corners of both box and lid with her knuckles, but felt only a few crunchy beetle shells and the notched lines of the Montaine family crest carved into the lid. The chest at the foot of Nissa's bed in Boxleyn was almost identical.

Here in her mother's room, cocooned in her mother's scent, Brierly better understood why Queen Golda had brought the spindle back from Conquisan. Her mother wanted Brierly back, Brierly wanted Nissa back, and for both, the answer was the spindle. The Prince made promises then went away. The spindle had proven power. But her mother had been unable to destroy the spindle.

But then, it wasn't hers.

As if in answer, a draft from the open door stirred the air in the room. The ghost of roses teased her nose. And she knew, Brierly *knew*, what her mother had done with the spindle.

All thought of sturdy shoes forgotten, Brierly ran through the castle. She'd thought yesterday that the servants' sleeping quarters were a strange place to store gardening tools. But now she remembered that old servant at Boxleyn, the one who had served at Estepel as a child, and even dusted the sleeping princess. What was her name? Senesca. She'd spoken of the strenuous shared daily routine of weeding out the briars.

Which room, which cabinet, had it been? A matchless stocking groped out of one room as if to plead, *Don't leave me behind.* And in this one, yes, an iron gardening spade, still caked with dried dirt. There was even an assortment of much-abused gardening gloves. She stuffed her fingers into the stiff leather. The cow who produced this hide must have been designed for grazing thistle patches. The tough leather sheathed her forearms up to her elbows. On closer inspection, these had probably started out as falconer's gloves. For a temperamental hawk, judging by the deep hash marks the talons had left in the leather.

Maybe not talons.

Her mother could not lay her daughter's body in the earth, because one day Brierly might revive. Yet she could make her a kind of memorial grave among the flowers she loved so much as to name her child after them. Even if it was a name Brierly had altered the moment she learned to talk.

The briars had long since choked out the other plants in the garden. Only the bones of the garden remained. Naked pots, stepping stones, and trellises poked out of the thick vines. But Brierly remembered the special spot where her mother tended her roses: along the wall of the castle. If they had not been so near the wall, Brierly never could have penetrated the thicket to reach the place they had once grown, not armed with only a spade.

She fell to her knees and hacked at the earth with her good arm. The spade struck something hard, but it was only a root. The briars stirred restlessly overhead. Brierly glanced up, but they stilled, and she went back to digging.

She might have called Arpien to help her. But while she might have been strengthened by his help, he might have tried to talk her out of it. Or the nosy vademecum sword would have an opinion. Or the Thorn King or through them the nebulous Prince, all telling her what to do when finally the means to defeat Voracity was within her reach. This was something she had to do alone.

Chunk. Her spade sliced into a root again. The vines swayed and flicked like annoyed panthers' tails. She would have to work quickly.

Clink.

Iron hitting iron.

Here it was, the repulsive, enticing four-inch rod of metal. She scraped at it with her spade, but could not cut it free from the roots and vines that surrounded it. No, that grew out of it, the same way roots burst forth from a moist beanpod. Could the acres of briars that swarmed around Estepel all belong to a single plant, sprung from this spindle seed?

She could hardly prick her finger through the leather gloves. And if she did, why fear falling asleep when she had never woken up?

Brierly tucked the spade in the ribbon cinched about her waist. "I will root you out, one way or another." Brierly clenched her teeth, grabbed the spindle, and heaved.

It didn't budge.

She drew away to wipe the hair from her sweaty face, but her hand was caught. A pale beige bracelet, the color of maggots, coiled up her arm outside her sleeve. She jerked back, and a dozen tiny teeth bit into the leather that covered her arm. The vine climbed even higher to the sleeve she'd pushed up around her upper arm. She braced her foot against the base of the briar plant and pushed backward. She heard cloth ripping, but it was her skirts, not her sleeve.

Her opposite shoulder throbbed as muscles just starting to heal threatened to tear.

The spindle sprouted another new vine. It twined around her right ankle alongside the crisscrossed bedraggled ribbons.

The years had taught Brierly that screaming produced earaches, not aid. So she didn't even think to scream for help. Help came just as surely as though she had.

"Hold still!" The vademecum sword bit through the vine around her right ankle, but another sprang up to seize the left.

"Arpien, above!"

Arpien brought up the sword barely in time to slice the vine that swept at his head. The vademecum sword was kept occupied in warding off attacks from the mature, thick vines. The new, pencil-thin vines were more sinewy and grew much more quickly. Cord after cord of spiky teeth burst out of the spindle and latched onto her limbs. Would they draw her down into this pretend grave her mother had dedicated to her? For the first time in years, here was a dream death that scared her.

She heard a woman's laughter.

Brierly had to take control. "It is my spindle! Mine to use or destroy. You have no power over me!"

"No, Brierly!" Even the Thorn King was having trouble pushing the briars back, for they knocked him down more than once.

The woman's laughter grew louder.

The Thorn King knelt at Brierly's side and gripped the top of the hand that was still holding the spindle. "You must give me your thorns. I can't help you unless you do."

He meant these thorns?

"Decide now!" His face, for the first time, was sharp and harsh.

"Take them!"

The vines unwound themselves from her body and snagged onto his. They gave up her right hand last, and only when the Thorn King twisted his hand under hers to grab the spindle from her and yank it out of the earth. The roots made a ripping sound, then snapped.

And still the vines attacked. The thorns began to disappear into his flesh.

"Run!" he shouted.

It was much like their flight through the briars a month ago, only this time Arpien led the way to the gates with his vademecum sword and the Thorn King came last. The briars whipped around them like trees in a storm, stirring up the sweet stench of decaying vegetables. All she saw through the tangle of snapping green vines were glimpses of Arpien's brown hair and the peripheral flash of triumphant fairy wings.

How would the Thorn King keep up, with that limp? Was he still holding the spindle? She turned back, and Arpien, who had grabbed her hand, turned with her. The Thorn King was a few paces behind them. He stumbled over a root that rose up to attack him. He recovered his balance and crushed it with his heel.

"I can fight them! Go!" A blast of air shot from the Thorn King's hand and cleared a narrow tunnel before them.

They were already through the gates before they realized that the Thorn King was not with them. Arpien tried to dart back inside, but the iron gates clanged shut. They sealed the pair of them out and the briars in. Arpien and Brierly could only watch as more vines twined up their friend's arms, one from the right, one from the left, and caught him up in the air a few yards from them.

The briars slammed against the gates, glanced off, and shook with a woman's howl of rage. Thorns aligned around the Thorn King like arrows. For a long moment there was a silence saturated with terrible anticipation, as though a hundred archers drew their bowstrings taut.

Brierly did not want to look into the Thorn King's eyes and see fear or justified blame, yet she could not look away. The face the Thorn King turned to her was full of such exquisite sorrow it leeched her of cynicism. Never had she seen mourning without even a touch of self-pity. His new wounds bled over his old ones, until he looked more creature than man. Yet for the first time in her life, Brierly thought she had finally seen Beauty.

His raspy voice pierced her all the way to the marrow.

"For one I love."

Then the vines blurred his body. She heard the wet impact of the thorns plunging into his flesh.

By the time the vines drew away, his eyes were already dull.

50

Arpien

"Come away, Brierly." Arpien's throat felt sore, clogged, and lumpy, as though he had swallowed a plateful of hard-boiled eggs whole. He wished he could throw up.

Brierly was a marble garden statue that had been abandoned outside the gates. He wrapped a palm around her left elbow—the uninjured side—and squeezed. Flesh and blood.

"Brierly, we can't stay. Those briars can't reach us now, but I'm not convinced that's a permanent condition." Even as he spoke the thorns gnawed the iron bars.

"Permanent," she said, her eyes locked on the corpse of the Thorn King. Then she laughed, and it raised every hair on his arm.

The hand he had placed gently on her elbow now yanked her into motion, mostly to stop that unnerving laughter. Had the Thorn King's death severed her final threads of connection to reality?

Something dropped from the Thorn King's half-curled fingers and rolled under the gates.

The spindle.

Brierly lunged back toward it. Arpien clamped his hand around her arm, more forcefully than he meant to.

No, exactly as forcefully as he meant to. "Now I know you are crazy. Leave. It. Would you make his death pointless?"

She shook off his hand with more energy than she had ever shown. "Exactly!"

Her eyes were fully aware and furious, all trace of laughter gone. "He died for this! I don't care if I pick it up with bare hands, a potholder, or fire tongs, we're not leaving it here."

Clang. One of the thorns bit into a rusty hinge. The gates swayed out and in, as though stirred by a giant's breath.

They could either argue or escape. Arpien snatched the spade from Brierly's ribbon belt, jabbed up the clod of turf under the spindle, and dumped it into his money pouch.

At first her Fleetsome Feet outpaced him down the main road out of Estepel, but her stamina gave out long before his. They ran a mile, jogged a second, and walked a third. Every time a pliable branch swayed in the wind, Arpien braced for attack.

"What do we do now?" Arpien said.

Brierly shrugged.

"Do you really think we can use the spindle against Voracity?"

"No."

Their flight had finally shaken the last spiky green pin from her long-suffering ballroom coiffure, and it unraveled completely. Tendrils kinked and snaked across her face. He couldn't see her expression.

"I had my hands on it, Arpien, and I could do nothing with it. Voracity never needed me to find the spindle, or regain control of it."

"Why did you insist we bring it with us, then? Why did you risk your life"—*and mine and the Thorn King's*—"digging it up? Are we going to take it back to Boxleyn? Try to destroy it? Mind, I don't think we can destroy it even if we chuck it into a volcano."

She jerked up short. His momentum carried him a couple steps past her.

"Why go back to Boxleyn?" she said.

"Because it's your home and it's under attack."

"Boxleyn has never been my home."

"Rosaria is. Don't you care what happens to Rosaria?"

"Why do you care what happens to Rosaria?"

"Brierly!"

"I'm not going back to Boxleyn, so you have no reason to go back there, either." She plunked herself down on the ground. Her tattered skirts billowed around her like a mushroom cap. It took several more moments to collapse into an ice-green pond, as though a painter had arranged the swirling folds for a portrait. Even in her petulance, Brierly's Gift interfered to force a kind of Beauty.

Arpien could taste the salt of blood from biting his tongue. He marched himself as far away as safety dared, hopefully far enough away that he could mutter about her without alerting those Fine Ears. Wait—let those Fine Ears overhear. If she hadn't gone after the spindle yet again, the Thorn King would still be alive. But a good quarter hour of muttering reduced that thought to another: if Arpien had better control of the vademecum sword, if he had turned back in time to help his friend instead of running for his own hide, the Thorn King might be alive.

He wanted to stay angry with her. A good slathering of righteous indignation was wonderful ointment against the effects of self-recrimination. And of grief. He had only gotten to know the Thorn King a day or two ago, if one could ever get to know such a mysterious man, yet in those few hours the Thorn King had seen as deeply inside him as Nissa or Kirren. All three, now gone.

Yet if he been the helpless witness to three deaths of people he cared about, how many more deaths had Brierly witnessed?

His tincture was wearing off, leaving him raw and exposed to the uncertainties of their situation. No food, no water, no horses, no shelter. Brierly didn't even have proper walking shoes.

His stomach growled. When a plump robin landed in the middle of the road, its red breast a bullseye, the only thing that saved it from being dinner were his lack of arrows and the fact that it seemed to be chatting with Brierly like a close personal friend. It bowed its beak to her in one of those avian jerks of movement and flew off. Another bird landed and did the same. Within the next quarter hour, a small infestation of rodents and birds paid their fealty to Brierly.

"Here," Brierly said to Arpien, and he saw that the forest creatures had not been paying the human court but dislodging nuts and seeds from their cheeks and beaks. A four-inch high hill lay at Brierly's feet.

Would they taste like squirrel spit? "I don't need to eat."

"No, that's my Gift." She filched his knife, split open an immature nut, and popped it into her mouth. "See, it's fine."

Hunger is the best cure for culinary qualms. The nuts and seeds proved chewy but spit-free and did much to tame the bear in his stomach and in his temperament.

"Look, I'm sorry. It's just that he seemed a good man, and to die like that—" Arpien swallowed. "He deserved better."

Brierly slit open another soft green shell and extended it to him. "Nut?"

He wouldn't force her to talk about it. He waved the back of his hand toward her. "Yours. You're eating like a bird."

"Somewhat literally, but it doesn't matter. I don't need to eat."

"Fairy Gift or not, I think—"

"I got them for you."

He accepted the nut and let her feed him a few more before packing up the rest in his upside-down cap. Maybe she'd take some later.

It had warmed considerably since their last journey from Estepel, but the night was still chilly. The darkness was unrelieved but for the occasional zap of an electric tree eel. They drew around the spot Arpien would have set a fire if he had flint. He tried to imagine a fire there, but it only made the cold seep more deeply into his bones. Was Brierly, with her experience in the dream world, having any better luck?

Brierly broke the long silence. "Explain it to me, please."

Arpien looked up but couldn't see her face.

"Why he did it."

Her tone was one he'd never heard her use before, like some nocturnal creature too vulnerable to bear the scrutiny of day.

"Did he really want thorns?" she said. "Why, when they killed him just as surely as any man? Was he suicidal? A madman?"

"He said he did it out of love."

"For Voracity?"

"You know for whom."

He heard her shift, as though she had pulled her knees up to her chest. "That doesn't make any sense."

It was the first time she had ever objected to something not making sense.

"What did we ever do for him?" she said. "I wasn't even polite to him. You can't say that deep down he knew I was a nice person. He knew my innermost song better than I know it. You overheard. Admit it, Arpien Trouvel. When I am not swaying people with a fairy Gift of Charm, I am a child of dissonance."

"Most of us are."

"I don't understand you any better than I understand him. What do either of you gain by helping me? I had an answer for you at least, but now—" she sighed. "You are an unruly figment."

"Call me a dream if you want to," Arpien said. "I'm used to it. But don't say you made up what just happened to the Thorn King, or you make his death meaningless."

"It is meaningless. So the Thorn King died for love. He's still dead. Is this your 'real world?' A place where death is permanent and love fleeting? A place where a man who did nothing but help us is punished for it? Where is the reason behind these rules? Is this world any more logical, reliable, or desirable than any other? Why should I fight for its existence? Why should you?"

Her next words were muffled, as though she had buried her face in the cloth of her ball gown. "No. I won't let it be real."

Arpien didn't know what more he could say. Gowsma's recipe of Patience-Constancy-Compassion-Logic was a cake that refused to rise. The memory of Gowsma's voice—and cane—drummed his head.

She may decide to sleep forever. No matter how much evidence you lay before her, if Brierly doesn't want to believe the truth, she won't. That is the human way.

For the first time, Arpien considered that maybe it was more merciful to let Brierly believe she was asleep. Then the fates of her parents, Nissa, Sentre Forest, the Thorn King, everything she cared about, didn't matter because truth could be rewritten for her taste. Death was some transient thing, a migratory bird that came, nested for a season, and flew away, year after year.

Right now he wanted to believe it himself.

He pried off his boots and made ready for a night of pretending to sleep.

He heard a crinkle. Oh. He'd forgotten.

"Brierly, the Thorn King wanted me to give something to you."

"What?"

He extended his hand toward the sound of her voice. Their knuckles brushed in the dark and she jumped back. The gift was knocked from his hand. He patted the ground in search of it.

"What is it? A message?" Brierly said.

"I didn't open it. He said it would explain the meaning of life."

"So the meaning of life is written on a piece of paper I can't read."

"I could read it to you in the morning, when there's more light."

"It doesn't matter. Leave it, Arpien."

As incompetent as he was to combat a maiden's tears, he almost wished she would cry. It would be real sorrow, at least. Then maybe he'd have the guts to shed a tear himself. But her denied pain bristled from her like porcupine's quills, stymieing his hopes of taking her in his arms and both offering and receiving comfort.

As exhausted as he was, it took him hours to fall asleep that night. He had next to no hope that the spindle would help them defeat Voracity, but he didn't dare try to dispose of it. Brierly's Fine Ears would catch him. Would she be able to resist reaching inside the pouch when he wasn't on guard? He quadruple-knotted the money pouch at his waist. Even that would probably do nothing to stop fingers that were Handy with Needle and Thread (and therefore knots). So he drew his knees up and slept with the bag digging into his stomach. Did he feel the spindle worming around, as it fed on the hacked-up clump of earth? Would roots and vines poke out of the bag like pins in a pincushion, and impale him? His abdominal muscles clenched in self-defense. It was impossible to relax enough to fall asleep.

And awake, he saw over and over the Thorn King's bloody corpse, arms stretched wide to embrace a death that, but for them, would never have happened.

51
Brierly

The most ironic part of Voracity's Curse was that Brierly slept forever but nowhere in the dream world could she find rest. The figments of friends and family brought no comfort. She whittled away some hours building a mile-high fortress of crystal, snow fox fur, and claws. It was grand and impenetrable, but when her masterwork of architecture was finished, there was nothing to entice her to stay.

She imagined Herren to keep her company, but his manipulated professions of love left her as cold and hard as the crystal fortress she had just built.

She joined a tribe of giggling snickle-footed imps and cartwheeled through an intoxicating field of purple impweed. Their antics failed to amuse her.

She became a shooting star.

She became a box.

Even the music dream couldn't satisfy her.

After slogging through countless numbing worlds, she found herself drifting in a vast ocean. The listless currents toyed with the lifeless tentacles of her hair.

I'm weary of pain. I'm weary of pleasure. How is it that after one hundred years of sleep, I'm so tired? Tired down to my toenails. My soul wants to scream but my lungs can't be troubled to do it.

Her ears submerged, she could hear the approach of the merfolk from many leagues away. Spinning wheels. She was so tired of fighting. She'd let them chain her to a rock again and leave her for good this time.

She didn't bother to open her eyes. Their voices echoed loud and distorted where they swam just a few feet below her back.

The tip of a trident poked Brierly's back.

"Is she dead?" That was the mermaid's voice, like ripples of moonlight on the water's surface.

A deeper voice answered. "You think Voracity would be in her current mood if she were dead?"

"She's dreaming she's dead?"

"Or she's dreaming she's asleep."

The trident punctured the fabric at Brierly's hip and scraped the skin. Brierly didn't flinch.

"Dead or asleep, she's got the mark of the thorn. Let's bring her in to pay her respects to her mistress," the mermaid said.

This time the trident jabbed her side with enough pressure to spin Brierly facedown in the water. The motion startled Brierly's eyes open. Otherwise she refused to move. She gazed down at the merfolk with half-lidded eyes. Their exquisitely crafted faces stared back up at her, statues of such cold perfection that they froze the insides. Their iridescent hair billowed around them like icy threads of gold spun by the dwarf on his spinning wheel. Strands of Brierly's own long hair drifted into her field of vision. When had she acquired the hair of a mermaid?

The mermaid crinkled her nose. "Look at those eyes. I think she is dead."

She dragged the tip of the trident across Brierly's throat. It cut a thin line, too shallow to kill, deep enough that the salt water stung the wound. Brierly's blood clouded the water between them and tinged the hair of the merfolk red.

"Are you dead, little flotsam?"

The merman grabbed the trident from the mermaid. "Stop that."

The mermaid flipped her strong tail.

"The Sleeper isn't like the other ones," the merman said. "She can fight back. Don't you remember last time?"

"Are you afraid? That was only because of the vademecum sword, and she doesn't know how to use that any more than the spindle." The mermaid burst out a single surprised laugh. "She is alive—I saw her eyes react."

She swished her powerful tail until she was close enough to cup Brierly's face in her hands.

"Enough," the merman said. "We have other duties."

The mermaid grabbed a fistful of Brierly's hair and towed her along, like a child dragging a rag doll to playtime. "Let's take her with us."

"It'll take too much time, and we have to get to the Voracity. She's in a fairyfunk about something, and you know what can happen when we're late. We can't kill the Sleeper here anyway. Not permanently. Leave her here. She'll come when she's ready to serve Voracity."

"And if not?"

"Then she'll serve herself and drift forever."

The mermaid traced a long blue tongue across Brierly's slit neck. At her touch Brierly could no longer repress her revulsion, and jerked away. The mermaid smiled broadly with blood-red lips and teeth. "Goodbye, little Driftwood."

Brierly grabbed her own throat as if to rub away the mermaid's fishy touch. The smooth skin was unbroken. Her hands pressed into the wounds in her side. Healed.

The merfolk were quickly vanishing into the now murky sea below. Brierly could only just make out the fading flash of their powerful tails. Maybe she did want to fight them. She paddled a few strokes after them.

Don't leave me alone.

She swam after the merfolk, even imagined herself a tail like theirs to try to keep up. The mermaid's ice laughter echoed in waves all around her. Then silence and darkness. Which direction should she swim? Maybe she had imagined the merfolk all along.

Water compressed her body from all directions, a blind mass of tangible weight that resented her presence and sought to rush into the vacuum that was her existence. No light filtered down from the surface. Which way was the surface? Why should she want to reach the surface? She plunged backward, sideward, forward, in all directions. Was there any up or down left? She strayed through an infinite nothing.

She drank up the sea. It tasted of salt tears. She drank up the sea. It tasted of honeyed wine. She drank up the sea. It tasted of nothing, and did nothing to fill her.

She took a sponge and wiped away the horizon. She meant to paint a new dream landscape, but she found herself back in Sentre Forest.

Was it storming? No, it was only the electric tree eels. They leapt from branch to branch above her. Their sinuous bellies glowed softly as they clung to the ferrus bark. The light winked out while they jumped, and sparked to help them, without hands, latch onto the next limb. The eels were most active now, at night, with more night coming on all the time. They chased each other, and from below it looked like even the eternal stars could not decide where they belonged in the sky.

By the light of their gently zapping storm, Brierly stared up at the tree above her and traced each branch to its own dead end. She might have stayed frozen like that forever, were it not for the mundane inconvenience of a root digging into her back. She rolled onto her side. The intermittent light illuminated a square of white on the ground some three feet in front of her nose.

The Thorn King's paper.

As with all things you try to ignore, it nagged at Brierly until she reached for the paper. It might be another didactic nursery tale, but she could not shun the last legacy of a man who had paid such a price to allow her to escape.

She glanced at Arpien's huddled form. He had balled himself about the spindle pouch. He flinched in his sleep. Brierly wanted to brush back the brown hair that had fallen across his face. She could almost feel the strands between her fingers, the warmth of his scalp as she soothed the nightmare away. But she dare not come so close to the spindle. It coaxed her in a voice more subtle than even her Fine Ears could detect.

Brierly slipped through the ferrus trees until she found an electric tree eel some dozen feet off the ground. Electric tree eels were excitable, but quick to form attachments. She deposited the requisite small talk in her most lulling voice before she said, "Lend me your light."

A tree snake would stair-step the grooves of the bark. The eel traveled down in a straight line. Its belly emitted a constant faint light as it adhered to the trunk. She stopped it at shoulder level and unfolded the paper.

The first part of the message was a number. Easy enough. ½.

The next word was short—only three letters. *C-U-P.* She could do short ones sometimes. *Cup. ½ cup?*

Then a long word. The letters scrambled like loose beads in a box lid. She took a deep breath and stilled them. It started with another *C. C-I-N...*another *N...*

The word snapped into comprehension. *Cinnamon?*

It was perhaps the very nonsense of the message that spurred her to keep trying to make sense of it. Brierly never could resist conundrums. After a good quarter hour she made out: *¼ cup whole cloves. 5 pounds whole cucumbers. Petals of 45 fireflowers, without the stems, picked at full bloom and dried upside down for at least 6 months.*

This was no old tale. This was the recipe for grandmother pickles.

In spite of herself, she laughed aloud. *Behold, you seek the meaning of existence, and it is grandmother pickles.* Only a person condemned to dream would find purpose in pickles.

Only a person who was awake could read.

Her heartbeat exploded out her ears. She looked down at the creased page again.

Fill crock to top with brine and seal.

The words did not come quickly, but they came, they stayed on the page, they read the same each time through.

Bury in ground for at least thirty years. Pickles dug up too soon will not have cured properly. They will have a bland flavor and will spoil soon after the crock's contents are exposed to air.

Arpien's voice: *So if you can read, that proves you're awake.*

If she had spent even one afternoon with Nissa in the library, if she'd made one serious attempt to look at the pages, she would have had her evidence right then. But even when Arpien held the book under her nose, she had been too busy telling herself it was impossible. Too impatient to let the atrophied part of her mind remember the skill of reading, the way her atrophied muscles had had to remember how to walk.

It took more faith now to believe she was asleep than to believe she was awake.

The dreadful permanence of the waking world came crashing down. It trapped her under immovable blocks of stone. She had wished for decades to awaken, but this was as frightening a prison as the dream world. *The waking world has consequences.* If she was awake, all Brierly cared about was dead or dying. They'd be gone forever, just like—oh spinning wheels, spinning wheels—the man she had pulled off the roof when Eusar tried to kill her.

She was a murderer. Perhaps she'd acted in self-defense, but it didn't change the terrible finality of what she'd done.

If she was awake, then Arpien was real.

The choking sound she made now was unlike any she'd heard in a lifetime of singing and speaking with animals. Her throat pulsed, seized, shuddered, entirely of its own volition. One hundred years of pent-up skinless emotion bellowed out of her, primal as giving birth.

The sound startled a spray of defensive sparks from the electric tree eel.

This ... this was so wonderful she was sobbing. So tragic she was laughing. "Pickles. Pickles and eggs."

The eel flung itself away from the crazy human. It latched onto a nearby tree with a lightning flash so bright it left a burning S shape imprinted on Brierly's field of vision.

I've cracked. Cracked like eggs. Eggs and pickles and pickles and eggs. All the king's horses and all the king's men ...

On the other side of the birth pangs emerged a creature she could not recognize as herself. A creature worth dying for.

But why, why? *I wear the thorns for one I love.* She'd done little enough to make Arpien love her, let alone the Thorn King.

A true creature of the forest, Brierly stood on shaky newborn legs and sniffed in this exhilarating, threatening world. If she was awake, Arpien was in danger. The only and irreproducible Arpien. In one instant she finally acknowledged the improbable, splendid reality of his existence and his love. In the next she acknowledged that she would inevitably lose it.

Time had always been Brierly's enemy, whether there was too much of it or too little. The waking world offered permanence, but not that sort of permanence. In its own way, it was still subject to the whims of disaster, politics, emotions, and time. Humans weren't meant to be anchors. No human was strong enough to ward off death.

And death—oh aye, if Arpien went back to Boxleyn and fought this war for her sake, he would die. Love only conquered in fairy tales.

Brierly succumbed to reality, and reality was more hopeless than illusion.

That night Brierly practiced the one skill she had perfected both waking and sleeping. She ran away.

52

Arpien

Even *this* rescue wasn't going how he planned.

Arpien knew she was gone before he even rolled over to look for her. There was an emptiness in the air that settled into his body when he breathed in the cold drab morning. The morning mist filtered the tepid light of dawn and cast the forest in repeating patterns of grey. He could not even see the sun through the blockade of clouds, as though it had come unchained from the Earth.

He would not follow her this time. He could not force her to love him. It violated the very nature of love. Even if he was convinced that her choices would take her into danger, they were still her choices to make.

Which left him with two choices for himself. First, leave this disaster of a fairy tale behind him and start afresh in some other kingdom. Second, return to Boxleyn, attempt to earn the Rosarians' trust after they'd imprisoned him and nearly killed him, and fight a battle in which the only possible result was fratricide.

He rested the vademecum sword in his lap. "Any ideas?"

It ignored him.

"The Thorn King said you'd tell me where I ought to go."

In a rush he remembered the night the Thorn King had filled the darkness with tales of the Prince. But he could not remember the stories he'd told, only the tragic brevity of their friendship. Why did such a man have to die?

Before Arpien could formulate an answer, the sword leapt from his lap and planted itself in a tree trunk. The buried tip pointed toward Boxleyn.

Arpien sighed. "I was afraid you'd say that. You do know there's nothing there for me. Brierly's past my reach. Nissa's dead. I'll admit I've a few people there I'd not see harmed. Cuz, Kendra, Gerret. But I can't see how my presence is going to turn back the strongest army on the continent. Or how I'm going to get to Boxleyn before the Conquisani army does, now that I'm on foot. Anyway, it's not really my problem, is it? I'm not Conquisani anymore, not Rosarian, and the two people I pledged to protect are gone. I belong to no one and nothing."

The blade vibrated in the trunk.

"You sound as backward as those mantizes. I'm not your human, you're my sword."

The blade went rigid, like a back stiffening in offense.

"Sorry, you're the Prince's sword."

The blade vibrated again, this time like a purring cat.

"You never want to take the easy route, do you?" He pried the sword loose. "Surly nut-hook."

Every step toward Boxleyn multiplied his problems, but the moment he surrendered to the sword's suggestion he felt stronger. "But I'll tell you this, sword. If you're expecting results you'd better help me. We both know my history as a rescuer."

The sword didn't answer, but it seemed to listen. What if it really were some kind of link to the Prince? The idea of such a powerful and immortal legend hearing his mundane complaints disturbed him. Especially when he remembered some of the things he'd called the vademecum sword. *Pretentious pigsticker. Bossy scrap metal. Inoperable, uncooperative, disobedient, misshapen paring knife.*

"Uh, sorry, sword."

He had a feeling that the Prince knew how he'd been treating his sword, about all his failings. Oh well. If the Prince had been witness to all his blunderings, there was no need to pretend to be a hero.

Arpien whittled down the miles to Boxleyn. He saw no one, not even many animals. No predators, no mantizes, and only a sprinkling of birds. He worried about Boxleyn, about Cryndien and Voracity, but mostly about Brierly. Sometimes his fears for her so consumed him that his feet turned back down the path of their own volition. But he did not know how to find her, and the vademecum sword wasn't going to tell him.

He was as alone as he'd ever been, but somehow not alone at all. Eyes seemed to watch him from behind the great hittal trees. He let the vademecum sword guide him on a winding but decisive path through the middle of the woods, convinced it knew what it was doing.

At least until it landed him in the middle of the Conquisani army.

Part Six

The truth will set you free,
but first it will make you miserable.
Attributed to James A. Garfield

We are such stuff as dreams are made on,
and our little life is rounded with a sleep.
William Shakespeare

5 3

Arpien

Arpien was having a row with his sword. All in a whisper, but none the less animated for that.

Worse, the sword seemed to be winning.

"No!" He shook the sword in the air in front of him, not as he would practice dueling positions, but as though to shake some sense into it. All his earlier feelings of sentimentality about this domineering toothpick were wiped away.

"This is your inspiring plan? Get captured by the Conquisani army?"

The vademecum sword rode the air in martyred passivity. When Arpien lowered it to the ground, the sword rose in the air, swiveled, and pulled him firmly three steps closer to the army. Arpien's heels dug up clods of earth before he could rein the sword in.

"You ... headstrong ... reforged ... mule bridle!"

The red teardrop jewel in the hilt of the sword hummed and burned. The Conquisani army was some two hundred yards below. They had set up camp in the valley, no doubt because the river cut through this low point. It took a lot of water to quench an army's thirst. Arpien hadn't seen or heard the army until the sword had pulled him over the crest of the hill. He hoped the army hadn't seen him either, at this distance, but they'd have sentries further out. It wasn't doing his nerves any favors to debate tactics with his sword on exposed high ground.

Arpien tightened both hands around the hilt and heaved, like a boy playing tug-of-war with no one on the other side. The humming intensified and sent vibrations up his arms.

"They'll see or hear you. Shut up! You're not an ill-intention-ometer. I don't want to go that way."

The vademecum sword dropped to the ground, the stone cold and silent. It gave up resistance so quickly that Arpien fell backwards on his rump. The hilt slipped from his sweaty grasp and clanged against a tree trunk some feet away. A crow tore into the air with a caw of ruffled resentment.

Arpien sat still as an undignified statue for several long moments, to be sure no one had spotted them. Especially Cryndien.

A hundred heartbeats passed without any further reaction from the sword or surrounding forest. Arpien walked stiffly, his hand on his tailbone, to where the sword had fallen. He suppressed a groan as he bent to pick it up.

It was stuck.

Not all of it. Just the tip. Which made it all the stranger, for he could grasp the handle and pivot the sword any way he wished. It wasn't lodged in a clump of ferny earth. The tip was hinged to the ground by its own willpower.

He pulled, he twisted, he rotated. Nothing.

"Oh, come on. This isn't even the right story. And there's not a stone in sight."

Arpien sighed and plopped down beside the sword. He winced as his tailbone hit ground.

"All right," he said in a low voice. "Can't we discuss this rationally? I'm willing to defend Boxleyn from my brother at almost impossible odds. But fighting the Conquisani army here? Completely impossible odds. What good will it do Boxleyn if I am captured or executed in the middle of Sentre Forest? Can't you at least let me bring them a word of warning before—?"

The red jewel flickered once.

Arpien thought over what he'd said. He felt like a foolish page boy. "Oh. You want me to scout their numbers and supplies so I can tell Boxleyn exactly what they'll be facing."

The sword came up easily in his hand this time.

It was nearing dusk, so he waited a few hours to have the aid of darkness. He hoped not to encounter anyone, but if he did, maybe in the bad lighting they'd mistake him for his brother again. He also hoped most of the army would be asleep. But he doubted anyone could sleep through the screaming.

At first it was so intermittent he thought he'd imagined it. A high-pitched shriek, there and gone in a couple of seconds. Fifteen minutes later, another. At the third shriek he could pinpoint its source at the far side of camp.

Arpien crept down the hill face into the valley. The angle was steep, and he braced his descent against the saplings that craned their necks out of the hill.

The woman's screams grew more agonized and frequent. Were they torturing a prisoner? But as he drew within a hundred feet of camp, he could see no woman, no poor tortured figure. Just the horses and the hunting hounds, and a few dozen men trying to keep them in order. The horses nickered and stamped. Arpien imagined that even Fearless would be aghast at their nervousness. It didn't befit Conquisani war horses at all. A few of the hounds added their baying voices to the screaming, an anxious chorus.

Maybe it was the overlay of hounds baying, but the screams did not sound entirely human.

Arpien didn't dare creep closer to the animals. That corner of camp already drew too much attention. But this was to his advantage, for it made it easier to approach camp from another side. He circled the perimeter and counted tents, supplies, men. Within fifty feet, he could hear familiar sounds: whetting stones on blades, the bawdy banter of seasoned comrades. Few slept, no doubt tensed up by the periodic screaming. Battle anticipation was on a slow roast, as they were still a few days from Boxleyn.

Speaking of slow roast, the smell of food was driving him mad. Campfire smoke curled around the naked forms of small wild game on spits.

Would anyone notice if he stole a fish or five?

He dared not go so close. Or did he? He was already within fifty feet of the Conquisani camp, and he'd not met a sentry or lookout. Maybe the vademecum sword was disguising him, like an invisibilifier.

Or maybe …

Had the entire Conquisani army used the invisibilifier?

It would explain a lot. Why set up a guard against an enemy that could not see them?

But Arpien could see them.

The vademecum sword helped him dodge from shadow to shadow. His hand was just introducing itself to the remnants of oatcake when the vademecum sword yanked him toward the center of camp. It dragged Arpien away from several other tempting crumbs and wove a zigzag through camp.

Arpien scowled at the sword. "I realize you're against theft, but my growling stomach may give us away."

The vademecum sword only dunked him under a table made of two wooden planks laid across a couple of barrels. Arpien reached up and grabbed a biscuit before the dictatorial cattle prod could jerk him along again. He had just opened his mouth to take a bite when the sword slammed full to the ground. Arpien slammed down with it. His funny bone took most of the impact. He sucked in a breath. The biscuit rolled from his fingertips. He heard footsteps pause, saw a fuzzy-knuckled hand reach down to pick the biscuit up.

Just then another scream split the air.

The boots turned back toward the noise. "I wish she'd get it done with already. How are any of us supposed to sleep?"

"Just thinking about it's enough to make me lose sleep," said another nearby voice. Arpien's neck muscles jumped. He hadn't even seen the second speaker.

"You think she'll survive the process?"

"Of course not. They'll chew their way out."

Thistles, what was going on?

The footsteps moved on. The scream must have driven the mystery of the self-propelled biscuit from the man's mind. The mud-streaked biscuit stood on end, cozied up to a fern. Arpien didn't want it now.

The sword kept him under the table a full quarter hour before hauling him along to the king's tent. Cryndien's tent was the biggest in camp, an octagon of canvas fluted with red and gold. Was the sword taking him to fight his brother? Half of him yearned for the confrontation, half dreaded it, but it mattered little as he'd never get past the Grey Cloaks.

No light shone through the canvas of the king's tent. The sword escorted Arpien to the back. He heard more voices and flung himself down again. He nearly clotheslined himself on the ropes. The voices drew nearer. In a few steps they would see him.

Arpien lifted a flap of the tent and rolled inside.

It was empty.

Well, now what? he mouthed to the sword, afraid to speak aloud and alert the guards outside. Was he supposed to search for something?

But here the sword decided it had said enough for one night, and pretended to be an innocent blind piece of scrap metal.

Arpien crouched in the dark. He patted the few furnishings in the room. Cryndien believed in traveling in style, but he also believed in traveling in speed.

Bump. A cot. A rack for weaponry. A wooden chest, and on top of that—sniff—a half-eaten pork pie. Arpien gnawed at the unbitten end as he continued his search with one hand.

Can I at least know what I'm looking for? Battle plans? The invisibilifier?

"How much longer will the yowling beast be? We've lost a half day of travel."

Cryndien's voice. No one boomed like Cryndien.

Arpien dove under the cot and pulled the blankets down several inches to cover him. He made certain he had secure hold of the pork pie. Would Cryndien notice it missing?

In the gap between the ground and edge of the blanket, Arpien watched ten feet enter through the tent flaps. The first set: knee-high boots that had seen plenty of travel, patterns of curling flame tooled in sturdy leather, buffed to a high shine. The second set: another pair of boots, ankle-high, generally clean but worn to suppleness, less gloss and no tooling. The third set: almost nothing was discernible of her feet, for her dress dragged the ground, and she moved with the stiff small steps of an old woman who'd been jostled on the back of a horse for far too many hours.

The final set of feet was brown, hairy, and small as pansies, but they came in a set of four, and that worried him.

A dog.

Cryndien nearly always brought his hunting dogs with him on campaign. His visit to Boxleyn had probably been the longest he'd been away from canine companionship. Unless you counted Queen Perturbance's lapdogs.

Arpien pressed his ear into the ground to try to see which dog it was. He might be safe if it was Harbinger. Harbinger had been Cryndien's favorite for years, allotted the honor of sleeping in the king's room. She was lithe and loyal and sharp-toothed, but she was useless on the hunt now. She'd lost most of her sense of smell a year or two ago.

"She can't give birth penned up in a moving cage," Voracity was saying.

Arpien sucked in a breath. That screaming had been a woman in labor? Why would Cryndien bring a pregnant woman on a military campaign? Or worse, cage her?

His sharp little inhalation had been soft, but the hound heard him. Arpien saw her feet freeze in position, pictured her cocking her ear.

The cot above him sank as Cryndien flopped down. The added weight made the gap between the blanket's edge and the ground shrink.

"Why not?" Cryndien said.

"A Devarish sow weighs hundreds of pounds," Voracity said. "She'll give birth, the cart will hit a bump, and she'll crush her babies against the sides of the cage."

A sow? At least the screaming didn't come from a human. Although it made little more sense that Cryndien would bring a pregnant pig along on campaign, either.

"We have the *bishlongya* still," Cryndien said.

"You only have two left," Voracity said.

Bishlongya? Where had Arpien heard that term before?

Thwack! The blanket swung toward Arpien. The dog must have slapped it with her wagging tail. Cryndien and Voracity carried on their argument, but Arpien only had ears for the snuffling noises just a foot for two from his hiding place. The three most powerful people in Conquisan stood in this tent, yet Arpien's undoing would be the dog.

"Why can't you stay here with the stupid sow and follow us later?" Cryndien said.

"Because you can't do without me."

The cot creaked. Arpien heard a gentle slap, as though Cryndien had pushed the dog away by her rump. The nose was back, snuffling, in moments.

"Is that so?" Cryndien said. Arpien couldn't see him, but he knew Cryndien would wear on his face the brilliant toothy smile of challenge.

"Assuredly so."

The scream pierced the camp again. Now that Arpien knew it was a sow, he could hear more animal tones in it. It still came painfully close to mimicking a woman's cries. Distorted and alien, not quite beast nor human.

A dog nose thrust under the blanket, the snuffles amplified by its nearness to Arpien's ear. The wet pimply surface bumped Arpien's cheek. The dog barked in surprise. It nearly deafened Arpien. The dog hauled back and tangled herself in her master's legs.

"Harbinger, stop it!"

The barking ceased immediately.

Someone would investigate under the cot now. But Cryndien said, "That thing has us all on edge—men, horses, and now even my dogs. She bit the fingertip right off the last of my men who tried to help her deliver."

"I told your men Devarish hogs do not deliver in the way of common dumb beasts. Yet the farmers and feed-growers among them treat her like a domesticated, earth-wallowing—"

"Just do what you can to shut it up, will you, or we'll none of us sleep tonight."

"At your command." The humility in Voracity's voice was like cheese-cloth. Other attitudes leaked through the porous gauze of obedience.

The tent entrance flapped open and shut.

The boots tooled in flame paced. "By my father's strong right arm, Bo, who's in charge of Conquisan? Sitral didn't talk to me like that three years ago when she came begging on the steps of the palace. She may be a consulan now, but she was nothing but a helpful hedge witch then. I can make her one again."

"Maybe you don't need her." It was the first thing Bo had said since they entered.

Cryndien punched the side of the tent. Not full force—it only rippled for a few panels. "No, that's the sting of it. She's right. I can't roll siege engines through Sentre Forest. I can't sail them into Rosaria's tiny harbor. I do need her weapons to fight Rosaria."

"Is Rosaria worth it?"

Harbinger thrust her head under the cot again. Arpien stiffened. If she had any sense of smell left, he would smell like fear. The dog sniffed at him and thrust her nose at his hands. Her jaw was too close to his neck. He could smell her hot dog breath.

But Harbinger didn't attack. Did she recognize him? Dismiss him as not dangerous?

Arpien didn't know how he felt about that.

"Harbinger, what is it?" Cryndien said.

Arpien shoved half the pork pie at the dog. She snapped it up between her teeth and ducked back out from the cot.

Cryndien laughed his booming laugh. Arpien heard the rasp of a rough hand scratching the bristly coat of brown fur. "Is that what you were after, silly girl? My dinner scraps?"

The hog screamed again. This one went on and on, until Arpien could nearly hear her vocal cords shredding.

"It sounds as though she's being eaten alive." Cryndien's voice was low.

"I think she is," Bo said.

The two bites of pork pie churned uncomfortably in Arpien's stomach.

"I can't listen to this, Bo."

Cryndien hadn't made a pet of an eight-hundred pound pig?

"I know," Bo said. "But this is what you've allowed."

There was a sharp silence, as though the hog had suddenly been put out of its misery, and then, so loud that Arpien's eardrums rattled, another scream.

"By all that's merciful, someone help her," Cryndien shouted. "She'll lose the child!"

His shout blended into the screaming, and suddenly Arpien was reminded of another night, five years ago. Arpien hadn't been allowed beyond the paneled doors, shut tight like a bite. Childbirth wasn't for men's eyes, and certainly not boys'. But the sounds drenched the northern wing of the Conquisani palace. A woman's screams, a man's shouts. The morning traced pale fingers over faces: a dead wife, a dead son, a widowed king.

Cryndien had not been married a year.

Arpien suddenly felt smaller, as though he were once again listening to secret family pains from the other side of the door.

The screams died away. Arpien heard liquid streaming into a cup, smelled the sharp fruitiness of wine.

Cryndien rummaged around for his sword and started to strap it back on. "The main body of the camp can wait here. I'll take the Grey Cloaks and ride ahead."

"No, you won't." Bo's tone could have been scolding or empathetic—there was no telling.

"Who would see us?" For a moment Cryndien's voice gave a stifled echo, as though he were speaking into a cup. "Besides, I'm king."

"And a king has a duty to stay with his troops."

"Yes, you know all about duty, don't you, Bo? Father would be pleased with you. You've done everything he ever asked of you. Look at me. A twenty-seven-year-old widower without an heir, our fleet so undersupplied we can barely maintain enough ships to keep control of the territories father died to gain, and I still haven't taken back this stupid forest that should have been ours a century ago."

Arpien heard a gulp of wine.

"Well, that will change," Cryndien went on. "In a few days Conquisan will hold Sentre Forest and Rosaria both. We'll have the hitall wood to repair the fleet. We'll make the provinces pay their backtaxes." He snorted. "Maybe then I'll have the leisure time to woo a pretty little enchanted princess, too."

"Hand me your wine for a moment and lift your arms," Bo said. The goblet clunked quietly on the top of the chest.

Cryndien continued his muffled monologue through the layers of military gear being peeled over his head. "Maybe I should have been the one to extract Princess Peerless from Estepel. It would have given me more leverage in negotiations. But Sitral was so insistent she'd be dead after one hundred years. And who'd have thought Fumbleshanks would have the guts to strike out on his own?"

"Drink your wine now."

"Do you think he's still there, Bo? Whispering Conquisani military secrets in the ears of his troublesome bride-to-be and his new friends at Boxleyn? Or do you think they saw him for the advantageous fortune-grasper he is, and drowned the pup like I should have years ago? No matter, they'll all be dead soon enough. Unless you want to keep Princess Peerless for yourself, Bo? I wouldn't—too batty by half. But Sitral says she's alive, if we can believe her this time, so we could still seal the old marriage treaty with you as the Conquisani prince."

"Thank you, no."

"Is there someone else you'd fancy? I saw you bumbling along at that miserable excuse for a ball with King Emol's plump little cousin."

"Niece."

"See, you know exactly who I mean. Nessa, wasn't that her name? You could do better, Bo, but she's young and pliable, and has the bloodlines."

"Which is why you killed her."

"Oh."

Cryndien had forgotten? Arpien clenched the handle of the vademecum sword.

"Right, sorry about that." Cryndien buried the moment in the last long swig of wine. "I feel a little muddled tonight."

"That's because I drugged your wine with sleeping powder."

"Oh? Nice of you." The characteristic intensity in Cryndien's voice was fading away like a drummer marching into the distance.

"Where'd you put the *bishlongya*?" Bo pronounced it as though he held a peach pit in the base of his throat.

The cot shifted, as though Bo were shaking his brother's shoulder. "Cryndien, you know you can't go to sleep wearing them. What if one slips out? Do you want to wake up in a crater?"

"Yes, yes, you fussy old nurse, they're in the pouch."

A leather bag nearly bopped Arpien on the nose when Bo hung the leather string over the wooden pole of the cot's edge.

He winced. *Bishlongya.* The fairy term for tornado seeds.

"You didn't like her all that much, did you?" Cryndien sounded younger when he was sleepy.

"Boot," said Bo in his general's voice.

Cryndien swung his calf up a few inches off the floor. Bo bent down to pick it up and pull off his boot. The smell of feet wafted over Arpien.

"Maybe it's just as well," Cryndien said. "I wouldn't want you to move away, Bo. You and the dogs are the only ones whose loyalty I trusss …"

The cot heaved as Cryndien's head hit the pillow. Bo pulled the boot off Cryndien's other foot, then swung both onto the cot. Cryndien was already snoring by the time Bo finished his unhurried patterns of laying out the king's clothes for tomorrow.

The center of light shifted and sent the shadows sprawling at new angles. Bo must have picked up the candle. The light drained away at the entrance flaps.

"Surround the tent and see that no one enters tonight," Bo said. "I don't want the king disturbed."

The orders sealed Arpien inside with the dog and the drugged king.

54

Arpien

Cryndien snored more heavily than Brierly. Even so, Arpien waited to a full count of fifty before rolling out from under the cot. By then his eyes had readjusted to the dim levels of light in the tent. Light from neighboring campfires peeked in the gaps and coated the canvas sides a pale yellow. The Devarish sow screamed its anguish into the night. It cut Cryndien's snore short. Arpien held his breath, but Cryndien's snoring pattern resumed on the next exhalation.

He would be a poor tactician indeed not to notice that he could kill the king of Conquisan right now. Nissa's murderer, his own would-be-murderer, lay drugged so senseless that a little pool of drool puddled at the corner of his mouth.

Harbinger lifted her head. A growl was just beginning to percolate in her throat.

But it wasn't the dog that made Arpien step back. It was the drool. It made Cryndien look too much like a little boy.

He tossed Harbinger the rest of the pie. That screaming sow had put Arpien off pork for months. Harbinger swallowed her growl and the pie, but continued to watch.

What if Arpien could stop the war without fratricide?

He peeked at the guards through the gaps of the tents. Five ordinary soldiers surrounded the tent. Bo must have something special in mind for his Grey Cloaks. Good. The Grey Cloaks had already seen Arpien pull this trick, though never with the right props.

He'd heard Bo lay out Cryndien's clothes, so finding them was not tricky, even in the dim light. What was hard was exchanging clothes with his brother without the guards hearing. Cryndien's boots were still warm and damp when he slid them on. Arpien had mixed feelings about seeing the midnight blue breeches and doublet on his brother. It was marked with so many golden scars of his time with Brierly. But it also stank from a week's wear, and who knew?—it could prove useful in confusing the guards. Arpien eased the leather pouch from the edge of the cot and tied the thong around his waist.

There. He had just stolen the greatest weapon in the Conquisani army.

Arpien's hair was the wrong color, but it was night. Most people would be looking at his crown, anyway. Cryndien always, always brought a crown with him, part of maintaining appearances. He had a thoughtful assortment of them, from formal concoctions crusted with gems from all over the empire, to simple brass circlets. Arpien fished in the chest for the lightest of the circlets. The crowns clinked together with unbearable loudness, but neither Cryndien nor the guards stirred. Harbinger cocked her ear, but it might have been at another scream from the laboring hog.

He slid the vademecum sword into Cryndien's ornate leather scabbard, tooled in the same flames as his boots.

Now the last garment in the disguise: an outer coat of swagger.

He thrust aside the tent flaps and rubbed his eyes. "I can't sleep with all that racket. I need a walk to clear my head. We will inspect the arsenal."

There was no response from the two guards at the front entrance, other than an initial jump. He saw this through his hands. He kept rubbing his eyes, in hopes it would further disguise his face.

"Well?" Arpien said. He envisioned the lashing of a lion's tail to help him get Cryndien's tones right. "Lead the way." He flung out an arm to point them along.

"Yes, Your Majesty," they said.

It was perhaps a little strange that they should lead, not the king. But he had no other choice, since he only had a general idea of the layout of the camp.

Arpien concentrated on mimicking his brother's gait. Powerful strides, decisive as lightning, face like thunder at all this delay. Some men bowed as he passed, which spared him from their close scrutiny. He recognized a face here and there, soldiers who had trained or served with him. This one had mocked his boyish lack of coordination, but that one had turned into a friend. He must stop this war this evening, or in a few days he'd be spilling their blood, or they'd be spilling his.

Most of his performance went unappreciated, as the attention of the entire camp was on the screams of the Devarish hog. Many men went to witness the gruesome entertainment. Others pretended to sleep or joke around their fires, but there was no ignoring the torturous sounds.

Not unless you had the help of sleeping powder.

They reached the arsenal at the far edge of the camp. The army had brought no siege towers, but there were several siege ladders on their sides, and ropes and grappling hooks, and stacks and stacks of arrows, and boxes and barrels of—food? Magical weaponry?

Only two men kept watch on the supplies. Everything was sloppily guarded tonight, as though the Conquisani army thought itself impervious to intruders. Arpien fussed with his circlet until he stood backlit before them. Arpien dismissed the guards to go see if they couldn't do something about that caterwauling sow.

"Sire, are you certain—"

"You think someone's going to come out of the forest and see us here?" Arpien snorted. "Go somewhere you'll do some good."

Either he was right about the Conquisani army and the invisibilifier, or they didn't want to cross him.

Arpien reached to his side and began to untie the leather pouch. One well-thrown tornado seed would greatly diminish the Conquisani army's arsenal. They would only have the men's personal weapons, the ones they kept at their sides at all times.

But the guards hadn't made it more than fifteen paces away when Arpien heard a familiar voice.

"I told you to guard the king. Why have you abandoned post?"

Thorns and thistles.

Bo.

Arpien's fingers felt like jostling hams on the leather tie about his waist. He dare not just tip the tornado seeds into his hand. He'd seen one no larger than a coin burn a hole right through a brigand's palm.

"Yes, General," one of the guards was saying. His voice sounded like Bo might have been towing him in by his earlobe, but sight proved they were just striding back toward Arpien. "We were guarding the king until just a moment ago, and he dismissed us. Ask him yourself."

Arpien shifted quickly so he was backlit again. But even if he could fool his brother's eyes, Bo would never believe this could be Cryndien out here by the arsenal. Bo had drugged the king himself.

Bo's gait stuttered a little, but he only said, "I see. Then you are dismissed."

Arpien froze in the stance he had borrowed from Cryndien. Should he run? Try for the pouch again? Draw his sword? His every muscle tensed like a fraying rope splitting off in all directions.

Bo didn't even pause in his stride. He grabbed Arpien's elbow, spun him around, and said, "Brother, walk with me."

Arpien went. His right hand tightened on the leather pouch. From the back, did it look like Cryndien and Bo were having a congenial family chat? But they said nothing for several dozen paces, as though each were challenging the other to speak first. The further they walked, the less certain Arpien grew of Bo's loyalties.

"Well?" Arpien finally said.

"First, suppose you tell me if our brother is alive?"

Arpien's anger at Cryndien mixed uncomfortably with the admission that yes, for a moment he'd had to talk himself out fratricide. "What do you mean?"

"You're wearing his things, so you were clearly in his tent. Cryndien was in no condition to put up a fight, fool that I am."

"Easy, Bo, I didn't touch him."

Well, not quite true. I dressed him up in very memorable gold-slashed breeches and doublet.

"Then you were there to spy? How long were you there?" Bo stopped walking and turned a finger on him. "It was you Harbinger kept trying to get at under the cot, wasn't it?"

Any lie Arpien made up would do more damage than the truth. "I'm here to end this war before it starts," Arpien said.

"By playing king? It won't be dark forever, 'Shanks. You can't order the army home by light of morning."

The hog screamed.

"What if Conquisan doesn't have the weapons left to wage war?" Arpien said.

"I won't let you steal them and give them to our enemies."

"As if I could carry a dozen siege ladders out of Sentre Forest on my back. No, Bo, we destroy them. Not the men. The weapons."

"How?"

"Are you with me?"

"How?"

Arpien was silent.

Bo circled him. Arpien turned to match his pace so the leather pouch would still be tied to the side farthest from him.

Bo considered the options aloud. "A fire? No, that could easily burn down your whole forest. Fairy magic, then." His eyes fell to Arpien's waist. "You stole the *bishlongya*."

Bo's eyes measured the distance. He lunged. Arpien sprang back and thrust out a hand to deflect Bo.

"Come on, Bo! You know this war is wrong."

"This from a boy who's trying to usurp the Rosarian throne with an incompetent princess. You and Cryndien are so alike."

"We're not the same at all. I'm not starting a war to gain it."

"No, but you are willing to join that war. On the wrong side."

"Cryndien and Voracity will only bring misery to these lands if they succeed. And yet you serve them both."

"I serve Conquisan. And unlike you, who ran off to chase cobwebs and legends, I stay here to minimize the damage our brother and that witch might do. What claim can Rosaria have on your affections? My spies tell me they've already tried to assassinate you twice."

"True. But there are people there I admire. But you misunderstand. I am no longer a man of Conquisan or Rosaria. I serve the Prince."

"You serve a nursery story."

Bo lunged again. Arpien evaded. But his escape from attack one direction led him into a trap the other. Bo knocked his legs out from under him with a sweeping kick. It paid to be lower to the ground, and Bo was a boulder. They grappled and rolled.

Arpien gained the upper position for a breath. "If you seriously meant to stop me, you would have brought those soldiers with you. But instead, we're talking philosophy. What does that say about your loyalties, brother?"

There were new sounds now on top of the hog's shrieking. Men shouted, horses whinnied, and dozens of frantic hooves beat the darkness.

Arpien forced a laugh. It would have been more effective if he had more air to squeeze out of his lungs. "You might as well join me. Because tomorrow morning, after I succeed in blowing up this arsenal, Cryndien's going to remember who drugged his wine and think you were in on it from the beginning."

This was clearly the wrong thing to say.

Bo's eyes disappeared in the shadows under his stone brows. He flipped them over in a mighty heave. Bo had always been the best wrestler of the three. He let out a jagged-edged whistle.

Arpien cringed as he recognized it. It was the call of no bird, but it would bring another grey beast.

But it was a white ghost who tore through the camp directly toward them. No—a panicked horse, her mane flying. Only her oncoming hooves convinced Bo to release Arpien. They broke apart to either side and rolled to their feet.

Had Bo summoned it? But what use was that, to summon a horse so frightened it galloped right past him?

Arpien took advantage of the moment of distraction to draw the vademecum sword. Bo drew his own sword in response. But Arpien only meant to slice through the troublesome cord at his waist. He held the pouch high in his hand, away from Bo. In his other hand he pointed the vademecum sword at his brother.

Bo froze mid-lunge.

Arpien had only to tip the pouch over, and he'd blow up the pair of them and the entire arsenal.

Bo's voice was measured and even. "Think about what you're doing, Arpien. Do you even know how the *bishlongya* work? You could kill hundreds of good men, men you've fought alongside."

"Did Cryndien think about the good men he'd kill when he planted the tornado seed in the roof of Boxleyn Palace? The unarmed men and women? The children? I know you saw the children there, Bo. I saw you talking to Cuz."

"Cryndien didn't plant the *bishlongya* in the roof of Boxleyn. I did."

The severed strands of the pouch dangled and tickled Arpien's wrist. *"What?"*

"There's a space between the roof and the domed ceiling of the ballroom. I found the entrance to it, through the library tower. I crawled inside and planted the *bishlongya* four days before the ball, so it would have plenty of time to feed on the people below and grow. I killed all those people."

There was some trick here.

"If the plan had worked, I would have killed you. So throw that pouch at me if you're going to attack anyone, Arpien."

That was it. The tornado seeds would stay dormant until they were taken out of the leather pouch. Bo was trying to infuriate him enough to make him throw the whole bag. It would be like playing a harmless game of catch-the-ball.

Arpien smiled. "I don't believe you."

Out of his peripheral vision, he saw a silhouetted blade of a man, dressed in drab colors that blended into the greyness of the dim light. "You should. I was with him."

It was always startling to hear a Grey Cloak speak. Shadows didn't have voices.

"Circle around slowly," Bo said to the Grey Cloak. Or Cloaks? How many did it take to necessitate the word *circle*?

Thistles, he'd waited too long. He'd never convince Bo to change sides in front of his men. If there had ever been a chance.

Had Bo really planted the tornado seed in Boxleyn?

For a moment Arpien revisited his old nightmare. He stood in the center of a thicket of blades.

A roan horse burst into the clearing and reared. All Arpien could see of the rider was a banner of iridescent hair. Arpien's attackers dodged the mare's flailing hooves.

"Good girl, Windried," said a familiar dulcet voice.

Windried whinnied in pride and settled to the ground.

Brierly wiped her tangled blond hair from her face and quirked a brow at Arpien. "Would you like me to save you now or does later fit better into your schedule?"

Arpien vaulted up behind her and kicked Windried into motion. "Now is fine."

The men in front of them scattered. Only Bo leaped for them from the side, but he was too late.

"Get the pouch!" Bo cried.

But Arpien countermanded with his best Cryndien boom, "Out of the way, stand aside for the king!"

A few men fled from the arsenal at his warning, but there were too many standing beside Bo to take the whole thing out without casualties. And Bo knew it. He ran for the center of the arsenal, as though daring Arpien to destroy him, too.

"Quickly, Brierly, head for the siege ladders," Arpien said.

"Windried says that's the wrong direction," Brierly said, but both horse and princess turned hard.

Arpien felt for the seeds in the pouch from the outside. The seeds were impossible to feel through thick leather when turned flat, but with a few shakes, they rattled about so he could feel their sides, like coins. He grasped one through the leather so it wouldn't go flying when he upended the pouch.

"Tell Windried to turn again," he said in Brierly's ear, "then live up to her name."

Arpien thought he saw a smile curve the edge of Brierly's cheek as she repeated the instructions.

Windried skidded and reared back around, turned away from Bo and his men. They were at a full gallop when Arpien launched the tornado seed toward the pile of siege ladders. It opened into a whirl of lights as soon as it hit the air.

He misjudged slightly. The seed had no weight. He undershot.

Good thing, too. The whirl of lights expanded and turned like a violent spinning wheel. By the time it hit the siege ladders, it was only six feet across, but it sliced the first ladder and kept going through a second, a third, ten all in a line. It chewed through barrels and boxes. Clouds of flour mushroomed into the air. A few of the barrels made unnatural popping sounds. Arpien wondered if they really had contained fairy Magic.

The whirl of lights didn't slow. Nothing it touched provided any resistance. For a terrifying moment Arpien thought it might roll on forever, as it threaded a six-foot-wide path of devastation through Sentre Forest.

Worse.

It came back.

Just like the whirl of lights at the Rosarian ball, it seemed this one could only go so far then stop, like a dog jerked up on a tether. It hovered midway through a stack of arrows. Bits of wood and metal splintered through the air. Then, just as abruptly, it reversed its path.

Would it demolish the camp? Leap back into his pouch? But it flickered out, like a snuffed candle but with no trace of smoke left behind, at the precise spot Arpien had launched it. Which was now, thankfully, some five hundred feet behind them.

Windried kept a punishing pace through the dark forest. They ducked low, Brierly into Windried's mane, Arpien into Brierly's. At this speed they would not be able to see branches.

"Are they following?" Brierly asked after several minutes of flight.

"I don't know. All I can see is your hair."

He captured the whipping tendrils in one hand and turned.

"I can't see anyone. Between the destroyed arsenal, the whirling lights, the runaway horses, and the screaming hog, I think we had enough diversions." Posing like Cryndien seemed like overkill now.

Brierly patted Windried's neck. "Windried, you can slow a little, girl."

The horse was trembling all over. Carrying two riders at full gallop was no easy task, but Arpien doubted all the tremors were from exertion. "Is she all right?" he asked.

"She saw some baby pigs eating their mother. It upset all the horses. Fools, to corral the horses so close that they could smell the blood."

Arpien swallowed his gorge.

The slower pace allowed them both to sit up. Now her weight pressed back into his. Arpien might have lessened his grip around her waist, but he didn't. He liked the way the knobs and curves of them fit together. Even if her hair did tickle his nose. And he needed the contact to reassure himself she had really returned to him, safe. That she wasn't some figment he had dreamed up because he wanted to see her again.

Was that how Brierly felt, all the time?

But yearning for her presence, even enjoying it, didn't explain it. "Uh, Brierly, not that it's not conspicuously gratifying to see you, but what are you doing here?"

"Investigating the invisible army."

So he'd been right. "You mean you couldn't see them?"

"A man with your prodigious vocabulary is asking me that?"

She was … mocking him. No, teasing. It felt strange. Nice.

"I suspected they'd used the invisibilifier," he said, "but they weren't invisible to me. Why? The sword?"

"Or because you're Conquisani, too."

"How'd you keep from getting caught if you couldn't see the army?"

"Windried. They captured her after Voracity used the invisibilifier on them, so I could see her. The device doesn't affect the vision of animals—she could tell me exactly where everything was. And of course I could see you."

It didn't negate the achievement in Arpien's eyes. She'd have had to sneak her way through the camp to reach Windried, and that without benefit of sight. Was her fairy-Gifted hearing that good?

"You're brilliant," he told her.

"It's a gift."

A gift or a Gift?

He didn't care.

"How'd you know it wasn't Cryndien?"

"I have a good ear for voices. There's only one like yours, even if you are auditioning to play your brother in the next Conquisani theater production."

That was a long way from *one of a thousand replaceable copies.*

"That still doesn't tell me what you're doing here," he said.

"I saw you were going to return to Boxleyn with or without me. It's not very complimentary, Arpien, to pledge your devotion to a lady and then prove your devotion to another is stronger."

"There's never been another woman."

"I mean the Prince."

Was he in trouble? Women were so good at saying everything was fine while plotting punishment.

"I couldn't go after you, Brierly. You made your own choice, and ultimately I had to respect that."

"Exactly. You let me make my own choice. And you made your own choice. If you had followed me, I would have thought you were a figment. Either you'd be one of Voracity's creations, made to destroy me, or one of my own, something I invented for my own gratification. If you left Rosaria, which is what I intended, you'd be proving the law of self-interest. But no, Arpien, you're an idiot, and you chose to go back to Boxleyn. There's nothing there for you and it's going to kill you."

"You sound happy about that."

"Don't you see? For one hundred years, everything existed either to please me or torment me. You made a choice that wasn't centered around me. It wasn't even centered around yourself. You and the Thorn King proved to me that there's another option. I never meant see you again, but I—well, I had to find out what happened to you. I used birds to track you."

Aye, he'd seen them.

"They reported that you were headed south. Back to Boxleyn. In that one act, you showed the Rosarians more compassion and loyalty than I've shown them in my whole life. And I'm supposed to be their queen. I saw then, finally, what kind of a person I was. I saw what kind of man you are when all the trappings are removed. Brave. Loyal. Generous."

Her voice had gone soft. Was she blushing? He couldn't tell in the moonlight. He was, all the way to the tips of his delighted ears.

When Brierly spoke again, her voice was its normal volume. "You were always too pig-headed to be a decent figment anyway."

"You don't think I'm a figment?"

She reached into her bodice and pulled out a flat white square. She didn't unfold it, but it had to be the Thorn King's message. He heard it crinkle in her hand.

"Unclog thine ears, Arpien Teric Elpomp Victor Trouvel, and I shalt testify unto thee the truth of the waking world. ½ cup cinnamon, ¼ cup whole cloves, 5 pounds whole cucumbers ..."

"You read the Thorn King's message?" He had to repeat it to believe it. "You *read* it?"

"Yes, and if you say *I told you so* I'll take back what I said about you being generous." She stuffed the paper back into her bodice so that she had both hands free to hold on to Windried.

"What was that? A code?"

"It's the recipe for grandmother pickles."

It felt good to grin at his friend's unexpected but effective choice, a welcome counterpoint to the gruesome memories of his death. "I never thought I'd be grateful for grandmother pickles," Arpien said. "So, that's it? You're awake now? It seems too easy."

"Of all the words in your vocabulary, pick anything besides easy."

Aye, she had fought hard to reach this place. But there was something he didn't trust about her complete change of attitude. If she could hide her troubles behind indifference, could she also hide them behind geniality?

Brierly whispered something into Windried's mane and patted her neck. "Let's see: horse, vademecum sword—no worse off than you were before we met. Better perhaps, seeing as how these clothes aren't ventilated by thorns. Just drop me off at the edge of the forest, and then you're all set."

"Set to do what?"

"Leave Rosaria."

"I'm not leaving."

"Yes, you are. Consider it a royal order if you want. I am still a princess of Rosaria. I've killed the Thorn King, Nissa, several family members, and one lackey, but I won't be killing you."

"You didn't kill those people."

She patted his hand with all the grandmotherliness her one hundred and seventeen years could bestow. "Arpien, we both know Voracity is going to win. How can Rosaria stand against the strongest army on the continent? An invisible army nonetheless?"

"If you thought it was so hopeless, you wouldn't be going back yourself."

"On the contrary." Her cheery tone was completely at odds with her words. "You've shown me self-sacrifice exists, and for that I'm grateful. But it can never win. People who die nobly are still dead."

Her zeal was a little too bright. "What are you planning to do?"

"Go back to Boxleyn and atone for what I've done."

"How exactly?"

She cocked her head. "I'm going to die."

55

Nissa

Boxleyn needed something to cling to, Nissa longed to give it to them. She started by hanging her embroidered pictures of the old tales around the palace. Within a day every last piece had been torn down and returned to her chambers. At least whoever had removed her scenes had not destroyed them—that was hopeful.

She screwed up her courage and went to speak to General Gapric. "Did you tear down my banners?"

"No." His straightforward tone made her feel the fool for asking. If Mathew Gapric had a problem with her décor, he'd address it with her head-on. "I don't believe we'll be saved by any Gnomes or Unicorns or Heroes from the old tales, but if my men do, I don't begrudge them their beliefs. Skill and steel count for a lot, but not everything. Men who believe in something fight better than men who believe in nothing. It doesn't particularly matter to me what that something is."

"So ..." The idea was so simple, she was almost frightened to ask. "Would you bear the Prince's standard into battle, even though you don't believe in the Prince?"

"Young lady, I'd order a banner of an enchanted mushroom ride before us, if it inspired my men to fight."

"An enchanted mushroom can't save anybody."

"Neither can a Prince who doesn't exist. But belief can."

Nissa bit her lip. It wasn't belief that saved, it was belief in the right thing. But if General Gapric would take her banner of the Prince into battle with him, maybe she best not argue the point.

"If I can make a new standard for you by the time the Conquisani army arrives, will you use it?"

"As long it doesn't distract my men from their work, certainly. I'm no believer of old tales, young lady, but that doesn't mean our goals are at odds."

It will be a war fought with spindles, and needles, and thread.

So Nissa fought. By day she organized people and supplies. By night she sewed a large banner of the Prince of Here and There, surrounded by her embroidered pictures of the old tales.

She was updating their inventory of grain in the market when a scream rang against the stone sides of the palace. Nissa turned in time to see a roan horse tear into the market.

Beside her, Kendra dropped her basket. Potatoes rolled over Nissa's feet and under a table, as though they too fled for cover.

"It's King Cryndien." Kendra tugged Nissa's hand. "Run, m'lady."

But Nissa only stared at the man in King Cryndien's white-and-flame-colored garb. A willowy woman in a raggedy ice-green dress rode before him. His arms kept a tight hold on her, but as a prisoner, or as someone infinitely more precious?

Nissa tugged against the pull of Kendra's hand. "No, Kendra, look, that's your brother with them. And Windried. That's not Cryndien, it's—"

Poor Aunt Perturbance would have been appalled by her lack of dignity. Nissa ran through the market, flapped her arms like a chicken trying to take flight, and whooped a greeting to her friends. Arpien sprang off Windried, picked Nissa up, and spun her in circles like a child.

Arpien set her down, and Nissa turned to hug Brierly. But Brierly still sat on Windried. She stared down at them with an odd expression of pain. Had she been hurt?

With graceful movements that belied any suspicion of a wound, Brierly slid off Windried. Nissa closed the gap impatiently, but then hesitated. Odd. With the normally calculating Arpien, the gesture had been spontaneous. With the normally casual Brierly, she felt restricted. She wanted to hug her, but she remembered Brierly's expression when Gowsma had hugged her—one of tolerance instead of pleasure.

Her friend was back from kidnapping and peril and all Nissa could do was stand there with her arms hanging at her sides like two boneless fish. If Brierly didn't want to be touched, Nissa had to show her relief another way. She beamed at her—thistles—did she actually bounce? "Welcome home."

Brierly flinched somewhere deep within her eyes.

"Back. I mean welcome back. Of course you think of Estepel as home—I just meant it was good to see you—and—"

"You're alive."

Of course. Her friends couldn't have known she'd survived the collapse of the ballroom roof. They'd had no good fairy to report on her.

Brierly reached out a hesitant hand, withdrew it, and laid it on Nissa's arm. "You're alive," she repeated. The slender fingers pressed Nissa's arm, as though testing her substance.

Alive.

Real.

The Sleeping Beauty had at last woken up.

Nissa threw her arms around Brierly. She squeezed like Brierly were a ripe apple and she a cider press.

"Aye, I'm alive! And you're awake!" She bounced again. "Good morning, Brierly Steward!"

She was so happy she even kissed Windried.

Yet even under the joy of their reunion rode an urgency. Arpien insisted on seeing Cuz at once with crucial news. Nissa sent Gerret flying to alert Cuz and his advisors.

Brierly turned Windried over to Kendra. "Take her to the stables, please, and see she gets a banquet of carrots, sugar, the finest in horse treats."

Brierly kissed Windried, too, and whispered into the horse's ear. "You should brag to Fearless and Neef. It will do them good."

Now that her separate relationships with her friends were restored, Nissa was able to see the change in the relationship between the pair of them. Unspoken messages passed between them, in the lift of a brow, the placement of an arm. Something had happened while they were away from Boxleyn—something they only seemed able to share with each other. Nissa had quietly but perceptibly been kicked out of the position of facilitator. Though from the tension between them, it seemed they needed some facilitation. Brierly was finally revealing a glimpse of her affection for Arpien, but she was also showing her annoyance. Arpien was in trouble.

Brierly noted her speculative glances. "Quit writing stories in your head. I'd like nothing better than to put the two of you on Fearless and send you away right now."

"Brierly, Boxleyn is my home. And Cuz needs me, whether he wants my help or not."

There wasn't time to write happy endings, anyway. There wasn't even time to let the two of them wash from their travels. The most Nissa could do for them was arrange for cheese and bread to be brought in to the Reception Room for the emergency meeting to advise the king. Arpien downed two goblets of much-watered wine before tearing into the bread as though he had not eaten since the ball. Maybe he hadn't. Were his cheeks thinner under the brown stubble? Even Brierly, with her Eat-Anything-I-Want-and-Still-Retain-a-Maidenly-Figure Gift, managed to keep pace with him for the first few minutes.

Between bites their stories poured out. Nissa swung her feet as she sat at the council table in a chair that was too tall for her. She could not keep her body still. Too much joyful relief spurted out of her. "Everything will be all right, now that the Prince is on his way."

"The Prince is on his way?" Arpien said through a bite of bread. He swallowed. "You found him?"

"N—no. You found him. Gowsma said you'd found the help you needed at Estepel. I thought—she meant you found the Prince, right?"

She looked at them.

They looked at her.

"You must have found him," Nissa said.

If belief didn't make something true, repetition didn't, either.

Nissa's feet wouldn't swing anymore. If her knees were hinges, they'd be rusted shut. "I don't understand."

"We found a man who said he could lead us to the Prince." Arpien wiped his mouth with his sleeve. It hid his expression when he continued, "He died helping us escape Estepel."

Nissa gasped. "What happened?"

But now Cuz, General Gapric, and the king's advisors were arriving. Arpien and Brierly had to begin their tale all over.

"You saw the Conquisani army with your own eyes?" General Gapric asked when they were finished.

"Not exactly," Brierly said. "They were invisible."

Garmar, King Emol's Ceremonial Chamberlain, pushed back from the table as though in disgust. "Evil fairies, invisible armies—this is clearly a Conquisani attempt to demoralize our troops. There are no such things."

"You can say that after what happened at the Spring Ball?"

"The Spring Ball was a tragedy. But a collapsing roof does not have to be supernatural."

"I saw the army," said Arpien. "And if you believe only what your eyes see, you'll be very dead when the army arrives tomorrow."

"How do we know we can trust you?" said the chamberlain. "Why would a Conquisani prince aid Boxleyn unless it was an attempt to infiltrate our defenses?"

Arpien was silent a long time. "Because I believe the Prince is telling me to help you."

"Prince—Bo?"

"The Prince of Here and There."

"Oh." Garmar sank back in his chair. "*That* Prince. King Cuzzar, the man hears figments talking to him. He's either a spy or loon."

Nissa saw a muscle around Brierly's eye jump, but she said nothing.

"I don't hear his voice," Arpien said. "But I believe he does tell me things. Your Highness, permission to draw my sword?"

It took Cuz a moment to realize Arpien was asking him. He shrugged.

Arpien drew his sword slowly, as though to minimize the appearance of threat. "This is a vademecum sword. The Prince forged it centuries ago, and it's capable of marvelous things."

Lord Darcet tapped his foot. "Yes, yes, we heard all about your wonderful sword last time you came."

"Then you'll remember I couldn't always get it to do those marvelous things I wanted. I still don't fully understand it, but I do understand why it wasn't working before. I don't tell it what I want it to do—it tells me what the Prince wants me to do."

He took a deep breath and closed his eyes. "Prince, show me where I should be. With the Conquisani army?"

He threw the sword to the northern wall, the direction the army would come from. The vademecum sword arced through the air, froze in midair before hitting some of the Montaine family tapestries, and spun back to the center of the room faster than Arpien had thrown it. It embedded itself in the center of the wooden table with a decisive thwunk.

Nissa was proud of Arpien's loyalty to the Prince, but did he have to dent the council table? Maybe she could cover the mark with a doily.

Nobles pushed back from the table with exclamations. "It's a trick!" "It's a sign!" "Where are the strings?"

"Shut up, the lot of you!" A high-pitched boy's voice cut across the commotion. "You all keep telling me I need to make decisions, so sit down and let me do it. I don't know if there's any such thing as a Prince of Here and There. But I do know Arpien was nice to me before I was king. Don't tell me that was a Conquisani plot—he had no way of knowing that I'd come down off the dais before"—he squirmed—"you know. So even if he is a loon, I'm making him second-in-command of our defenses. General Gapric, you better listen to him better than you do me."

"Your Highness, I don't think that's wise."

"I don't give a dried-up raisin about wise. If we're as bad off as you say, we should let him help us."

There wasn't a lot they could say after the king issued a command, yet they continued to say it, talking themselves round to the idea of accepting Arpien's help. Then came another debate of exactly what kind of help they ought to accept. After many circles one of them thought to ask Brierly's opinion on their course of action.

"And you, Princess Brierly?" the armsmaster said. "You have firsthand knowledge of our enemy. What do you recommend?"

"Stockings." Brierly nodded her head sagely. "There's nothing more chafing to the spirit or the feet than a shortage of clean stockings in the middle of a long journey."

"A journey? You suggest we rush out to meet the enemy?"

"No, no, I mean when you escape. There's no way to defeat Voracity. If you stay, you're all going to die. Stockings, gentlemen." She dipped her head to Nissa. "And lady."

Arpien's chair squeaked on the wooden floor as he rose. "Your Majesty, I beg your leave to consult the princess?" Arpien escorted Brierly from the room with hasty decorum.

From there the discussion led to the logistics of defending Boxleyn.

"I don't care about the details," Cuz said. "Just put me somewhere I can dump boulders or boiling oil on the heads of those Conquisani myself."

Was he right to be angry? Of course. His mischief was sometimes unkind, but this, this could turn into self-justified cruelty if it continued.

"It may not be wisest to let you fight, Your Highness," General Gapric said. "It depends on what strategy my new second-in-command, *as appointed by you*"—he pressed into the words as a baker might dough—"advises. And on what Lady Nissa says."

"Why does it matter what Nissa says?"

"Because you're her ward."

She wondered if the horror on her own face was as comical as the horror on Cuz's.

"I assumed you realized. Lady Nissa is now your closest living relative, so she assumes responsibility for you."

"She's only five years older than me!"

"She's reached the age of majority."

A month ago. She was to go from being a king's ward to having a king for a ward in less than a season?

"But—I'm the king."

"Yes, Your Highness. You are also twelve years old. You decide matters of state, but you need guidance. That's why you have us. And a guardian, until you turn seventeen yourself."

Five years. She and Cuz sat like condemned prisoners trying to accept their sentence. If frogs could turn into princes, could brats turn into kings? She wouldn't just need a fairy godmother to manage this transformation—she'd have to be one.

Cuz jabbed a royal finger in her direction. "If you even think of assigning me a bedtime, I'll order the rat catcher to empty his traps in your bed."

Nissa didn't respond. This was not the time for their own battles for power. But how did anyone expect her to command the respect of Cuz? He'd barely listened to anyone in the family, and she, as least of them, had been the butt of his jokes a dozen times in the last year.

Even if they survived the next few days, they'd never survive the five years after that.

56

Brierly

As soon as they were away from listening ears, Arpien whirled and scowled down at Brierly. "What exactly are you trying to accomplish in there? I thought you were done playing the simpleton."

Brierly scowled back up at him. "I'm the only person in there giving wise counsel."

"Why are you angry?"

"You know what you two are doing? You're giving them a pretty dream of rescue to hold onto, a dream Voracity's going to destroy. These people need to wake up!"

"Is that why you came back? To make scared people more afraid than they are already? Thistles, Brierly, these people are willing to fight for your country, and you're throwing that back in their faces."

"They need to know the truth, no matter how ugly that is. Isn't that what you've told me for weeks? Some of them can still get away."

"You'll only be making it easier for Cryndien to bring down Boxleyn, and then Voracity will control your country anyway. This is not the sort of message your people need to hear from you right now."

"You want me to lie to them," she said.

"The Prince may still come. I know this sounds crazy, but my sword tells me not to give up."

"Does your sword have any specifics on when we can expect its master?"

"Brierly, if we fight without hope, we're defeated before we start."

The tartness drained out of her. She felt like an old lemon, shriveled into a hard, tasteless, pimply rind. "I'm afraid of hope."

She had not meant to admit it to him.

"If something happens—" She sucked in a shuddering breath. "Humans aren't meant to be anchors."

He lifted her chin to meet his eyes. "Maybe someone else is."

But to hope for that frightened her most of all.

"To believe in anything takes risk," Arpien said. "Perhaps the risk of disappointed hopes is greater than the reward of fulfilled ones."

"How'd you read my mind?"

"I'm not always the paragon of obtuseness you think I am."

Of its own volition, a corner of her mouth tugged up at his choice of words.

A corner of his reflected the gesture. "Anyway, it was something Gowsma said, a long time ago."

"I doubt the Prince wants to help me."

She'd deliberately pricked her finger on the spindle. For anyone else, the action was nothing—a mild physical injury, soon healed. But for her, it was a flagrant disregard of the sacrifices her people had made to safeguard her. Spinning wheels burned, livelihoods lost, all for her, and she went and pricked her finger anyway. The chance for peace between Conquisan and Rosaria ruined, because of that one decision. Money spent importing textiles that could have been spent feeding the poor or building roads. Her parents had treasured and guarded her, and she had simply used her Fleetsome Feet to sidestep their silly rules. She remembered the old servant's description, how the old Stewards dried up like dead roses, mourning their Cursed daughter.

It was the good daughters who earned rewards. The kindly milkmaids who helped old ladies carry heavy baskets who earned gold and magic rings. What was she? A spoiled princess who'd done nothing to earn the Gifts she did have, let alone any favors now.

She was afraid to ask the Prince to return for fear he was weak or non-existent. But she was more frightened to ask for fear he'd laugh. *Why should I help you, you ungrateful narcissist?*

"Horseradish." Arpien tipped her head up again. "I know you were listening to the stories the Thorn King was telling about the Prince. We found you snoring in the feasting hall."

"I wasn't snoring. I only fake snoring sometimes."

"You snore, old lady. Sonorously. But my point is that you know the old tales. Of course the Prince wants to help you."

"Then why hasn't he?"

"You're awake, aren't you?" He dropped his hand and shifted uncomfortably. "Look, I know I'm not Herren ..."

Spinning wheels, she'd insulted him. "That's true, you're not."

"The Thorn King told me I'd never be a king."

He did?

"I want you to know that I understand why you didn't choose me. I'm stiff, I'm quick to temper ..."

"You're passionate, but quick to ask forgiveness."

"I lecture too much ..."

"With too large a vocabulary."

"I disappoint even myself ..."

"Because you're far too hard on yourself."

"I come across as overbearing ..."

"And protective and kind and intelligent."

"I get caught up in my own ideas and forget to listen ..."

"As evidenced by this conversation."

"And I know that you wanted to marry him, not some arbitrary descendent of his, a cheap copy of what you lost ..."

"Ah, there you have it wrong." There she'd finally gained his attention. "Your great-grandfather was a fine man, Arpien, but I knew him for a single evening. Yes, I took a liking to him. But what I felt for him, that's the cheap copy."

He looked as though she'd thumped him on the head with a bag of flour. Then he beamed like a little boy.

"I shouldn't have said that," she grumbled. "Now I'll never get you to leave."

"You weren't getting that to start with," he said. His deep voice triggered heat all through her. He leaned closer, but it was only to capture her hands. He pulled her forward so gently that a butterfly could have beaten him off. Not Brierly. He watched her expression closely, and rested his forehead against hers with that same butterfly touch. "You have no earthly concept how much I want to kiss you."

Don't. I'll break. That pesky bird was flapping around in her ribcage again.

He must have felt her panicked pulse. "Don't worry. Your fairy godmother pounded that lesson into my skull quite literally."

"Lesson?"

"Patience. Of course, my skull is thick."

So he did kiss her—on her hands. But the gesture was so tender that when his lips grazed her knuckles she didn't know whether to laugh at the discovery of a dozen new ticklish points on her skin, or quit breathing entirely.

"I'll save higher hopes for later. And Brierly"—he gave her hands a gentle squeeze—"there can be a later. Don't be afraid of posby blossoms."

Wait. Did he just compare her to his horse?

A damsel who didn't hold court with sympathetic forest creatures on a regular basis would have taken greater offense. As it was, Brierly just smiled and rolled her eyes. How very Arpienlike, to say exactly the right thing and then exactly the wrong thing.

Arpien slipped back into the council, but before she could follow the Brierly faction burst into the atrium. They fell upon her with exclamations of relief. Her enthusiasts were not so many in number as before. Through the excited babble she gleaned that some of the courtiers had fled Boxleyn immediately after the Spring Ball. A few had joined the Boxleyn guard.

"See?" they said to each other. "I told you they'd return. They're right out of the old tales. They have to win."

You need to let them know there's hope.

I will not lie to them.

For the first time she looked at their anxious faces and saw people, not a company of dolls. She owed them for their misplaced devotion. She could use her Charm to make them laugh off their fears, but that was no kinder than scaring them with a blunt prediction of defeat.

"I do not have the power to save you. But I promise that I will die before I let Voracity take Boxleyn."

"An easy promise," said Gamel, the son of Lord Darcet. "Voracity doesn't really exist, does she? Neither does the Prince. It's just us against Conquisan, isn't it? Bloody and unromantic. All these tales about you and Arpien, they're just puffery to make us believe we're going to our deaths in some heroic burst of glory."

An outcry drowned Gamal's words.

"Voracity is no tale," Brierly said. "As for the Prince ... " Never in her life had she wanted to believe in something so much. "As for the Prince ... "

The doors to the Reception Room slammed open and Cuz skulked out. A few of the courtiers nodded to the brat king. Most did not bother. Nissa followed a few steps after him, then stopped and chewed her lip.

Brierly knew what answer to give. "As for the Prince, ask Nissa."

If the courtiers had barely acknowledged Cuz, most of them hadn't noticed Nissa at all. They looked around in surprise, as though Brierly had told them they'd find an elephant behind them. The legend wanted them to listen to Lady Overlooked?

"Nissa has been studying the Prince of Here and There for years. Nissa, tell us why we should believe the Prince is real."

Nissa opened her mouth and squeaked.

"She even sounds like a mouse," Lady Miranda said.

Brierly stifled the giggles with a pointed look. She caught Nissa's elbow before she shrank away and gave it a squeeze. "Tell us."

Tell me.

Nissa held her eyes as though she heard her unspoken plea. She turned to the others. "Would you like to see my embroidery?"

Only six of the Brierly faction followed them up to Nissa's chambers to hear about her embroidery. One got bored and left, but her report sparked the interest of three others to come see the display for themselves. Over the course of the day, no less than thirty people dropped by Nissa's chambers. Some were simple gawkers, out to view the legend returned. Some marveled over Nissa's skill with a needle but nothing more. But some lingered, and listened, and watched Nissa lay the embroidery squares out on the floor in dozens of patterns. As she did, she spun a tale of adventure and love and wonder that rivaled one of the Thorn King's.

A few of the ladies so embraced the new tale Nissa revealed that they offered to help sew the new banner of the Prince Nissa described. Brierly's sharp ears picked up Nissa's murmured, "A sewing circle may help after all, Cuz."

Most of the visitors were ladies, but men, too, found excuse to wander in. The armsmaster came by to scold them all for being idle while the Conquisani army drew nearer. But General Gapric pulled him from the room with advice about the exercise improving morale.

Brierly listened to her formerly meek friend give her people the hope Brierly herself could not. Nissa made belief in the Prince sound both exciting and imminently reasonable. As for that violent purple bruise that distorted her right eye, her confidence transformed her face from something pitiable to something indomitable. It was in itself a kind of beauty. A beauty related to that of the Thorn King.

57

Arpien

"I can't believe you brought the spindle back with you," Nissa said. Again. She'd been repeating the phrase like a whip-poor-will ever since Arpien had outlined their escape from Estepel.

Yes, well, neither can I, Arpien wanted to say, but didn't for Brierly's sake.

Not that you'd think it affected Brierly by her behavior. Brierly-who-knew-she-was-awake was not all that different from Brierly-who-thought-she-was-asleep, at least not when it came to sidestepping conversations. She sat tailor-style on the floor of Nissa's parlor and addressed all her comments to Albertus. Every few minutes Albertus launched his tiny haunches into the air, snatched a chair cushion or pillow between his teeth, and dragged it beneath another chair. The pair was redecorating.

Arpien knew his lady too well by now to believe her indifferent.

"Why would you even search for it?" Nissa said. "How many times has it nearly killed you, Brierly?"

Brierly kept her back to them and pointed to the right. "No, Albertus, the one with the fringe should go there."

"Brierly?"

"It's not what you—" began Arpien.

"I asked Brierly," Nissa said.

It still jarred him when Nissa looked him square in the face. The massive bruise across her temple and brow had turned the skin a variegated green/yellow/purple. The scaled effect made it look as though she were turning into a dragon. She still couldn't open her right eye all the way. Nissa assured him the swelling had gone down a great deal. The thought only sickened him. Why wasn't she dead? Arpien steeled himself never to flinch when he saw her new face, but that didn't stop the urge to give Cryndien and Bo matching injuries.

Nissa's words drew his attention away from the anger he wouldn't show. "I want to know what's so magnificent about this spindle that she keeps courting suicide."

Albertus minced back to Brierly's side. Brierly scratched his head and rewarded him with scraps of her dinner. The three of them had dined in Nissa's parlor instead of the dining hall, in hopes of having a more private conversation. Not everyone in Boxleyn was ecstatic at their return. But Brierly wasn't conversing, she was studying furniture with her canine consultant.

Just when Arpien had decided Brierly wasn't going to answer, she said, "Voracity said she'd give you back if I gave her the spindle."

Tiger-cub Nissa retracted her tiny claws. "Give me back? She never had me. I was—" She looked down and to the side. The furrow between her eyebrows looked like a tiny letter z. "I don't know where I was. Someplace safe."

"Safe? You nearly died," Arpien said.

"I know. I can't remember, but there were no evil fairies there."

"I know that now," Brierly said. "But I couldn't find you anywhere in the dream world and—yes, Albertus, the square one would contrast well there."

Albertus got a running start and leapt at his new target.

Nissa sat down in front of Brierly, so close their knees bumped. "You tried to risk your life for mine?"

Behind them Albertus jumped and missed five times.

"It's no different than what you did up on the dais," Brierly said.

Nissa took her hand. "It's very different. All I did was get you out of the way of Voracity's magic. You would have tried to use her magic to bring me back. Brierly, there are worse things than death. Don't face them for my sake."

Arpien cleared his throat. "Uh—I suppose you won't be happy to hear that we also brought back a *bishlongya*."

Nissa raised her brow.

"Tornado seed."

She wasn't happy. Arpien felt like he was facing down a ferocious kitten.

Albertus's teeth finally clamped on the pillow. He gave a muffled bark of triumph and dragged his kill to Brierly.

"You've got to get rid of them," Nissa said. "Both the spindle and the—*bish-bishlonja.*"

Arpien decided now wasn't the time to correct her pronunciation, and went back to referring to them as *tornado seeds*. "How? The spindle's indestructible. And the tornado seed might be our best weapon against the Conquisani army. One already took out a good portion of their arsenal."

"You are not going to try to defend Boxleyn with the very weapon that destroyed most of my family. Did you try the vademecum sword against them?"

It was too dangerous to palace architecture and residents both to do this inside, so the trio claimed their horses from the stables and rode well into the park. Nissa chewed her lip the entire ride there. Perhaps Windried really had been bragging to Neef and Fearless about her heroics, because Fearless marched within one hundred feet of the posby bushes without more than a slight hitch in his pace.

They dismounted in a wide-open space, not a witness in sight. Arpien untied the money bag that held the spindle and the leather pouch he'd filched from Cryndien's tent. He wound the strings around each, and laid them out on the ground, like two coffins awaiting burial side by side. He wasn't about to take the fairy weapons out of their coverings.

He drew the vademecum sword and concentrated on the Prince to make it sharper. The sword hummed in a tone Arpien had never heard it use before, and the money bag answered it. They argued like a nest of wasps.

Nissa's eyes were round. "Uh, Arpien, I don't think you should wait any longer."

But it was to Brierly Arpien turned. Her long fingers clutched the cloth at her neckline. It bunched up, but there wasn't quite enough to cover the vulnerable line of her throat.

He held the handle toward her. "Are you ready? We could do this together."

She didn't take her eyes from the pouches. "I don't think I can."

Couldn't use the vademecum sword? Or couldn't destroy the spindle?

Either way, protectiveness surged up in Arpien's chest and spread through his fingers, into the sword. Nissa was right. This spindle had cost Brierly too much, just as a tornado seed had cost Nissa.

He brought the sword down like an executioner.

Shreds of cloth, colorful embroidery thread, and leather splintered into the air. The scraps exploded outward some ten feet.

Nissa tucked her face into her elbow. But Brierly just stood. One hand still clutched her neckline. The other reached forward, fingers splayed, as though to deflect the spray of fabric and leather.

The scraps halted midair, hovered like snowflakes too light to fall. The tornado seed, freed of its binding, spread into the grass like a perfectly circular spill of iridescent wine. Five inches, ten. It sucked the shreds of fabric and leather into its flashing surface. Fifteen inches. The spindle in its clump of dirt rolled into the circle. Brown-black humus flaked from the metal spindle and sank into the pool of spinning lights.

The waspish humming grew louder, to a pitch that made Arpien's ears pop. Would the two magics cancel each other out? He'd never thought of disposing of the spindle this way.

"Arpien!"

He could barely hear Brierly over the buzz. She stood as before, one hand at her throat, the other outstretched.

"Do something!"

What was she asking him to do? Destroy the spindle or save it?

It did not matter, for even as he raised the sword the spindle drank in the tornado seed. It slurped in the pool of lights as a frog would a fly. The whirl of lights made an odd little crackling sound. Then all that remained was the spindle, naked, black, and smug.

Brierly knelt down beside it. Before her knees touched the ground, Arpien putted the spindle out of the way with the tip of his sword. Nissa tackled Brierly—or tried to—while Arpien trapped the spindle under the flat of his sword.

"I wasn't going to touch it." Brierly shook her shoulders, but Nissa clung to her back like a resolute bear cub.

"Then why were you reaching for it?" Nissa said.

"I was just curious."

Arpien and Nissa exchanged glances.

"I wasn't going to touch it."

Brierly's glare haltered both of them.

"Fine. You clean up. I'll go round up the horses." She exhaled audibly through her nose and stalked away.

Arpien glimpsed three horses on the horizon, and sighed. He really should be used to walking by now.

"Why didn't it work?" Nissa said. "It's the Prince's sword. It ought to be stronger than Voracity's spindle."

"It's Brierly's spindle, too," Arpien said. "Maybe she's not ready to give it up."

"But she hates the spindle." Nissa plunked herself onto the ground and peeled off her right shoe and stocking. She extended the limp stocking to Arpien. "Here."

"Thanks, Nissa, I usually don't wear stockings embroidered with flowers."

She balled up the stocking and tossed it to him. Or at him—with Nissa's aim it was hard to tell if she meant to hit his shoulder or it caught there on accident. "No, put the spindle in it. Unless you brought another pouch?"

The most dangerous fairy weapon in Rosaria was tucked away in a bulging stocking, guarded by dainty embroidered daisies, by the time Brierly rode up on Neef. Windried and Fearless trailed close behind. Arpien and Nissa mounted and they rode away from the scar of earth without a word.

It was Brierly who broke the silence. "You're right. I do hate the spindle."

Nissa opened her mouth and closed it. "Oh. Fine Ears, right?"

Brierly nodded. "But you're also wrong. I wasn't going to touch the spindle. Why would I do a fool thing like that? I can't use it. Can't destroy it. I know it's still Cursed with sleep."

She was talking too fast, piling up words like a makeshift barricade.

"But maybe it's best ..." Brierly jutted out her lower jaw. "I want you two to hide it. Hide it and never tell me where."

She spoke to both of them, yet it was Arpien's gaze she caught. He gave her a sad little smile, and nodded what he hoped read as encouragement. The air between them was full of the dream they shared but never spoke of.

She nodded back and kicked Neef ahead a span. "Just don't bury it in the ground. I'd hate for old Senesca to have to add weeding to her list of chores again."

58

Brierly

Brierly spent the next few hours in the stables. She helped the grooms lay out the equipment for the horses and prompted Fearless to give advice as the only experienced war horse in residence. Neef told a few dazzling and completely fabricated war stories of his own. Neef had perfected the art of Conquisani boasting to the degree that he might have given a tip or two to Arpien.

Just as Brierly's reading skills had atrophied in the past century, so had her writing skills. But she was the only person in the stables just now who had ever learned to write. She crimped the quill in her hand and blotted numbers and figures to carry up to the Reception Room, where Arpien and General Gapric were planning Boxleyn's defense.

Between inventorying for Nissa, altering one of Timothy's old outfits for Arpien, and giving motivational speeches to animals, it was dawn of the next day before Brierly slipped up to the roof to visit with her old friends, the spotted pigeons. A fifteen-foot chunk of the roof had caved in. The remaining squared-off stones jutted into midair. The hole looked like a gaping mouth with teeth knocked out in a brawl. Brierly peered all the way down to the dusty ballroom. The sickness she felt had nothing to do with heights.

The pigeons drew her attention away and circled about her in delighted reunion. The chicks boasted they could fly now, and proved it proudly, if a bit unsteadily. Brierly praised their efforts, but even their enthusiasm could not stop her from glancing to the horizon for the Conquisani army. Which was ridiculous—did she expect to see an invisible army coming?

The chicks pouted, as much as beaks can pout, at her distraction. What could be more interesting than their new flying skill?

Brierly gasped. True, she couldn't see the invisible army, but the birds could. She could use them as her eyes the same way she had the horses. In fact, the birds would be more useful, as they could scout out troop movements from overhead. "Show me how you can fly to get Arpien," she said. The three chicks tore off like hawks in search of prey.

Only when Arpien burst onto the roof, sword drawn, did Brierly realize he might think the pigeons were warning him of a threat to her life again.

"Oh, sorry," she said.

Arpien exhaled and sheathed the vademecum sword. He crossed over to her and put a hand on her shoulder as if to confirm she was whole. Strength seemed to flow from his fingertips into her body. "What's wrong?"

"I just had an idea."

At first Arpien seemed surprised at her interest in military tactics. No wonder, when until recently she had made a point of being oblivious to danger. The merit of her ideas wiped away his surprise, and soon they were debating the defense of Boxleyn like two generals. Within minutes they sent the two oldest birds off to survey the approaching enemy. Arpien outlined what to look for, and Brierly translated it into bird terms. Arpien had spent most of yesterday analyzing the strengths and resources of the Boxleyn guard, and of course he already had an estimate of what the Conquisani army might do. Arpien had an excellent grasp of strategy, and Brierly a knack for unexpected tactics. It reminded her of the game of jumpstones they had played their first day at Boxleyn. Only this time, they didn't need Nissa in the middle. If not for the fact that the future of Rosaria rested on their success, Brierly might have outright enjoyed it.

Arpien observed it, too. "We work well together. Especially now that you think I'm real."

"Now that you think I'm real."

He raised a brow at her.

"You finally got rid of the pedestal that stood between us."

Arpien nodded. "I'll accept that criticism."

"Not criticism. Teasing. You have no idea of your true merit, do you?"

He blinked, then his mouth tipped in a tiny smile. "I'm willing to listen to you enumerate my many virtues."

His humor was all the more precious for its rarity. Especially now. She gave him a twisted smile. "No, sir, I have decided that the way to handle you is to humble you when you get cocky and compliment you when you are too hard on yourself. In short, to always do exactly what you need and the opposite of what you expect."

"Definitely female thinking. Can we get Nissa to explain this to me?"

"Nissa's busy." They sat on the ledge and she explained the embroidery. "She's changed so much, even in two weeks."

"We've all changed." He reached over and claimed her hand. Her left hand, she noted, although it meant reaching farther. Did he worry that her right arm still hurt? A bruised shoulder was least of the sensations that registered just now.

Her pulse leapt, but as he did nothing more than settle their joined hands in his lap, she let it comfort her rather than panic her.

"Three days ago you were coming back to Boxleyn to die," he said. "Now you're planning a brilliant defense. And what you said about the spindle—I think that was really brave."

She snorted. "It was brave to tell you to hide it from me?"

"It was brave to ask for help." He studied their joined hands. "Believe me, I know what a hard thing that is."

She expected him to say something about the Prince, perhaps even wanted him to, but Arpien let the silence stand as he held her hand.

"I admit I find Nissa's arguments appealing," she said. "But there are so many stories out there. How can you tell the real ones?"

He toyed with her fingers. "Well, lately I've been talking to my sword. Would you like to borrow it?"

The pleasurable tickle of his hand distracted her for a moment from the significance of his offer. For all Arpien had badgered his sword over the past two months, he was possessive of it. It was an offer she had to accept, if only out of recognition of what it meant to Arpien.

"I should warn you, it doesn't respond to everyone. But I think it listens." Arpien unbuckled his sword belt and helped her fasten it around her waist. Perhaps the dim light of dawn accounted for the clumsiness that hindered both their efforts.

"I'll just"—Arpien cleared his throat and stepped back—"leave the two of you alone to talk this out."

Brierly settled against the door to the library tower and drew the vademecum sword across her lap. Brierly had long experience conversing with unusual partners—animals and inanimate objects both. But how was she supposed to address this one? As a sword? As a link to the Prince?

"Are you there?" she whispered into the near-darkness. "If you're there, will you come back?"

Of course there's nothing there. You're talking to a figment.

Was it the sword talking? Or her own doubts? "It was my fault. Don't hold it against them."

Her parents had spoken of the well of warmth and understanding they felt when they spoke to the Prince. Brierly only felt the immense empty space of the air around her, the hollowness of the wind, her smallness compared to the sky.

What's better, Brierly? The fleeting satisfaction Voracity offers? Or the permanent rejection of an absent Prince?

For a moment Brierly imagined Voracity as empress, not as a hag, but in full form. Beautiful and terrible and cruel and exhilarating.

The vademecum sword clattered against stone as she darted for the ledge. But she didn't vomit. She clung to the stone wall and shook like a kitten on a windy fence.

The return of the pigeons provided a welcome reprieve. At least until they reported that the Conquisani army was right outside the gates of Boxleyn.

59

Brierly

An hour into battle and still the Prince had not come. One by one arrows sent her birds plummeting from the skies into the chaos below. Only by exerting all her Gifts could she convince them to venture out again, and again, until the last failed to return.

So this was the duty of a queen.

Without her animals she was blind to the movements of the enemy below. General Gapric ordered her back to the inner palace. If the Rosarian royal line fell, Cryndien could invite Voracity into Boxleyn, and the kingdom was lost. It hurt to obey. They'd lost their eyes on the northeast corner of the palace. Now more people would die, because of her failure.

Permanence was a terrible thing. Soldiers fell and did not rise. In the makeshift ward in the east wing, she watched a servant, too young to have been pressed into battle, breathe his last. Somewhere off the page, a mother or father waited to hear of their son's fate. (*That, sir, is infinity.*) No amount of imagination could make the vulnerable chest rise again. Arpien led a losing battle against an invisible enemy. He could ward off a thousand blows and fall to one. For both strategic and personal reasons, Cryndien would target him.

All of it was her fault.

Having lived without guilt for so long, she had no barriers against its tidal return. If she hadn't touched that spindle one hundred years ago, she would have married Herren, the issue of Sentre Forest would have been settled, and there would be no war. There'd be no reason for Arpien to be out there risking his life for her and Rosaria now.

Come to think of it, Arpien wouldn't exist at all.

The shocking thought snapped her out of her paralysis. She had made a ruinous choice, and a price must be paid.

She didn't hold any noble hope that she could offer her personal surrender and Conquisan would call off the attack. No, she was thinking instead of an unwatched battlefield. In the waking world, General Gapric was right, she was of little use in battle. But in the dream world, she was a toughened warrior with one hundred years of combat experience. If she proved a big enough pest in the dream world, it might distract Voracity's attention from the waking world. Perhaps it would even disrupt the magic that protected the Conquisani army.

There could be no running away this time. She'd have to willingly endure, because each minute she drew Voracity's attack would draw it away from Boxleyn. Could she be as brave as the Thorn King, and endure the pain to save her friends?

She retired to Nissa's chambers to seek the dream world. Nissa was in the sitting room, hunched over her embroidery. She raised bleary eyes to meet Brierly's.

"Nissa, haven't you slept?"

"I wanted to finish the banner of the Prince. General Gapric said if I finished it, he'd carry it before him into battle."

"Too late for that. The army has retreated inside the walls."

The needle slipped. Nissa sucked the tip of her finger. "Thistles, I sew too slowly."

Brierly plucked another needle out of Nissa's basket. The easiest way to steal a moment to sleep was to help Nissa finish. "We can still hang it from the high tower. I can do a dirty job of finishing it up for you. It won't match your artistry, though."

Nissa rubbed her eyes. "That's fine."

Brierly asked Nissa to describe what parts of the banner were left to do, then sent Nissa to the table to eat some stale toast. By the time Nissa had choked down two pieces, the banner was finished.

Nissa dropped her crust into the pot of gooseberry jam. "How—?"

Brierly shrugged. "Fairy Gift."

On the rare occasions she pushed her Gifts to their limits, she tended to scare people. She'd forgotten that. Nissa closed her mouth, nodded in her Nissa way, and accepted the miraculous.

Brierly packed Nissa off to the tower to hang the banner. It was perfectly plausible Brierly stay behind, to keep the Rosarian line spread out. Look what had happened last time the rulers of Rosaria clustered together. The moment Nissa was gone Brierly dove into bed, like a knight charging into battle.

Something was wrong. The world did not shift.

She deepened her breathing, let her pounding heart slow. Minutes dragged by, marked only by the phalanx of worries that marched through her head. She flopped over, beat the sweet-smelling linen pillow into submission, and settled again.

Make ready, Voracity.

She only saw the back of her eyelids. She'd heard of this phenomenon, but it'd been decades since she'd experienced it herself.

The Sleeping Beauty had insomnia.

60

Nissa

By the time Nissa clambered onto the roof of Boxleyn Palace with the heavy banner, her hands were slick with sweat and her heart thunked against her ribcage. Which–she told herself–had nothing to do with the sounds of battle below.

Nissa discovered how quickly you could envision your own death—method, funeral, burial—in the two seconds it took her to realize that the figure who rounded the tower with blade drawn was not an enemy soldier, but Rosarian.

"It's just Lady Nissa, Your Majesty," he called over his shoulder. Cuz and another eight guards rounded the tower. Nissa could not decide if the sight of her pudgy-cheeked younger cousin in battle gear amused or depressed her.

"What are you doing here?" she said.

"Guarding the hole in the roof." Cuz rolled his eyes. "I told General Gapric I wanted to *fight,* but neither of you would let me."

"Your Majesty," said one of the guards, "the attack at the Spring Ball left a great breach in Boxleyn's defenses. It is essential we cover the gap."

From above, the hole was only fifteen feet across. General Gapric had explained that Conquisan had planted the magic in the narrow space between the domed ceiling and the roof. So while the thin tornado had devastated the ballroom, it had not altogether destroyed the integrity of the roof. Still, seeing the crumbly, jagged wound in reliably sturdy Boxleyn Palace jolted Nissa with sick excitement, as though residual magic might suck her in.

"What are *you* doing here?" Clearly Cuz delighted in accusing some-one else of being too soft to defend the palace.

"I—General Gapric said I could hang this banner to help morale. That is, if I have your permission."

Her tone of deference assuaged his wounded pride. "Let's see it then."

Two of the guards took the weight of it from her arms. She looked up to thank them and saw that one of them was Gerret. He winked at her, and he was once again the easy-going big brother of her maid.

The guards unrolled the banner. "This isn't Rosaria's standard."

Cuz scuffed his toe against the stone roof. "More of Nissa's fairy tales."

"Old tales," she said. "And while they do contain a few fairies, most are about the Prince."

"Which prince?" one of the guards said.

Cuz rolled his eyes again. "Now you've done it."

Perhaps the guards were as restless as their king at this menial assignment, and the banner provided a needed distraction. Whatever their reasons for listening to Nissa's stories, she saw hope dawn in one pair of eyes, and then another.

"You really think he's coming back to Rosaria?" Gerret said.

"He promised he would." Nissa looked up at him with a smile that then froze in half-conscious fear. The grey-cloaked soldier behind Gerret was not Rosarian. He raised his sword to stab him from the back.

The change in her expression must have warned Gerret. He whirled to face his attacker. The hilt of a dagger blossomed in the other man's chest, and he fell to his knees, face stunned. No one ever defeated a Grey Cloak, but more than that—

He thought he would be invisible.

Nissa could see him. So could Gerret.

Two of the Rosarian guard collapsed at Nissa's feet in a pool of blood. A third Rosarian guard chopped the air, until another Grey Cloak felled him with a single swift lunge.

For all that he was five years younger than she was, her bratty cousin had not frozen. But even weeks of practicing with Arpien left Cuz little match for a soldier full-grown. Cuz's movements blazed with fury, but his blows did not meet their target. Then she realized Cuz could not see his attacker.

Yet Cuz remained alive. How?

She thrust herself in front of Cuz, to his high-pitched protests. She looked up into his attacker's face and met stone-grey eyes that were dead to fear, dead to pity, dead to anything outside his mission. Yet he did not strike.

"You won't do it, Bo."

Her words goaded the statue to life. Bo seized Nissa's upper arm with bruising force and hurled her aside. Nissa smacked onto the stones and rolled. The roof gave away beneath her.

She scrabbled for higher ground. The stones at her feet loosened and plummeted to the ballroom floor five stories below. Cuz yelped her name as she slid backwards toward the growing abyss. Her sweaty palms left a glistening double smear on the stone, marking the track of her doom.

Her body jerked to a halt, feet midair. The crushing strength of the hand that saved her could not be Cuz's.

It was Bo's.

Bo's hand was as slick as hers, and she slipped an inch further into the hole. She tried to kick her legs up onto the roof. The stone at her knee shifted alarmingly.

"Hold still," Bo said.

She obeyed, even though the stone at her knee continued to grate free. As it gave way beneath her, Bo grabbed her scalp with his other hand and hauled her up by her hair. Her nose wound up jammed in his armpit as he rolled them both away from the expanding hole and onto stable ground.

It was not the picturesque princely rescue of her fantasies. Sheer relief outweighed all else, including the alarm she ought to feel in the arms of the man who had helped kill her family and who knew how many of her countrymen.

"Let her go." Gerret added the encouragement of a sword tip at Bo's throat. The Grey Cloaks stilled their blades.

Bo released her. Nissa sat up but did not walk away, now more afraid for her enemy than of him.

Where was Cuz? There—alive, if shaky. Only two of the Rosarian guard remained. The Grey Cloaks had lost only one man, but there had only been three of them to begin with, plus Bo.

"You have every right to kill me," Bo told Gerret evenly. "But I'm certain my men would retaliate, and you cannot survive that."

"I cannot let you go." Nissa had never heard Gerret sound so intense.

"Then I surrender."

"The general of the mightiest army in the known world is surrendering to me?" Gerret said.

"Only myself. My men will report to my brother. You will let them go, and they will not kill anyone on their way out."

"General." So the Grey Cloaks were not sworn to silence. "Use the girl as a hostage."

Bo barked with laughter tinged in self-contempt. "When everyone here has seen that I cannot even let her *accidentally* die? I am a dog with no teeth. No, men, return to my brother and tell him I have disobeyed his orders. Then he will not waste lives trying to avenge a traitor." He turned his eyes to Gerret. "Do you accept my terms?"

The Grey Cloak took a step forward. "Prince—"

"Will you make me repeat my order?"

Bo did not raise his voice, but the sudden weight of command behind it snapped the assassin's jaw shut. They had all been wrong, Nissa realized, to think of Bo as a mere unwilling shadow to Cryndien.

"They can see us. Cryndien needs to know that."

Bo looked at Gerret again. "Do you accept my terms of surrender?"

"I—well, yes."

Bo gestured crisply at his men, and they vanished like a whisper around the tower.

"You'd do better to guard the broken window on the first floor than the hole in the roof," said Bo.

"Why do you help us?"

Bo answered Gerret, but his eyes sought Nissa's face. "Because Cryndien finally asked me to do something I cannot do."

Nissa's cheeks flushed, both because of the speculative glances Gerret was giving the pair of them, and because Nissa knew the truth now. Bo hadn't really saved *her*.

Gerret withdrew his sword a foot from Bo's neck. "We will escort you down to the dungeon."

"*No!*" Cuz waved his own sword where Gerret's had just been. "He killed my parents. Your king and queen. He killed Eusar. And Timothy." Cuz's voice shook. "Now I'm going to kill him."

Nissa surged to her knees. "No, Cuz! He could have killed us both today, and yet we live. Don't return mercy with lack of mercy."

Nissa reached out to lower his wrist. Cuz flung her hand away, and snapped the sword back to its position. The blade nicked Bo's jaw, but Bo did nothing to resist.

"I return murder with murder," Cuz said.

Cuz drew up short, as if startled by his own claim. He stared at the trace of blood on his blade as though he did not realize until now that he had cut his prisoner.

He still couldn't see Bo.

"I—I meant justice," Cuz said.

"It would not be justice. He surrendered. Gerret accepted."

"Gerret is not king!" Cuz's round shoulders rose and fell with great heaving breaths.

"No, Cuz, you are. This is when you decide what kind of king you will be."

No one did anything to intervene, not even Bo, who watched Cuz with level resignation. Over the course of a wordless minute, Nissa watched Cuz's frenzy abate, measured by the rise and fall of those half-childish shoulders.

He stepped back, not lowering the sword, but no longer on the offense. "I will at least have the satisfaction of locking him in his cell myself. And throwing the key into the moat."

Nissa couldn't help a smile of nervous relief. "We don't have a moat."

"I'll build one."

Before she left, she unfurled the banner over the edge of the wall. Gerret left her in the charge of three other guards on the first floor. She thought Bo might say something to her before he was taken to the dungeons, but he did not.

"Go outside, spread the word," she ordered two of her new guard. "I've hung a banner on the palace wall. Anyone who looks to the Prince for help will be able to see the enemy."

61

Brierly

Permanence was a terrible thing. Only when you came to value one world above the others did you worry about losing it.

Brierly buried her head under her pillow, but the feathers could not block the sounds of battle from her Fine Ears. She squeezed her eyes shut, but she still saw a dozen images of Nissa captured, the servant boy breathing his last, a bird arrested in its flight by an arrow, and Arpien. Arpien whisking off his cap—*I humbly beseech your permission to save you.* Arpien on the practice field, meeting his opponents blow for blow, and moments later modifying his approach to build the confidence of a bratty boy. Arpien brushing a shard from her hair, heedless of the dozens that gleamed in his own.

How foolish. The best way to help Arpien was to enter the dream world, and here she was, so worried about him she couldn't sleep.

Once before she had escaped the waking world by knocking herself out against the stone wall. She tried it again, and only succeeded in making herself see double. She ricocheted dizzily to the floor. High-pitched yaps dissolved into words.

What are you doing?

"Trying to fall asleep."

Madam, pardon the observation, but my nephew has more sense, the poor flea-brain.

Albertus went on with other observations about the intelligence of his nephew, but Brierly didn't listen. She wouldn't be much good in any world if she brained herself. If she got herself drunk and passed out, her thinking would be muddled in the dream world. She didn't favor drunkenness anyway.

There was one guaranteed cure for insomnia. Possible only for her, and only because of Gowsma's Gift and Voracity's Curse.

Albertus dodged flying clothes as Brierly dug through Nissa's chest. *What are you looking for?*

"A spindle. Arpien and Nissa hid it from me, the overprotective idiots." She tried to forget that it had been her suggestion. But this was different. She didn't want it for her own sake, but for theirs.

It's in the library.

"How do you know?"

I saw her put it there. Since my poor Queen's demise, no human has stepped up to give us the proper deference due to Royal Lapdogs. Lady Nissa at least remembers to bring us dinner scraps. Scraps, I tell you, when we used to dine at the king's table. Just yesterday, as I was following Lady Nissa to remind her of her duty, I saw her hide something in the library. Allow me to escort you there.

Albertus minced down the hallway, head high with the importance of his mission.

As they neared the queen's chambers they heard Squeezie whimpering at the queen's door. Squeezie's ears perked up at their approach, and wilted as they came near.

Albertus gave a brisk bark. *She's not coming back.*

You're not a good dog, Bertus. You said a dog should have only one master, and now you—

Don't you dare lecture me on loyalty, pup! I served the queen well for seven years. She was everything. But what use is a dead master?

She'll be back. Squeezie turned back to the door and resumed whining. Brierly had never liked the queen, but his keening pierced her chest. *Queeeeeenie. Queeeeeenie.*

Albertus gave a scornful sniff and minced on. *Nothing but dander between your ears.*

There were human traces of a deadly skirmish on the roof, and more of the roof had collapsed. She could not even tell which side had lost, for the enemy slain would be invisible to her. As well as any of the enemy survivors, but no one attacked her. Brierly paused beside the bodies only long enough to confirm that they were beyond help. There would be many more dead bodies if she did not stop Voracity.

Albertus sniffed a metal ash bucket in the library. Brierly dumped a daisy-embroidered stocking onto the hearth and picked at a hole in the toe with a fire poker. Dark earth spilled out from the wound. In the semi-dark, the spindle had already started to sprout thorns, like an old potato sprouting anemic shoots in the cellar. At the moment, she felt no attraction to the spindle, only repulsion. The cloying stench of rotten vegetables saturated the air.

Pricking her finger once had brought all this trouble. Could pricking her finger again cure it?

She might imprison herself in another century of sleep. In one hundred more years, Arpien would be long dead, and there would be no true love to wake her and make endearing over-rehearsed speeches. But if by condemning herself it meant Arpien and Nissa lived and Rosaria endured, she'd accept the cost.

She'd learned that much from the Thorn King.

She dragged her fingertip across the spindle and drew a single red drop of blood.

Brierly plunged into her old nightmare of the night of her birthday ball. The hand holding the spindle went icy numb, Voracity rose up in full form, and Brierly raised a bloody hand to defend herself. She imagined a shield. She imagined guardians of fire.

Nothing changed. Why in this dream did Brierly have no power?

Then she realized. This was still the waking world.

"Brierly. How kind of you to invite me," Voracity said.

Brierly had seen Voracity in full form before. Many times. She was still inhumanly handsome, alien and exquisite. Her magnificent wings still fell about her in a dazzle of mesmerizing lights. She was still simultaneously repulsive and appealing. But never, not even on the dawn of Brierly's one hundred year Curse of sleep, as her innocence shattered about her, had Voracity looked so terrible.

"I didn't invite you!"

"You Stewards have never understood proper etiquette. The invitation is still in your hand."

Brierly looked down. The small thorns she had seen sprouting from the spindle were now shooting into long vines. She flung the spindle away, but the vines twined around her wrist. They wound round and round her arm, tying the spindle into her wet palm. Wet because as the vines grew, so did the thorns, and they found purchase in her flesh. Whatever thorn she tore loose with one hand merely sank into the other and left an open gash.

Brierly quit struggling and forced her breathing to slow. *Concentrate. Take control.* She imagined the thorns withering away. The only result was that the thorns took advantage of her stillness to bind her arms to her sides.

"They're my briars. The Thorn King said so," Brierly said.

"Yes, they are your briars. You have planted and watered each one, and so you die by your own hand. I should no longer be surprised by how often you humans repeat the same idiotic choices. Dogs returning to your own vomit, isn't that the phrase? You created the briars, but I own them. Or did the 'Thorn King' forget to mention that? All briars in this world belong to me, as does anyone who bears their mark. You, my dear, most certainly bear their mark."

Voracity eyed Brierly's numerous puncture wounds, the crimson stains that spread across the fabric of her dress. "He is no master of the thorns. I am."

Fear bit into Brierly, as tangible as the thorns that stabbed into her body as the vine wound ever tighter. She squeezed out her words between gasps for air. "It's not—supposed to happen—why here?—Spindle—should send me to the dream world."

"The spindle was never meant to send you to sleep. That was Gowsma's interference last time. The meddlesome twit. No, the spindle was made to do one thing: bring me to you in full form so I could do with you as I will."

Arpien, Nissa, all of Rosaria would be harmed if she failed now. "I won't—let you—"

"Let me?" Voracity's wings swelled up hot and red. "Even now, as you bleed to death before my eyes, will you not see me for who I am? All I asked of your parents was that they honor me, recognize my power. I might have given you a mighty christening Gift. Far more formidable than Beauty or Music or Chatting with Rodents. But all the Stewards could ever see was their beloved Prince and those mindless fairy puppets of his."

"If you wanted—recognition—why disappear from my dreams?"

"As long as I left you alone, you grew more self-reliant, and less and less of a threat to me."

Brierly could think of no retort, nor did she have the air to deliver one. She could no longer tell whether the stabs of pain shooting through her were due to the thorns or loss of circulation. The bookshelves grew grey and indistinct, covered over by a field of colorful sparks.

"Gowsma isn't here now, little Steward, to tamper with your Gifts. I'd like for you to at last enjoy my full christening Gift to you."

Brierly roused momentarily as something slammed into her shoulder and drove the thorns deeper into her left side. No, she realized muzzily, she had passed out and fallen to the stone floor, and was in danger of passing out again. Her mind willed her arm to lift, but her arm refused to obey.

Her Fine Ears outlasted the rest of her senses. She heard a thousand crystal goblets shatter. Voracity's voice seared through her like victory call of a fiery trumpet. "Look on her! The last Steward lies dead on the floor, killed by her own briars. The line is destroyed, and you could do nothing."

Who was she talking to? Arpien? But there was no one else in the room.

A breath later Brierly left it herself.

62

Nissa

Nissa made for the east wing. She towed the three guards Gerret had assigned her behind her. She could at least do some good carrying and fetching for the doctors. For a time she was almost too busy to think of anything but which room needed more water and who to send for extra needles. But it was amazing how many thoughts could rattle around in the human brain at once. Buried under the commotion lay the nagging feeling that she was still neglecting her duty. By the Prince, what else could she do? Her swollen fingers ached as she tore ball gowns into bandages. Bo had bruised her twice—once to imperil her and once to save her.

From outside and overhead came the sound of a dozen windows shattering at once. The whole of Boxleyn Palace rumbled and shook. A lady at Nissa's side dropped a crock full of bloody cloths. The crystalline sound of breaking glass mixed with the duller sound of cracking pottery.

"What weaponry is this?" the lady cried.

Nissa was torn between her own desire to flee and her need to know what new danger had come. With shaking hands she cracked open the window to look out. A thin shadow slipped through the narrow gap. A snake? She jerked the window closed, but the beast bit her with improbably long fangs. She spasmed backwards.

"Get out!" She back-ended the lady into the hallway—a generous backside was useful sometimes—and slammed the door. The wood vibrated with the impact of fangs on the other side of the heavy wooden door.

"Block this door!" she ordered her guard. An emaciated brown-green leaf slithered into the gap under the door. The guard jabbed at it with his sword, and it retreated. Only then did Nissa understand that what she had seen was no snake, but a vine of living thorns.

Did that mean Voracity was here within the walls of Boxleyn Palace? How could that be? Nissa yet lived. Not for long though, if Voracity had enough power to attack them with briars that were ripping bits of Boxleyn apart as a kraken would a ship.

Nissa tried to block out the sounds of more glass shattering, heavy things falling, screams. *You'll do no good if you panic.*

Her thoughts turned to the imprisoned General of Conquisan. Perhaps her own part in the battle for Boxleyn was played out, but not his. The moment her feet set on a course toward the dungeon, she felt a palpable relief. It was faint but undeniable, as though she had fit a final gear inside a broken clock, and now it ran again.

"The keys, please." She held out her hand to the guard at the dungeon entrance. He held out the keys over her open palm but did not release them. "He can help us."

The guard shifted on blocky feet. Nissa recognized him from the stables, shoeing horses. He was burly enough to bounce Nissa back up the stairs like a stuffed leather ball, but he was also new to the guard and uncertain in his duties.

She finally dredged up his name. "George, do you believe I would do anything to harm Boxleyn?"

"No, m'lady. It's him. How can I trust a man I can't see?" He nodded toward the first cell. The torchlight barely illuminated the still figure who sat within, once again the watchful granite statue. Could George even see Bo's shadow?

If she tried to wrest the keys from his hand she'd look like Squeezie when he took it into his fluffy head to play guard dog. So she did what she'd done all her life—she called the servant by name and said please. As though "please" were truly the magic word mothers told their children it was, the keys fell into her waiting hand.

"Thank you, George. You may wait at the top of the stairs." She included her own three guards in her glance.

She'd wanted privacy to speak to Bo, but now that she had it, she had no idea how to begin. She busied herself flipping through the ring of keys, and tried one after another in his lock. Without looking directly at Bo, she knew he had not stirred from the boards that served as a bed on the far wall. She felt his eyes intent upon her, which made each failed attempt to open the door more embarrassing.

"They're not even wet," he said.

What? Oh, Cuz had threatened to throw the keys into a moat. Was Bo joking? But his face bore the dour expression she had grown accustomed to.

The fifth key turned and clicked inside the lock. The door swung open without even the whisper of a squeaky hinge. The Boxleyn dungeons were as well-maintained as the rest of the palace, a legacy of poor dead Aunt Perturbance.

If Nissa had detected a hint of amusement in Bo's voice, there was none to be seen in his face, rough and chiseled by shadows.

"Why?" he said.

"Voracity is already inside the palace walls. As that was your primary objective in killing Cuz and me, I conclude that you'd gain little in our deaths at this point."

"Voracity is here?" Bo rubbed his forehead. "Then I have betrayed my brother for nothing."

Nissa drew herself up to her full undaunting height. "I am of little political consequence, but I would not call my life nothing."

"That is not what I meant."

"Of course not. Twice now you have tried to destroy my family. Twice now you have failed to complete your mission—on purpose."

"That does not make me your ally. Maybe Arpien has forgotten he is Conquisani, but I have not. I will not fight against my men or my king."

"Then talk to him. Get him to abandon his quest for Rosaria."

"At the very moment of his triumph? You are naïve."

Nissa had always looked younger than her years, and borne the condescension of others—cruel or well-meaning—as a natural course. For no reason she could name, she needed Bo to recognize her as an adult.

"Are you coming out of there or not?" Her indignation echoed as petulance in her own ears.

He rose and obeyed with that slow watchful sadness that brought again to Nissa's mind a trained brown bear. Nissa shut the cell door behind him more adamantly than she'd intended. In one of those surprising precise movements of his, he caught her wrist and turned her forearm to the unsteady light of the torch on the wall. For the first time, Nissa noticed the three tiny beads of blood that were drying along a shallow white inch-long scrape on her arm.

"That scratch is from a thorn." There was no question in Bo's tone. Hadn't he witnessed Voracity's tactics for three years?

"Yes." She looked up into his eyes, searching for—what?

"Lady Nissa, do you know what it means if the thorns are here? It means Voracity is not only here, she's here *in full form*. That means Brierly and Cuz are dead, and Cryndien has declared himself king of Rosaria."

He was still holding her wrist. The contact both gave solace and sought it.

"If they were dead, I would be Queen of Rosaria," Nissa said. "Your brother would still have to kill me before he could invite Voracity into Boxleyn. She must have found another way in. There is still a chance."

"Against a fairy in full form? The most I can do for you is secret you away from Boxleyn before my brother kills you."

"Then return to carry out his atrocities?"

"The shadow does not question the man who casts it."

"Yet you are willing to cross him, three times now, for my sake." At least, she'd like to believe it was for her sake. But some truths must be acknowledged, no matter how painful. "Bo, I am sorry, but I am not Kirren."

He sucked in a breath and released her wrist.

"I do not ask you to protect me, just to do what is right," Nissa said.

"Whose version of right?" He shook his head. "I only know duty."

"Oh posh. If you only knew duty you'd hack off my head and have done with it."

"Why should you trust me?"

"I don't. I trust the Prince. I think—" This would sound ridiculous to Bo, but out with it. "I think he wants me to let you go."

"I have cursed the Prince since I was twelve years old. He would never tell you to do anything for me."

"Obviously it's been too many years since you read *Tales of the Prince*." There was no time for this. "You'll pardon me—I'd love to debate literature with you but my kingdom is under attack. I've told you what I think you should do, but you're free to choose your own course. I'm hardly big enough to stop you."

"What will you do?"

"I believe," she said, "I already answered that when we parted in the ballroom."

63

Arpien

For hours Arpien stood with the soldiers of Rosaria, directed their arrows, told them where to overturn their kettles of boiling oil that they might hit their unseen enemy. Immune to the invisibilifier, only he could see the suffering of his countrymen when a Rosarian weapon struck true. He stored up pain that would be managed later, should he live. In the present, the sorrow of it transmuted to battle anger. For however many Conquisani fell to a lucky blow, ten times that number perished among the Rosarians. While they'd held the outer wall, the losses had been even. But now, reported General Gapric, Brierly's pigeons had been shot down, leaving Boxleyn half-blinded. Conquisani scaled the northeastern walls unseen. Hand-to-hand fights spread over the battlements. No, it was not accurate to call them fights—it was slaughter. Only when the man next to you fell did you realize you had to lash out with your sword in a gambled hope that you would strike your enemy before he struck you.

Anger built in Arpien. *This is the expense of your empire, Cryndien.*

Perhaps because the Rosarian army was blind, it heard the new threat before it looked for it. Above the din of battle, there came great crash, accompanied by a swarm of high-pitched tingling as a million shards of glass zinged into each other. Something bit into Arpien's ear. He flicked it away like an insect, and the back of his hand came away with a thin streak of blood. The Conquisani soldier he was currently fighting was not so lucky – the hailstorm of glass left a three-inch shard embedded in his forearm. Arpien took advantage of his opponent's shock to knock the sword from his hand.

He whirled in the direction of the noise. Vines poured from the broken windows of the library tower on the roof of Boxleyn Palace. Even given the distance, the way they snaked down the side of the tower was all too familiar. These were Voracity's vines, the same kind he had battled at Estepel, the same kind that had killed the Thorn King. Voracity could only be inside Boxleyn if she was invited by one of the rulers of Rosaria. Which meant Cuz and Nissa and were dead. And Brierly—

No. She can't be. I will kill Cryndien if he let Voracity have her.

Panic and rage filled him to the eyeballs, and for a moment he and every Rosarian soldier on the battlements saw only the terrible writhing of thorns that signaled their demise. But from the east tower hung a square of cloth so large none could long overlook it. It was Nissa's banner. Even those who did not recognize the Prince of Here and There soon understood the meaning of the banner from the shouts.

"Look to the Prince!" cried a voice that sounded like Gerret's. "Look to the Prince and you will see your enemy!"

One by one the defeated cries terror of the Rosarians turned to cries of revelation and triumph. Somehow turning to the Prince negated the effects of the invisibilifier. For his part, seeing the banner of the Prince reminded Arpien to seek him through the vademecum sword. As he did, the sword sucked away his panic and a good portion of his rage. Whatever was going on with Brierly, the sword was telling him to trust the Prince. Like a compass needling to a new north, it jerked Arpien around and pulled him down from the battlements. If the Rosarians could see the Conquisani, they didn't need him there.

It's leading me to Cryndien. He was certain of that much, although the sword wasn't telling him what to do when he found him. Strategically, he already knew the answer. If he killed Cryndien, the battle would end. Bo would not prolong a war he had never wanted.

The Conquisani had broken through the gate, and now soldiers flooded through the entrance, a tide pushing against the Rosarian ground defenses. The vademecum sword cut a jagged path of safety though the flashing weapons. Arpien only had to listen to it to know when to dodge right or duck left. He was through the gate just in time to see Voracity land beside Cryndien. The sight froze him in midstep.

She was no hag, but it had to be Voracity, because it could be no one else. In her full fairy form she looked both human and inhuman. She was younger in build, although she had always had that unnaturally straight spine, the erectness of one used to commanding attention. She had grown at least three feet in stature. The eyes were still gold, though now they burned like smoldering honey. You could suffocate in those sweet, coal-crusted eyes. Her hair was still short and white, though its texture had changed, and it blew as a single indefinable tuft, not a series of strands.

All this Arpien took in in a glance, because it was impossible for his eyes to linger on anything save her magnificent cloak.

He called it a cloak because it flowed down her back and cupped her shoulders, though it was made of no material Arpien knew. What fabric flashed geometric patterns of color and light? What fabric left holes in his vision because his eyes did not know how to translate what he saw? The cloak was both there and not there. When he looked slightly to the side he could perceive it with more definition, the same way a star seems brighter when you do not look directly at it. He could not ascribe a shape, or a size, or even a consistent pattern to it. He only knew that staring at the cloak made him feel drunk.

Even sitting on his horse, Cryndien barely reached Voracity's eye level. If being so close to a fairy in her full form intimidated Cryndien, he did not show it.

At his nod Voracity waved her hands in a gesture that was either a spell or a signal. A dozen baby pigs frolicked out of the woods on stubby cloven hooves. Could these be the Devarish pigs, born only days ago? By their size they were at least three months old.

They paused by Cryndien and rooted their snouts at the air. They gamboled closer to the walls of Boxleyn. With each step they grew larger. Uglier, too. Hog hair was by nature stiff and coarse. What covered these animals looked as hard and sharp as metal toothpicks. Twisted yellow-red tusks jutted from misshapen mouths.

Arpien gripped the vademecum sword, prepared for their attack. Most of the hogs passed him by, perhaps instructed to attack only Rosarians. Only one paused level with Arpien. It sniffed the air, turned, and unnatural green eyes fixed on his. Before Arpien's eyes the hog swelled to the size of a horse.

Arpien's stomach cartwheeled with a combination of nausea and hunger. He gripped his sword. "Go away, you great spoiled sausage."

The Devarish hog stamped a foot and turned away. Arpien watched it charge forward to join its brothers. They gained speed together, charged the gate, and plowed through Conquisani and Rosarians alike with squeals of delighted hunger.

The horror of it gave way to rage again. Arpien was a weighty force, a boulder catapulted toward his enemy. Every wrong Cryndien had committed swelled up in his memory and gave him an unstoppable momentum. He disarmed Cryndien's personal guard almost as a second thought, so focused was he on his brother. He was vaguely aware of Voracity's expression of amusement, the same one she'd worn in his dreams when he proved a paper prince. Cryndien dismounted, drew his sword. There were no speeches, no taunts or readings of wrongs. It was as though both brothers had long known this confrontation was inevitable, and now that it was here there was nothing left to do but cross swords and see who survived.

Arpien's blade rang against his brother's.

But it was not Cryndien's. It was Bo's.

"Bo, I will cut you down too, if you stand with him. You've supported his evil too long."

"That I have," Bo said.

Arpien blinked. Cryndien took advantage of the moment to bring up his own sword to attack Arpien, but here again Bo raised his blade to block the attack.

"Bo, what are you doing?" Cryndien said. "The Grey Cloaks tell me you refused my direct order to kill Lady Nessa and the brat-king, even under my direct command."

Nissa and Cuz were alive?

"Now you defend Arpien, which makes you three times a traitor."

"I defend you both," Bo said, "against committing fratricide. Against her." He nodded toward Voracity, who barely bothered to feign a look of innocence.

"She has proven a better ally than you today!" Cryndien said.

"No. She uses you for her own ends."

"As I use her for mine."

"She exacerbates every fault you have, Cryndien. Taking Boxleyn by force would have been unthinkable three years ago. I know you feel that Sentre Forest is yours by treaty and perhaps it is, but not the rest of Rosaria. You must call our troops back."

"A traitor and a lunatic!" Cryndien was working himself into one of his classic rages, but there was something besides distilled rage in his voice. For years, Bo had been the only person Cryndien really trusted, and therefore the only person who could leave him vulnerable. His anger was the stronger for it. "I am glad Father is dead. He can't see how you have turned against me and your country. Just like Fumbleshanks did months ago."

"Can't you see, brother, it was you who forced his hand?" Bo said. "You are ambitious, proud fools, the pair of you, but I'll say this for Arpien. He did not sit by silently when you went astray. I have not failed you today, Cryndien, I've failed you for years before this day. Today I mean to set things right. I will not let you two murder each other, and I will not stand here quietly while Sitral persuades you to do wrong again."

Both Cryndien and Arpien stared. Could this be quiet, unquestioning Bo?

Voracity at last came to her own defense. She sighed and swatted her hand in front of her face, as though Bo were a fly trying to land on her nose. "Your brothers have sided against you, Your Highness. Why should you be surprised? The desire for power is universal. You can trust me because we benefit each other. But you are different, Your Highness. You take power not only for yourself, but for the good of your country. Your father would be proud to see how you are taking initiative to further Conquisan's interests this day. The Rosarians have long stolen the fruits of the land that is rightfully Conquisan's. Don't let your brothers steal it away from Conquisan again."

As she spoke, three of the hogs disengaged from their feeding among the troops. They nosed Cryndien out of the way and circled Bo and Arpien. They smacked their lips in hunger. They were still growing— feeding on something in the air—growing even as Arpien watched. The nearest one was now larger than a carriage.

"For the good of your nation, for your own safety, Your Highness, your brothers must die."

Now Cryndien stared at Bo with a rare stoic expression. Arpien gripped the vademecum sword. Voracity gestured, that same small flick of the wrist she had used to summon the hogs.

The Devarish hogs lunged forward.

64

Brierly

A murky blue-grey world pressed in around Brierly, as in her last dream chasing the merfolk. She floated in an ocean without floor or surface. She struggled to breathe. She expected to see vines of thorns constricting her rib cage, but when she looked down she saw none—no blood, no vines, only the spindle in her hand. She flung it away. It spun in slow circles and stilled about ten feet from her.

How do you sink an object in a world that has no up or down?

"You can't rid yourself of it that way."

A man stood above her. Or below her; maybe she was upside down. But he wasn't floating, he was standing as though on an invisible reef. His back was stooped under the mottled red cloak. His voice was raspier than she'd ever heard it. If he were to sing her life story now, it would sound of desert sand.

"Am I dreaming? Or dying?" Brierly said. For there was no other way the Thorn King could be here.

"Yes."

His thorns were gone, as were hers. Only when she floated closer to him did she see the full extent of the damage they had wrought. They had left behind dozens of festering puckered holes, like cankers.

She swallowed. "That's why you're here. Because you died, too."

He nodded.

Brierly added saltwater to the ocean that engulfed them. "I'm sorry. It's my fault."

"Yes." But there was no accusation in his eyes. "Don't cry, Brierly. I was glad to stay behind, so you could escape."

He was drifting away from her, or she from him. The grey waters dimmed his features as they moved further apart.

Brierly reached out a hand. It felt like someone had tied horseshoes to her wrists. "Don't leave me."

"That choice is not mine, but yours. But you only have moments left to make it. Will you give me your thorns?"

"I did. That's why you're dead."

"You still hold on to one." He pointed to the cold object she clenched in her hand.

The spindle.

Her final, her first, thorn.

"How did it get back into my hand?"

"There is no way you can rid yourself of your own thorns. But I can. You saw me do it at Estepel."

"No!" She clutched the spindle in a protective embrace. "If it's my spindle, so be it. I deserve it. Too many people have died because of me. I won't let you!"

"Beloved," he said, "I'm already dead."

Then she couldn't hurt him anymore.

He held out a wounded hand to her. "Trust me. Please."

In his face she saw Beauty.

How could she deny this man the only thing he asked of her?

Her hand trembled with weakness, fear, relief. "Then I give it to you, forever."

She had been wrong; he was not past the reach of pain, though he was dead. Even holding the spindle made him cringe, as though he held the handle of an iron pot straight from the fire. When he took the spindle from her, she felt the pull of threads. It was as though unseen yarn wound around the spindle, and the twisted fibers that made it originated somewhere deep inside Brierly's very soul. The unsnappable threads that always allowed the spindle a path of return, like a spider climbing its own strand of silk home.

The Thorn King pressed the spindle between his hands, one tip in the center of each palm. The spindle spun, faster and faster, until it whirred with the sound of angry wasps. Each rotation wound the strands and brought Brierly closer. She dug in her heels, but to what? The ocean had no traction.

The spindle bit into the Thorn King's hand. He groaned.

An invisible strand snapped. She didn't see it, she felt it, as though it were tied around a rib. Brierly jerked back an inch.

Red curled from the Thorn King's hands, like tendrils of smoke from a snuffed candle. Still the Thorn King pushed his hands together. The spindle started to bend. Brierly felt another thread snap, and another.

Then in one sharp motion, the Thorn King's hands clapped together. The points of the spindle jutted through the backs of his hands. The Thorn King cried out. The spindle spun ulcers in his hands. The holes grew, as though he held a tornado seed. Then, as the spindle had swallowed the tornado seed back at Boxleyn, when Arpien tried to destroy it, the spindle drank in the Thorn King. Hands, arms, body blurred as he drained away with one final horrific cry.

No.

Brierly was left alone with her spindle again. Only a single thread connected them now, spindle to her fingertip. And her fingertip started to blacken.

No. No. No.

The spindle began to vibrate. The thread that attached her fingertip to the spindle unraveled into separate fibers. They drifted away like dust motes. Her Fine Ears picked up shrill harmonics. They swept up and down the scale, until they honed in on one pitch.

The spindle shattered.

Brierly threw her arm over her face. She kept it there for protection, not from shrapnel, but from the blistering light. She felt the pressure of the resentful waters dissipate as the ocean evaporated around her. She took a full minute to raise her nose from the crook of her elbow, for fear the whiteness of the light might sunburn her eyeballs. Through furiously blinking eyelids, she saw she was no longer alone.

A conundrum: How do you describe the indescribable?

With other people's words, because your own fail you.

Nissa would have defined him as a Rescuing Prince. He stood before her, whole and perfect. He wore clothes so white that a laundress would lose her job trying to clean them, for the purest soap and water would make them dirtier. The gleaming gold embroidery on them surpassed even her best fairy-Gifted work. Strength and power exuded from him, more than could even be ascribed to his well-formed physique. She pitied the warrior who offended him, as much as she suspected even the most timid rabbit who stood under his protection would be unassailable. Even his shadow would cast the shade of safety.

Only he had no shadow, because he himself was the source of light.

He took in her expression, threw back his head, and laughed as though they shared the best joke ever told in the banquet halls of a dozen kingdoms. His voice rang through her like a thousand bells rewriting the symphony of her destiny.

The light dimmed just enough that she could bear it without squinting. Only now could she make out the crown of gold upon his head. Wrought in the ornamentation were tiny thorns of pure gold.

But it was the eyes, those empathetic eyes, that gave it away, even now that he was smiling.

"The Thorn King," Brierly said.

"The same. And different," he said. "I am the Prince."

Brierly didn't know whether to hug him or sink down in the deepest curtsey before him. So instead, she burst into tears.

When he moved to embrace her, she grabbed his golden sleeves in her fists and shook him with all the vehemence of her relief, anger, and love. Like the child woken from the nightmare, striking out at her father. "Where have you been?"

But she knew where he'd been. He'd been watching her dreams until she woke up. He'd been walking in the briars, ensuring they never quite took over her tower. He'd been waiting one hundred years to cut for her a path through her own thorns.

Gowsma was right. He'd never truly left her alone.

She sank down at his feet and clung to his knees with all the strength in her.

His hand brushed the top of her head. "Do you think to keep me here?"

She jutted out her chin. "Yes."

"You have it backward still. I'm the one who never let you go."

She'd given up on him, but he hadn't given up on her. Her tears subsided, and she released her death grip on his knees.

A smile hatched on her face like a baby chick. It fought its way out through the cracks and shook remnants of hard shell away. "You did send my true love to save me."

"Aye. True love saved you."

Brierly wished she could tell Nissa about the genuine Rescuing Prince. Nissa could at last finish embroidering the mysterious silhouette who rescued the Sleeping Beauty.

"Nissa has her own work now, just as you have yours." He offered his hand and helped her rise. "Your parents and their parents before them, all the way back to the founding of this kingdom, swore to serve as my Stewards, whatever the cost."

"Steward. I thought it was just a name."

"Don't underestimate a name, Brierly. I choose mine very carefully." His eyebrows flashed up and down like a mischievous boy's. "And I enjoy a good symbolic pun."

She laughed. Her Prince had a sense of humor. But of course he did. He was perfect.

He sobered. "Will you do the same, Brierly? Serve as my Steward?"

"But you saw me with that spindle." He knew everything about her. "I'll fail you."

"Then you give me your thorns. What is your answer, Brierly? There isn't much time."

Would she serve the one who died for her? An easy choice. "Aye, I will serve you, and gladly. Just tell me what to do."

"You remember I'm a gardener, Brierly?"

He looked no more a gardener now than he did a juggler. *Warrior,* perhaps.

"That too," he said.

Could he read all her thoughts?

"But I prefer making things grow and blossom. I know a garden that needs pruning." He held out his hand. "Shall we?"

65

Arpien

The Devarish hogs lunged toward Arpien and Bo. Arpien dodged the deadly twisted tusks, but Bo was not so fortunate. From the corner of his eye Arpien saw a body knocked to the ground. He heard Bo's cry, quickly cut off, as the Devarish hog gored him through his chest. But no, as Arpien rolled to his feet, he saw that the victim was not Bo, but Cryndien.

Cryndien stood before Bo and protected him with broken body. The hog jerked back and shook Cryndien's impaled body from shriveling tusks. Bo surged up with a cry of denial to catch his brother in his arms, but his leg collapsed beneath him and he could not reach him.

Death took Cryndien before his body hit the ground. The abruptness of it captured his last living emotion on his bloodless face: profound surprise.

Cryndien.

The sight of his inseparable older brothers, the injured one even now dragging himself to reach the dead one's side, hit Arpien like a blow. Whatever their flaws, there was a bond there that Arpien ached for but had never shared. Bo's grief and failure was written so plainly on his face that Arpien had to turn away.

Turn away to see Voracity's face as she studied the three brothers. Studied them with the same calculating expression you might study a board of jumpstones when your opponent has trounced your key piece. Voracity caught Arpien's eyes on her and rearranged her face into cool respect. "Hail King Arpien."

"What?"

"King Cryndien is dead without issue. That makes you his heir."

"Bo is Cryndien's heir."

She dismissed the crumpled figure with a sideways glance. "This is not a king, but a shadow of one. He lacks ambition and resolve. You have the will to rule a kingdom. Empire, rather, for you may harvest another two kingdoms this day, if you accept my help."

"Don't dare play friends with me. I have years of evidence otherwise."

"You seem to think I hate you, and I never did. No, we were never friends. But that was your decision, not mine, as you chose not to befriend Cryndien."

Chose? As a youth he had longed for his eldest brother's notice as he had no other's, especially after their father died. Cryndien had shut him out with a flashing grin and booming words that struck him down like a storm. Even as Arpien had struggled to become more like Cryndien to please him, Cryndien had rejected him, until Arpien struck out on his own. Now it seemed Voracity wanted Arpien for that very reason. He was like Cryndien, and she needed a human to influence. Her powers here were indirect. Arpien shuddered at the notion that he would make a more suitable pawn for Voracity than Bo. "I will not kill a brother to gain a crown."

"You were willing to a moment ago."

That blow struck harder than any magical one. "I only wanted Cryndien to spare Rosaria."

"You knew he would never agree to that, and you would be forced to kill him."

"That was never my intention!" Was it? "If a king is bad, it is our duty to remove him from power."

"Exactly why you should kill Bo now. He too will make a bad king. You know he is a follower, not a leader. Conquisan will lose its empire under his lack of resolve. The lords will rebel, and civil war will follow. Killing one man now will spare the lives of many later. You, Arpien, are strong enough to take up the reins of the Conquisan. That is why Cryndien feared you."

Cryndien, afraid of little Fumbleshanks? A lump of laughter hardened and died in Arpien's throat, as flashes of insight proved Voracity's statement. Why else had Cryndien worked so hard to belittle him?

He looked down at the expression of surprise frozen on his dead brother's face. Perspective spun, and Arpien saw himself as Cryndien must have. The brother who constantly challenged his authority. Who increasingly criticized his political decisions. Whose growing skill as a swordsman had to be checked by the warning attacks of the Grey Cloaks. Whose fascination with the old tales indicated a clear ambition to be king himself. An ambition that eventually led him to turn traitor to his own country.

It was not a clear picture of himself, for Arpien knew what motives lay beneath the perception. If his motives were not as evil as Cryndien feared, nor were they as selfless as Arpien had once believed.

For the last time in his life, Arpien measured his own course against what Cryndien would have done. "You are right. I have thought all those things, and more. Perhaps I am the least of the three."

Voracity's understanding smile flickered.

"But I was told something by a man I trust. I think his prediction was not merely a foretelling but a course of wisdom for me to freely choose. I will never be a king."

The vademecum sword hummed in his hand. Voracity sized him up another long moment, then called down sentence with a wave of her hand. "Then you have freely chosen to die alongside your brothers. Kill them both," she ordered the Devarish hogs.

The hogs moved to obey, but not so eagerly as before. Arpien deflected two of them with a shaking hand. Why was his hand shaking? He felt more certain of his actions than he ever had, and the hogs had shrunk a foot as Voracity held them back. The vibration in his hand worsened, until he realized it was not his hand's fault, but the sword's. The vademecum sword jerked his hand in a slash in front of him. What had ripped? The air?

Ripping air was a small enough wonder to ponder compared to what happened next. Between the jagged flaps of air poured green antennae, multi-faceted eyes set like dark jewels in triangular heads, fangs, long sleek limbs with jagged ridges like saws.

The mantizes were here.

The first mantiz through the portal of ripped air tilted its head at the nearest Devarish hog. The hog snorted and huffed. Beady eyes stared at multifaceted ones as the beasts sized each other up. Even an eight-foot mantiz would be no match for a Devarish hog. The muscled density of bristly flesh, the twisted tusks would bludgeon and tear apart such slender limbs.

But mantizes kept pouring through the hole.

Mantizes hunted in packs.

It took three mantizes to corner, paralyze, and dispatch each Devarish hog. The green limbs were slender, but they were quick. And Devarish hogs, it soon became clear, only knew how to wreak havoc in the same vicinity as others of their kind, not organize any kind of mutual strategy.

When the last mantiz emerged from the slit in the air, Arpien found himself, vademecum sword still raised, shoulder to shoulder with the last few towering bugs.

He had, wittingly or no, joined a pack.

Arpien was under no delusion that he was the pack leader. Mantizes, by instinct or long practice, needed no instruction from the human. He matched his strategy to their own as his new pack cornered the last Devarish hog.

If the mantizes were not natural ground fighters, their ability to isolate and surround their enemy made up for it. If he were not as quick as a mantiz—and certainly he lacked the poisonous fangs—he could help hold the Devarish hog in a tightening circle of bodies. And if a Devarish hog trampled one mantiz in the attempt to reach another, the hog's massive body rippled and shrank even as it struck the blow. Just as it had when Cryndien took the blow for Bo.

Then he understood. Devarish hogs fed off greed, fear, even an understandable self-concern. To take a blow for another, such camaraderie was not only incomprehensible to such a beast, but poisonous.

A few of the hogs charged the human troops. Why attack the humans now, when the mantizes were the greater threat? Yet as the soldiers fled before the twisted tusks, the shriveled flanks of the beasts grew plump as autumn hams again.

"Hold your ground!" Arpien shouted to the human troops. "Think of the families you are trying to protect!"

It was no guilt trip—it was strategy. If the Rosarians fought to protect land or a building, these were not bad reasons, but they were reasons of self-interest. Fighting for loved ones turned their injuries into ones of self-sacrifice.

Arpien's request was not without cost, for more than one man who turned back fell to the trampling cloven hooves. But if those men's bravery didn't fry the Devarish hogs away to flaky nubs, like overdone bacon, at least it counterbalanced any growth allowed by the men who retreated.

Yet no sooner had the Rosarian troops sent up a rallying cry than their cheers turned to shouts of confusion. The earth under them trembled and gave way. Pools of metallic flickering lights spilled out of the earth and drained away again. Massive clods of dirt churned up around them. The pools of light mounded as no natural water ever could. The surface strained as though some bulky creature flexed powerful muscles to break through it.

One fairy emerged from each pool. Troops scurried out of the way. Arpien couldn't imagine any fairy here at the invitation of Voracity was favorably disposed to Rosaria, or to him. The pools draped the shoulders of each form, until Arpien realized they were not pools, but robes like the one Voracity wore. A fairy with cobalt hair flung his robe out behind him and leapt into the air. Finally Arpien realized he'd misnamed it again—the dazzling, imperfectly perceivable lights were wings.

Three of the evil fairies dove at him, arms outstretched. They grabbed a mantiz in each powerful hand, spiraled dozens of feet into the air, and dropped them. The mantizes plummeted to the earth. Saw-tooth limbs flailed in the air. The flailing continued after impact. A sign of life or the last twitches of death?

Arpien raised the vademecum sword and rushed to the mantizes' defense, a reaction he would neither have predicted nor judged wise. He drew up short as one of the evil fairies slammed down into the earth in front of him. He felt the impact as two more fairies closed in from the right and left. There was no good stance to take, but as Voracity was the threat that Arpien wanted least at his back, he whirled to face her.

"Mind the sword," Voracity ordered the others. "But the prince is only paper."

Arpien chopped at the fairy nearest him and found only air. He tripped headlong, rolled and recovered. The fairies' smug expressions told him he had not tripped over his own feet. They were toying with the paper prince.

A blade sliced into his back. Pain robbed his breath, then vanished as quickly. He whirled in the direction of the new attack, and found only a flash of dizzying winglights and another piercing attack from behind. His knees buckled at the agony, but he used the vademecum sword as a crutch to keep from falling. Blows from his barely seen enemies fell before he could pinpoint the location of each attacker.

It was his nightmare, brought into the waking world. Voracity stood back and watched the others have their amusement with a vaguely impatient expression on her stunning face. Her wings thrummed in orange squiggly lines.

Suddenly the pattern of Voracity's winglights shifted to violent ice blue. "What's she doing there?"

Voracity extended her wings behind her and somehow, stepped backward through them. As her body dissolved she barked an order. "Confiscate the sword. Kill the wielder." Her impossible wings glittered in the air a few seconds after the rest of her vanished, then they themselves swallowed each other up.

Without Voracity, the briars paused in their disassembly of Boxleyn Palace. The reprieve made little difference to the Rosarian army outside the gate. It made little difference to Arpien, as the giant winged figure before him raised a final killing blow.

66
Brierly

Garden. Brierly never would have described it as such. It was a maze of the thickest briars she had ever seen. Far more intimidating than even those outside Castle Estepel. Thorns as long as rapiers. Vines as thick around as a man's thigh. Worse, these vines were dead. The sweet rotten stench of them lay heavy in her lungs. But they were also alive. They grew, they moved, they reacted. They were more like predatory animals than plants. Thorns aligned like eyeless heads to watch them pass.

She saw creatures slinking within the vines—a foot, an eye, a tail. Here and there a vine whipped around one of the creatures, a snake sinking teeth of thorns into its prey and swallowing it whole. Brierly never got a clear sighting of the creatures, but they didn't look human. Their screams were just human enough to scrape the courage from her bones.

But the Prince stood here beside her, so she didn't escape into another dream. "Do you recognize this place?"

"Are we going to her fortress?"

He nodded, and tugged her forward by the hand.

The vines slithered around them, but left a path open. They must have passed through a mile of briars before Brierly saw through the tangle to the stone fortress. The fortress gave the impression of impending weight, an inevitable fall. Even as she watched, Brierly saw a chunk of the building crumble off. Before it hit the ground three vines shot out and caught it. Thorny fingers wedged and tied the block back in place. The stones shifted to receive it, but the stone distorted the face of the wall instead of strengthening it. It swelled like an abscess ready to burst.

"Is Voracity's fortress really a prison?" Brierly said. "Do you make her live here?"

"It is a prison of sorts. But she chooses to stay here."

"Why would anyone choose to live in a place like this?"

The Prince regarded her soberly.

"This is the garden we're going to—prune?"

"One of them."

Brierly thought of the servant, Senesca. The old woman still bore the scars from weeding the briars outside Castle Estepel as a child, and those briars were nowhere as virulent as these. Brierly sucked in a breath. She'd promised to serve the Prince. She seized a vine and pulled.

The vine pulled back. Brierly fell nose-first in the dirt as the vine dragged her into the thicket. The Prince laid his hand on the vine. A jolt ran down its length and into Brierly's hands. It felt soothing to her, but it must have irritated the vine, because it released her. Brierly scooted back.

"I see I'm going to have to teach you my way of gardening," the Prince said.

Brierly rubbed her hands. "I'm listening."

"How do you defeat thorns?"

That sounded much more like a question than an answer.

In one accord all the vines stretched for the sky. In hunger or in welcome, Brierly couldn't tell. They blocked out the sun. Only it wasn't really a sun, it was a pale silvery orb. Not the moon either. A source of false light.

The briars bowed down around a tall graceful figure.

Voracity.

"You do not understand the rules," Voracity said to Brierly. "You are mine completely now. You cannot stand against me."

If that were true, why had Voracity rushed back to her fortress?

"Maybe someone else can," Brierly said.

Only then did Voracity see the Prince a few feet behind Brierly. Voracity dropped back a step and covered her head. When the Prince did not attack, she slowly lowered her hands.

"You came to fight," the fairy said. "Fine. Fight. No matter who wins, I will make you pay dearly."

"My Steward is going to fight for me."

Brierly choked. Why chance the fate of Rosaria to the prowess of someone who had one hundred years of defeat to her name?

Voracity scoffed. "Your Stewards are weak. Why do you place your faith in them?"

"You've got it backwards, as usual."

Uh, you're the Prince. Crush her.

The Prince laid a hand on her shoulder. "I'm right here with you. How do you think she'll win?"

Brierly didn't have time to answer. She was too busy dodging the three-foot-long thorn that came hurtling at her chest.

She avoided it by turning into a mouse.

A mouse wasn't a small enough target. Voracity flung thorn after thorn around her. Brierly scurried right and left as their razor tips bit into the ground. In seconds Brierly was caught in a cage of thorns.

"How do you defeat thorns?" asked the Prince.

Wasn't he supposed to be telling her that?

She turned into a shadow and slipped between the thorn bars of her cage. But this was a mistake, as the shadows of the vines could twine around the shadow of her soul. She popped into her own flesh again.

"What is your name?" the Prince said.

Never underestimate the power of a name. "Steward," Brierly said. Was he reminding her of her vow?

Briars shot out of Voracity's hands. Brierly sprouted wings and launched into the air. The vines chased her. She flew in circles. The pursuing vines tied themselves in knots.

She could still see the Prince below. She flapped closer to him, certain that if she lost sight of him she'd be dead. He cupped his hands around his mouth and shouted up at her. "Your other name."

She frowned. The moment of distraction cost her her right wing. One of the thorns pierced the feathers. She wanted to scream but it was quicker to vanquish the wings. She plummeted toward the hungry thicket.

Spinning wheels. She reversed gravity.

Not her best idea, as now she was soaring away from the Prince. She switched gravity back the right way and grabbed ahold of a dingy storm cloud. "My name is Brierly!"

"No," he said.

A flock of thorns pierced the cloud and she let go. She twined her limbs around a bolt of lightning—ouch—and slid to the ground. "No?"

"Your true name."

It was all too familiar. Voracity was attacking her, and instead of interceding, he quizzed her with useless conundrums.

"Do you trust me or not?"

Brierly flushed. Aye, she did trust him. Then let her listen. He wanted her true name.

She gasped. Not her nickname. What she was christened.

She raised her hands and aimed for the briars.

"My name is Briar Rose."

Petals flew out of her fingertips like a swarm of avenging butterflies. Single petals seeded themselves in the hard vines and bloomed. The roses grew so large that they choked out the thorns. The thorns shed from the vines like scales. The earth swallowed them down in little pits of steam.

Voracity redoubled her attack. Briars collided with petals in the air. The petals stripped the thorns from the vines like devouring locusts. Naked limp vines drooped and fell over.

Voracity turned and fled to her fortress. Her power was thorns, and thorns had no power anymore.

The thorns were not the only thing the petals destroyed. Brierly aimed higher and the petals embedded themselves into the walls of the fortress. Roots spread through stone and mortar. The fortress cracked and crumbled. Voracity braced the disintegrating building with a web of supporting briars. Brierly targeted these, too. The briars bloomed and thorns rained from the fortress. It sounded like hail hitting the ground.

As Brierly/Briar Rose flung petals, she saw the Prince beside her. Only, in the corner of her vision, sometimes he looked like the Thorn King. When the Prince stood beside her, the petals she threw were pure white. When the Thorn King stood beside her, the petals were blood red.

When her briars failed, Voracity plucked the roses from her fortress with her own hands. She screamed as her hands closed around each blossom. The rose petals pierced Voracity's flesh as the thorns had pierced Brierly's. Voracity tore a white blossom from the wall, smeared with her own blood. It floated to the ground and took root. The bloodstains sizzled away, and the petals gleamed as white as before.

"Long ago she made her choice. Now the petals are poison to her," the Prince said. "You see what you must do."

Brierly sprayed the petals directly at Voracity. The petals swirled around Voracity in a great red and white funnel.

The Prince put a hand on her shoulder. "Stop."

He took exactly one step back. Brierly went with him.

The weakened fortress shuddered and swayed overhead. Any moment before this, Brierly would have dodged out of the way. With the Prince beside her, she stood rooted as the fortress crashed down around them. A stone block as big as she was smashed in front of her. It rolled and bumped gently against her toes.

The fortress was gone. In its place stood a magnificent rose garden. Wild but not unplanned. And not a single thorn anywhere. Fragrance rolled over her like incense. She sucked it into her lungs. The breath of life itself. How was it possible to feel so spent and energized at once?

She walked in the garden with the Prince. The rose vines rearranged themselves into tunnels and arches to let them pass. The very rubble left from the ruined fortress shrank into pebbles. Within the fortress's blackened heart they found Voracity. The fairy shrank and faded like her place of power.

The malignant glare Voracity cast at Brierly was enough to turn her stomach. But it was only a passing glance compared to the hatred Voracity fixed on the Prince. At last Brierly understood that the christening Curse, the killings at the Spring Ball, the one hundred years of torture, none of it had been out of hatred for Brierly. By herself Brierly was no true threat to Voracity. In the same way Voracity was no true threat to the Prince. But rather than surrender, Voracity had struck against the things he loved.

Voracity raised a bloody hand and pointed at Brierly. "She's dead anyway. Bled to death in the waking world." Voracity kept her eyes on the Prince, as though she searched for any sign of pain to savor. "She's the last Steward, and you've lost her. And with her the entire realm."

"Have I?"

The earth rose up and swallowed Voracity down, like the wave from Arpien's childhood nightmare.

Watching it made Brierly lightheaded. She sank down at the Prince's feet.

"Well done, Steward," he said.

"But you didn't need my help. Why ask me?"

"Because in doing what I asked, you've given me what I value most of all."

"Are Arpien and Nissa all right?"

"What is my name?"

She was beginning to understand the Prince's way of answering in questions. Somehow he was both here beside her and there on the battlefield with them.

She smiled, but she was too tired to respond in words. Her weakness couldn't be from this battle. She'd drawn on the Prince's strength, not her own. Maybe Voracity was right. But only half right, as she was about a lot of things. Brierly thought she might have died in the waking world, though she certainly didn't feel lost. In fact, the only thing about death that bothered her now was being parted from Nissa, dear friend, and Arpien ...

Meeting the Perfect Prince did not diminish her feelings for her imperfect one. If such a creature as she were loveable, how easy it was to love Arpien. In very different ways, both her princes laid claim to her heart through their kindness, goodness, and their pursuit both gentle and relentless. She wished now that she'd had the courage to say more to Arpien. If there was anything she'd learned from the Thorn King, it was that love did not mean self-protection.

So tired. She could feel time dripping through her fingers, brief yet infinite. "Could you ... tell Arpien ..."

"I know, daughter. Rest."

She sank into a dreamless dark.

67

Arpien

Arpien thrust the vademecum sword into the fairy's abdomen—as high as he could reach. The fairy arched backward and opened his mouth to the sky. A fairy scream was unlike any sound Arpien had ever heard. It was the sound of a thousand whetstones grinding the metal of a thousand blades. It was the sound of luxurious silk torn between wolf claws. It was the bellow of a dozen shrill organ pipes. The pitches writhed like snakes cast into a fire. Conflicting resonances shot through the vademecum sword and into Arpien's arms. Arpien's ears dripped with warm blood. He clung to the vademecum sword with both hands. His knuckles whitened, and he called to the Prince for help with all his might.

The Prince did not come. But something else did.

The evil fairy exploded.

Without blood (did fairies have blood?) the fairy shattered apart, like glass when a singer hits a certain pitch. Glimmering shards of fairy zinged past Arpien. But no, these were not pieces of a dead fairy. Pieces of living fairies burst out of the white-hot vademecum sword and expanded into a fleet of whole fairies. Two score fairies took to the skies.

It looked like the Prince had finally given his loyal fairies permission to appear in full form.

They seemed to be relishing it.

Arpien peered up at the soundless storm overhead, soundless because all he could hear was the piercing ringing in his ears, left from the evil fairy's scream. Their conflict lit the sky in a dozen clashes of lightning that was not lightning, of arrows that were not arrows, of wind that stirred the elements but not the air. Stray fairy weapons slammed into the earth below and created craters ten feet across.

Arpien would never again think of fairies as wispy and delicate sylphs who lounged around on spotted mushroom caps.

He started as Bo touched his arm. Bo was standing now. He favored his left leg heavily, but he was up. Arpien could only hear ringing, but he read his brother's lips and his intent well enough. All around them troops stopped to stare at the celestial battle. It would be an ideal moment to order them to stop fighting, when the heat of battlelust turned to the cold rush of awe.

"Lay down your swords!" He could feel his voice more than he could hear it, a series of vibrations in his own skull. "The battle has been won by forces you and I can never match."

Perhaps persuaded by the sword that had magically imported legendary warriors twice in the past hour, all soldiers within earshot paused to consider him.

Bo declared something inscrutable beside him. The gaze of the soldiers shifted to the banner of the Prince that hung over the walls of Boxleyn. Arpien shifted his own gaze there as well, just in time to see the east tower burst open with thousands of red and white moths.

They streamed down the walls of the palace and through the grounds of Boxleyn. The briars shriveled at their touch. Millions of moths wove through the frozen ranks, a swirling blizzard that obscured enemy from enemy. No more than ten feet to his left a soldier swung a wild sword at this new invader.

"No, wait!" Arpien said. He knew that scent.

Beside him Bo caught one of these creatures between two of his fingertips.

"They're rose petals," Arpien said.

When the air cleared a few moments later, it revealed two entire armies dropping their weapons onto the ground. Many dropped to their knees as well. Bo would try to describe to him, much later, the sound of so much metal dropping onto a cushion of silken flowers. Weapons, bodies, warriors, all were blanketed in petals ankle-deep like snow. Snow and blood. The rich flowery fragrance saturated the air, heady but not cloying.

We've won. The thought seeped into every pore, like the scent of roses around him. *Brierly, Voracity's gone. You're safe.*

His hearing returned slowly over the next hour. He was impatient to rejoin Brierly, but there was too much to be done with the troops on the ground. He, Bo, and General Gapric, along with the vademecum sword, seemed to be the only ones who could bring order to the bewildered warriors. He'd never believed the fighting would end before one side was demolished. Still, too many were dead, and the injured needed attention. He kept Bo close at hand to show a visual sign of unity to both sides. And because Bo was a useful aid in repeating and answering the reports Arpien couldn't hear.

After the fighting ceased, one of the most important things that had to be faced was confirming that Cryndien was dead. His charismatic brother didn't look himself at all, all waxen and still and small, like a snuffed candle stub. Was it natural to feel more kinship in death than in life?

Bo braced himself on Arpien's shoulder, but Arpien couldn't tell which injury made him do it. "Now that he's dead, what do I do?" Bo said.

Arpien's hearing was returning by then. He wanted to pretend it hadn't, because he had no good solace to give his brother, and felt he had no right to mourn the man as Bo did. "Be king," Arpien said quietly.

Bo didn't shed tears for Cryndien. "It was supposed to be the other way. He wasn't supposed to die for me."

"Then be a king worth dying for."

It was with a face of stunned stoicism that Bo accepted the fealty of the surviving leaders of the Conquisani army as they witnessed Cryndien's dead body. Bo already commanded the loyalty of the army. But steadiness and calmness were not virtues that would impress most of the nobles back in Conquisan. Even the nobles here on the battlefield seemed dubious of this new king, who accepted their fealty from a sitting position because his leg had given out again. A proper Conquisani king would have stood, no matter the pain, and performed all the proper bows and gestures. But maybe it was time for Conquisan to have a different sort of king.

His hearing restored, Arpien left Bo to sort out Conquisani politics while Arpien helped sort out Rosarian. Troops of both sides greeted him with fervor: exuberance from those who had become believers in the Prince during the battle, and respect from many others at the wonders they had seen him perform. The sword had performed the wonders, Arpien kept repeating, but some people seemed as deaf as he had just been. Not everyone rejoiced as he passed, but those were wise enough to hold their murmurs of trickery or sorcery back until later.

Although the mantizes had fought alongside him, he was unnerved when the whole cadre surrounded him. For long moments Arpien and the mantizes stood stuck in a cycle of political preliminaries, like courtiers trying to shoo each other through a doorway. *You first. No, you.* Not for the first time since the battle ended, Arpien wished Brierly were there beside him. Not only would she be able to communicate with the mantizes, she would doubtless delight in interacting again with any creature so deliciously fierce. In fact, it surprised Arpien that Brierly hadn't slipped past the protective guards to join him on the battlefield.

The mantizes were saying something to him. Shouting, virtually, he realized as their antennae flipped and swayed. He took a logical guess that it was a statement of peace—they weren't eating anyone.

Arpien considered, then bowed the *Full Bow to Honored Emissaries of Dangerous but Allied Nations, as well as Tamers of Large Wild Cats.* "For your service, I promise to help safeguard the lives of your offspring. We will only take your egg sacs after your children are hatched. Anyone who does otherwise will answer to this sword."

The vademecum sword hummed firmly. Perhaps it provided the necessary translation, for the mantizes all tilted their antennae in identical gestures toward the sword. Taking their cue, Arpien extended the sword. Its tip dragged against notches of air with a ripping sound. The mantizes disappeared through the slit left behind, then the slit stitched itself shut and vanished.

"Handy trait, that." Arpien tried not to feel awed. "One day you'll have to tell me how you do it."

Diplomacy with the mantizes completed, Arpien now wanted to thank the fairies for their aid. He'd been surprised that the good fairies lingered. Perhaps they meant to ensure the evil fairies would not return. They made themselves useful by healing the wounded and filling in craters, both repairs managed by a mysterious warm breeze that emanated from their wings. Mysterious because they weren't flapping their wings, exactly—the useful wind just sort of came out. Most of the people gave the fairies wide berth. Wise, given what destruction they'd just seen them cause. He overheard one of the braver souls asking a fairy about the Prince.

He struck out for a cluster of fairies on the battlefield. One saw his approach and flew the last few yards to greet him. She landed beside him with a cheeky grin. Although *land* wasn't quite the right word, as he couldn't discern even the barest outline of feet or legs under that robe. She towered a good four feet above him. The muscles of her long arms were as powerful and graceful as a lion's under her yellow skin. Her hair was an even sunnier yellow, though it was not hair so much as it was smoke, thick and opaque, curling softly upwards.

None of this was noteworthy compared to her wings. In the sky, the fairies' wings had been confusing. This close they were bedazzling, enough to thoroughly mesmerize and befuddle the human brain. They were not at all like bird's wings, made of flesh and feathers. He wasn't convinced they had any substance at all, at least not a substance that could fully materialize in the mortal realm. Geometric patterns blinked into and out of existence, like a message he'd forgotten how to read. Her wings were very thin, but also somehow very deep, an optical illusion popping off the page and then slipping out of the mind's grasp again. At the moment, her wings flashed a dizzying pattern of glowing orange and gold triangles, a new pattern that must mean happiness or victory. For fear her wings would scramble his brain, he forced his gaze up to her triumphant face.

A blue eye squinted down at him. "Don't you recognize your old Gowsma?"

He gaped and she beamed all the wider. So that's what she looked like in full form. No wonder the Prince set limits on how often fairies could appear that way. Human minds would warp from looking at them.

"It's just—you're so—"

"Beautiful? Thanks."

He was going to say *bigger and scarier*. But he wasn't going to contradict *beautiful*.

The only thing familiar about Gowsma was the riot of fuchsia flowers growing in her smoky hair. Only a few of the flowers were in full bloom. The majority were buds just beginning to open. This observation made him peer more closely at the exquisite face.

"Why, you're younger than I am!" Arpien said.

One of the male fairies–the one with mahogany skin and brown buckeyes at his wrists–covered a snort. Gowsma glared at them in turn, her smoky hair flipping to one side like an annoyed cat's tail. "I am centuries older than you, young legs, so don't sass me. And you"—she whirled on Buckeye—"you would do well to remember that without the intervention of the youngest of Brierly's godparents, she would have died a century ago."

"Without the intervention of the Prince, you mean." The buckeye fairy raised a firm but gentle brow.

Gowsma's wings faded to a reprimanded pink.

"You'll have to forgive our impetuous Gowsma, human prince. She's always been sensitive about her youth."

He bent down and seized Arpien's left wrist. Arpien's hand flopped back and forth in the fairy's unbreakable grip. "You are Arpien Trouvel, the human that belongs to this vademecum sword. I am Frendan, one of Brierly's godparents."

Gowsma put her hands on her hips. "Frendan, are you trying to throttle the lad?"

"I'm shaking his hand. You're not the only expert on human greeting rituals."

"That's not how it's done."

Frendan released Arpien, who did his best not to rub his tingling wrist. He started to accord Frendan the same bow he had the mantizes, but in mid-gesture switched to the more welcoming *Full Bow for Potential In-Laws*. Interestingly enough, it did not require much modification.

"Thanks for coming." One must say something, even to a legend.

"My pleasure to fight beside you, human. You fought with bravery and honor."

"The Prince was right about you." Gowsma's eyes sparkled. "But then, he always is."

"So, I'm finally good enough to marry your goddaughter?"

The fairies said nothing.

It took daring to joke with fairies in full form. It was a bit like tickling a mountain lion. "Uh, I mean, no one's good enough, but do we have your approval?"

Gowsma's wings lost their sheen. "Oh child." The fairies exploded into a swirl of stars, and winked out.

Arpien scanned the battlefield. All the fairies were gone. But here was Nissa, clutching her side as she ran through ankle-deep petals. Arpien closed the last few dozen paces between them.

"Brierly—I found Brierly in the tower." Nissa clung to Arpien's arm and tried to get her breath back. "Arpien, she bled to death."

The thought was more disorienting than a fairy's wings could ever be. The Prince would not grant them unbelievable victory and taint it with devastating defeat.

Arpien ran a few steps toward Boxleyn Palace, realized Nissa would never be able to keep up with him, and barked an order at two of the nearby Rosarian soldiers to guard her. Even though he ran faster than Nissa, his feet still couldn't break that sluggish nightmare pace. He slogged through petals, slippery but so light that the more quickly he ran, the more petals took to the air. He zagged through the blizzard of snow and blood.

He burst into the atrium and took the stairs three at a time.

The tower library was choked with dead vines. Brittle thorns crunched into dust under his feet. He saw Nissa's squashed stocking first, the one with the embroidered daisies. Dirt streaked the library carpet, but the spindle was nowhere to be found. He followed the trail of dirt around a bookcase.

Brierly lay in a pool of her own blood. Vines encased her slender body, snakes that had squeezed the life out of her. Now they were as frail and lifeless as their victim. Arpien fell at her side and tore the vines off her.

He took her cool, graceful hand in his but could not feel a pulse. He pressed it to his lips and tried to recapture the last time he had kissed her. He didn't realize until he saw the sheen of moisture on her hand that tears of loss and denial ran down his face. What was this drop of red on the tip of her index finger?

She must have done it again. Pricked her finger on the spindle. Why, Brierly? He'd seen how the spindle called to her. Perhaps she had meant to sacrifice herself to save them. Whatever she'd meant to do, he'd never hear the explanation from her own lips.

You'll never be king, your brother will breach the walls of Boxleyn Palace, and Brierly will die before Cryndien crowns himself king. Perhaps fortune had changed for Boxleyn and Cryndien afterward, but all this paled next to the soul-jarring realization that Brierly was dead. He no longer cared about being a king, not without her.

He heard a man's footstep on the rug behind him. Arpien waved the intruder away without turning to see which of the Rosarian authorities had been sent to confirm Brierly's death. "Leave. Please. This is a private grief."

"No. It is no private grief."

The tone was so sober that Arpien could not be angry with him for disobeying orders. Arpien turned, and was glad he had not pressed the issue. This man wore authority like an old familiar cloak.

Arpien had never met this man before, but he knew him well. He'd seen him in the old tales. He'd spoken to him through the vademecum sword, which was purring at Arpien's side.

There was no need to exclaim his identity. It was plain for anyone with eyes to see.

Awe mixed with grief. Arpien felt he owed the Prince a more exuberant greeting, but the weight upon him was too heavy. Arpien smeared his face into his dirty sleeve, but did not apologize for his tears. There were tears in the Prince's own eyes.

"I'm grateful, Your Highness, for what you've done. But if you'd just returned a little sooner, she'd still be alive."

"She chose to serve me, no matter the cost."

"But I loved her."

The Prince of Here and There knelt on the opposite side of Brierly's body. He smoothed a tendril of hair from Brierly's cold face. In the tenderness of his touch, Arpien saw a love for Brierly that made Arpien's feel boyish. The Prince's was not the sort of romantic love that made him jealous. It was the sort of love that amazed him with its strength, amazed him more when he saw it reflected toward himself, as the Prince turned that understanding gaze on him.

It came to him in flashes. Imagine the rich red robes as a bloodstained cloak, vines of thorns around his now unscathed head.

Arpien sat back on his heels. "But—but you died. You died."

The Thorn King—the Prince—smiled sadly. "I died." The smile grew into something triumphant and joyful, like the sounding of a thousand golden trumpets. "And I live."

Arpien started to reach out and seize his hand in glad welcome, but it hardly seemed proper. "I never thought to look on your face again, friend. Er—Your Highness."

"You may call me friend," he said, bringing his own hand up to finish the warm handclasp.

The laughter in the Prince's expression bloomed in Arpien's chest. His friend was alive. Was that thought any stranger than the notion that he,

Arpien, was a personal friend of the Prince of Here and There? It was a device you'd only hear in the old tales. Some of which happened to be true.

And some of which were false. He could not forget whose body lay lifeless before him. "I thought you'd give Brierly her happy ending."

"I did."

"Death?"

"You still don't understand?"

"Make me understand. Please."

"Give me your thorns."

"I have no thorns." Even as Arpien said it, he felt something digging into his chest. The briar leash.

"But it was destroyed when we escaped the merfolk." For the first time he was aware of how it cut off his air.

"Not destroyed. Hidden. It's been choking you slowly for years."

"Then yes, take my thorns. I don't want them."

"Give me the sword."

Arpien handed it over. It was, after all, the Prince's sword.

The Prince sliced the briar vine off Arpien. He took the fragments from the ground and twisted them into a circle. This he placed on his own head, a crown of thorns over a crown of gold. He looked more like himself as Arpien had first known him. Arpien winced as the still living thorns dug into the Prince's brow.

"Doesn't that hurt?" Arpien couldn't help asking. But he knew. Someone had to take the thorns.

"Yes. But this is what I choose to do. Your thorns destroy me, and I destroy the thorns."

What did you say to such sacrifice? Arpien bowed his head in the position of fealty, vassal to lord. "Thank you, my lord."

"Lord, aye. And friend."

"What happens now?"

"Conquisan will go to Bo, Rosaria to the child-king Cuz. Nissa will help him until he comes of age. I will divide Rosaria in half, as I promised long ago, and give Sentre Forest to one who will rule over it as I would want. Arpien Trouvel, I choose you to serve as my Steward. Do you agree?"

"B—but—why would that be necessary? You're back."

"Today's battle was only a shade of the battle to come. Voracity is but one of her kind. I am not back to stay yet. Although I never truly leave, either."

You'll never be a king ... but he might rule as one of the Prince's Stewards. Half a kingdom. The joy of serving a Good Prince. Exhilaration zinged through Arpien's veins. "I'll do it."

And yet—

"You've kept one last thorn," the Prince said. "Do you feel it?"

Aye, there was a thorn, still lodged deep in his chest. Not one of evil, but of hurt—his loss of Brierly, at the very moment a future together had finally seemed possible.

"Do you trust me with even that?"

Arpien nodded. He was not giving away his love of Brierly, but trusting the Prince to ease the pain of it. "May I kiss her farewell?"

The eyes, capable of such profound sorrow, now sparkled with— amusement? "Wouldn't you rather kiss her awake?"

Arpien snapped his head up. The Prince opened his mouth and exhaled an invisible power. The tangy fragrance of wild roses twined around Brierly's battered body, like the healing music from Brierly's dream. Only this was more substantial, the reality instead of the imagining. A tendril of living breeze danced through Brierly's slack lips and filled her chest. Her colors shifted. Pale red rushed into her lips and cheeks while the red bloodstains on her gown leached away, leaving her dressed in gleaming white.

Arpien was so astounded watching her heal that he didn't see exactly when the Prince vanished. Or had he gone? Arpien directed an intense burst of gratitude to wherever the Prince was now—here or there—and supposed the Prince wouldn't mind if he saved the philosophical debate for a time less filled with the miraculous gift of *her.*

Arpien leaned over and woke his princess with a kiss.

Her eyelids fluttered open.

"How do you feel?" Arpien inquired gently.

Her eyes danced and sparked, blue-green galaxies exploding into light. "Awake."

Her fingertips traced the side of his face, his brow, as though she reveled in the reality of him.

"I thought you'd died," Arpien said.

"Just because people die, it doesn't mean they have to stay dead."

Arpien beamed at her. So many words to exchange, but his first order from the Prince was to kiss Brierly awake. He continued to do a very thorough job of it.

Just to guarantee that there was no question this time.

ACKNOWLEDGMENTS

An acrostic poem to express my extreme appreciation:

Working with Steve Laube of Enclave Publishing has been a priceless education and true pleasure. Steve: your instincts for the written word and passion for the power of Christian speculative fiction inspire me.

Artist Kirk DouPonce: you captured so much symbolism in this beautiful cover.

Kindest and most supportive of parents: thanks for letting me talk off your Fine Ears.

Insightful beta readers: your editorial suggestions were so helpful.

Noble Poets, Hook Line and Sequel, Nickel Plate Arts, and my fellow Enclave authors: thanks for fostering a community of artistic exchange.

Genesis Contest judges and organizers: thanks for the wonderful encouragement and feedback.

Best friend and travel-sized version of me, Sherry: you not only saw the birth of this idea in college, but your example led a Brierly to the real Thorn King.

Encouragers, mentors, and fellow soldiers at conferences, including Joyce Magnin at Montrose, Cec Murphey at Write-to-Publish: you are my creative caffeine.

All my young'uns at Conner Prairie: thanks for our many discussions about books, teaching me about spinning, making me laugh, and not putting your socks in the microwave anymore.

Unsung heroes, my fine teachers: thanks for believing in young people, including me.

The real Thorn King, teller of true tales, and the real Prince, rescuer of my soul: what I capture here is only the echo of a rose. But take it as my reply to the love letter you wrote first.

You: if you read this far, you must have read the whole epic novel, for which I am profoundly grateful. You could have chosen to take a nap instead. Hopefully a shorter one than Brierly ...

About the Author

Sarah E. Morin is an author, poet, and euphoniumist. She is the Youth Experience Manager at an interactive history park near Indianapolis, Indiana, where she mentors 100 youth volunteers. She also writes and performs original monologues and spoken pieces for conferences and local organizations.

Visit her Facebook page: www.facebook.com/sarahemorinauthor

Visit her web site: www.SarahEMorin.com